THE SLEEPER

DR. MICHAEL BREUS
SEAN PLATT

STERLING & STONE

THE SLEEPER

To David.

ONE

Houdini

The walkie crackled.

Standing in the shadows, a young man leaned against a dark wall on the building's roof and touched his earpiece to seat it more firmly.

A female voice said, "You dream you're in an elevator."

"How much longer?" the young man asked her.

"Fifteen seconds. Twenty seconds."

He dropped his cigarette, then ground it out with his toe. The action felt performative: something a character would do in a movie. It was a filthy habit. He'd only chosen smoking because it was so cool — so showy. He should have picked up drinking instead, like Dad. Pills like Mom. Smoking was barely a vice. It took decades to kill you. He should have chosen a more self-destructive habit. At this rate, he might live to see thirty, and obviously that was no good.

He peeked around the corner.

The structure he'd leaned against housed an elevator to the roof. That was good; it made the building's architecture a bit surreal. Rooftop elevators were rarely seen in real life.

1

Same for the floor indicator mounted above the elevator door: a sweeping brass hand instead of a digital readout.

Everything up here felt like a cliché. Like something made-up. Reality itself, in this place, felt almost fake. Which, of course, was the whole idea.

To ram the unreality home, the young man's fellow Tailors at the Bespokery had added surreal touches to make this seem less like a real building and more like a parody of one. They'd changed the signage to look like something from the 1950s. They'd enlarged the doorway, then skewed it into a shape you'd see in a funhouse. They'd even decorated the lobby for Easter before the subject arrived, despite Easter being months away. A massive animal — more *hare* than *bunny rabbit* — loomed as the centerpiece. He'd seen it on his way up. It truly was the stuff of nightmares.

No wonder the Bespokery had chosen this place for tonight's job. It was a mindfuck — and their subject, thanks to prior intrusions, had a mind that was already half fucked.

The young man hugged his jacket tighter, but it was a motion born of habit, not cold. In truth, the air up here was practically nonexistent. Tonight's was the kind of non-weather a person never really noticed. Seventy-two degrees Fahrenheit. Forty percent humidity. No wind and dead calm. It was nighttime, with only streetlights and stars to see by. But bland was good.

Unremarkable weather vanished into the background, making the strange building stand out more. Besides, on too warm a night the subject might notice heat. Too cold and he'd shiver. Too dry and he'd feel parched; too humid and he'd sweat. The Bespokery needed for the subject to feel none of those things. No bodily sensations — or anything to remind him that he *had* a body.

Too much reality would spoil all the fun.

The young man could feel the elevator's motor humming through the wall. Waiting, his eyes went to the mirror — the strangest object on the rooftop. He reminded himself not to look at it for long. Like the Arc of the Covenant, staring directly at that goddamn thing could drive a person mad.

"You dream you reach the top floor," said the woman's voice in his ear.

Under his breath, the young man muttered the next bit of tonight's script: *"And a calliope plays."*

"Repeat?"

But he didn't need to respond. A second later, the elevator's car reached the roof. No ding to announce its arrival, instead the Bespokery had installed a calliope sound that added to the surreality.

Hearing it, the young man felt almost as unreal as they wanted the subject to feel. His eyes went to the moon, momentarily convinced he could float up to it if he wanted to.

Careful, he reminded himself.

"You dream you exit at the rooftop," he told the earpiece as the doors opened — as he caught sight of the subject.

"Don't interfere," the woman reminded him for the tenth time.

The young man frowned. He'd obey, but in truth he wasn't sure non-interference was smart. The subject might need nudging, even if that complicated things for the Bespokery. The woman on the walkie — nominally the young man's mentor but in reality something else, and worse — acted like she could see the future. Obviously she couldn't ... and oftentimes people, like the subject, weren't so predictable.

"I'll only approach him if I have to," the young man replied.

"*Don't interfere.* We've talked about this."

He hugged his coat again, wishing he hadn't already ground out his cigarette. Although nobody would see him do it, flicking a cigarette aside could be his Cool Hand Luke way of flipping her the bird.

The subject moved away from the elevator. Despite his orders, the young man thought about tackling him — taking the subject out instead of doing this the complicated (and, in his mind, far-from-certain) way. A simple tackle-and-concuss would be so easy. Dazed as the guy was, he'd never see it coming.

Well, not *dazed*. *Deluded* would be a better word. *Misdirected* would be another. Right now, the subject thought he could turn invisible. He thought he could beat King Kong in a fistfight. In truth, he couldn't beat anyone. Three surprise smashes and there'd be brain and blood everywhere, then this problem would be solved without the need for so much Houdini.

He supposed the Bespokery had its reasons for doing things their way, but there was so much to be said for the simple ways. The old-fashioned ways, as it were.

"*Did you hear me, O'Brien?*" the walkie asked.

He should say *Yes, ma'am*. Or was it *Yes, sir*? He couldn't remember whether Baynes bristled more at being addressed differently than the men or at the patriarchy implied by "sir."

O'Brien glared at the subject, then gave his superior a response that wasn't exactly by the books. "You dream that nobody's about to kill you."

"*Don't.* That's an order."

Now he wanted to disobey just for spite. "This isn't the military anymore. I don't take orders."

"Then let me ask you a question."

O'Brien regretted his smart mouth immediately. Her voice had turned icy, tolerating zero bullshit. It was the same tone she'd used when she'd killed before, turning family against itself.

"Can you fly?"

He didn't answer, finding himself somewhere between obedient and cowed. But he would obey, and he supposed that was all she cared about.

He moved away from the wall, watching the subject as he left the elevator. The subject had splayed his fingers, looking down at his hands. He studied them for a while. Too long, really, as if he found them strange to look at. Which he would. One of the Tailors had spiked his night-stand water with a drop of hallucinogen. Instead of five-fingered and normal, he'd be seeing those hands as rainbow-colored, with too many fingers.

"You dream you're—" O'Brien began to report.

"I asked you a question," Baynes interrupted.

"I'm sorry. I won't interfere. I hear your order."

She paused just enough to scare him. "Then continue."

He drew a deep breath, trying to reset. She'd crawled all the way up under his skin. It was that sorcerer's trick of hers, melting his resolve into simpering fear.

He swallowed, then went on. "You dream you're doing a reality check."

"Is he using the clock?"

O'Brien shook his head. There was a digital clock mounted on one of the air handlers — a strange place for a clock, to be sure. The Tailor controlling it was watching the subject's head, changing the clock's display every time he turned away and looked back at it again. Sometimes, the clock's time shifted. Other times, it displayed odd, foreign symbols.

"No. He's checking using his hands. I don't think he's noticed the clock." O'Brien kept watching. Waiting. Something was wrong. Despite staring for a long time at what must look like psychedelic hands, the subject still hadn't moved more than ten feet from the elevator.

O'Brien said, "He knows."

"He doesn't know," Baynes replied.

"I'm telling you, *he knows*. What if he holds his nose and tries to breathe? What if he tries to relocate?"

"He didn't try to relocate when they were chasing him. Remember, he thinks he's new to this."

O'Brien stayed hidden, still watching.

For a while it seemed the subject would count his fingers, decide that there were ten of them, then realize the truth.

If that happened, he'd run back to the stairs and there'd be a fight — a real one, not one for show.

Seconds passed.

The subject kept staring. Kept watching his hands, trying to decide. Or maybe he wasn't trying to decide; maybe they'd overdone the LSD and he was simply high. Either way Baynes was right; the subject didn't know. If he'd known, he wouldn't look so peaceful. Armed men and women had chased him here. If he thought that'd actually happened, he'd be afraid. He'd be rushing right now, or trying to hide.

But he was doing nothing of the sort.

Instead he stared. Finally looked up, then noticed the mirror.

He walked over and looked closely at what should have been his reflection, but O'Brien could see from here that it definitely wasn't.

"You dream you find a Magic Mirror," O'Brien told Baynes. Staring into the mirror was definitive. It meant the subject hadn't realized the scam. He believed all this surreality was actually happening. "It's a go. Send them up."

"Copy," said Baynes.

Seconds later, footfalls thundered up the stairwell. The Tailors had been just a half flight down, waiting for Baynes to give the signal.

O'Brien barely heard them coming. He'd kept watching the Magic Mirror despite warning himself not to. Its screen was showing the subject a bad trip instead of his reflection: shadowy whorls and sprites cavorting like demons. The display kept changing, shifting from one nightmare to the next. At the end it reflected the subject back to himself, as a gnarled slenderman: long and black, elongated into something terrible.

The stairwell door burst open, a group of Tailors arriving with guns drawn.

The subject turned from the Magic Mirror to face the newcomers. He wasn't afraid; his face looked downright pacific. This was no big deal to him anymore. He'd checked his hands. He'd looked into a mirror and found his reflection strange. Maybe he'd even seen the clock, the display different with every glance. Why would he care, after all those checks, that people were running toward him with pistols?

"*Pop,*" said the young man to himself. "*Pop, pop, pop.*"

The Tailors fired their fake rounds, muzzles flashing. Then the subject, neither shot nor bleeding, looked up at them and smiled.

"I know what this is," he told them. "I know what you are."

The gunners advanced.

The subject stepped backward without hurry, hands not even raised, stopping when his heels struck the short wall at the roof's edge.

He stepped backward onto the ledge, exactly the way the Bespokery's advance work had trained him to do.

A wind finally stirred. His hair lifted. His shirt flapped like a cape behind him.

"Can you fly?" asked the lead gunman.

The subject smiled.

Then he tipped on his heels and fell backward into the night air.

Goddamn. Baynes had been right. O'Brien was shocked despite all his preparations. He hadn't believed a man could be so easily trained.

Wanting to see, he sprinted to the building's edge, grabbed the concrete, and looked down. He had plenty of time. They were twenty-six stories up — according to Baynes that meant seven or eight seconds of free-fall.

There was no way to see the subject's face from this far up, but O'Brien swore he could see it anyway. Full of fear. Betrayal. Disappointment. Confusion most of all.

It wasn't supposed to be like this, the falling man would be thinking right now. *I did my checks and made sure. I wasn't supposed to fall. It's not supposed to be real. I was absolutely certain I'd be able to fly.*

And yet the subject hurtled toward the unforgiving concrete, surprised to realize his life was about to end.

The body fell.

And fell.

And—

TWO

Blustering Tactics

Ash jolted upright in bed, propelled as if by a massive spring. He suddenly wasn't tired at all — as if he hadn't just been sleeping, or maybe had never been.

At first there was vertigo: that odd sense of being somewhere new and unusual. He'd fainted once, after being left unattended in the Afghanistan field hospital and trying his legs much too soon. The feeling now was like waking from that.

He remembered looking up at the canvas ceiling and wondering if he'd gone to the circus. Not that he'd been in his best mind that day ... or, really, ever since.

Now, there was no tent. Today he saw walls, end tables, and morning sun through draperies instead of plastic windows flapping open to sand.

Whose room was this? Was it his? For long seconds he had no idea. Ash knew only that he was an officer of some sort, though he was still too sleep-fogged to be sure which branch, which agency.

But then that certainty, too, faded and he remembered that he *wasn't* an officer anymore. Hadn't been for years.

It was all coming back with a less glamorous reality.

He had a job at Workman Precision Fabrication, drilling holes in steel plates. His name was Ash Sanders. He was thirty-six years old, honorably discharged so he could commit his dishonor in a civilian way that was so much worse.

The bulk of his confusion passed. The room was no longer unusual, but instead where he belonged. He was at home — though still breathing hard with his heart pounding, brain spiked with epinephrine and cortisol. Despite the sounds of children lining up for school buses in the street outside, Ash still felt pursued.

Watched. Surveilled. Chased, maybe. In danger, probably.

He told himself: *Relax.*

But he could only settle his mind so far. It lingered on a dream that refused to dissolve the way dreams were supposed to and usually did.

He hated dreams, and had as few as he could manage these days. Ash had a simple solution to keep them at bay. Booze slaughtered his dreams for the first half of the night, and the weed kicked in to help him forget whatever came later. A single Nyperal tablet kept him immobile while he had those unremembered dreams, so he barely ever sleep-walked like he used to. Or sleep-did anything else. Anything *worse.*

You weren't supposed to drink while on Nyperal. On any benzodiazepine, according to Dr. Irving. You might stop breathing, then never wake up again. Still Ash faithfully drank his nightcap, wondering if the doctor was right.

He woke up every morning anyway. *Every goddamn morning,* without fail.

A woman's voice said from Ash's right: *You're okay. You're safe, Ash. Remember? Sunshine makes everything better.*

It was a stupid thing for her to say, and yet he always felt instantly better. That idiotic little koan somehow soothed his jangled nerves every time.

A smile tweaked the corners of his mouth. He turned to the bed's other side.

"You always—"

But then Ash stopped, looking at the vacant pillow and undisturbed sheets as the smile fell from his lips. The remaining fog departed and then he remembered everything.

The dream, he thought. *I fell. I died.*

If only he'd been that lucky.

"TELL ME," the doctor said.

"I didn't bring it up to talk about the dream," Ash replied. "I was making a point about the fact that I'm dreaming at all. I shouldn't be dreaming, should I? I thought the meds were supposed to solve that."

Dr. Irving nodded. Her legs were crossed at the knee, a pad and pen at home in her lap. She barely broke eye contact. The woman was a chameleon, which was probably why she was so highly regarded outside of her pro bono work with the VA.

Ash had seen the way Dr. Irving adapted to whatever personality happened to be on the other side of her conversations. Back when she'd been helping him with more mundane sleep issues, when Emily was still around, Ash had even complimented her on it. She'd told him that adaptation was a handy skill for a psychiatrist. Every patient was defensive, despite their best intentions. It was her job to adapt and navigate around those defenses. Every person was two people, she'd told him: social armor first, then the human being hiding within it.

You needed to learn a person's unique weaknesses … so you could slip a blade through the gaps.

Slipping a blade through the armor struck Ash as a terrible metaphor, considering her profession was meant to help people through hard times. Still, Mina Irving never flinched. Awful or not, the metaphor was spot on. If she'd tried to reason with Ash whenever he became defensive (like he was now, though not on purpose), she'd never have cut through to the core of his issues.

The best way to confront him was to say nothing, then stare like an expectant parent. Instead of pointing out the obvious, she needed only to fall silent and let him realize on his own that filibustering solved nothing.

I want better meds, not to tell you what's inside my head, he'd come here to say.

She understood, but was having none of it.

"It was nothing," he told her. "Just some dumb dream."

"Ash. When you first came to me, you were in crisis."

"I'm still in crisis."

"The antidepressants you're on repress dreaming. Nyperal reinforces your otherwise-lacking REM-state atonia. You—"

"So many big words."

Mina stopped speaking and stared at him again.

Ash kept forgetting how smart she was — how very much the chameleon. In real ways, she knew Ash better than he knew himself. He'd mocked her treatments at first because he'd found her explanations condescending. He'd insisted she explain the medicine and science behind his treatment, not the dumbed-down version — everything from the field's background all the way up to present-day sleep studies conducted in her lab. He'd insisted she speak to him like a scientist, not an idiot. He wanted to know the psychological research behind it all, without having to simply swallow whatever she gave him like a good boy.

Acknowledging his dislike for simple talk, Mina had spoken to Ash more like a colleague than a patient from the start. But now, his little jab seemed to imply that he wanted things both ways — or, more accurately, *neither* way.

So did he want big words or small ones? More relevantly, did he want help or not? Some days Ash honestly didn't know.

Mina resumed after making her point. "But despite *any* pharmaceutical treatment I give you, it's important to keep in mind that your subconscious mind is sort of a jerk."

"Just mine?"

"Everyone's. Sometimes the subconscious mulls your past and frets about your future, but other times it has definite opinions and insists on telling you all about them. You can try to drown it out with denial and repression, but the mind is persistent. It finds ways *around* your repression. It's like trying to hold water behind a leaky dam. Water won't be confined, and neither will the things your subconscious refuses to bury. You're not stupid, Ash. Don't pretend you don't see the point in discussing a dream strong enough to shove its way past everything we've done to keep them from coming."

"It's my understanding that with enough antidepressants, dreaming stops entirely."

"It's my understanding that I'm the doctor, and you agreed to stop diagnosing yourself online."

Caught, Ash played with a small empty vase on the end table. "Everyone does that."

"Maybe everyone checks WebMD. Not everyone has their whole psychological make-up worked out, certain they know everything about how their brain works. We've talked about this. Over and over. And yet you keep telling me that you feel like someone's watching you and won't listen when I say it's trauma-mediated paranoia. You have what are clearly panic attacks, then insist they're no big deal. So let me ask you a question: How is Emily? Have you visited her? Have you spoken with her?"

Ash was looking down. He took out his wallet and begun looking through it when he realized a lecture was coming. He'd forgotten he had a library card. And a punchcard from Baskin Robbins. There was even a hand-written note tossed into the middle that meant nothing to him: *Mariana Jordan.* No phone number, though. If he'd met "Mariana" at a bar and hit on her, he'd done it poorly.

"Ash."

He looked up, wallet spread.

"Please pay attention."

"I am paying attention," he said.

She didn't bother to contradict him. "You're self-destructive."

"Self," Ash repeated.

"Yes. *Self.* But because you won't look it in the eye, that self-destructiveness manifests with a real possibility that you might end up harming *others* as well. Even setting aside the obvious, you've nearly caused three minor accidents at work, and—"

"Nearly." He had the verbal retaliation of a parrot.

"You know how this works: We talk and they let you keep your job as long as I keep saying you're making progress. Don't threaten to find a new doctor again. We both know the VA is your only choice."

Ash closed his mouth.

"So. Yes. After we talk, if I think it's warranted, we can increase your medication. *If.* But right now you're on a not-insignificant dosage and dreams are still leaking through.

14

Whatever your subconscious keeps trying to show you must be pretty important, and we're *still* not looking it in the eye. We can't just put a bandage over it. Things will only get worse if you keep pushing it away."

"That's what beer is for."

"*Physically* worse, too. Am I right to assume you're still having migraines?"

Defeated, Ash looked at the floor.

"I'm guessing a bunch of psychosomatic stuff as well. Back pain. Nerve pain. More panic attacks complete with tachycardia. I assume you know the term 'tachycardia'?"

"Rapid heart rate," Ash recited. "But—"

"Given your family history, it's never a good idea for you to be tachycardic. Are you looking for a heart attack?"

Yes. Yes, he was.

"You have talk to me if you want it to stop," she told him. "You know you do."

Ash shook his head, resolute as a kid refusing to eat his vegetables. "We've discussed everything that matters. This is supposed to be aftercare."

"We've discussed what the court *insisted* we discuss," Mina corrected. "In excruciating detail. What you've never talked about — even before the trouble, when you were still coming to me voluntarily — is all the stuff that kick-started your sleep disorder in the first place. Your plea deal didn't require us to discuss your trauma overseas, which I think we both know is the real problem and always has been. If you want to feel better, we have to stop talking so much about *what* happened and spend some time talking about *why* it happened. You didn't so much as sleepwalk before Afghanistan, did you?"

Ash said nothing, so Mina persisted.

"We need to talk about things like your incident with the IED. What was it like, when the bomb went off?"

15

"I don't want to talk about that."

"Exactly. *You don't want to talk about it.* But what do you think: it just *goes away*? There's a famous expression in psychology: 'What you resist persists.'"

"I'm not resisting it," Ash insisted.

"Was that what last night's dream was about? About Afghanistan?"

Discussing the dream seemed suddenly appealing, now that Ash could use it to prove her wrong. "Not in the least. I was in the US. In some American city."

"*This* city?"

"Maybe. I don't know. There were tall buildings."

Mina made a note.

"This isn't about my fear of heights."

"With all due respect, Ash, you don't have the slightest idea 'what it's about.'" Before he could rebut, she said, "What happened?"

"I was on a roof. This guy came up through an elevator."

"Anyone you know?"

"I'm not sure. He might have been Russian."

"What makes you think that? Did he speak Russian? Was he waving a Russian flag?"

"He just was."

She made another note on her pad. Ash resisted the urge to comment. Sometimes in dreams, you just *knew* shit. Everyone knew that.

"Then what?" she asked.

"These people appeared. They were walking toward him like zombies. They …"

He couldn't remember all of it. He remembered the others with their arms forward, but not why or if those hands had been holding anything. They could have been reaching out to strangle the Russian man, playing pat-a-cake, holding guns— even making profane hand gestures for all he knew.

"They were chasing him?" Mina asked.

"Just kind of plodding forward. Like they were after him, but couldn't move fast, or didn't want to."

Mina made another note.

"A woman was there. Not with the zombie-people. She was just observing or something. Watching him walk to the edge."

"He went to the edge?"

Ash nodded. "And stood on it."

"Then what?"

"The woman told him not to do it. She said …" Ash was groping for details.

But it was another black hole. He didn't remember why the dream had frightened him — only that it had.

He focused, if only so they could move past this. And as he did, details returned that had eluded him upon waking.

"She said that the Russian guy didn't need to do it," he told Mina.

"To jump?"

"I assume. She said 'You don't need to do it, because …'" He thought harder. "Because you have the real one.'"

"'The real one'?"

"I don't know what it means!" Ash snapped.

But there was something else — something he was just now realizing that he couldn't repeat even for his therapist.

The woman in the dream hadn't been anonymous. Ash had recognized her. She'd said something else in a whisper after the "real one" comment, too. She'd told the man on the roof, *Wait for dawn. Because sunshine makes everything better.*

"And then?" Mina asked, breaking his reverie.

Ash blinked up at her. He didn't like these new revelations. Not one little bit. He chose to ignore them, pretending it wasn't repression.

"Then he jumped," he said. "That's all there was to it."

"Nobody pushed him?"

Ash shook his head.

"So it was a suicide."

"No. After he jumped, he felt free."

"But he jumped from a building," Mina pointed out.

"While feeling free and happy," Ash added.

"Was *he* happy?" Mina asked. "Or were *you* happy, watching him do it?"

Ash didn't answer right away. He'd just remembered his thoughts from moments after waking, when he'd looked back on the dream:

I fell. I died.

At some point the jumper had stopped being an anonymous Russian and become Ash himself.

With the realization came one last bit of dream recall: a dizzy sensation of flapping through the air, hurtling toward a rendezvous with concrete.

Ash answered her obliquely: "I think I sort of *became* the guy at the end."

"You became the jumper?"

Ash sighed, not feeling outmaneuvered so much as tripped-up. He nodded. "Then I died."

"You actually hit the ground."

Another nod.

"Did you feel it?"

"It was just a dream."

"Sensory 'feelings' are just nerve impulses. Accomplished dreamers sometimes report feeling all sorts of things."

"I didn't think you could die in dreams."

"You can," Mina told him. "It's just not common. Most

people are so afraid of dying that fright wakes them up before it happens. The fact that you actually died in your dream makes me wonder if you're afraid at all."

Ash shrugged. "Isn't that a good thing, to not be afraid of dying? We all have to do it eventually, right? Might as well be prepared."

But Mina didn't look convinced. "'Good' is contextual. If you had terminal cancer, I'd agree it was 'good.'"

They both knew what Mina had left unspoken.

Ash became the jumper. Ash jumped. Then he died, and was perfectly fine with it.

"I'll increase your meds," she told him.

THREE

Conspiracy

The boy is happy.

He's found a trophy: a bit of detritus left behind by the Americans that can either be kept or sold.

He takes it to his mother.

Ash does not speak their language, but she seems to say, "That is not yours. It is theirs. Give it back to them."

The mother will not be a war profiteer any more than she will be a freedom fighter. This is the forgotten demographic. In an occupied land, not everyone in opposition actively fights. Most are quiet, wishing only to live their lives.

Disappointed but dutiful, the boy runs toward the tank with the Americans standing all around it while holding his prize, yelling what could only be, "WAIT! WAIT!"

But the soldiers see only a local running right at them with an explosive device.

And …

ASH PINCHED the bridge of his nose, setting askew the black-frame glasses he used for close-up work. He closed his eyes and sat that way for a while before opening them again with a yawn.

Fatigue was heavy tonight, but sleep evaded him. The world outside the window was dark and silent, barely even there.

Live long enough with insomnia and nothing feels real anymore.

And then Ash thought: *Well? Is it real?*

Being awake this late messed with a person's head unless they were used to it, and Ash never got used to anything anymore. He honestly didn't know.

Obeying a ritual whose origin he'd forgotten, he held his hands in front of himself. He pushed the fingers of one hand against the palm of the other, half-expecting them to go right through.

Then looked at the small digital clock beside the keyboard. It was 2:28 a.m.

He looked away, then back again. Still 2:28.

Wondering just what the hell he was doing, Ash let his gaze drift toward the reading chair across the room. A worn copy of *Pride and Prejudice* sat on the small wooden table to one side, a bookmark like a tongue between its pages. A teacup and a desiccated teabag on a spoon were beside the book. There'd be a dried-out lemon wedge still in the cup if Ash walked over and peeked inside to see it, sitting atop a dark brown stain of evaporated tea.

But he definitely didn't want to see that. Not now. Maybe not ever again.

"Am I awake," he asked the reading chair, "or am I dreaming?"

He thought again of his dream from the night before. He wasn't supposed to be dreaming at all, and yet recently it was happening more and more.

He dreamed most often about Emily. Or about killing

himself — though of course his mind buried suicide inside metaphors that weren't subtle at all.

That's what last night's dream had to be about. Ash was half Russian on his mother's side. The slowly-encroaching crowd on the rooftop represented everyone who'd silently (and not so silently) judged Ash for what he'd done. There was no shortage of those people around here.

Kill Ash Sanders! String him up! Slit him open and let his guts fall out! the people in his dreams seemed to scream at him. He knew where they were coming from.

He dreamed despite the antidepressants. Despite the booze and the slow-release edibles. On the nights between dreams, Ash couldn't sleep at all. Either because of his resolve not to dream, or his fear of what might happen in the real world as he slumbered.

Even asleep, Ash could destroy a life. That much, he knew better than anyone.

He'd barely rolled over at night since the verdict, let alone acted out his dreams. Despite that — despite the drugs that now kept him immobile at the times a sleeping man *should* be immobile — Ash felt sure he'd wake up in a neighbor's house someday, beating a stranger in his sleep. His hands had done worse, and not always for God and Country — not even always awake.

Everyone must secretly be afraid of him now. Except for Daisy Zhao, the one friend who'd never flinched.

Technically she had been Emily's friend. But then she'd become Ash's a while back — and somehow, impossibly, stayed that way.

When he didn't dream of suicide or his own death, Ash dreamed of Emily. But rarely the good times; instead he dreamed of them at their worst or Emily at *her* worst: alternative miseries like rotten little presents from his mind.

Ash saw versions of reality that might exonerate him if

they were true, but he didn't believe them. And even if he did — even if he *was* able to forgive himself — done remained done. Misery was misery, regardless of who was to blame.

But more and more, Ash found himself dreaming of Afghanistan. Of the boy with the IED that nobody (not even the boy) had realized was an IED until it was too late. In the end it didn't matter that the soldiers shot him. Everyone had ended up dead except for Ash and Chuck, who'd been fifty feet away smoking a cigarette when the bomb exploded in the child's hands.

The dreams played a hundred ways. Sometimes Ash saw things from the boy's perspective, and others from the mom's: first surviving the blast and then collapsing with grief. Sometimes Ash was himself in the dreams, and other times he witnessed the horror show from some outside perspective.

Dr. Irving liked that last one least of all. Third-party views of horrific events were the brain's way of disassociating from them — of trying to believe none of it had happened ... or at least not to him.

In today's session, Ash had told Mina about a double-whammy: a dream that was both suicidal *and* disassociated. She'd seemed to think that starting the dream as an outsider was even worse than if he'd been the jumper the entire time.

The boy is happy. He runs to his mother, who sends him back to the soldiers.

"Return it," she says, and he runs toward the tank with the Americans standing all around it.

Toward the truck with the Americans standing all around it.

Toward the van with the Americans standing all around it.

Ash, pinching his nose in combined fatigue and exasperation, felt his brow furrow. Was it a tank that day, or was it a truck? He'd lost the truth of what inspired his dream. He saw now that he'd started to think of the vehicle as a *van*, and yet that felt most incorrect of all.

A troop truck, fine. A Jeep, fine. An eighteen-wheeler? That seemed a stretch in the narrow streets, but again: fine. Same for a tank. But a van — like a band on tour — tooling through a war zone? Never in this lifetime.

So why did he keep picturing it that way?

Because you aren't thinking straight. You haven't really slept in days. Even though you technically slept last night, that wasn't really sleep. That was Hell with your eyes closed. It's all Hell. You're dead, man. Dead and gone.

Ash let his eyelids drop. Like holding his hand over a flame for self-punishment, he now invited the visions, hoping their savagery would make him sick with all the fear and guilt he deserved.

Again he saw the boy. The mother. The soldiers. And the van.

Large.

White.

No windows, not even on the rear.

A logo on the side that looked like a crescent moon carved into long and sharply curving slivers. A lone word below it: *ArkTek*.

That was strange, Ash thought as he opened his eyes and returned to the reality of his quiet nighttime office. His visualization skills were usually poor, and yet his mental image of the van was clear enough to print out and place in his hand.

It felt like he could walk forward in his imagination and read the VIN from any of the inside door panels. He saw it as a civilian fleet vehicle: the kind of thing an exterminator or cable company sent out on jobs.

But that couldn't be right ... it had been a canvas-topped troop carrier.

It almost had to be.

But the van, he could almost see it even with his eyes closed, seemed to disagree.

Ash opened his laptop. It took him a while to close the many windows and tabs from his last late-night session two days ago. He had a way of falling into a fugue when diving down internet rabbit holes, working punch-drunk and on autopilot. Half of what he clicked out of now, he didn't remember opening in the first place.

He gave each page a glance anyway before hitting Command-W to close them, fascinated by the idea that some other part of himself — an Ash doppelgänger — had explored these things while his higher mind was somewhere else.

Strange, how little sense he could make of them now. He'd have to invest some serious research just to grasp the questions that must have led him to open these tabs. The headlines were foreign, like dispatches from another land:

Mathematician Candace Wurtzman Honored: "This Changes Everything."

From Cloud Formation to Earthquake Prediction: Twenty Chaotic Systems the Wurtzman Conjecture Now Allows Scientists to Predict.

Privacy Concerns Raised — Why Hackers are Calling a Recent Math Discovery "Second Christmas."

On one tab, Ash found a YouTube video called *Be Afraid*. At the risk of falling back down the rabbit hole, he scanned the image and skimmed the description.

A middle-aged man wearing glasses sat behind a well-ordered desk in a bright and sterile-looking room that was nothing like the mess Ash had made of his. It struck him as a doctor's consultation space — maybe the den of a well-heeled lawyer. The man seemed professional, but more informed and educated than someone with a formal degree. A guy who knew things — a man the average Joe and Jane could trust.

Ash had apparently stopped the video about a third of the way through. He hit *Play* and the man resumed speaking in a calm, academic manner.

"—Congress. But did it even make it to the floor? Of course not. You have to understand a lot of mathematics that almost nobody understands to even *begin* to comprehend the ... the shall we say 'diverse and potentially problematic' spectrum of what's now possible. That's not your average congressperson or senator. So after the right people felt enough lip service had been paid to Jensen's concerns, the inquiry was quietly dropped from the docket. See, the Wurtzman Conjecture is like a set of Russian Dolls. Even Wurtzman herself doesn't know how deep it goes. I'd bet there aren't a dozen people in the field who could actually tell you how it all works, but do you know what?"

The onscreen pundit plucked an iPhone from his desk blotter and held it up. "I don't know how *this* works, either, but I can still make calls, use apps, and everything else. I could probably even figure out how to jailbreak it and install software to read the ID of any NFC antenna nearby — and use *my* phone to snoop on *your* phone. I could sniff out vulnerabilities in public wi-fi like you'd find at your local Starbucks, then use that weakness to steal enough personal data from the people around me to hack accounts and apply for fraudulent credit cards." He shook the phone in demonstration. "All without any real technical expertise at all."

He lowered the phone and kept talking.

"And now, thanks to Wurtzman, we've got this new

wrinkle. Now, instead of using a plain old jailbroken iPhone to steal a few bits from iffy wi-fi, I might be able to *decrypt secure wi-fi on the fly.* Those NFC antennas people use for tap-to-pay purchases? What if now, instead of just reading the ID of the device itself, I can use Wurtzman-enabled software to steal credit card numbers? It's only been three months since Wurtzman published her conjecture, and we're already seeing malware that uses it being passed around on Telegram and through the dark web. You can stop worrying about the future, folks. The stuff you need to worry about is already here."

He shook his head.

"Hackers don't *care* how the Conjecture does its decryption — which experts are now starting to admit makes child's play of even 128-bit security. They don't *care* how it can make predictions from massive and messy datasets, or why it's able to find order in what scientists were calling 'chaos' just months ago. Does the Contingency have the potential for great discovery? Absolutely. It might flat-out *solve* black hole physics. It might revolutionize supply chains in a way that more or less ends world hunger. We might even have the tools now to address climate change in a meaningful way. But with all that good comes a lot of bad ... and right now no one is discussing the dangers of the Wurtzman discovery. *No one.*"

Ash stopped the video. That last bit was no longer true. The video had been published three months ago, and anyone who didn't live in a cave knew there'd been plenty of worry since.

Congress still hadn't gotten out of its Barcalounger to investigate much, but the private sector was abuzz. Relatives kept contacting Ash to insist he upgrade his phone software. Insisting he upgrade his smart doorbell and security systems. The last two months had seen a boom in the home wi-fi business as well, as every ISP sent out crew after crew to security-patch its customers' routers.

Ash closed the video and looked at the one just beneath it: *Before Letting Your ISP Touch Your Router, Do This.*

He smirked, remembering a bit of this video. It recommended everyone check any repair tech's IDs twice (and ideally call the company to verify they actually worked for Verizon or AT&T or whoever) before letting them near your equipment. Conspiracies begat conspiracies. You couldn't allay your fears about internet vulnerability because the criminals were in the "repair" business too — not fixing your router so much as hacking it further.

Ash himself was split on the issue. Privacy had never been at bigger risk, sure. Personal information — in electronic form, at least — had never been more vulnerable, sure. Still, Ash wasn't ready to go into full-freak mode over any of it. The idea that fake technicians were going door-to-door masquerading as the real things in order to build backdoors into routers wasn't far from the wackos who thought vaccines were a cover to implant microchips.

There was a fine line between being cautious and going tinfoil.

He closed the rest of the tabs. He really, *really* needed to start staying away from the internet when suffering from insomnia.

Once the screen was clean and fresh, Ash opened a new search and entered the word his mind kept seeing on the day of the IED, stenciled onto the side of a van: *ArkTek.*

No relevant results returned, at least on the first three pages. The closest in matches were Biblical: either Noah's Ark or the Ark of the Covenant.

So he entered *ArkTek Afghanistan* and got even fewer results.

That made sense, because he was imagining things.

When he'd seen that kid gunned down and the bomb had exploded, it'd happened beside a truck or a Jeep or maybe a tank — definitely *not* a windowless white van with a moon and some weird word on the side.

Ash's memory had probably overlapped two separate memories, was all. In stressful situations, people jumbled their memories. You were just as likely to remember seeing your boss rob the liquor store as you were to recall the real bandit's face.

Still Ash sat back, unsettled.

If he could just figure out why that word (ArkTek) and that logo (a sliced-up crescent moon) were so familiar — where he'd seen them, if not overseas — he'd at least have the seeds of his closure.

But for now, the issue hung open like a screaming throat.

More exhausted than truly tired, Ash removed his glasses and rubbed his face with both hands. "Go to sleep, asshole. You're out of your mind."

More and more, the second thing felt true.

But the first, until morning, eluded him.

FOUR

Sanderz

Ash felt the drill press wheel push back against his palm as metal chewed through metal on the platform before him.

His eyes found the simple act of watching it happen difficult. Everything in his field of view was slightly fuzzy, as if seen through dirty contacts. The shop's background drifted in slow motion. Voices nearby were deeper than they should be whenever he had his hearing protection off, or so he'd noticed when clocking in.

His drive to work had felt like a slow slalom, as if the car was on benevolent ice that rocked it instead of turning it sideways.

This must be how it felt to operate machinery on NyQuil. He'd read the warnings, but you could probably get to the same place by never closing your eyes.

And so his mind wandered to inebriated places.

The shop's work was strange once he thought about it: metal yielding to metal. And yet somewhere in the building, specialists worked with lasers. *Light* cutting through metal was even stranger. Thinking about it now, Ash started to wonder if this whole crazy world was in his head.

Maybe he wasn't even awake right now. Maybe *that's* why nothing felt real.

It would explain a lot — like the notion that he and everyone else lived on a big rock revolving around an even bigger fireball in an infinite void.

Existence was trippy. Ash's new theory was that maybe it just *seemed* trippy because everything was actually in his head. After all, how could he know? It was an oddly heartening thought. It implied that maybe, at some delightful point in the future, he'd snap out of the nightmare he'd been living and awaken somewhere better. Somewhere more logical, where light always lost when it encountered metal.

"ASH!" boomed a voice above the cacophony.

The drill bit punched the last of its way through the plate, dropping his wheel arm like falling through a trap door. Ash turned toward the short but somewhat round man with a reddish-brown beard who'd come up beside him, safety glasses and ear protection on.

Not exactly smart, sneaking up on someone working a deadly machine who can't hear or see you coming.

"YOU OKAY MAN?"

Ash nodded. He hadn't entirely heard, but this was something Chuck asked him often nowadays. It was getting a bit irritating, but still better than the death stares he got in his neighborhood.

"WHEN IS MRKBRK?"

"WHAT?" He hadn't gotten the last word from context.

Louder: "WHEN … IS … YOUR … BREAK!"

Ash's head turned. DeShawn was watching the two of them. He seemed to make sure both men were looking at him, then pointed somewhat angrily where a watch would be if he wore one. He mouthed, *Take five!*

His body language said he wasn't granting a break to be kind, but instead for safety reasons.

Ash stepped back, then looked from DeShawn to Chuck, then back to DeShawn. The foreman was standing with his beefy arms crossed, staring at them like light boring through metal.

Seeing his eyes, Ash got the impression this wasn't really a *break* so much as a five-minute taste of his imminent firing.

"FORGET HIM," Chuck said once they were settled in the break room.

Knowing Chuck, this would be a fifteen-minute break instead of five. DeShawn wouldn't care because the less time Ash spent fucking things up, the better.

"I'm so fired," Ash replied.

Chuck sort of shrugged. Everyone knew Ash was a dead man walking around here, but the risk of a PR nightmare had thus far stayed the company's hand. Most of the shop's news-watchers had long ago decided that Ash was a monster, but a surprisingly large number of them seemed to have his back: those who believed he'd done nothing wrong — although security footage, if Ash had any, would have strongly disagreed.

"You look like shit," Chuck said.

"I *feel* like shit."

"Yeah, well, you look it." Chuck sipped coffee from a mug that read, DRILLERS DO IT DEEP. "Nightmares?"

"I was just awake all night."

"Better than nightmares."

"They take turns. One night I sleep in Hell and the next night I don't sleep at all. I can't decide which I love more."

Ash got up and walked to his locker. He pulled a flask his father had given him for Christmas from the interior pocket of his jacket and raised it in silent offer.

"Yeah, *that* seems like a good idea right now," said Chuck.

Ash drank anyway. Then, as he returned the flask, a piece of paper he didn't remember sticking to the side wall of the locker caught his eye. Someone had secured both top and bottom of the paper with tape, so it ripped as he pulled it away.

It was a printed web article. A more sensational one than anything reported by the likes of CNN or the Associated Press.

SANDERS GETS AWAY WITH MURDER, the headline read.

It was hardly the first jab Ash had received, even at work. He looked down at the paper, nodding. "It's nice to have something to read."

Chuck snatched the article, then crumpled it into a ball. He tossed it into a wastebasket beside the grease-covered coffee machine.

"I'm sure it's about some other Sanders," he said.

"Like Winnie the Pooh."

"What?"

"Winnie the Pooh. He's got *Mr. Sanders* written over his door."

"Who knows that?" Chuck asked.

"*You* do."

Of course Chuck did. The man had a memory like the Library of Congress. "Yeah, but I have an excuse for knowing shit like that. I have a kid. What I don't get is why *you* know it."

Ash didn't reply. Emily, always one for advance preparation, had started reading parenting and kids' stuff the

33

second they'd started trying to get pregnant. Not that they'd made it far.

"Pooh fucked up the E, though," said Ash. "I think it was upside-down or something."

"Like a schwa?"

"A 'schwa'?"

"An upside-down E. *Schwa*. Didn't you take grammar in school?"

Ash laughed a little. Chuck was awful at making Ash feel better on purpose, but excellent at getting the job done on accident. He was strange — not at all like the other machinists. Chuck had always been odd, even when they'd been grunts together overseas. He knew all sorts of useless trivia, like schwas and what Pooh had above his door. Like his blue collar would have been better off with its owner in the library.

"But it wasn't the upside-down E that made the sign wrong," Chuck went on. "There wasn't a schwa. The S was backwards at the end. It looked like a Z. 'Sander*zzz*.'"

Ash wasn't sure. "I remember it being the E."

"No E." Chuck shook his head. "It was backwards S, backwards N."

"I'm pretty sure, Chuck. Emily put posters in the den for 'inspiration.' As if it might encourage my sperm and her eggs, all who'd look at that poster and see what they were missing." What was supposed to be levity left him like acid.

"I could look it up if you want," Chuck told him.

Ash glanced through the window into the shop and saw DeShawn staring at them. It had been at least five minutes. Ash should have been fired a long time ago, Chuck too for that matter, but because everyone liked him so much, seemed immune to downsizing. Almost like he and DeShawn had struck a deal.

34

No, Ash didn't want Chuck to look it up. Not only was it a stupid thing to spend time on, but thoughts of Pooh were too close to thoughts of Emily and the kid that would never be born. That path was paved with memories Ash tried to avoid and the *almost*-memories his brain had invented to color the blanks he still had in the worst night of his life.

For now, he could still take solace in the *dream* version of events. Ash had been strangling a serial killer to save Emily's life in his dream. In reality, her neck had been in his hands.

"Look, man," said Chuck as if reading his mind. His eyes ticked to the wastebasket, where the crumpled-up news story still sat like an accusation on top. "Guys fuck around. Guys blow off steam. You know nobody here thinks you did it on purpose."

Ash laughed: just one sarcastic bleat.

"Okay, so some do. But look who we're talking about here. Sonny beats his wife and it's not like *he's* doing it in his sleep. Ray, Jerome, Hitch, Junior … their families all hate them, and they're not fucking up marital bliss in *their* sleep, either. Only angel around here is Charity Goddard."

"It's not a question of whether I *did* it."

"Yeah. I know. It's a question of whether you *meant* to do it. Whether you were in your right mind when you did it. Whether you have a diagnosed condition … which, on the official record, Selina made clear you do."

"Right." Ash almost laughed. "Selina was a *great* help."

"You say that, but she was. Listen. You got a raw deal, but you couldn't help it. It wasn't great when you pulled your old girlfriend's hair out by the roots, sure, but at least what you did to *Mindy* got you to a sleep clinic. It cost you one breakup, but at least you got a diagnosis. One that Selina and the rest of HR have had in your file forever, by the way. Thanks to Mindy, you were *already* on-record. Officially, legally and medically, everyone knew you were a sleepwalker long before … *you know*."

"Technically, I have 'sleep violence.' It's a REM behavior disorder, not—"

Chuck barely heard. "That shit with Mindy happened — what? — like a full year before you even *met* Emily. People understand sleepwalking, so they're able to understand what you have if they've got half a brain. Emily knew you had it. Selina confirmed it for the world with her testimony. I vote you owe her a thank-you card."

Ash was less than mollified, but he liked Chuck's attempts at soothing a lot better than pity or blame. In a weird way, Chuck discussing Ash's killing of his wife in such casual terms felt refreshing. Most people were afraid to talk about it — and when someone finally did, they couldn't keep the horror out of their eyes. Chuck and Ash had seen a lot of terrible shit together. In a twisted way, they were used to it.

Chuck flapped his hands in a *what-do-you-want-from-me* sort of way. "You're a *vet*, man! A fucking hero! We did shit for this country that nobody should have to do. And what thanks did we get? I got PTSD and you got what you got. People want to blame you for what you couldn't control — what war did to *you* while *they* were back home watching football — then fuck 'em!"

Ash tried to look grateful. What Chuck said was technically true, but that didn't make it easier when people Ash didn't even know shouted at him on the street. Or when he considered eating his service pistol, or when he'd had to drive into work with *MURDERER* painted on his car because there'd been no time to cover or remove it. The first R and D had been written backwards, the way Danny wrote *REDRUM* in *The Shining*. It'd either been some weird homage or a mistake, like Pooh with Mr. Sanders.

Oh. Right. Speaking of Winnie the Pooh, something had occurred to Ash. Despite his reservations a moment ago, he pulled out his phone, did a quick image search, and immediately found what he'd been looking for. He turned the screen to show Chuck.

"How did you know?" Ash asked. It did indeed read *Mr. Sanders*: backwards N and backwards final S, but not a schwa in sight.

"So we're really going to keep talking about a cartoon named after taking a shit?"

"I was as sure about it as you were, but I was wrong and you're *never* wrong. Last week you were right about the date of that party I thought was on the fifteenth, not the twenty-second like you said. That party was over a year ago. I can't remember you ever forgetting anything … Do you have a photographic memory or something?"

For a moment Chuck looked like Ash had found all his porn. But then the expression vanished and he shrugged. "I've just always had a knack."

"Can I ask you something?"

"I think you're going to ask no matter what I say."

"Do you remember that day in Kandahar?"

Chuck took a long sigh: *You really like to torture yourself, don't you?*

"I do if we're talking about the only 'day in Kandahar' you'd ever bring up out of the blue."

"*How well* do you remember it?"

Chuck's half-smile finally broke. "Better than I'd like."

"Were we traveling in a truck? Or was it a Jeep?"

"It was a troop carrier. Not that anyone went home in one."

"An APC?"

"No, it wasn't armored. Why?"

"So it wasn't an eighteen-wheeler?"

"Why would it be an eighteen-wheeler?"

The break room door opened. The cacophony of the shop floor filled the previously quiet room like an assault, and DeShawn's angry face appeared in the crack.

"You girls finished doing your makeup? I said 'take *five*'!"

Chuck stood and put his protection back on, but Ash still needed a moment. His thoughts were suddenly and unexpectedly spinning, foggy and troublesome.

He hadn't asked if the vehicle was a white van with logos on the side because that was even more ridiculous than it being a semi. But that wasn't what had him most confused right now.

Right now (though it was surely because he was so sleep-deprived), Ash was starting to wonder why he'd asked Chuck about Kandahar in the first place ... because a burst of near-photographic memory of his own had just insisted that even vault-memory Chuck wouldn't know the answer about Kandahar.

How could he? Out of the blue — and contrary to all memory and evidence — Ash was suddenly sure that Chuck hadn't even been with him in Kandahar that day.

FIVE

Shadow Figures

"You're not sleeping," Mina told him.

"I already said that. It's literally why we're here."

"No," she said, waving a dismissive hand. "I'm not trying to tell you something you don't already know. I'm saying *that's* the answer. You're not sleeping enough, and that's why you're paranoid."

"I'm not paranoid."

Mina resettled the pad on her lap and looked at him seriously. "Ash. You just told me that you've started to wonder if your best friend — the person you rely on most for support because you went through your traumas *together* — might not have been in Kandahar with you."

"Might." Ash felt himself backpedaling. "And he could still have been in *Kandahar*. Still in my unit, even. Just maybe not in the same place as I was on that same day. *Maybe.*"

"The day of the IED." Her face became half stern. "The day that boy was shot and your friends were killed."

"Right."

"The day you constantly think about. The day that haunts you. The day that's somewhat of an obsession."

A little annoyed now: "Yeah. That day."

"The day you refuse to let yourself think too much about."

"There are a *few* days I'd rather not think about."

"The day that arguably started everything. The day that's probably the reason you developed sleep violence in the first place."

Ash sat back, feeling cornered. "You know it runs in my family. My dad—"

"And *you* know that REM Behavior Disorder — the reason you act out your dreams — is often triggered by traumatic events. In our first session you used a very *specific* word, and it wasn't 'walking.' You referred to your state as 'sleep-*patrolling*.' You woke up in your kitchen holding a baguette like a rifle. It took Emily five minutes to convince you that nobody was crouched just out of sight and waiting to attack."

"I know what I told you. Because *I was the one who told you.*"

"You're regressing, Ash."

"This is very kind and compassionate of you. Thanks so much."

"Do you know why I do this work?" she asked with a hard stare.

Ash knew the core of it, and had enough respect to not be a smartass.

Mina continued. "My mom had nightmares so bad, eventually she committed suicide. I was eight years old. That's not something you hear about often — nightmares ending in suicide. My dad wouldn't talk about it for the longest time. Eventually, he told me that she didn't do it because of the nightmares themselves. It was because she didn't think anyone or anything could help her stop them, and she couldn't face the thought of dealing with them every night for the rest of her life, which was how she felt. *Real* was irrelevant."

Mina took a beat to make sure she still had Ash's full attention, then continued.

"Real or not, they scared her enough that she could barely function. We think she might have had undiagnosed schizophrenia — some sort of underlying condition, dissociative at the very least. She started taking over-the-counter stimulants to try and stay awake. She'd go days without sleeping, but that only made it worse when she finally slept. The mind *needs* to dream. And when it can't, all those accumulated dreams eventually come in a flood. My mother was so sleep-deprived by the time she had her inevitable 'nightmare avalanches' that she'd basically lose the ability to tell reality from what was inside her head. It meant her 'nightmares' felt constant. She thought some horrible vision might show up while she was watching TV or shopping. She tried to handle everything by herself and made things worse. The right piece of advice from a therapist could have helped her navigate the worst of it, but she never had the chance. Eventually she found a different way to escape. I went into sleep work for people like her, Ash. People like *you*."

"This is volunteer work for you," he replied lamely.

"Yeah. *Volunteer*. I'm not doing it for the pay. Don't you think that makes it *more* — not *less* — likely that I actually give a shit? My brothers are both veterans. What you did for the rest of us? What you had to go through? I don't underestimate it. Those constant offers for you to come to my sleep lab at the university, outside of the VA program, *for free*? I mean them. But you know the expression. You can only lead a horse to water. And you are one stubborn goddamn horse, Ash Sanders."

She crossed her arms and sat back. He almost felt bad for her — okay, he *did* feel bad for her — and in some obscure way what the doctor had said felt unfair. This was *Ash's* therapy session, not hers. She was supposed to remain dispassionate and help him no matter how difficult he made things. Her display of vulnerability and emotion was unprofessional. It had to be in violation of some sort of therapist's code.

But Mina wasn't an ordinary shrink. She had the degree, but not the practice. The VA had paired them because he had a sleep disorder and her specialty (to the extent of not one but two PhDs, plus an impressive award whose name he'd forgotten) was sleep. Or more specifically, *dreams*. She usually did lab work, not therapy. She was, Ash kept having to remind himself, sort of winging it whenever he detoured from his sleep disorder into neuroses better treated by psychotherapy. Or when he was being an asshole.

"I'm sorry," he said.

The words seemed to trigger Mina into embarrassment. She shuffled, eyes down, eager to compose herself. She wasn't supposed to lose her cool, but truth was her mother may as well have been the late Emily Sanders. Her brothers, both of whom she'd told Ash had severe and dream-incurring PTSD, could have been Ash himself. So yes. He *was* an asshole.

A flush of guilt climbed up the back of his neck. On a primal level, Ash was thumbing his nose at the closest thing she had to undoing the tragedies that had befallen the people she loved.

"No, *I'm* sorry," she said, trying and failing to disguise the wiping-away of covert tears. "But you frustrate me,

Ash. I shouldn't let you, but I do. You aren't even trying. Maybe it's because you don't think you have anyone left. If you had children, I'd be telling you to stay strong for them, but I can only tell you to stay strong for yourself. And it's clear that you couldn't care less about that guy. Is it too late? Do you even want to get better?"

It wasn't the fairest question, both manipulative and out of line. But despite that, her query hit him in the stomach. Maybe it was stupid ... or maybe there was still a compassionate human man hiding inside him after all.

"Okay," Ash said. "I'll want to get better. I'll try."

THROUGH UNSPOKEN AGREEMENT, they ignored Mina's a-bit-too-personal sidebar. She was mortified, and Ash was embarrassed almost as much. Still, something in the room changed after that, with a more honest road now paved between them.

"So you think Chuck *was* there and I'm just imagining things," Ash said. "That day in Kandahar."

Mina shook her head. "That's not for me to say."

Ash gave her a face: *Oh, come on. Cut the bullshit.*

Mina relented with a sigh. "I only know you've shown me photos with both of you in them. And that we read the incident report together."

He'd forgotten about that. Mina had helped him requisition the report so he could stare his history in the eye. She'd felt trying to ignore what he'd seen would only trigger his subconscious mind to work harder against him. Surrender might offer release.

It was Ash's turn to sigh. "I was so *certain*. Chuck stood up in the break room, and I looked right at him, and then it was like I was watching TV inside my head. *He wasn't there.* All of a sudden, I was one hundred percent sure I was alone that day."

"Are you sure now?"

He frowned and shrugged.

Mina recrossed her legs, less intimidating now that she'd set her notepad on the end table. "Maybe it would help to stop thinking in terms of true and false."

Ash made a face.

Mina continued. "Both versions of the day in Kandahar — one with Chuck and one without — feel equally true to you, right? But you know they *can't* both be true. That's not the way 'true' works. One has to be true and the other has to be false — and it's disconcerting to get them confused. So I suggest you stop thinking in terms of 'true.'"

"How the hell else should I think of it?" Ash asked.

"Our brains aren't passive. We *think* we're seeing directly through our senses, but we aren't. What we think of as 'our experience of the world' is actually a highly creative process. The brain uses a lot of information — from your senses, yes, but also from memories and expectations and its own understanding of what certain things 'mean' — to create the world it shows you."

Ash looked doubtful. Mina persisted.

"Think about it. Your *eyes* only see a pair of flat images … but when an object is in the exact same place in both of those images, your *brain* decides that object is far away. When an object's position is different between the images, though, your brain decides it's close to you. That's why depth perception is harder if you cover one eye: your brain can't compare two pictures and has to rely on one. Your *ears* might hear a police siren decreasing in volume, but your *brain* says, 'the police car is moving farther away.' The brain's a storyteller, Ash. It accumulates all sorts of data, and only some of it comes from the senses. Your brain interprets that data to tell you a story. *The brain's story* is what comprises our experience of the world. It's easy to think we're getting 'raw, objective feeds' from our senses, but that's not how things work."

"Deep," Ash said, trying to be sarcastic.

"I'm serious. You don't have the full truth of that day in Kandahar even if that's how it seems. You can't. You saw and heard and felt a limited amount, not *every single tiny thing* that happened. When you look back on that memory now, your brain is filling in the gaps — but the brain is sly; it presents all that gap-filling as if it's true. It's not, though. The same goes for the present moment. For instance." She pinched the fabric of her blouse between her fingers. "What color is this?"

"Blue."

"Okay. And what's 'blue'?"

"I don't understand the question."

"Colors don't happen in the world," Mina said. "Like depth perception, colors happen in the brain. Your eyes take in a certain wavelength of light, and your brain shows you blue. But 'blue' isn't a thing outside of the mind. Bats 'see' with sound. Do you think a bat experiences 'blue' in the same way you do when it looks at my shirt?"

"Where are you going with this?"

She settled back. "I'm saying the brain *always* adds to objective experience. It *always* skews what you see depending on a lot of factors, and only some of those factors are sight, sound, and the other senses. To some degree you see what you expect to see. If you notice a man behind you in the shadows and you're afraid, you might see a knife in his hand. If you notice the same man after a wonderful party, you'll decide he's holding a beer. All sorts of invisible biases come into play when you look back on your memories, but that's also true of what you're experiencing right now. My point is this: You said your memory of Kandahar, when you looked at Chuck today, felt like watching TV inside your head. But *everything* is like watching TV inside your head: then, now … even what you anticipate in the future."

"So what you're saying is, I'm wrong about everything so why even try."

She laughed. "I'm saying that even though it can be unnerving when memories and experiences don't jibe, it's actually not too crazy that they wouldn't. You're not comparing two objective facts, which is how it feels. In reality, you're comparing two reconstructions made by your brain. We act like our eyes are a window on the real world, but evolutionary biology tells us the brain only shows us the most adaptive *version* of the real world — whatever version it thinks will best help you survive, so you can pass on your genes."

Mina leaned forward.

"You're not unusual, Ash." She sounded so earnest. "Not because your memories sometimes conflict, anyway. Your brain is doing its best, but *your* brain in particular has been through a lot. It's like an air conditioner struggling to keep up during a heat wave. Give yourself a break. Thoughts are just thoughts. You're bound to have fantasies here and there, both good and bad."

Mina took a breath as if nearing a sticking point. "The same goes for your dreams, which are *always* constructed. *Always* nothing more than fantasies of the mind."

"Wait. Are you seriously conflating my fucked-up Kandahar memory and my dreams?"

She leaned back and crossed her arms with a shrug. "Why not? Both are fallible. In both cases you have to be vigilant, lest they deceive you."

"That's different." He shook his head. "You can easily tell a dream from reality."

"Are you sure? Have you ever had a lucid dream?"

"Yes." He frowned and corrected himself. "I mean no. I don't know why I said yes."

"Lucid dreams feel as real as you and me talking right now. What if *this* is a dream?"

He laughed.

"I'm serious. Most people never think to check whether they're in a dream, which is why most dreams aren't lucid. If you don't check, you'll never know the truth until you wake up."

"How the hell do you check to see if you're in a dream?" Ash asked.

"You try to fly. Or breathe with your mouth shut and nose plugged, or look at yourself in a mirror. A common check used by lucid dreamers is to look at the time on a digital clock, then look away and quickly look back. If the clock's display changes, you're dreaming. You can try to read the same bit of text twice without it changing."

Ash looked at the headline of a magazine on the table between them, and as he did so Mina laughed. She'd never before laughed in their sessions. The sound was warm and friendly — a laugh he'd like to hear more.

"I'm not saying you're dreaming right now," she told him. "I'm just pointing out that what you *think* is unquestionable might not be. The fact that you 'remembered' Chuck not being in Kandahar doesn't, in itself, mean he wasn't. Unless there's some big conspiracy against you, I'd say the pictures and official record prove that your mind was deceiving you today — but not with malice; it was trying to protect you in a maladaptive way we don't understand."

"So I'm cracking up?"

She shook her head. "You're *sleep deprived.* Sleep deprivation is as effective a form of torture as waterboarding. Literally. It screws with your judgment. It can make you paranoid. It can make you see things."

"Does that also mean you think the people I said were lurking around my house …?"

"I can't say." Mina made a noncommittal gesture, dismissing the more paranoid delusions he'd made the mistake of telling her in the past. "Maybe people really *are* lurking. You do have some infamy after … Well, *after.* But yes, you could be imagining all of that, too."

"What about …" This felt stupid now, but he pressed on anyway. "What about the people I've seen *inside* my house?"

Yeah. Ash was just now remembering that one. He'd told her in a moment of weakness about the persecutors he sometimes saw inside his perimeter, but until now he'd allowed himself to forget them — along with the embarrassment of having seen such paranoid things in the first place.

But she'd been honest with him today … and he'd promised he'd be honest back. And try harder.

Mina looked thoughtful. "You said you see them as you drift off to sleep?"

"As I *try* to sleep, yeah."

"I suppose that could be what we call 'hypnagogic imagery.' Usually it's shapes and colors behind the eyelids in Phase One of sleep, but if you think your eyes are open, you might see shadow figures."

"I read about shadow figures," Ash told her. "Supposedly they're common with sleep paralysis."

"Uh-huh. And did you 'read about it' on WebMD?"

Ash tried to look cowed.

"You don't have sleep paralysis, Ash," she said soberly. "That's kind of the problem."

Ash resisted a hard sigh. In their first session pre-trial, Mina had explained that particular bit of bad wiring in his psyche. People with REM Behavior Disorder tended to act out their dreams because the mechanisms that normally paralyze a sleeper during Rapid Eye Movement stop working. Ash had once woken to find himself doing pushups. Fighting assailants who weren't there. Dancing on one occasion, and of course pulling out his ex-girlfriend's hair on another. That time he'd woken to her thrashing and screaming. The next day there'd been a breakup. Then a sleep doctor.

"If I had to guess, it's not hypnagogia," Mina said. "What you're seeing are probably delusions of persecution. Manifestations of guilt. The less you sleep, the more that's likely to happen. You're subconsciously turning allies into enemies, and it's worse when you can't sleep and your defenses are down. Today your best friend became suspect. If you don't already, you'll probably suspect me next. You need to sleep. *Need*, with a capital N."

"The Nyperal …"

"The new dosage I prescribed on Monday will need time to take effect," Mina said, nodding. "Nyperal induces REM-state atonia — paralysis during REM sleep, the way things are supposed to work. Now. I just said you don't have a problem with sleep paralysis, but that *could* change now that you're on a higher dose. It's possible you'll wake up unable to move. But it's harmless, so don't fight if it happens. It'll go away in a minute or two."

Ash nodded. He'd prefer never moving again to moving any more at night. He was a sleep-murderer, living in constant terror that he'd do it again.

"Your antidepressants should be repressing dreams, but

they're obviously not working well enough. I don't want to up the dosage there, especially after increasing the Nyperal. I'll consider some options. For now I think emergency measures are worth the risk. We'll reassess as we go, but for now I want you to get a night or two of solid sleep no matter what. Getting you deeper into sleep deprivation strikes me as the highest risk on your table right now, so let's do whatever we can to get you some Z's."

She took a moment, nodding to herself before she finished her thought. "I have a sedative in mind that won't interact adversely with your other meds, but I'm only giving you an RX for two days."

"Two days?" Ash had never heard of such a short prescription.

"It's got a high potential for dependency and abuse — so yes, just two days. Two days of solid, dreamless sleep will do wonders." She scribbled on a prescription pad, ripped off the top page, and set it aside to send in later. "I want you to take one of these tonight and tomorrow night. Get a couple days of sleep, feel better, and then we'll talk again."

Ash looked at her, his doubt showing.

"The world will feel right again, at least for a while." Mina smiled. "You'll see."

SIX

Deprived

Defying Mina's explicit instructions, Ash waited a full day to fill his new prescription.

He simply got busy. It wasn't intentional. Unless it was *subliminally* intentional — something Ash had to admit felt possible after hearing Dr. Irving's diagnosis that his mind might be fucking with him.

You're trying to turn your allies into enemies. You want to be hated because you hate yourself.

The first part was a revelation, but the second like acknowledging a blue sky or stating that two plus two equaled four. Ash was once a proud man — proud to the point of arrogance. War had broken him, and post-war aftermath had shattered the brittle bit of himself that remained. He'd forgotten what it was like to see his face in the mirror and not want to strike it. Wring a neck that deserved it, for a change.

Still, Mina had sent him off with a bit of blunt-ended positivity: The fact that Ash now accepted what his psyche might be up to was an excellent sign. In the past, he would have remained in denial.

No, he would have told Mina in the past, *It's NOT my mind fucking with me. People really ARE after me. My old friends really HAVE become enemies. You don't know what you're talking about, Doc. I've got people stalking me 24/7. The sky IS falling. You're the crazy one, not me.*

Surrender, Mina had said as he left her office, was its own form of healing.

Still, for whatever reason (forgetfulness, a full schedule, or more self-sabotage), Ash had forgotten. He'd snapped out of a daydreaming haze on the evening after their appointment with an *oh-shit* revelation: Mina's office had sent the sedative prescription to his usual Walgreens but he'd neglected to pick it up. He'd been too absorbed with driving to Taco Bell, eating Taco Bell, then spending a half hour on the toilet because of Taco Bell.

Between Taco Bell and the toilet, he'd also noticed a windowless white van on Warner Boulevard. He'd then gone miles out of his usual way to try and catch what turned out to be a delivery van for a seafood distributor, making the restaurant rounds. The logo on its side was a shrimp wearing a chef's hat. Why? Was the shrimp planning to cook his friends and eat them? Was it a bad shrimp? A genocidal shrimp? Maybe the shrimp had made a deal with humans to save its own exoskeleton: *Help us eat your family and we'll let you live.* To a veteran, collaborators were the worst sort of shrimp.

Maybe he'd gone on that van-chasing errand so he'd forget the real errand. Maybe. *Just maybe.*

After being waylaid by the shrimp conspiracy (and maybe a little out of his mind; maybe Mina was onto something with the *sleep-deprivation-makes-you-crazy* thing), Ash had pulled out his phone and searched for the word *ArkTek* again.

This time after finding nothing, it felt essential that he

pull out a pen and sketch the sliced-up-moon logo on the back of an old oil change receipt. *That's* what he'd done wrong the first time, he decided two blocks away from the Taco Bell — the reason he'd found nothing. He hadn't made a sketch to use for a Google Images search!

But instead of ArkTek and persecutors, Ash's search yielded French bakery logos. Apparently he wasn't artist enough to draw a crescent moon differently than a croissant.

He felt defeated. Insane. Tired, and like nothing made sense. So he parked on the roadside, closed his eyes, and rested his head on the steering wheel while traffic roared by.

"Chuck was there," he'd said aloud, trying to convince himself. "And it was a troop truck, not a white van with a logo on the side."

He'd never talked to himself before the trouble began. Doing it today in his car hadn't made him feel any saner. So he'd driven home, and on the way he saw ten more white vans. But they weren't ArkTek vans, if ArkTek vans even existed. They were internet service provider vans, installing the security patches required to keep Wurtzman hackers at bay.

AT&T. Verizon. Comcast. T-Mobile. Women and men in company uniforms parking at curbs, walking up and down the block with tablets.

Despite knowing better, Ash's exhausted mind had gone to the conspiracy videos on his desktop. The people he saw in uniform weren't *really* the employees of internet service providers — they were obviously part of the big machine, exploiting security vulnerabilities to … to control everyone's brain or something.

In the car by himself, his bark of laughter sounded downright manic.

So he'd gone home. Made a microwave dinner. He'd then done an admirable job of ignoring his now-abrogated doubts about Chuck, and the likely truth that his neighbors were plotting against him. He hadn't at all wondered how many not-actually-part-of-a-conspiracy ISP workers were in his area, waiting until he fell asleep to break in and persecute him.

Ignoring paranoid thoughts ended up consuming Ash's evening. Only six or seven times did he find himself unable to resist temptation, standing from his armchair to draw back the curtains and peek outside, needing to be sure no one was watching him through binoculars.

Instead, outside, Ash saw pedestrians pretending they weren't part of something insidious. Once he saw a white van with a crescent-moon logo out of the corner of his eye, but he made himself decide it probably hadn't actually been there.

"Go to bed," he told himself. "You're drunk."

Except that he hadn't been drinking.

That's when he remembered the prescription. Mina's instructions had been clear: *When you take the new pills tonight, it's very important not to drink.* Compassion had kept her from pointing out the obvious: in addition to helping Ash sleep, the sedatives would double as a test of his suicidal tendencies.

Her advice, if Ash inverted it, practically gave him a recipe for death: take both pills at once, then drink a bottle of whiskey. They'd know in the morning if he really wanted to die.

Ash realized what his hands had been doing while he'd been thinking: they'd grabbed garden ropes from a box at his feet and begun idly tying nooses.

Horrified, he dropped the noose.

It landed in the box atop three others: four chances to swing, just in case pills and whiskey didn't do their jobs.

Jesus. And to think: Mina knows this. She knows I'm suicidal, depressed despite the meds, and not thinking clearly. Who the fuck ties nooses? It seems like everyone — including me — wants me dead.

So what if Mina's prescription really *was* a test? Something more nefarious than looking out for his well-being? Why would a responsible physician give suicide pills to an obvious depressive?

Dr. Irving probably *wanted* him to kill himself. She wasn't his friend after all.

No. Mina was his enemy.

You're paranoid. You've been paranoid all day. You're losing your mind to exhaustion.

Mina's voice followed his own: *Don't be surprised if something happens tonight that makes you suspect me next.*

He almost laughed.

Ash hated himself and hating yourself was a solid reason to get shitfaced, so he did.

Alcohol puts you to sleep. It represses dreams.

Maybe that's what happened next. Or maybe not.

His night was populated by visions, but even the next morning Ash had no idea if they'd been dreams or genuine things.

He remembered being on a rooftop, chased by what looked like *Matrix* agents.

He remembered *watching* someone be chased on a rooftop, same as his dissociative dream from days ago. Was he either of those people? He hadn't a clue, but even after the fact the rooftop dream felt real. Although it seemed unlikely he'd been on a real-world rooftop during the night, it felt *entirely* likely that he was having a flashback to something real.

So *had* he dreamed it? Or had he instead relived a memory?

He remembered handling an IED.

He remembered being in a tank.

Neither of those things had happened in life, but both felt as real — as much like memories — as the rooftop.

Mina had been right today. Every experience now felt like closed-circuit TV. Everything he did was fly-by-wire. So was he really *living his life* these days, or was he instead lying in a gutter somewhere, living through a psychotic fugue?

What was real?

What wasn't?

He should have picked up the drugs and used them.

He'd lost the ability to tell the difference.

Live long enough with insomnia and nothing feels real anymore.

In the morning, Ash had no idea whether or not he'd actually slept. He'd gone so long that the world right now might not be happening.

Mina's voice: *If you never think to check whether you're in a dream, you just might be.*

Ash looked in the mirror. He was still ugly. Still reprehensible. Still something an intelligent being would step on, then wipe up the smear with a tissue. It had to mean he was awake.

So he went to his job and operated machines that could be deadly even for someone paying close attention.

Chuck pulled him aside again. *Chuck*, meaning the man who was only pretending to be his friend and hadn't been in Kandahar. Or Afghanistan. Or the war. Or even in the Army.

"What's the matter with you?" Chuck asked him once they were in the break room. His voice wasn't playful this time.

"I might be dreaming," Ash told him.

"Are you drunk?"

"Not currently."

"You told me you felt better. You said your doc gave you something to help you sleep."

"Mrr," Ash opined.

Chuck shook him. "Maybe you're having some sort of reaction. You're still doped-up the night after."

"No," said Ash.

"*No* what?"

"I'm not doped."

"You can't know that."

"I never took the pills." Ash rubbed his face, wishing he could remember how to sleep.

Chuck looked around. He'd pulled Ash into a corner, his eyes worried someone might see Ash in his current condition. "Are you sure you didn't take the pills?"

"Mmm-hmm. I never picked them up."

"*What?*"

Chuck was being silly. "I never picked them up," Ash repeated.

"Why the hell not?"

"I was busy. I'll get them today."

"How long has it been since you slept?"

"I don't know, Chuck. Maybe I'm sleeping right now."

"Listen to me." Chuck's eyes darted around the room. "You—"

He reached for Ash, but Ash didn't like it.

"DON'T TOUCH ME! STOP TOUCHING ME! LEAVE ME THE FUCK ALONE!"

Chuck backed off, hands up, his face a mirror for Ash's insanity.

Seeing it, Ash took a breath. He wanted to prove he was cool and calm before he spoke again.

"Chuck."

"What?"

"I'm serious."

"About what?"

"I think I'm dreaming."

"You're not dreaming."

"That's what you'd say if I *was* dreaming," Ash told him.

Chuck exhaled. Then he looked to the coffee machine, and the stack of magazines right next to it. He grabbed a magazine at random, then handed it to Ash."Read."

Ash looked down. On the cover was a collage of someone's family photos below a headline: *The Killer Next Door.* And a subhead: *A Small Town Mourns Four More Random Murders as the World Asks: What's Making People Do It?*

"Is reminding me of my shit supposed to make me feel better?" Ash asked.

"The article isn't about you. It's about the Freak-Outs."

"Then why did you give it to me?"

"Can you read it? The headline?"

"Of course I can read it!"

"Read it again."

Ash's lip twisted. "You think I'm stupid? Fuck you, Chuck."

"Just do it, dammit!"

Ash did, then looked up with challenging eyes.

"And?" Chuck asked.

"And what?"

"When you read it the second time, were the words the same?"

"What's *that* supposed to mean?"

"Was it?"

"Of course it was!"

Chuck reached for Ash again, but this time Ash didn't

lash out. "If the words stayed the same, you're not dreaming. Do you understand?"

Ash blinked. This felt like déjà vu.

"Do you understand?" Chuck repeated.

Ash felt himself relax. Yes, reading the same thing twice was one of the *am-I-dreaming* tests Mina had told him about just yesterday. Interesting that it'd come up now, so randomly.

It was, in fact, as random as the recent rash of Freak-Outs.

Ash opened the magazine. He had to; it'd just occurred to him that the Freak-Out epidemic proved he wasn't the only one going crazy lately.

But before he reached the piece, Ash spied something interesting: a story about another potential Freak-Out who'd gone to the top of a building and jumped off. That in itself wasn't too strange. What made it strange was that security camera footage showed the man calmly stepping to the building's edge, then smiling as he tilted back into the fall to concrete.

The man hadn't been suicidal. Not a soul in his life had seen it coming.

"You don't need to read the whole magazine," Chuck said.

But Ash was transfixed. The story was so *familiar*. He wondered if he'd read it before. He may have; the magazine was dated two weeks ago and he liked to read on break.

He looked up and said to Chuck, "Hey. How did you know that?"

"Know what?"

"The thing about reading in a dream."

Who gives a shit? Chuck implied with a shrug. "I don't know. I probably read it somewhere."

"And you *just* remembered it. *Just* now."

"Jesus Christ, Ash. Yesterday you were telling me how freaky my memory is. I remember strange shit; what can I say?"

"You remembered Pooh."

"No, not poo. I meant 'shit' as in 'stuff.' How fucked-up are you?"

Ash watched Chuck's big, friendly eyes.

"Ash. Dude. You need to go home. *Now*. Before DeShawn sees you."

"Before DeShawn sees what?" DeShawn asked from the doorway.

Ash and Chuck both froze. DeShawn looked intently at Chuck, who seemed to be standing in the way of a serious ass-chewing.

"Hey, boss." His tone pretended innocence, but wasn't remotely convincing.

Then, after a few silent seconds, Chuck got the message and left without another word. He had to slide his moderate girth between the floor manager and the break room wall to do it.

When Chuck was gone, DeShawn turned his gaze on Ash.

"So tell me. What *exactly* is DeShawn gonna see that he won't like, Sanders?"

Ash's eyes flitted closed, open, closed, open. Maybe he should have made a point to fill his prescription after all. Maybe then he wouldn't be fighting so hard to stay upright and stable. Maybe if he'd done as he'd been told, he wouldn't be waging a war to stay awake while his boss glared at him.

DeShawn waited. And Ash wondered: *Is he angry? Is he even here?* What was the term Mina had used for phantom figures that came at the onset of sleep?

In Ash's mind, the supervisor's eyes widened like a cartoon, with pupils like teacups. His face melted and his arms dripped to the floor like hot wax.

Then he was just the boss again, furious and fed-up.

"DeShawn saw enough weeks ago. Pack your shit, Sanders. You're fired."

SEVEN

A Whisper Through Fog

Ash watched noon come and go on the dashboard clock of an Uber because DeShawn wouldn't let him drive home. He went so far as to threaten Ash's severance pay if he refused to surrender his keys. Even nemeses don't let nemeses drive insane.

"You know what, man?" Ash told the driver. "That's my Walgreens up ahead. Can you pull in and wait just a sec while I grab a prescription?"

The driver waffled. "We're not really supposed to do that."

"I hear you. But I'm sort of losing it, if you know what I mean. Last night AT&T home-invaded me and decoded my internet. They surrounded my house from like two to four a.m. I looked out the windows and saw them waiting for me to sleep. They're probably following us right now. I know this isn't a dream because of your clock up there. But see, if I don't go to Walgreens *right now*, I won't sleep for another four days. Have you ever been waterboarded?"

The driver stopped, against regs or not. Ash was surprised he didn't drive away as soon as his passenger went inside, but that was probably because Ash had left his bag in the car. The driver wouldn't be rid of him if he sped off now.

Ash had dry-swallowed one of the lonely pills in his vial while still inside the drug store, and by the time he tossed his wallet onto the kitchen table it seemed to be taking effect. Ash could tell it was the drugs, not natural fatigue now taking him over. He knew because his "just tired" state was exhausted and wakeful in unison. His mind usually refused to shut down: the soldier's curse, with his head on a swivel.

But this was different. With the sedative's help, his mind and body crashed in tandem. He barely made it to the bed before collapsing face-up atop the comforter.

Despite Mina's promise of quiet, uneventful rest, the so-called hypnagogic hallucinations came in spades as he faded.

He heard his front door open. Then footsteps.

It had to be Chuck.

Chuck who was in Kandahar; Chuck who wasn't in Kandahar.

The shadow shape behind "Chuck" could only be Mina.

Then his mother.

Then Emily, God rest her soul.

The ghouls surrounded him, and Ash found he couldn't move. He was halfway to dreamland, paralyzed like the good doctor predicted.

"You're not here," Ash either said or thought to them.

The room faded.

"Pleasant dreams," whispered one of the ghosts as he finally went under.

. . .

HE RETURNED to the world as if rising from the dead.

Even at his best, which Ash hadn't been for a long time, he typically woke to use the restroom several times a night. He hadn't slept uninterrupted since he was a kid. This morning, however, it felt like someone had broken into his mind overnight and burgled its contents. He had no memories — not even a timespan *absent* of memories — after he'd seen the ghosts.

How much time had passed since he'd gone to sleep? One second, three weeks … there was no way to tell. He remembered nothing.

"Fuck," was all he could think to say.

Ash rubbed his cheeks, trying to get his head straight. His uncomprehending face was dough in his hands; he pawed and pressed it as if preparing to bake.

Having gone to sleep before noon, seeing what was clearly sunrise beyond the drapes struck him as not only wrong, but flat-out impossible.

It must be *evening* sun, not *morning* sun … right?

But Ash knew it wasn't; sunset happened on the other side of the house. Still, nobody slept that long uninterrupted. His bladder should have exploded.

Shit. Maybe it did.

He peeled back the sheets and comforter. Everything was dry.

But he needed to piss like a racehorse. So he did. And did. And *did*. By the time it was over Ash figured he should be desiccated entirely: a raisin in human form. There was no way that much liquid could have come from one man. Surely his blood had turned to powder.

He looked in the mirror. Still ugly.

Ash, said a voice. It came like a whisper through fog.

Unsure if he'd heard anything for real or not, Ash frowned. It'd been *like* hearing a voice, but not. He stared at his reflection. Then, unexpectedly, something happened.

But what was it? The thing he'd seen had been in his eye's corner, impossible to pin down. Had the mirror *itself* changed? Ash had no idea.

He scratched at the almost-memory, but it was already gone.

He turned away, but then the voice came again.

Mirror. Yes. A magic *mirror.*

Again like a whisper. He didn't want to think about it. He was still tired. He didn't feel like playing guessing games, especially with himself.

"Go to bed," he told his reflection. "You're …"

"Awake," said someone else.

He stopped, frozen in his too-bright bathroom.

Very, *very* clearly, Ash was sure he'd just heard Emily's voice — the woman whose last words to him had only been sounds: a baffled and betrayed sort of croak before dying.

Confused, Ash turned away from the mirror, toward the bedroom, catching sight of the shining-bright window.

"Sunshine makes everything better," said that same voice.

He turned in a circle, convinced all at once that he wasn't awake after all. Maybe, like Mina had half-joked yesterday, he was dreaming right now.

If so then he'd been dreaming for a long time — all of the terrible past few months. Maybe Emily wasn't even dead; maybe he'd dreamed her murder. That actually made sense. It was absurd to think he'd killed her in his sleep.

It was even *more* absurd to think someone else had broken in and killed her with Ash unwaking beside her. The whole thing was *so* absurd, in fact, that his mind labeled it as a dreamsign: an unusual or impossible occurrence that proves a person might be dreaming.

If Ash was hearing Emily, wasn't that a dreamsign?

Weird, he thought. *I actually don't know the word "dreamsign."*

But of course he knew it. He couldn't *think* a word (let alone use it correctly) if he didn't know it. It was LaBerge's word.

Steven LaBerge. Except … how the hell did Ash know who Steven LaBerge was?

He did, though. LaBerge was a dream researcher. The guy who, back in the 1970s, had put lucid dreaming on the map.

But I haven't studied lucid dreaming! Never cared to. I've never even had a lucid dream. Except for this one. This lucid dream I'm having right now.

Then, as suddenly as it'd begun, the moment shattered.

Suddenly Ash knew the truth as certain: That it wasn't a dream after all. He *had* killed Emily. He'd killed her and then he'd been fired from his job and then he'd slept for an entire goddamn day on his back, sick with Taco Bell and goddamned lucky that he hadn't choked to death on his puke.

But … *the voice. Emily's voice.*

How had he heard her so clearly, if the world around him now was real?

Unless he was insane.

Strangely at peace with that answer, Ash returned to the bedroom. But upon seeing his bed, he froze again. Because he was quite certain he hadn't pulled the covers over himself before falling asleep … and yet just a few minutes ago he'd peeled the covers back to see if he'd peed the bed.

And come to think of it, the pill bottle was now in the bathroom even though Ash had left it on the nightstand.

And the framed photos hiding his internet router were askew. Ash was fastidious about keeping all the frames perfectly parallel, so who'd gone and messed them up?

YOU did, dummy. You were asleep, and you sleepwalked. You have a disorder, remember? You woke up, you moved the pills, you messed with the photos, and then you pulled back the covers and got back into bed. You probably even used the bathroom. How else could you have held it so long?

That would have made sense if it was possible. But Dr. Irving had increased his Nyperal dosage. She'd even warned him it might be too much; he might wake to find he couldn't move at all.

Irving was wrong.

But Ash, whose ears still remembered hearing Emily's voice just moments ago, didn't buy it.

He stepped forward, but stopped when his bare foot registered something on the floor. He looked down to see his phone, presumably where he'd dropped it.

Played with your phone last night, too, huh? What else did you do without knowing, Mr. Sanderzzz?

He picked it up and sat on the bed. Then, on impulse, he called Mina. His call went to voicemail, so he left a message. His mouth turned out to be more worried than his brain, so the message sounded too frantic.

But maybe that was okay. He'd need her help if he'd finally lost his mind.

He hung up, then reached for his laptop and googled the name of his sedative. Under Side Effects, it read, *May cause visual or auditory hallucinations.*

That was it. That was the explanation. It was the drugs, not his head, now messing with him.

The only problem was, a deep part of Ash didn't

believe the drug was at fault any more than it believed he'd sleepwalked. The logical answers were plenty logical, sure. The only problem was they didn't feel right at all.

He forced a laugh.

But nothing felt funny right now.

EIGHT

Intruders

Ash practically ransacked his home in search of evidence that he'd been sleepwalking. He discovered only a backyard hose off its hook, but that could have happened days ago. A coyote could have knocked it free. Or a dog. He didn't have security cameras unless he counted the smart door-bell, which saw only his stoop.

It was unnerving, not to know what he'd been up to.

His phone rang.

Mina, returning his panicked call. "What happened?"

Ash wedged the phone between cheek and shoulder. He needed both hands to check the liquor cabinet. Maybe something was askew in there, and either way maybe he should have several glasses of whiskey. He was already descending from his earlier agitation. Still frightened on some level, but also a master of repressing his emotions. This had become a problem to solve — no longer a psychological crisis he couldn't drink away on his own.

"Nothing. I'm fine." Then, pre-deflecting, he added to his lie. "I finally slept. For a crazy-long time."

"That's good. But what's this about Emily?"

"Nothing. I thought for a second I heard her, but it was just an auditory hallucination."

"Your message sounded really freaked out," Mina said.

"It was a *vivid* hallucination."

"Well, what did you hear her say?"

"That thing she says. The juvenile thing I hated."

Mina waited. She was going to make him say it.

"'Sunshine makes everything better,'" he finished.

"Why do you hate it?"

"*Because it's juvenile.* Look. I'm fine. Sorry I called."

"Are you sure?" she asked.

"I just wanted to know if the stuff you prescribed causes hallucinations. But I looked it up, and now I know it does."

"Oh." She sounded unconvinced. Maybe even disappointed. "Was there anything else?"

Yes, there was, Ash thought. *I've been sleepwalking. There's no proof besides a few tilted frames and a moved bottle, but when I went out to check the hose, I saw fresh footprints in the yard where the sprinklers were running. Not coyote footprints. Not dog footprints. Human footprints, and I haven't been out there for days — not while I was awake, anyway. I'm starting to wonder if I had a dream last night, even though I'm not supposed to be having dreams. Two dreams, actually. In the first, people were in my house again, like I dreamed — or hallucinated — the night before. You know, the previous night? As in: the night before I took the drugs that cause hallucinations? The second dream didn't feel anything like a dream. Or like waking life. It was more like someone was beaming a television broadcast into my brain. It even had interference glitches. I remember trying to shut it out, then realizing it was coming from inside me. And, sure, I may have spent a half hour or so parting my hair to see every inch of my scalp in the mirror, doing acrobatics with a second mirror to make sure I got it all, looking myself over just in case there was a scar there. You know — a scar on my scalp, where someone might have implanted a microchip? Of course there was no scar. I'm not crazy. Only crazy people believe the conspiracy videos. Oh. And yes, in case you're curious, I did a YouTube search and found a few people saying that the Wurtzman shit might make brain chips possible. Nothing can decode electrical signals as complex as the brain's without the Wurtzman Conjecture, you know. And sure, the TV broadcast in my brain was — how should I say it? Well, I was really damn sure for a while that I was seeing* my own thoughts played back at me. *And by a broadcaster inside my head who'd gone to all the trouble of splicing them together in a highlight reel that was pretty much ready for its debut as a conspiracy video of its own. So sure, I did consider whether my thoughts were being stolen. But I can't see how they could be, so now I'm going to try and forget all about it. Long story short? All's well here, Dr. Mina Irving. This wife-killer is on his non-working meds and doing* jesssssss fine.

"No, there's nothing else," Ash told her.

He hung up before Mina could express another nugget of empathy, then put his phone on *Do Not Disturb* for good measure.

ASH GOT DRESSED and took a walk around the block to get some fresh air.

He couldn't stay inside anymore. The dreamy, hallucinatory haze that had followed his disorienting (and possibly pathological) sleep marathon and maybe-sleepwalking, combined with memory of the article he'd scanned the other day about the weird epidemic of Freak-Outs, had him thinking that maybe *he* was a Freak-Out in progress.

"Freak-Out" was the politically inconsiderate name the media had given to the unexplained epidemic of random people doing randomly terrible things with zero warning beforehand. Applied to Ash? Yeah. It felt about right. He'd *already* murdered someone without cause. He'd be the Freak-Out kingpin when they all shared a prison block.

You did what we never did, Mr. SaNderZ, the other Freaks would say. *You, like Pooh, are our motherfucking hero.*

Relaxing walks were supposed to include calm, daisy-fluttering breezes past friendly neighbors holding lawn-watering hoses behind white picket fences. But Ash's neighbors all hated him. They didn't wave or smile while watering their begonias. They glared as their children pointed at him instead.

What's more, most of those same neighbors had banded together a few weeks back to try and get him ejected from his house. Apparently his Not Guilty By Reason of Clinical Sleep Violence verdict hadn't cleared his name in their hearts like it had with the jury.

After the block failed to evict him, the die-hards tried something else. They wanted Ash to forever need to register like a sex offender, introducing himself as the man who'd strangled his saint of a wife to neighbors for the rest of his life. City Council had denied that particular request on the grounds of civil liberties, but it was obvious that the voters felt otherwise.

So, cutting the walk short, Ash came home and got into his car.

Soon he found himself driving by Chuck's house, waiting to see if he could spy on his only friend through the window. But then he remembered that Chuck was at work, of course, and so he drove to the shop to sit in the parking lot.

He did this until Lloyd, the elderly guard, tapped on his car's window and told him that he'd always liked Ash, and he didn't blame him for lingering like this, but two managers had already spotted his car and said (Lloyd quoted), "Make him leave or shoot his ass."

So he went home again, where he discovered a team of strangers in his living room.

Ash was so startled upon finding them that he felt sure he was hallucinating. He'd entered through the side door like always, finding a middle-aged woman and a younger man wearing what looked like AT&T uniforms messing with his wiring.

Adrenaline had been building all day like a percolating tea kettle. Finding strangers in his home was (in technical terms) the last fucking straw. He didn't even think before retrieving the bat he kept beside the door for just such opportunities.

Ash shouted. When the interlopers merely stared at him, Ash annihilated two of his own lamps and advanced like Babe Ruth planning to call his home run.

"I SAID WHO THE FUCK ARE YOU! ARE YOU FUCKING DEAF? I ASKED WHY THE FUCK YOU'RE IN MY FUCKING HOUSE!"

To cap his questions, Ash slammed the bat down on the top of a small wooden end table. He expected his weapon to rebound, but either the table was weak or Ash had summoned the strength of a junkie on angel dust. Instead of bouncing off of the top, his blow split the table like a karate chop.

Milliseconds later the woman was holding up both palms, shouting for Ash to calm down, please just calm down so they could talk.

"*Talk?* What's there to talk about?" Ash took his left hand off the bat, reached into his pocket for his phone to call the police, then fumbled it to the floor because he was right-handed.

It was a clumsy move. Embarrassing, really.

The woman almost reached for it, so Ash returned his

hand to the bat and shouted, "WHAT THE HELL ARE YOU DOING IN MY HOUSE?"

"Easy! Easy!" she said. "I'm Seneca. Remember? We spoke yesterday! You said you liked my name?"

Ash took another big step toward the woman — *Seneca*, apparently — twirling the bat in preparation for a swing. These assholes simply weren't getting the picture.

Seneca had some guts. She barely backed off, reaching into one pocket while keeping the other palm out like an olive branch.

"Hands where I can see them!" Ash demanded.

"If you'll just—!"

Ash swung the bat. Home Invader Seneca ballet-stepped back so that instead of crippling her reaching arm, he turned his television to shards instead.

Then, as he followed through, he was tackled from the left side. Sneaky boy; he hadn't noticed her partner waiting to leap.

They hit the ground hard together, avoiding a concussion against the coffee table by inches. Once down, the other man made himself a blanket, pinning Ash instead of disarming him.

The woman then knelt next to the men, her expression clear: *Are you going to behave? Or do* we *have to be the ones to call 911?*

Ash didn't speak. Apparently satisfied with his silence, she finished reaching into her jacket. She withdrew a small tablet instead of the pistol he'd expected and showed him its screen. It just so happened to display Ash's signature in a box, implying he himself had signed the thing.

"We're here to update your modem and router. That's all," she said. "I told you about this when we came over yesterday. The new security upgrade can't be downloaded.

It requires new hardware. Do you remember, Mr. Sanders?"

It was strange, being manhandled and womansplained in unison. A SWAT team hadn't taken him down, shift workers had done it. The woman's everyday, tech-support tone made an odd counterpoint the recent violence. They should have run regardless. They should be calling their bosses — and the cops — right now.

"I don't know who you are," Ash said.

"Is this your signature?" Seneca asked.

"Yes, but I don't know who you are."

She stood. "For Christ's sake let him up, Paul."

Paul backed away, but seemed reluctant.

Ash took his time rising. The intruders watched him get onto all fours before sitting up, then slink over to the couch.

"Do you remember us now?" Seneca asked.

Ash looked at her, taking his time to consider the question. She looked upper thirties, maybe lower forties, attractive in a practical way, trim but with a toned look that bragged of athleticism. Shoulder-length red hair and a confident hardness to her face. He looked at his tackler. Paul looked almost angry. Cocky, perhaps. Young and smooth-skinned with only a ghost of acne. Twenty-five at most, but with the kind of face and thin-limbed body that would still look young at his retirement party.

"You're with AT&T," Ash said.

"No, we're with a digital security firm *subcontracted* by AT&T. Our techs have been in your neighborhood for the past few days, installing expansion cards to patch vulnerabilities in your connection. Do you know about digital ransom?"

"Of course I know about digital ransom."

"Not something you want. You said it happened to your friend Gail."

Ash thought. Although he didn't recall telling these people about it, Gail had had her hard drive's contents encrypted and held for ransom. The FBI got her out of it somehow, but not before she lost all the precious family photos she'd digitized before tossing the original albums.

"You entered my home," Ash said.

"Like you gave us permission to do yesterday." Again Seneca flashed the tablet with his signature. "You said you couldn't be sure you'd be home, and to use your hidden key."

Dammit. They knew about the key. He must have done this yesterday after all: not just sleepwalking, but sleep-conversing and sleep-signing and sleep-giving-away-his-vulnerabilities like candy. He swore. Now *he* was the asshole. The *criminal* asshole, and there was no reason for them not to press charges.

Confession was better than an assault charge, so he crumbled and said, "I sort of have a condition." He took another long sigh. "I don't remember meeting you."

"You signed—"

"I know I signed." He'd apparently also rearranged parts of his house and played with the hose. It wasn't entirely out of the realm of possibility that he'd sleep-authorized utility work. Once, when his somnambulism had been particularly active, he'd alphabetized Emily's spice rack.

"Look. I'm ..." Should he apologize? Probably, but it was too weird.

So Ash stopped speaking and said nothing more. He stood, then walked into the back yard. He stared across the fence, deeply lost in more than thought. Life was falling apart even more than it was already in pieces. And to

think: He'd felt optimistic for the first time in forever just
… just however-the-hell long ago it was that he'd had that
honest chat with Mina.

He let them do their work, staying away from them out
of embarrassment.

The techs finished an unknown time later. The woman
came through the patio door, surprising Ash while he was
thousand-yard-staring in the opposite direction. She asked
for his signature again, this time to verify the upgrade. He
did as she asked without comment. He couldn't speak. He
couldn't say thank you. It was too strange, like facing
someone after walking in on them masturbating.

Ash returned to the living room to find they'd tidied
up. The TV was back upright. The shards, while not gone,
had at least been swept into a pile. The batted-down
photos of his cousins and grandparents were back on their
stands where they belonged.

Ash was shocked to discover that he wanted to break
down and cry. He—

His self-pity was interrupted by the sound of a rumble
and slam: a van's sliding door closing. He went to the door
— perhaps to shout one final apology; he didn't know —
but the techs' van was already moving.

A crescent moon logo was on its side, cut into slivers.
Below it was the company name: *ArkTek*.

NINE

¥°∂ß in the Morning

Ash would have read too much into it, had he not resisted the urge.

Truth was, there turned out to be nothing suspect or menacing about ArkTek at all. Ash was starting to admit that seeing the name didn't, in and of itself, make it a notable name. Besides, the only time he'd seen it at all (if he *had* seen it) was in a memory Chuck and Mina had both told him was false. So once he got right down to it … why the big deal?

Was ArkTek important? Ash would have bet the farm on it yesterday. After poking around a bit, he was starting to realize it was ordinary. Nothing to see here, folks.

Google searches for *ArkTek* were coming up fine now. Ash didn't know how he'd missed them the other night, but considering the way he'd authorized repairs in his sleep, he was probably mistaken about a *lot* of things over the past few days — search results included.

The company website came up first. Visiting it, Ash learned that ArkTek did exactly what Seneca the Tech had said: firewall and security services, currently specializing in remediation made necessary by hackers' exploitation of Wurtzman math.

"For fuck's sake," Ash told himself after an hour spent investigating what had turned out to be an ordinary IT firm. "Give it up already."

And then he did, now humbled by the fact that he'd attacked people after inviting them into his home. All the fight he'd had in him — all that paranoid, investigating, gotta-figure-this-out spirit — had finally left him. He was beyond help. Totally out of his mind. He'd gone from sleep-murdering to sleep-contract-signing. He'd probably get a call from the bank soon, letting him know he'd bought a Jet Ski in his sleep.

So why should he bother to be determined? Why put forth the effort? He'd gotten himself all worked up about a conspiracy involving ArkTek only to learn it was an ordinary company. He'd assaulted two people for no reason. He was lucky they hadn't been angrier. He was lucky they weren't going to sue him for assault … although, of course they still might.

Ash Sanders, ladies and gentlemen: A real piece of human garbage. A man whose thoughts, opinions, and actions are definitely not to be trusted.

He burned the day watching nonsense TV on his laptop, seeing as he could no longer watch the annihilated living room screen. Despite the fact that he'd woken at noon, he tried to retire at ten, hoping the sedative would make it possible.

He managed the first few hours without dreams, walking down the stages until he was lost in long, slow, delta wave slumber. Every hour and a half he climbed up a little, but never fully woke thanks to the drugs.

But the dreams didn't stay away for long. They began

around three in the morning and were even odder — and more memorable — than usual.

The first wasn't dreamlike at all. Instead, it was like something aired over broadcast television. The mental images were interrupted every few minutes by static, split by blips of horizontal interference. Sometimes the dream even rolled bottom to top like an old VHS tape with tracking problems. Somehow the whole thing felt both alien and familiar: something sent *to* Ash *from* Ash, as if stolen and then relayed back through a tower in the real world.

Soon after, the image cleared and Ash found himself watching those same TV-like images inside his dream, now on an actual television. He was in his grandmother's house. She had an ancient and enormous floor model: a bulky tube inside what looked like a 1940s radio cabinet.

Ash was sitting beside Nana on the couch. The dream was multi-sensory — enough to smell the reek of mothballs clinging to the upholstery.

"This is a good episode." Nana nodded at the thought-stream they were watching. "It's the one where Alexi goes to Prague. After that, Chloe and Ishaan meet in Constantinople to exchange a Faberge egg."

"Constantinople doesn't exist anymore, Nana."

Nana's face looked like she'd sucked on a lemon. "It's not the only one."

Ash watched the onscreen program — the real dream, whereas Nana's living room was something else. The living room had stopped seeming dreamlike. It was more vivid and more real than any dream Ash had ever had.

"Just because I'm a dreamsign doesn't mean I'm wrong!" Nana snapped after reading his face. "Don't get smart with me, Ash. I know I'm dead. I know that makes me a dreamsign. But that's no excuse to disrespect your elders!"

"How do you know Mina's word?" Ash asked.

"'Dreamsign' is *LaBerge's* word. Everyone knows that."

Ash looked back at the TV. The program there — the dream within this dream — really did look like television. The camera work was shaky, the resolution questionable. Had someone filmed what he was seeing? Why did it look like a broadcast?

Ash realized he was *thinking*, which was strange. Usually in dreams, he accepted whatever happened as if it was perfectly normal.

He found himself wondering what time it was.

He looked at his wrist, but he wasn't wearing a watch. That's when Emily's huge clock — inherited from her grandfather — began to chime four a.m. in the other room.

The other room meaning his bedroom in the non-dreaming world, where the real clock lived.

"Don't look at me that way," Nana scolded, snapping Ash's attention back to her. "*You're* the one who let her put that clock there. *You're* the one who decided Ishaan and Chloe should meet in *Istanbul*."

She used the modern name reluctantly, as if liberals were forcing her to change. "Alexi probably wanted to go to Kyiv, and wouldn't that have been better? *You're* the one who looked right at the thieves and invited them to steal whatever they wanted. What can *I* do about any of that? I'm dead. *You're* the oneironaut."

"I'm the *what*?"

Nana didn't appreciate the interruption. "You don't like it? Well, then why don't you get up and spin something about it?"

"What are you talking about, Nana?" But he sort of knew, didn't he?

Spin something about it.

A nonsense phrase that made sense deep down inside his mind, where Ash couldn't reach it.

Nana rose on her cane. She flapped her wrinkled hand at him as if exhausted by his youngster's shenanigans, then hobbled out of the room.

Ash stood to go after her. Then, without knowing why, he began to turn himself in a circle, spinning like a ballerina.

"Time to wake up," he mumbled to himself. "Time to see the real world."

He closed his eyes as he spun in place.

Then he opened them again and found himself in the waking world.

He was now in bed, on his back with his sheets up to his chin. He'd snapped from dream to awareness with zero lag, fully awake in a second.

Ash put his feet on the floor. He sat up, annoyed. Three to five a.m. had always been a fragile, hard-to-sleep time for Ash. He knew the clock's gong had been real; it really was four a.m. Getting back to sleep was going to take forever.

He swore. The damn sedative hadn't worked. *Now* what was he supposed to do?

He stood, not even a little tired. He went to the bathroom and splashed water on his face, trying to shake the unreality. His dream had been lucid; he'd known he was dreaming while he was dreaming or else he wouldn't have told himself to wake up.

He'd never had a lucid dream before. How the hell had he done it now?

It didn't matter. It was over, and now he was awake. *Wide fucking awake* at—

He glanced at the small digital clock beside the sink.

—at ¥°∂ß a.m.!

He swore again. He'd never get back to sleep. He wondered if he should even try, or just give up. Maybe he should just brush his teeth, get dressed, and call it an early morning. It was so annoying. He'd thought it was four, and that was bad enough. But now it was ¥°∂ß?

He was *never* awake at ¥°∂ß a.m.!

(¥°∂ß?)

Ash did a double-take. He glanced at the clock again, but the display had changed. Instead of being ¥°∂ß, the time was now π∆œ.

Ash blinked. He held out the index finger of his right hand, then pushed it against the palm of his left hand.

Instead of stopping when it met flesh, his finger went right on through.

That's two failed reality checks. I'm STILL DREAMING.

Lucidity snapped back like a rubber band. He hadn't actually woken; he was still in the dream. What he'd just experienced was called a *false awakening.* Another phrase he shouldn't know.

A sound from outside caught his attention.

Ash rushed to the window. His backyard was chalked with lines, marking-up like a baseball diamond. There were people out there: the repair people from ArkTek. Only now instead of wearing service uniforms, Seneca and Paul looked like Men (and Women, he supposed) in Black.

Black suits. White shirts. Skinny black ties and sunglasses.

I want to be outside, Ash thought.

So he spun in a circle. Soon enough he found himself right where he'd wanted to be, because spinning was one way to teleport inside a lucid dream — not that Ash knew he knew that.

Dream Seneca and Dream Paul saw Ash arrive and startled. They'd opened up the big green junction box in the corner of his property and had been meddling inside. They were yanking out wires. Making mischief. A fun-sized satellite dish sat atop the box, spinning in lazy circles. Seneca was holding something like a walkie-talkie as if testing its connection.

"What are you doing?" Ash asked them. "Why are you here?"

Because they were his dream figures, it meant they were actually part of Ash. They answered the way his subconscious mind would answer:

"Because you're supposed to stop us," said Paul.

"Why?"

"Do it for Ishaan," Dream Paul answered. "If you just stand there dreaming, we'll have it soon!"

"Ishaan?" Ash remembered the name from Nana's living room but knew no one by that name in life. Or at least … he didn't *think* he did.

Seneca stood up straight, drawing a pistol and pointing it at his chest. "Easy, now," she said. "You don't want to end up like Alexi."

She tossed the walkie-talkie thing to Paul. It'd become more complex — a sophisticated sort of comm device. Ash understood, from somewhere deep down, that he needed to get it away from them. He couldn't let them turn the thing on, or use it, or finish what they'd started … no matter what.

Why? But it was no use asking. These were things his deep mind knew, but about which Everyday Ash had no idea.

"Easy …" Dream Seneca repeated. "You don't have

the slightest idea what's happening here."

But that was a trap. A misdirection. Ash saw it now. This was *his* dream. These people were merely representations of himself, or something his sleeping mind wanted him to understand. If *they* knew what they were doing, it meant by definition that *Ash* knew what they were doing, because they were him.

Except that he didn't know. He had *no idea* what they were doing.

Get the device he's holding, instinct told him. *It all starts there.*

Seneca saw Ash flinch toward Paul and raised her gun. The gun became a banana, and her face became fearful. So they ran. And Ash chased them. They were fast, so Ash made himself faster.

The pair of techs hurdled his fence. Ash followed. Soon all three were on the dark nighttime streets, passing neighborhood landmarks that, in the dreamscape, had acquired odd new features. The Wattersons' lawn was filled with pink plastic flamingos. Elvira, Mistress of the Dark, was grilling steaks where the corner mailbox should be.

Seneca and Paul had widened the distance. So Ash, who knew from deep inside how to control the dream, flew toward them like Superman.

The gap narrowed. Then the world turned rubbery: his mind threatening to wake up for real this time.

Hold onto the dream, Ash told himself. *Hold on, because you have to catch them.*

He focused, demanding clarity. The rubber underfoot became concrete again.

He lunged and caught Paul by the ankle, half-pantsing him. The device Paul had been holding skittered out of his hand and between Elvira's legs.

Ash's head whipped toward it.

Paul, seeing Ash's distraction, kicked him in the face.

Ash learned something then: *Yes, Virginia, there is pain in dreams.*

Bleeding freely, Ash crawled onto to his feet as Paul scrabbled up and resumed sprinting.

But chasing Paul was harder now. Ash could no longer fly. Running was winding him now the way it would in real life, his legs burning.

The dream began to dissolve. Ash clung to it as best he could.

He ran, and ran, and ran, and—

TEN

Dreamsigns

—ran.

Ash realized, in a blink, that he'd just woken up.

Outside. Woken not in his bed, but running through the streets of his neighborhood like a madman.

And yet, awake now, he still didn't stop running. Instinct wouldn't allow it.

Oh shit. My sleepwalking. My acting-out. The medications didn't help at all — because here I am, at it again.

But … he wasn't just *acting out his dreams*. His mind kept insisting something was different this time. Because he still hadn't stopped. He was still running as hard as he could, as if everything depended on it. Even though that was crazy.

*Stop running! For fuck's sake, Ash, stop running or everyone will think you're crazy! Well. Craz i*er.

But no. His legs refused. Because something was different this time.

Once in the past, Ash had dreamed himself into a breakdancing contest. Another time, he'd climbed a rope for hours on end. He'd woken while dancing and climbing, but without music or a rope to ascend. The real world was

cooperating this time. Ash was acting out his dream, yes …
but somehow, *two other people were acting it out with him.*

Two very real people thirty yards or so ahead. All three
of them were sprinting through dark streets as hard as they
could.

Confusion came, thick and heavy.

I'm chasing real people, but I was dreaming when I started
*chasing them. If I was asleep, how did I know they were there? Is
this real, or is it all in my head?*

It's both.

His legs kept churning, but he was losing ground.
Finally, Ash was starting to flag.

Of course you're flagging. You just woke up, har-har.

Ash was fast, but the people ahead of him were faster.

Because you're out of shape, old man.

The thought made no sense, because Ash had never
been in good enough shape for this. Still — and maybe this
was sleep talking — he kept getting a feeling that he was
slower now than he used to be. That if he'd only kept
training—

KEPT training?

Ash had *never* trained. The most he'd run was a 5k with
Emily. Or maybe it was a 10k. Or a tiny triathlon. That
was three years ago. Five years ago. The course they'd
taken went through a park in Boston, where they'd been
visiting. In Hawaii, where they'd had their honeymoon.
Fiji. Palm Springs. Their honeymoon in Vail. It was all of
those things, and not a single one of them. He must be
getting lightheaded. All of his memories seemed fake right
now, dry of oxygen.

Finally empty, Ash slowed and then stopped entirely.
He bent at the waist, put both hands on his knees, and
waited for the dizziness to pass.

Thirty seconds passed. The worst of his hypoxia went away, but the confusion was plaque left behind.

Ash raised his head. The people he'd been chasing were the techs from today, he knew even from here that he'd been right about that. He could still see the kid two blocks down. Seneca, who was in better shape than Paul, was a half block beyond him. They were in hoodies now, Seneca's flopped back to reveal the same crimson hair he'd seen this afternoon.

It meant his brain had been *half* aware, but only half. He'd identified the people correctly, but his lucid-dreaming mind had dressed them as clichés instead of as the run-of-the-mill burglars they appeared to be. Ash himself wore only sleep shorts.

That meant *some* of what he believed moments ago was true, but some was false.

He looked up at a nearby street sign. It read STOP. He looked away, then read it again.

Still: STOP.

So he inspected his hands. He tried to put the fingers of one through the palm of the other, but unlike in the bathroom earlier, his finger now stopped instead of going through. He plugged his nose and mouth, then found himself unable to breathe.

All of his reality checks were coming up green. He was awake this time, sure and certain.

"What the *fuck* is going o—?" He started to ask nobody in particular. But before he could finish, he spontaneously heaved and threw up in the bushes.

A light came on in a nearby house. He retreated around a corner, feeling like he was forgetting something and unwilling to flinch until he knew what it was.

I almost did it, he thought as he pondered, looking ahead

again to where his targets were no longer visible. *I nearly caught the bastards. I had that goddamn kid by the leg.*

The thought repeated: *Had the kid by the leg.*

Which led to: *Elvira. I tackled him while we were passing Elvira, who'd been added by my dream.* And that's when he had it. That's when Ash realized what he'd forgotten.

He wiped his mouth, tossed off his fatigue, and turned to jog back the way he'd come.

Some of what he'd seen while chasing the techs — like Elvira, the Men in Black clothing, and all those pink flamingos — had been the substance of dreams.

But other things — *important* things — Ash was now sure had been real.

ELEVEN

Same as Kandahar

Ash found the thing Paul had dropped exactly where he'd expected it to be: under the corner mailbox, which his dreaming mind had shown him as the Mistress of the Night.

In waking reality, the device wasn't exactly the same as Paul had held in the dream, but it was close. It was bigger than a modern walkie-talkie but smaller than an older one, though it had no obvious mic or speaker. An odd metallic shape was bent back across its rear — probably an antenna.

Ash turned it over in his hands. The device was matte black with no apparent controls or markings. A screwed-on door on its back was probably the battery compartment. He supposed the thing used batteries because—

Ash tilted his head. He'd almost remembered something: something not quite in the center of his normal cognition, but instead on an alternate track.

In the dark, with the strange device in his hand, he tried to focus — to locate that other track of memory.

There'd been a man. Something about a piece of plastic, and …

But no. The memory was gone, and showed no signs of returning.

So Ash went back home, hopping the backyard fence to reenter because he hadn't taken his keys. The yard was in disarray, but just like the other elements of his dream, his mind's translation between real and unreal wasn't perfect. His dreaming mind had shown him the right things but done so in exaggerated, surreal ways. The backyard wasn't chalked. He'd added that detail for unknown reasons … but there'd been two uninvited people meddling back here. That much was true.

The junction box was open, but there was no satellite dish on its top. The tools he'd seen in the dream were mostly gone, a lone screwdriver left behind. The house itself was dark, meaning he hadn't turned on lights like he'd thought. The sliding glass door was open halfway. That must have been how he'd come out to the patio, seeing as he couldn't really teleport.

He peered into the box. He'd always assumed it was the power company's, but now he saw it was for lower-voltage matters: phone, cable, internet, maybe other utilities. Unsure how to decipher what was inside, he put the junction cover back in place at least until morning, when he'd be able to see.

He retrieved the left-behind screwdriver. He was about to pocket it when he thought to use it on the battery hatch of the black walkie-talkie thing. He really wanted to see those batteries.

Why do I care about the batteries? I know what's inside. It's just a normal pair of double-A's. And the thing only uses batteries because—

"—because if we do not use double-A batteries, we must make a

custom charging dock," says the tall man with the crooked front teeth and Russian accent — an accent that turns make *into something like* meek. *"That in itself is not a problem. It is okay to make a dock. I can 3D-print it same as the case. But I have learned that the more you fabricate to do your job, the larger the trail you leave behind. We are supposed to be quiet, yes? So we will use batteries same as remote control." Then he — Alexi — screws on the battery case and says, "Now turn it on, Ash, and I will turn on the transmitter."*

Ash blinked. He remembered the moment clearly but had no idea when it had happened. Or where. Or with whom.

With *Alexi*, yes … but who the hell was that?

Alexi. You know: Alexi? *Alexi with his crooked teeth, with his weird love of buttered noodles. He was barely taller than you, and you joked about it like a rivalry, as if height was something you could control.*

Ash remembered. But of course he also couldn't.

Alexi. You know: Alexi? *Alexi falling from the top of a building. Striking concrete, failing to fly.*

Ash stared at the walkie-talkie thing, trying to eke more from his mind. Nothing came. Thoughts of this device and the man Alexi were sugar on his tongue.

But it did make him wonder: had Ash once known about the device in his hand? He'd certainly wanted it badly enough in his dream. He'd certainly wanted badly enough to get a hold of it while chasing Paul the Tech—

(Mike. His name is Mike, and he's not a Tech.)

Ash frowned, wondering where any of this was coming from.

Turn it on, Ash, and I will turn on the transmitter.

He closed his eyes. Bunched his face. He couldn't figure it out. Couldn't get at any of it. Notions came and went, but they were all snowflakes on the wind.

Transmitter, he heard inside his head.

Inside the house now, Ash found his head turning until he was facing the corner. Facing the bookcase. Facing the router perched on its top.

Pieces of an indistinct puzzle tried to assemble in his mind. He mentally ran through his encounter with Paul

(Mike)

and Seneca from earlier today. As things turned out, he'd been right to doubt them. He'd been right to pick up that bat and start swinging. They weren't from AT&T after all, nor from one of their subcontractors. AT&T and its subcontractors didn't come back to customers' homes in the middle of the night.

His mind showed him the white van.

The sliced-up crescent moon logo on the side.

And ArkTek.

Yes. ArkTek. Same as ArkTek was maybe in Kandahar. Except: That was a troop truck in Kandahar, wasn't it?

Why would an American utility van be anywhere in Afghanistan?

But Ash was starting to suspect the van had nonetheless been there, sure as anything. Somehow. Some way.

Maybe on the day of the IED, or maybe another time.

You're crazy, Ash thought to himself. *About* himself.

Maybe that was true.

Or maybe not.

Turn it on, Ash, and I will turn on the transmitter.

It, meaning the walkie-like thing. *It* wasn't the *transmitter.* The way Alexi had said it, they were two separate things.

Ash pulled the router from its place behind his family photos. He knew enough to understand that the modem received the internet signal and the router spread it around the house. You didn't need to use a router with a modem (you could plug directly into the modem), and likewise a router could be used for any kind of network — not just internet.

Alternatively, a router could be used to keep tabs on an existing network.

Plugged into the back of Ash's router was a small peripheral with no markings — a fat black teardrop hanging from a short plastic lead.

He unplugged the thing and heard a ding from the device Paul the Tech had dropped, which Ash had left on the couch.

He plugged it back in: *Ding*.

Then unplugged it: *Ding*.

Transmitter. Receiver. The two were connected for sure.

He doubted that what he'd found was a listening device. Audio bugs were tiny. Same for spy cameras. So this was something else, linked in his mind to a memory that felt like it belonged to a stranger.

He thought of the Russian. Alexi had helped design the things, but he'd been frustrated by them … Concentrating, Ash felt sure he had.

Because Alexi hadn't been able to make them work. Only Tailors could do that.

"What are you trying to get from me?" Ash asked his dark living room.

"That's what I wish you'd fucking figure out already," replied a voice behind him. "*Starting to piss me off.*"

Ash turned with his fists ready for battle, but his assailant was prepared this time.

In the shadows he saw the young man he'd so recently been chasing, now with Ash's own bat cocked and ready.

Ash hadn't locked the slider behind him, and the kid had the feet of a ninja.

Ash swung his fist.

The kid swung the bat faster.

TWELVE

Masterminding

Alexi turns the device over and over in his hand. It's small, black, and shaped like a teardrop. It's not the hardware that is failing, *he says.* It's the algorithm that's the problem. But do you want to know a secret? Maybe I am glad it cannot work.

Static.

A cascade of images comes to the fore, tiny but fragmentary vignettes, incomplete and absent of context:

A woman with dark skin and feline eyes, with eyeliner drawn to make them even more so. She boards a private plane. Nobody knows where she will go.

Hands, though it's not clear whose, slide over sheaves of paper. One plucks up a pen and scribbles equations. Nothing is coming together. There's a missing piece.

Someone's voice: They won't stop at watchers. This is the only way.

Somewhere else now. A foreign city. Ash, if this is indeed Ash, has already trained someone to keep an eye on Chloe. There was no deception there. He followed orders, knowing they will verify his work. They all tie each other's leashes, or so says the part of the agreement that higher-ups will admit to.

He hands a small thumb drive to a man in a hood. Anonymized. It is unclear where the man in the hood will go next. Where he will hide it. But that's the point.

So who has the real one? *someone asks. No answer. That, too, is the point.*

A short film of Emily in their kitchen.

Static.

A short film of Emily looking Ash in the eyes very seriously, the moment bittersweet like a parting. Ash knows he might not remember. But will she?

Static. The background of the last scene was somewhere they'd never visited, certainly not together.

The Indian Ocean far below the wings of a plane with no officially filed flight plan. Headed east or west? The sun's direction is not obvious; whatever steers this vision does not know.

"Ash," *says Emily.*

But no. Even in this in-between state he knows that Emily is gone. Of course he won't answer her call.

"ASH."

Her presence is a torment. He's losing his mind. He is sure she's gone, because he killed her.

He mixes this disjointed past with the present timeline, then and now blending in a tragic collage:

He went to work. He got fired. Then he shot some kid in Kabul. Or was it Kandahar? He rode in the van, ran from the van. No: the truck; *it was a truck that day, not a van. DeShawn yelled at him. Then Emily died. After that he got married. It's impossible to tell the past from the future, the future from the past. Now from then. Real from fake. Real might not even exist anymore.*

Emily shakes him, tired of him ignoring her. "Ash! Come on, buddy, wake up!"

But Emily never spoke to him like that. Never called him buddy. *Where was he? Where* is *he?*

It's almost like the person harassing him now is—

. . .

"CHUCK?"

"Come on, buddy!" Then Chuck seemed to see Ash stir and said, "Wait. Can you hear me? Are you okay?"

Ash was lying face-up on a hard and unforgiving floor. He didn't think he was in his bedroom, which would make sense if he was just now waking up. Even if he'd rolled out of bed, his bedroom's floor was hardwood and this felt like tile. The lights above were fluorescent and offensive.

Chuck was kneeling over him, his head haloed by an overhead bulb like a saint in a Renaissance painting.

"You okay, buddy? You got a concussion?"

Silly Chuck. You couldn't just *ask* someone if they had a concussion.

"Are you supposed to sit up?" Chuck asked. "I just know I'm not supposed to let you fall asleep."

Ash found his mind returning. As it did, he discovered new affection for Chuck, who had a mind like a vault but was simple in so many ways. With his fuzzy beard and small, somewhat-dull eyes, he was like a talking bear from a storybook. His medical advice might kill the patient, but at least they'd die in the arms of someone friendly.

Ash allowed himself to be dragged into a sitting position. After that, things cleared a little.

At first, his surroundings didn't make sense. From where he sat on the floor, the world was a forest of metal chair legs and the fatter, duller legs of a few round tables. The soundscape was a world of muffled machine noises, unrelenting and not far away.

"I'm in the break room," Ash decided. "The break room at work."

Chuck nodded. "There you go."

"Why am I in the break room?" Hadn't he just been

somewhere else? Like … not in this building at all? Had he been at home? Or had he been elsewhere in the building, talking with DeShawn?

DeShawn. That's when he remembered.

Ash had been fired. So why was he here?

He looked at Chuck, fixated on his cherubic appearance. Chuck's baby face was warmed by a reddish-blond beard. He struck Ash now as distinctly bloated, any potentially chiseled features lost to an abundance of water in the system.

"I'm not supposed to be here," Ash said, feeling a bolt of panic he couldn't localize.

"It's okay," Chuck told him. "You didn't take a break in the morning."

"No, I mean …" He felt a need to wave his arms and reset the conversation, but he didn't know which version was correct.

Fired. Pills. Home. Dreams. INTRUDERS? Chasing. Device.

!! BAT !!

He might as well have been hit by one, considering how hard his head was throbbing. And yes, as memory returned Ash grew even surer about his firing. The guards had thrown him out of the parking lot, and yet now here he was, dressed in workshop coveralls with grease-smudged hands.

"I told you not to do that," Chuck said, looking vaguely upward.

"Do what?"

"Try to fix the buzzing light. It's not loose in the socket. It's a piece of shit."

Ash followed his gaze. One of the overheads — a can light not far from the second long fluorescent — was flickering.

"Are you seriously telling me I was trying to change the lightbulb? That I *fell*?"

Chuck shrugged. "You're not still on the chair, are you?"

His mind was clearing. *No. It wasn't a fall that did this. Someone hit you. Hard. And it felt like minutes ago.*

Ash surveyed the room. One of the chairs was canted sideways all the way over to the sink, as if thrown there.

Ash moved to stand. Chuck made noises of protest, spotting his rise like a climber's partner.

"Maybe you should stay where you are."

"Who brought me here?" Ash asked.

As the wrongness of everything crept further into his awareness, he heard the way his simple question had become more like a demand. But he did need to stay put. Chuck was right about that one.

"What?" Chuck asked.

"Who brought me here," Ash repeated.

Chuck waited to see if this was a put-on, then, *"You, dude."*

"I was at home. DeShawn fired me yesterday." He corrected himself. "Two days ago, I mean."

"I didn't hear anything about DeShawn firing you."

"Chuck. You were *right here*."

But no, Chuck hadn't been. DeShawn had shooed Chuck from the room before dropping the hammer. Who'd seen it, other than DeShawn himself?

"Did HR talk to you or something?" Then, more timidly in that hairy-bear way of his: "You hit your head pretty bad. I think you're confused."

"I think I know if I'm fired!"

Chuck held up his hands. "Okay, okay, fine. You're fired. So why did you come in this morning?"

"I didn't! Someone …" The rest sounded preposterous.

Someone dragged me here. From home. After a burglar hit me in the head with a bat. Yeah, that's what happened. It's afternoon now, right? So I must have been on my living room floor for a few hours, and then someone broke into my house (again), stripped me naked, dressed me in work clothes, and brought me here. They threw me onto the ground so I'd think I fell from a chair, not got whacked with a bat. It's a conspiracy, Chuck! And no, there must not have been a more sensible way for … well … for whoever it was to do … well, you know … whatever they're trying to do. Blame the new math. It's making all sorts of fake technicians put equipment on our routers to spy on us. Knocking me out, bringing me to work, and probably erasing the day in between? That's just the most logical next step. And no: It's not overly complicated. Makes perfect sense. This kind of thing must happen all the time.

Chuck had wandered over to the shop window. DeShawn glanced into the break room as he passed by. He didn't particularly look like someone who'd masterminded whatever happened to Ash in the past forty-eight hours.

Yes. Masterminding. That was a much better explanation than Ash being mistaken or deluded. The complicated chicanery, invading and knocking-out and dressing up, was without question more likely than the alternative: that Ash was so sleep-deprived and over-drugged that he was … what was the medical term? *Losing his fucking marbles.*

"You must've misunderstood. DeShawn probably just *threatened* to fire you again."

"He said 'You're fired.' It couldn't have been clearer!"

But despite Ash's certainty, the bizarreness of it all was like a river eroding its banks. He could barely stay angry or indignant. He'd never been so sure of something, and at the same time found it so preposterous.

DeShawn made a gesture that seemed to mean, *Hurry it up in there.*

"Then he must have changed his mind," Chuck said.

"He didn't change his mind! I …" But now Ash was fighting to remember. Maybe he had a concussion after all. Phantom baseball bats could do that to a guy. "I even drove into the lot yesterday and sat in my car until Lloyd came over and told me DeShawn and the others said to 'shoot my ass' if I didn't leave."

Chuck put on his best *Let me humor you for a bit* expression. "So let me get this straight. You're saying you were fired?"

"Yes!"

"But you still came to work the next day, *after* you were fired? You weren't home sick like I was told yesterday? Instead, knowing you were fired, you drove here and sat in your car?"

"Yes …"

"Why?"

Ash pinched the bridge of his nose. "I don't know. I wasn't thinking straight." He was starting to wonder which was more probable: that the whole world was insane, or that it was just him.

"Okay. So are you thinking straight *now*?"

"I …" *Not at all.*

Chuck gave him a patient look. "Ash. My man. You *just* took a fall. Kind of a bad one. If I had it on video, I'd be winning ten thousand dollars right now. I think you should go to an urgent care."

That actually wasn't bad advice. Whether it was a bat or a tile floor, he'd still taken a blow.

"Want me to call someone?" Chuck asked.

Inspiration struck. "*Yes!* Mina! Call Mina Irving."

"Your *psychiatrist*?" Ouch. Even Chuck's answer made Ash look unreliable. "I was thinking more like a medical doctor. For your head?"

Ash tried to shake the head in question, but stopped

when stabbing hot irons lanced his neck and skull. "Not to *help me*. To *corroborate* me. Call Mina and she'll tell you I'm telling the truth. *She* knows I was fired. She—"

Ash stopped. He'd spoken with Mina on the phone, but he'd said nothing relevant during their call. Only that he'd slept ... and even *that* would have to be taken on faith, since Mina hadn't seen him in person.

In truth she might *not* believe it — might think he was lying and sleep-deprived, approaching lethal levels of confusion. He must have sounded nuts to her yesterday: first with his panicked message, then with his unconvincing assurances that he was fine.

Come to think of it, Mina might be the *last* person to give Ash a medical thumbs-up right now. Let alone to corroborate his weird-ass story.

"She *what*?" Chuck asked.

Ash touched his head, where he'd supposedly hit the floor. This wasn't good. Chuck would never believe Ash because everything that might vindicate his version events was at home, and ...

He was starting to get an idea.

"Chuck. How much of the day is left?"

"Dunno. Like an hour?"

"You got any flex time left for this week?"

Chuck shrugged. Within shop tolerance, they were always allowed to borrow flex hours from the future if it stayed within a pay period. Apparently his shrug meant yes.

"Do me a favor?" Ash hated the plea in his voice.

"Sure, man."

"Clock out. I need to show you something."

THIRTEEN

Check the Tapes

Maybe Chuck should be his therapist.

On the drive back home, he managed to make Ash feel more centered and less nuts — despite today's intense level of strangeness — than Mina ever had. Compared to Chuck, Mina was a real pain in the ass, making him confront things he didn't even want to think about: Afghanistan and the bombing (which had kicked off his REM disorder and sleep violence), Emily's death (the result of said sleep violence), the fact that just about everyone thought he was a murderer and thus hated him (even Mom sounded uncertain), and the relationship Ash had with his parents (including that wavering mother).

Chuck, on the other hand, was willing to toss a big freckled hand in dismissal at even the worst of Ash's atrocities with a smile on his round face.

Wooed by Chuck's bedside manner, Ash spilled his guts. He told Chuck every detail of what he believed had happened. In the passenger seat of Chuck's shitbox LTD with the sun shining down on him, Ash was even starting to accept some of that qualifier: what he *believed* had happened. But now, even his belief was changing.

A half hour ago, Ash had been as sure of prior events as he was of his name, but the normal world had painted a sheen of no-bullshit over his certainty. Maybe what Ash believed *wasn't* real after all. Maybe, as sure as he'd been that Chuck was the crazy one, Chuck's version of events had been right all along.

Because: Hadn't Ash "woken up" once already only to realize he was still dreaming? Was he really so sure now? It certainly didn't *sound* like truth coming out of his mouth. It sounded like the kind of thing that happened in dreams.

Ash had entered his weirdest sequence of events from something he *knew* to be a dream, then had found himself in the break room in a blink. Was it really that nuts to think he'd never stopped dreaming?

Chuck listened to everything with pleasant acceptance. He'd known Ash for a long time. He'd stood by Ash's side in literal life-and-death situations — and it seemed to Ash that, despite his buddy's cheery demeanor, Chuck must have a few mental scars of his own. Surely the bombing had given him terrors as well. Nobody came through what they'd seen without some emotional upset. And maybe *that's* why Chuck was so cool about this now: he knew, firsthand, what it was like to mistrust your own mind.

Ash said, "Park down the street. If anyone's in my house, I don't want them to know we're coming."

Chuck nodded again, still accepting. This was a mission of espionage, after all.

Chuck popped the trunk. He went to the rear and rummaged unseen for a while, before stepping away with a tire iron. He handed Ash another fetched item: a crowbar. The gesture was strangely touching. *I don't actually believe you, but if you're about to fight your demons, I'll stand at your side and fight them with you.*

They surveilled Ash's house from behind a hedge. A woman walking by with two small white dogs glared at them suspiciously until she was around the corner.

They waited, watching while Jose from next door trimmed his orange trees. When finished, Jose tucked the short limb saw he'd been using into his belt. The look was not fashionable. Jose's T-shirt was tucked into shorts worn above pulled-high tube socks. The ensemble was accented, as always, with a bulky fanny pack. As Ash and Chuck watched, he began watering both tree and lawn with a limp green hose.

Jose waved when he saw Ash looking. The errand stopped feeling like espionage after that.

Cars passed. The drivers inside stared at the two men who, once Ash thought about it, were the definition of hiding in plain sight. A kid on a bike rang his bell. Ash's attention drifted to a large van parked outside the Ramirez home — a delivery service dropping off Sofia's weekly floral bouquets.

It felt like every person was watching them. Assessing them. Following Ash.

They climbed the fence and entered his property through the rear, heading straight for the junction box. It was screwed-down and sealed tight.

Ash searched the grass briefly for more left-behind tools, found none, then got on all fours to look for for subtler signs of work: clipped ends of wire, stripped-away insulation. But he found nothing.

The back door was closed and locked. The young male intruder — *Paul or Mike?* — had apparently secured the slider after beating the homeowner unconscious.

Ash peered through the glass, cupping his hands around his face.

He did the same at the other backyard windows, scoping as much of the house as he could see without entering. Nobody seemed to be inside.

"Okay," Ash said. "Let's go around to the front."

They did, this time walking through the gate instead of climbing the fence. Ash retrieved his keys and opened up. Chuck followed, and they made a quick, military-style search of the place like they might have done together during their Bad Old Days.

"There's nothing here," Ash reported.

Chuck didn't reply.

Ash checked the router. There was nothing plugged into its rear. He scouted everywhere to find something amiss, giving extra time to any place where the device might have fallen. But of course there was nothing. Retrieving his dropped device was probably why the kid had come back in the first place.

"They cleaned it all out." There wasn't even blood on the rug, despite what Ash had matted in his hair near the wound. "They must have cleaned it all up after knocking me out."

"Ash …"

He scampered to his bedroom and grabbed his laptop. Knowing it was pointless, he ran his anti-spyware program, then the antivirus.

Nothing came up — not on the machine, and not on the network. It was almost as if nobody was spying on him at all.

Chuck followed Ash as his search frenzy increased.

"They even straightened the pictures! They were knocked crooked," Ash said.

"Wasn't that in your dream?"

"No! That part was real. It was after I sleepwalked the first time."

"You're sure?"

Maybe. It all ran together.

"Look," Ash said from the master bath, though Chuck was still in the front room. "My pill bottle was moved."

"You *said* it was moved," Chuck told him.

"No, I mean it moved again! It was moved the first time. Now it's moved back."

"So it's where it was to begin with?"

"Well …"

"And you said the pills were moved when the pictures were knocked sideways?"

"They're good," Ash mumbled under his breath. "I'll bet they even wiped their fingerprints."

"Fingerprints?"

"Wiped everything. Makes sense. This is covert work. They couldn't wear gloves while pretending to be technicians because it would look funny. So they had to come back to wipe everything down. How do you lift fingerprints, anyway?"

"Ash …"

Ash stopped, an epiphany dawning. It must look like someone had pressed pause on him.

"What?" Chuck asked.

"The doorbell."

"What *about* the doorbell?"

The home's previous owner had explained, when Ash and Emily bought the place, that he'd wanted a smart-home system but decided the monthly monitoring fees were excessive — and, in the end, something he could do without. He really just wanted to catch the neighborhood kids stealing his packages, which happened all the time. So he'd made his own doorbell cam using a motion-activated camera installed behind the bell plate, then run it to a tiny flash drive storing thirty hours of footage on a loop.

If you ever think one of your packages is missing, just check the tapes within a day or so, before it's overwritten, he'd told Ash. *Little shits think they can get away with everything.*

Ash remembered being amused that the man had used the word "tapes." That was, perhaps, the only reason he was remembering it now. They never had trouble with stolen packages, but "check the tapes" became a private joke used whenever he or Emily lost anything.

Drilling a hole through brick to place the drive inside would have been too hard, so the man told Ash he'd fished its wire behind the siding. The drive was inside the front-porch mailbox, in a hidden compartment lest the mailman get thieving ideas of his own.

Ash rushed for the front door.

"What's going on?" Chuck called behind him.

Ash explained. His hands were inside the mailbox seconds later, trying with meaty fingers to tweeze open the small inner box containing the drive.

"I didn't know you had a doorbell cam," Chuck said.

"Why would you? I barely knew it."

"You just don't strike me as a doorbell-cam guy."

Ash saw Chuck's jittering fingers from the corner of his eyes. His voice was strange. His PTSD must be acting up. If Ash was right, Chuck's paranoia would ratchet up as well.

Ash's fingers were also shaking, but his from anticipation. The camera's view covered the porch — for package thieves — but also the street beyond. The wide-angle view would show last night's chase. And Ash returning. He'd been holding the comm thing when he passed, and he'd cut through the front yard, passing closely enough to see with the included infrared. He'd even been holding it in the hand closest to the camera.

The footage would show the techs arriving. And leaving. It would show their van, with ArkTek on the side.

Ash peered into the dark mailbox, trying to see the small and stubborn latch. In the neighborhood around him, he could hear the rat-a-tat from a sprinkler. A truck accelerated a block away. Then he heard a big *THUMP* from somewhere behind him: oafish Chuck, accidentally knocking over something large and soft.

"Chuck ..." Ash extended his free hand while the other kept fumbling the latch. "Hand me your phone, will you? I need a flashlight to see in here."

When Chuck didn't respond, Ash said, "Chuck?"

He turned to see Chuck lying just inside his foyer, unconscious or dead.

As his mouth dropped open, something sharp and smelling of rust slid its slow, menacing way across Ash's throat like a warning.

"Step inside and close the door," said a familiar voice — sterner and more menacing than ever before — icy and professional. "This might get messy."

From the corner of his eye, Ash saw the man about to kill him.

Jose, his tree-watering neighbor.

FOURTEEN

Autopilot

Jose pushed Ash into a dining room chair and, putting some distance between them, slid the saw back under his belt. This done, he drew an unlikely item from the dorky fanny pack he always wore: a long, slim black pistol with a silencer screwed into the end.

Ash looked down at Chuck. He was still unconscious on the floor, his chest rising in a slow, even cadence. Then his gaze shifted back to the man aiming the gun at him — the man who'd knocked Chuck cold. He found himself unable to accept what he was seeing. He'd known Jose since he and Emily moved in. The man had lived on this block for twenty years at least ... or so Ash had been told.

Jose still wore his blue and white patterned shorts, neatly ironed and secured around his slim waist with a belt. His socks were almost to the knee: not compression, just uncool. Over them were brown sandals. His shirt was covered with math: swag from one of his son's academic competitions. He'd topped it all off with a floppy, pansy-blue hat to shade him from the sun.

The sleek black weapon in his hand was as incongruous as his gaze, which was made of ice.

"Jose …"

"Save it!" Jose snapped in a voice totally unlike his usual friendly drawl. "Unless you're about to tell me who you handed off to, I'm not interested in anything you have to say."

"*Handed off* … What are you talking about?"

"*You know,*" he sneered. It was like they'd had this conversation before, only this time Jose considered himself proven right. "You can't fool me. Somehow, *you know.*"

"Look. I know what people say about me, but Emily—"

"What?" Jose inched forward. His head cocked slightly, probably subconsciously, as if eager to hear what came next. "*What* about Emily?"

"I have a condition! I was fucking *asleep!* You think I'd have ever hurt Emily on purpose? I loved her more than anyone!"

Jose rolled his eyes, no longer interested. He pulled a phone from his pocket, tapped through something complicated onscreen, then swiped once before holding the phone to his face. A few seconds later, Ash heard a female voice on the other end.

"Yes. Yes. It was Sanders." He eyed Ash, nodding at a question from the other side. "Oh, don't worry about that. I'm pretty sure he's already noticed something's different about 'Jose' today." He said his own name with audible quotes. "What? Because I'm standing in front of him right now with my weapon drawn, that's why."

Now the voice sounded angry, or at least surprised.

Half-watching, Ash glanced at Chuck. Jose seemed to have forgotten all about him. Chuck could probably tackle their assailant and commandeer his weapon, if he would just wake up.

Listen to yourself, said an insistent, chiding inner voice. *Read his body language and stop being stupid. Does this really look half-baked to you? Do you really think this is the first time that man has held a gun?*

There was zero jitter in Jose's arm. No hesitation on his face. Who *was* Jose, really?

"He's got a camera inside the doorbell," Jose explained to the phone. "It apparently saw more than you want anyone to see." The caller tittered; Jose replied with his hackles up. "Things were too far gone for that. He was *retrieving it,* so I stepped in while I still could. What if he'd —?" An interruption stopped him. "What? No, no, I don't think so. Listen to me. It—"

The woman on the phone interrupted Jose again. He looked annoyed enough to shoot her.

"Well, what exactly did you *want* me to do?" More tittering. "No. No. Look. I think he's breached. What? I don't know. A gut feeling. I'm thinking we handle this the old-fashioned way. Unless you want to get Tailors over here for a re-fit? Yeah. Exactly. So you tell *me* what other options we have."

The conversation continued. Ash was trying to pay attention, but it was hard to ignore Chuck as he stirred. Chuck was their best chance to wrestle this clusterfuck back to normal. Every so often he'd twitch on the floor, and once it almost looked like he'd rearranged his legs into a more comfortable position. And so with more than half his mind on Chuck and the urgent need to signal him, Ash caught only bits of Jose's exchange as he talked about "mnemonics" and "waveforms" and, most troublingly, "security and disposal" with whoever was on the other end of his line. Ash didn't know how those ideas connected, but "disposal" at least seemed clear.

The people I chased last night. The thing I got from one of them, then had taken back with the help of a bat to the head. Either that was all real, or all of this — here and now — is just another part of the dream.

His eyes went to Jose's shirt. The words *WHAT ABOUT* hovered above a complicated mess of equations. At the shirt's bottom was *DIDN'T YOU UNDERSTAND?*

Ash looked away from Jose, then back. The words on Jose's shirt were the same. That meant he wasn't dreaming. This was real … and it meant last night had been real, too.

"Fine," Jose was telling the phone as Chuck groaned softly and rolled over. "I *could* just get this over with, but if you think you can get something out of Sanders, be my guest. I'll keep him warm for you. Yeah. No worries. No worries *at all*, your highness."

With a long-suffering sigh, Jose used his free hand to pull a zip-tie from his pocket. He leaned toward Ash.

"Sure," he told the phone while he stared into Ash's eyes. "Yeah. *Oh*, I'm listening. Yeah, and I'm doing it right now. You want him tied? Fine. I'll fucking tie—"

Before Jose could finish his sentence, someone didn't so much as *kick the gun out of his hands* as *clamped it hard between two feet.* That pair of feet twisted the weapon free, then somehow tossed it into the air with movements that were downright prehensile — something only a chimp should be able to do.

Milliseconds later (just as Ash reached the surprising conclusion that *he* had been the one to take Jose's weapon, apparently on instinct), his thieving feet hit the floor. He bolted upright without thinking. The motion was all ass and calves, his bent legs straightening like a pair of thick whips. A concussive motion, both hamstrings striking the chair hard and fast enough to send it flying backward.

The gun seemed to hang weightless in midair. Ash stood to full height while it was still airborne, his eyes catching every nuance as time crawled.

No. Time's the same as ever. It's you who's moving fast.

But how? Ash couldn't even play hand-slap games with his nephew. His coordination was pitiful. He would never be a quick-draw ... or so he'd thought before realizing how much time he had to grab the flying gun by its muzzle and slam the stock into the hollow below Jose's chin in the same upward arc.

The adrenaline second passed. Time returned to normal, the chair finally slamming into the kitchen island fifteen feet away. Ash found himself blinking at what he'd just done as Jose staggered back.

Turning the gun around to hold it correctly — now that Ash was aware of his actions — was clumsy at best. The awkward metal thing clicked against his wedding ring and he nearly fumbled.

He gaped at Jose's injured face and started to say he was sorry. But then Jose came at him for a tackle.

Ash's mind waited to be struck, but his body had other plans. He parried left on autopilot and Jose missed him entirely. Ash shoved Jose hard as he passed — into the knocked-back chair, reducing it to kindling.

Jose was up quickly, this time drawing the limb saw from his belt. At some point Ash had snagged the zip-tie (perhaps from Jose's hand as Ash smacked him with his own pistol; who knew) and was now holding it as if preparing to use it.

But how? Why? Ash had no idea. He was technically in control of his body, but only in the strictest sense. He was operating out of habit, every motion greased. But where had Ash *built* such deadly habits? He wasn't coordinated or practiced in anything. He could barely shuffle cards.

The saw flashed. Jose jabbed, then swiped. Ash felt his shirt catch as Jose came in like a conquistador swinging a sword, then dodged back just in time.

Seconds dilated. Something in his brain clicked, showing Ash every aspect of the skirmish as if someone had paused it for analysis.

Go left. Go right. Try this.

This turned out to be a complicated maneuver involving the zip-tie — one Ash wouldn't have bet on in a thousand years. The next time Jose swiped, Ash wrapped the thing with the tie, its blade in a hard plastic loop with Ash holding the tie at both ends.

The saw hung up, but Jose managed to hold his weapon. This was both anticipated and desired.

With the saw bound, Ash pulled both hands toward his chest hard in a rowing motion. Jose stumbled forward, and as he did Ash turned one elbow into the fall and shattered the other man's nose.

Jose collapsed, then stopped moving.

But now there was someone behind him. Ash spun to see Chuck standing behind him, watching in shock.

"Chuck. Thank God. I think—"

A kitchen towel whipped around Ash's neck from behind, then pulled tight. He could smell the copper scent of blood over one shoulder: Jose, breathing in his ear.

"I knew it," Jose told him, but it came out more like *eh do id* thanks to the nose job Ash had given him. *"I knew you were just playing stupid."*

Ash's hands whipped back, trying to snag Jose, but Jose wouldn't be fooled a third time. The towel twisted, tightening.

CHUCK! Ash tried to shout, but he could only croak.

He'd been exerted, with emptied lungs, when Jose began to strangle him. His limbs flailed, but to no avail.

Chuck remained right where he was, dumb. He must still be concussed; his eyes were so confused. Still he looked around at his feet, obeying some deep instinct to help. But where was the gun? Ash had lost it in the melee.

Think. Do something before you suffocate.

Ash was larger than Jose. Maybe he could shake him loose.

But nothing doing. Jose counter-shook, then shoved them both forward until Ash's face smashed into the kitchen wall with Jose to his rear.

Another bleat of instinct took over. Ash waited for the impact, then for the few inches of rebound physics inevitably demanded. Fighting pain and hypoxia, he stuck a knee into those inches and shoved his body backward.

He shoved harder once the gap opened, after he got a foot on the wall instead.

Off-balanced, the pair staggered away from the wall. But Jose still had his grip on the towel and quickly recovered. He braced, leaning in, and managed not to trip.

He was pissed off now — and able to just do it all over again.

"Oh," Jose said warningly, "FUG JOO!"

He shoved Ash toward the wall much harder this time, meaning to break his skull. But some dormant part of Ash had *wanted* Jose to try again, because as Jose shoved him hard forward, Ash torqued backward. He raised one leg and then the other, effectively running up the kitchen wall in an end-over-end circle.

Ash's weight loosened Jose's grip as his feet skittered across the ceiling. Ash landed behind his enemy, the towel twisted free and draping his shoulders like a scarf. Then

Jose, still a slave to momentum, struck the wall all by himself.

Ash pulled away, gasping but unhurt. He put his foot on Jose's neck, determined not to let his opponent get up again this time.

But then a shout from behind: "HOLD IT!"

Ash startled toward the sound, ready to fight, but he lowered his hands and smiled at the sight of Chuck, aiming the gun. His expression sharp and focused.

Then his smile collapsed.

Because Chuck wasn't pointing the weapon at Jose.

FIFTEEN

Figneligrakbint

"Do ed," said Jose: *Do it.*

He was rising again now that Chuck had Ash covered with blood from neck to crotch. Ash's eyes darted between them, unable to believe the last turn of events. Chuck was dazed, right? Chuck was confused, right? Chuck, of all people, was not his enemy.

"Chuck ..." Ash said.

But Chuck wasn't making eye contact. His gun didn't waver. It was centered on Ash's heart.

"I said *do it*," Jose repeated.

"CHUCK!" Ash shouted.

Chuck took one hand off the gun and stooped for the phone Jose had dropped when Ash attacked him. Unlike Jose, Chuck didn't make the mistake of looking away.

With his eyes almost entirely on Ash, he entered the same complicated sequence of taps Jose had used to unlock the phone earlier. It brightened to life, the call still connected but muted by the lock.

The same female voice cut in, yelling.

Chuck waited for an opening, then spoke. "Hey. It's

me." He spoke quietly to calm her, his eyes darting to Jose. "No, he's still here. Pretty bloody, but here."

More words from her end: a question.

"*Sanders* happened," Chuck answered. "No. No. I don't think he's breached. Not all the way. But unfortunately for 'Jose,' he did manage to remember some old tricks."

"*Chuck!*" Ash blurted. "What the f—?"

Chuck raised his aim to Ash's forehead, and Ash went silent.

"Instinct?" Chuck guessed, answering another of the phone-woman's questions. She seemed to be asking about Ash and his strange new abilities. Or perhaps not *new* abilities, strange as that sounded. What had Chuck called them? *Old tricks.*

"*You're* the mnemonist; you tell me," Chuck continued. "H.M. learned to walk around his neighborhood even *after* losing his hippocampus, just from repetition and habit. Maybe it's like that. Or maybe it's like I said; Sanders wasn't embedded well enough; I don't know. You'd better come down here and check him out. But from what I've seen, he doesn't have a clue. At least not a conscious clue."

H.M. Why did Ash know those initials?

Half of Ash was drifting away to somewhere else, now remembering himself saying words he hadn't remembered before: *H.M. was the real-life* Memento. *Surgery to eliminate his seizures gave him anterograde amnesia, and he lost the ability to form new memories.*

But when had Ash studied abnormal psychology? When had he studied the brain?

The answer, of course, was never. He'd gone to college on the GI Bill, gotten a B.A. in business, then ended up machining steel because he was good with his hands and the recession had dried up all the office jobs by the time he returned from Afghanistan.

Yet, like seeing a double image, Ash now seemed to recall a different version of his past that was incompatible with the first, where he *had* studied the brain and memory — and a whole lot about it.

Unbidden, inside his own head, Ash heard Emily saying, *Sunshine makes everything better.*

He'd hated the way she used to say that to him when he was angry, or annoyed, or otherwise bothered. A juvenile answer to complex problems.

So why had he been thinking about it so much recently?

Training. Words. The lab. Endless meditation and focus exercises. The games we played, and the World Memory Championships.

None of it had context for Ash. They were all naked concepts — a bucket full of untidy loose ends — and now that something was opening inside him, the flow of phantom recollections refused to stop. He was bombarded with unbidden memories as he stared into the barrel, each one unfolding like a freshly solved puzzle.

The key. The triggers.

"Everyone has a trigger, Ash. They gave every one of us a trigger so they could control us. If you know the triggers, there's always the way out."

He couldn't remember who'd said the last thing, yet knew it anyway. But what was a *trigger*? What might someone want to control, and why did the concept evoke both fear and hope within Ash now, as he recalled it? It invited the image of a hook more than the actuator on a firearm: a mental failsafe upon which an emergency helmet would forever be hung.

Ash imagined a dark-skinned man with black hair saying those words, though Ash had no idea

(Ishaan)

who the man could possibly be or what

(Ishaan)

his statement could possibly mean.

Chuck was squinting at Ash in suspicion. He ended his call without telling the mystery woman on the other end where to find them, or even saying goodbye.

"Maybe you should have a seat," he said.

"*Chuck.*" Ash looked around to indicate their situation: man with gun; man at gunpoint. Surely Chuck must see how bizarre it all was. "Come on. We're friends."

"No, Ash. I'm afraid we're not." He gave him a resigned sort of shrug. "For what it's worth, I regret that things had to turn out this way. I planned to *become* your friend, if I was going to play one forever anyway."

"*What?*"

"I don't actually know you. Our 'friendship' has always been one-sided."

"What about Afghanistan? All we've been through!"

Chuck shook his head and another bit of fragmented *something-like-memory* returned. *Anything can be a trigger, if it's unique. A word. A gesture. Everyone has one, Ash.*

"I wasn't in Afghanistan. I just met you six months ago."

Ash felt his face twist. His first tour was almost three years ago now, and Chuck had been there the entire time. They had been best friends ever since they met in Afghanistan, thanks to an unbreakable bond forged in the fires of death and healing.

"I know it's hard to accept," Chuck said.

"You're crazy."

"No, Ash. *You're* crazy. That's why you were so easy."

Instead of requesting an explanation, Ash allowed the anger to fuel him. Someone was fucking with him and had been for months — or, if Chuck was somehow right, *years*. He had to do something. But what?

Jose was using paper towels to staunch his nose's bleeding, relying on Chuck to handle the situation. He wasn't paying attention, and was only about two feet from Ash's right hand. He was also unarmed. Ash had lassoed away both saw and gun.

Ash's arm flashed out and grabbed Jose, pulling him between Chuck and himself as a shield. Then, before Jose could thrash and free himself, Ash pawed the counter until he felt the knife block.

He removed the butcher's blade and held it to Jose's throat.

Now with a hostage, he started to walk toward the door.

"Ash …" Chuck sounded tired. Fatigued from all these shenanigans.

Ash shook his head like an angry metronome. "I don't know what the fuck is going on, but I'm done with it."

"You can't go outside," Chuck said. "They're watching the house by now."

"You're bluffing."

"Jose isn't your only neighbor. Who else might you be wrong about?"

"This is insane. Jose has been here for years."

Jose gargled a laugh, despite his compromised position.

"Who else, then?" Ash asked. Chuck was tracking them both with the pistol, looking for a clear shot. "Who else has been watching me?"

"I can't tell you that." He still hadn't lowered the gun.

"DeShawn," Ash guessed. "DeShawn is part of this."

"He was paid," Chuck corrected. "Not 'part of' anything."

"The Uber driver. He asked some funny questions."

"I'm not going to tell you, so stop asking."

"You called Jose," Ash accused. "You told him to come."

Chuck shook his head. "He was listening. Your home is constantly surveilled. Look. Put down the knife, okay? Put down the knife and we'll talk."

"TALK NOW!" Ash jabbed at Jose with the blade. Jose jerked in his arms as fresh blood started to drip.

Chuck shook his head again. "You can't understand."

"Oh, I don't know, Chuck. I'm pretty smart."

"I mean: you don't have the *capacity* to understand. Let him go. The people who are coming will explain everything."

"Bullshit. They'll kill me."

Another lie from Chuck: "Nobody wants to kill you, Ash."

"BULLSHIT!"

"Not yet, anyway," Chuck added.

Jose apparently still had some fight in him after all. He had been dragging his feet like a lifeless lump: playing weak, acting like dead weight. Now, though, he stiffened and hooked one leg behind Ash's, causing him to stumble toward the closed front door as he reached for the knob.

He couldn't shake free of Ash, but he could duck to give his partner a clean shot … and did.

Chuck fired his weapon, nearly hitting Ash's shoulder as Ash flinched sideways.

Jose seized Ash's knife hand in both of his and slammed it hard against the door casing. Ash's grip broke, the knife rattled free, and five seconds later their positions were reversed: Ash in front, Jose behind, and the blade on Ash's neck for a change.

Chuck still held the pistol, but now he used his other hand to pat the air for calm — and it was *Jose*, not Ash he wanted to soothe.

They're not on the same page, Ash realized. *There's dissension in the ranks.*

"Don't kill him," Chuck told Jose. "The Tailors need him."

But Jose's manner had changed. Chuck's takeover had lit something in him — something Ash didn't understand. Something, between these men, had shattered a fragile allegiance.

"Fuck you, man!" Jose barked. "You were going to let him kill me!"

"Nobody was killing anyone. You're fine. I'm fine. We're all fine. Now *put down the knife*."

Jose's hand jerked and drew blood, nicking Ash to one side of his Adam's apple. "I know how this works! Things didn't go cleanly, so now you need a Cleaner. The boss shows up, and she'll wrap up *aaaaall* the loose ends. Don't tell *me* to be calm. Me and Mr. Sanders here, maybe it's us two from now on."

"I'm on your side," Chuck told Jose, though he still hadn't lowered his gun. "Nobody's going to 'clean' anything except the mess you keep making on the floor. You've lost too much blood. You're not thinking clearly."

Jose shook his head; Ash felt the motion against the back of his own. "I'm thinking just fine. He *had* me and you didn't do shit to stop him! Clean up the mess, right?" Jose shook his head again. "No way. *We* go. Him and me. *You* want him, you can have him after he gets out of my car five miles down the road."

Jose pawed at the door. He'd open it and drag Ash away, and after that things would be much more complicated.

Then Ash remembered: *The trigger. Everyone has one.*

Without knowing what he was doing or why, he felt nonsense syllables rise to his lips. Instinct told him that because mnemonic triggers were hard to develop, most of the organization's grunts used the same one.

All he had to do was to say the secret word, grabbing Chuck by his mind.

"Figneligrakbint," Ash hissed. "Shoot him!"

Chuck's eyes went blank as the trigger commandeered him. He fired a single bullet through Jose's forehead.

Jose went limp.

Then Ash slipped through the dead man's arms and ran out the door, knowing he only had seconds before Chuck returned to his senses.

SIXTEEN

Neighbors

Ash had slept with a loaded pistol in the nightstand drawer ever since he'd come back home. He'd wanted it under his pillow, but Emily hated guns. If they ever had kids, she'd told him, he'd need to buy a safe and keep it under lock and key.

But they never had kids because Ash murdered her. Since *then*, he'd slept with guns wherever he wanted — including in each car's glove compartment.

As he exited the house, Ash forgot Chuck's warning that the neighborhood might be watching him the way Jose had been. He ran right to where Emily's car was still parked in the driveway, one side of his head covered in Jose's blood, brains, and bone.

Then he remembered the warning all at once.

He froze with his hand extended toward the handle. His head jerked like a bird's. He was suddenly sure he'd see black sedans arriving when he looked back, or maybe that big white van with *ArkTek* on the side. There'd be shadow agents running at him with weapons drawn, every one of them wanting him dead.

But instead he saw nothing. The street was quiet. Chuck had either been bluffing or wrong. Nobody had noticed. Nobody cared. Thanks to Jose's silencer, even the bullets they'd fired inside were whispers.

Still, a too-long beat passed as Ash listened to the air, his attention on full alert. Bluejays flapped their wings in slow motion. Every tick of wind-swept branches and bird-song struck him as unfathomably loud.

Then, quite suddenly, life returned to an adrenalized throttle. And he thought: *You're out in the open. Soon they'll start shooting. Soon they'll swarm, coming for you in legions. You made a mistake. You fucked up, Ash Sanders, because you're no longer the man you used to be.*

His mind showed him flashes of a dark-skinned man. A woman with feline eyes. A tall man with disorderly teeth. And—

Shit. He'd pulled the handle and found the car locked. Of course it was. You didn't just leave an unlocked car sitting around for everyone to ransack.

But then he remembered: Emily's key was on his chain, and his chain was still in his pocket.

He fumbled. He stabbed the lock. Once inside, he practically lunged for the glove compartment. Seconds later his fingers were wrapping the comforting weight of a blue-steel Beretta: clip in, safety on, double-action with a round already in the chamber.

A flash intruded: another of those unasked-for almost-memories. It was a vision from long ago, fragmented by time. He saw himself holding this exact pistol, aiming at a faraway target. He'd known he could shoot, but he'd forgotten how well and who'd taught him to do it. He'd had no conscious answer to those questions before now. If someone had asked, he supposed he'd tell them he'd never needed to learn. Ash Sanders, born a deadeye.

But now a truer-feeling memory came:

Emily, spooning him from the rear as he sighted down the barrel, back then entirely platonic. Her breath had been so close to his ear. And she'd told him: *Not too tight. Not too loose. Pull slow and smooth. When the hammer falls, it should almost surprise you.*

Emily. Shooting guns. Beyond ridiculous.

Someone was sprinting right toward him.

Ash sprung from the SUV's cab, swinging the gun to confront the on-comer. His keyed-up mind showed him a tall assassin, almost upon him.

But then it was just Baine Collier, the 17-year-old who lived across the street. A football was hopping its oblong way around Ash's feet. Baine had lost it, was all — and now he had a gun in his face, Ash threatening to kill him for his fumble.

Baine flinched, raising both hands as he ducked low. Ash saw only terror before losing sight of the kid's face as he curled up to protect his middle. Baine was six-two, more tall than broad, with a mop of perpetually untidy hair. They'd had many engaging chats. It was a good kid now cowering into a ball on Ash's front lawn, begging his neighbor not to shoot.

Before Ash could retract and apologize, someone elsewhere started yelling. Ash looked up. He saw a stern-looking woman driving by in a red Kia who'd slammed her brakes and opened her window upon seeing what he'd done.

Alarms brayed in Ash's head. He didn't think; he swung to point the gun her way instead. Her hands went up and she flinched out of sight. The car rolled forward slowly, her foot startled into leaving the brake.

Then he saw the rest of them.

His entire block was out, it seemed. Two men were

walking a large dog fifty feet away. Raymond Bonaveu had looked up from waxing his car. Lettie MacDunnah — her PTA nose perpetually in everyone's business — had turned toward the shouts as she came outside three doors down to grab her paper.

Every one of them struck Ash as a potential plant. Each of them a silent enemy.

Stop it. They're just regular people.

That's right, countered a new and skeptical voice inside him. *Just like Jose. And Chuck.*

The onlookers stared. Finally some came hesitantly forward, thinking him ill, but Ash swung his gun to confront them.

Who were they, really? Were they *all* fakes?

Someone had been watching him for a while now, and now he knew who it was.

It was all of them. Every one of his neighborhood regulars, a liar and an enemy.

That couldn't be true. *Wasn't* true. But Ash had stopped believing in everything.

"Ash?" Raymond called from two doors down. He'd stepped forward, needing to verify an unlikely scenario. "Ash, what's going on?"

"STAY BACK! STAY WHERE YOU ARE!" Ash shouted, rounding on him.

He must be a sight. He was panting, his shoulders rising and falling in panicked heaves. His eyes were wide and wild. His hair was in corkscrews, his shirt was ripped, and he was covered in blood.

Behind him, the front door was still open … and if anyone looked too closely, they might just see the legs of a corpse inside.

"Mr. Sanders?" asked Lettie MacDunnah.

Conflicted, Ash swept his weapon from one member of

the neighborhood to the other, moving in a slow circle to make sure he'd spotted them all.

His neighbors flinched when the weapon reached them. A few ducked for cover.

"I'm sorry …" Ash said, his certainty evaporating in all this bright-sun normality. "I'm just … I'm just …"

But what could he possibly say? Chuck could emerge and give chase at any moment. There was no vindication left now for Ash Sanders. This part of his life was over no matter what came next.

He only knew one thing for sure: He had to go. *He had to get away.*

Ash barely lowered his weapon as he slipped inside the vehicle. Then started the engine, burning rubber as he sped away.

SEVENTEEN

Version A and Version B

Think.

Except that he *couldn't* think. Ash could only focus on the mechanics of driving while he tried to ignore everything else inside his head.

His thoughts were moving too fast. Worse, he seemed to have two independent lives at once now like a single man split in half. Even the things he'd been sure about were starting to fall apart.

Everything had unanchored. Events had stopped existing with any sort of *when* or *where* and instead now only *existed* ... simply *there* in an indistinct miasma.

Afghanistan. Chuck. Me and Emily. Was that two years ago? Or only one?

How long ago was Kandahar? Ash kept flashing back to the bomb, to the kid, but now that memory was glassy and hard to hold. After a while he could barely remember the white van the soldiers had been standing around.

The van with the logo. The van Ash was starting to think he'd been *inside* rather than standing away from.

Or maybe that recollection had happened somewhere

else. Or maybe there *was* no bomb, or a different *kind* of bomb. There, in Kabul. There, in Kyiv. In Paris?

Ash had seen the van in Paris, where of course he'd never been.

It was all so hard to carry — ironic, since the same memory had refused to leave him just days ago despite furious attempts to forget it.

Everything was slippery. He had the distinct sense that if he didn't keep replaying the scene in Afghanistan, he'd lose it forever.

But when the hell did a person lose only *one* memory?

When the memory is a dream. Or when he's losing his mind, dipshit, like you are right now.

How could anyone ever be sure that a memory was true, and not just a small-scale hallucination? What *was* a hallucination other than a false now, or an artificial past?

Ash knew from the brain science he'd never studied (where he'd learned about H.M. and anterograde amnesia, apparently) that even "rock solid" human memories got things wrong all the time. Eyewitness testimony, in prosecuting crime, was notoriously unreliable.

The robber had blond hair.

Are you sure? Think closely.

And everyone learns later that the robber had *black* hair. The clerk had blond hair, and the witness's brain conflated them while he was absorbed in the moment.

Why did Ash remember his gun-hating wife teaching him to shoot?

Was it possible (and he should think carefully about this) that he *was* losing his mind right now? Was it possible he'd done something horrible back at his house — something he was only remembering in the way he wanted and needed to, instead of remembering the truth?

Because really, Ash's version of recent events was insane.

In Ash's crazy version of reality, he'd wrestled a limb saw from his mild-mannered, high-socks-wearing dolt of a neighbor using a kitchen towel. He'd done it because that same mild-mannered neighbor, after years of living peacefully next door, had suddenly become an assassin bent on killing Ash for unknown reasons. During the fight with the assassin, average-guy-Ash had run up a wall and across a ceiling like a movie stunt.

And what did Ash's version say happened when he'd nearly been dragged away? Why, that's when Ash had used a nonsense word on his friend Chuck, who'd *also* become an assassin today.

Upon hearing the magic word, Chuck had shot the guy from next door who grew the prize begonias. *Of course* he had; Ash had been controlling him like a puppet.

Ash had done that with a *word* in his version of events. A goddamn *word*. A word that Ash had conveniently remembered at exactly the right time.

Yeah.

Well, that was Version A of what'd happened. Version B was much simpler. In Version B, Ash Sanders — a man who'd killed his wife for no reason — had flipped out and killed his neighbor for no reason, too. The End.

Ash knew what the cops would say when they saw the evidence. They'd say Ash Sanders was the country's latest Freak-Out.

Like the housewife who'd Freaked Out two weeks ago in Seattle. One afternoon she'd simply put down the cake she was baking, gone to a local political rally, and stabbed her state senator in the throat.

Like the Boise accountant last month who'd Freaked

Out while a prominent client was in his office. Instead of signing incorporation papers with the accountant's fountain pen, the client had ended up dead with the pen in his eye.

Face it, buddy, Ash thought. *You're losing it. They'll say you're Freaking Out, and they'll lock you up in a nuthouse same as the others.*

Trying to disbelieve it, Ash drove on.

He drove in a daze until, quite suddenly, he realized where he'd been headed all along. He hadn't meant to go there; his subconscious mind had brought him on autopilot. *The man's not in conscious control of his faculties,* the courts would say.

Instead of the VA, Ash had arrived at a small gray building on the edge of the college campus.

He forced himself to breathe. He tried to believe he was safe, and that the place he'd reached was one he could now enter without a problem.

It was a hard thing to have faith in. Something inside Ash had come undone today, and he hadn't yet decided what it meant. He only knew he'd felt pursued for the entire trip, and that feeling of pursuit was hard to shake. His route here had been beyond paranoid. He'd acted like a Hollywood hero, repeating things he'd seen in movies to shake any possible tail. He'd made unexpected turns and backtracked unnecessarily, always watching out for vehicles behind him that did the same.

Maybe it had worked. Or maybe he had no idea what he was doing. Even seeing nothing in the rearview gave him no reprieve.

Besides. They'd do better than just *follow him,* wouldn't they? They were more advanced ... whoever "they" were.

The car is probably GPS-chipped, said his paranoia. *"They" could be anywhere, in no hurry because you no longer have to be near someone to track them.*

Nonsense, Ash told the voice. *Look for yourself. Nobody's here. You'd be dead already if there was.*

But that was only true if "inside" wasn't part of this.

Ash considered the gray building. Did he really expect to find friends in there? No. He'd come to confront more of his enemies.

The internal voice almost guffawed at his resolve.

Listen to yourself. It'd be hard to find a more average Joe than you, Ash. If you hadn't earned some notoriety by murdering your wife, nobody would even know your name. You're an anonymous cog in society's big wheel. You're not special; you're America's average. Do you know the main characteristic of depression? Sure you do; Mina's told you over and over. It's a sense of meaninglessness, Ash. A sense that nothing you do matters. What have you done to escape that meaninglessness? You've made a fantasy world for yourself in which you're the hero who must break free. But that's not true, is it, Ash? Really, you're just sad and in sore need of purpose. You think you're Neo, seeing the bars of his prison for the first time, destined by fate to break free. But it's bullshit. You punched a clock and slept in on weekends before getting yourself fired. Nothing you do DOES matter … just like everyone else in this fucked-up world.

Ash felt the weight of his gun, tucking it into his waistband as he prepared to exit. Maybe things looked bad, but he couldn't believe this was all in his head. Not without a fight.

How could it be a lie? It was so … *real.*

So … *visceral.*

That's what schizophrenics said, about the phantoms only they could see.

He looked himself over. He'd been wearing an overshirt during the melee, so he'd stripped it off. Early in the drive, he'd pulled into an alley, poured the remains of a water bottle on the clean part of the shirt, then used it to wipe most of the blood from his skin. He now straightened his hair with his fingers, plucking away small bits of what was probably Jose's skull. Then he looked in the vanity mirror. He met his own eyes, forcing himself to take a few deep breaths before exiting.

"Take it easy," he said aloud.

He checked the gun as he stepped into the sun, hiding its protruding butt under a pullover that Emily always kept in the rear. He couldn't help looking around suspiciously, but he made himself move normally while climbing the stone steps.

A simple sign hung above the door: *SCIENCES*.

Once inside, Ash drew a folded business card from his wallet. It hung up on some other scraps inside, its extrication causing him to fumble his license and a pair of credit cards onto the floor. Plus the scrap of paper with the unknown Mariana Jordan's name and nothing else. *That* gem seesawed down like a feather on the wind: proof that he hadn't been firing on all cylinders these past few weeks.

But that was a lie, right? He hadn't been forgetting things, blacking out, and a little out of his mind lately or anything.

No. Not at all. He was entirely sane. Entirely sane to do what he was about to do: enter an academic building with a loaded gun in his belt. The word *Columbine* didn't come to mind or anything.

I'm not crazy, Ash throttled his doubts. *It's Version A all the way, baby.*

He slipped his license, credit cards, and the note back into his wallet, then re-stowed the wallet in his pocket. This done, he inspected the card he'd tweezed out with both hands. Whether Version A or B turned out to be correct, he'd find out soon.

Mina had given him the card weeks ago, suggesting he call to book a formal sleep study at her lab. It'd be free, she'd assured him: part of her quest to help sleepers in need.

The card directed him to room 114: to Mina Irving's sleep lab, just down the hall.

EIGHTEEN

Please
_____

Dr. Irving's sleep lab looked no different from the outside than the many anonymous-looking classrooms along the hospital-like hallway. The building itself was silent — either temporarily devoid of students or not a place used for classes. There were people inside some of the rooms, but the doors were closed and all were studiously quiet with the atmosphere of a library.

Above the knob of room 114 was a tall rectangle of glass embedded with fine wire, postered-over from the inside so Ash couldn't see through. To the right of the doorframe was a tarnished brass plate with a placard affixed to it:

Dr. Mina Irving, M.D.-Ph.D.
Dr. Bryan Waters, Ph.D.
Sleep Sciences

GRADUATE STUDENTS apparently didn't get their names on the door, though Ash had heard from Mina about a few of them. He knew a fair amount about her lab and her work because asking her questions was an excellent way to avoid discussing his own issues.

Ash opened the door. A woman in her early twenties looked up from a sheaf of papers and, after a respectful pause in which he was supposed to go first but did not, said, "Hi! Can I help you with something?"

"I need to talk to Mina Irving."

"Dr. Irving is with a subject right now. Would you like to leave her a message?"

Ash shook his head. He'd been trying to keep a new and rather insistent emotion at bay, and right now it felt like that emotion might tear through his carefully held facade of calm to rat him out.

"It can't wait."

The woman gave a helpless little shrug. "The experiment she's running is a real-time thing. I'm afraid she can't step away."

His eyes went to the only other door in the room.

The grad student noted his glance. "Sir?"

Ash moved toward the door.

"Sir?"

He crossed the room and had his hand on the knob before the woman rose and reached him. He almost punched her when she touched his arm. Now that the worst of his *flight* response was over, indignation was taking its place. Adrenaline pumped harder by the second, making him want to *fight* instead.

He'd come here on autopilot, but now he had a hard-set purpose: He suspected — but was not entirely sure — that he might be furious with Dr. Mina Irving. After all, who was closer to him these days than Chuck and DeShawn? Only Mina, of course.

She was the one tasked with improving his mental state.

She was the one who was supposed to banish the nightmares and help him sleep.

She was the one supposedly helping suppress his sleep violence, or at least his sleepwalking.

And yet, how well had she done with any of those things? *Not* well.

Maybe she'd done it all on purpose. Maybe she, like Chuck, wasn't on Ash's side after all.

"Sir! I'm sorry, but I can't—!"

Ash turned his head to face the grad student. As he stared, her hand lifted from his. She leaned away, as if afraid.

"I'm a patient," Ash told her. Then he opened the door and entered despite her protests.

He found himself in a dark foyer of sorts. There was no light fixture in the small space or windows to the outside. An intermittent light bled out from behind a fabric drape hung over the window in one of two additional doorways. The drape was imperfect; air conditioning from a vent made it sway, leaking fluorescence.

Ash drew back the drape and peeked into the room. It was fully lit and reminded him of a lunchroom: a round table surrounded by school-issue chairs, a vending machine and a coffee pot. A sizable Indian man and diminutive white woman were sitting in silence at the table, each immersed in a book.

He let the drape fall back into place. The room returned to darkness.

The door through which he'd entered the foyer opened then, striking him in the rear. He shoved it closed before the nosy grad student could enter, then turned the thumb lock. The knob rattled, now useless. The woman thumped against the door, now calling him *Hey!* instead of *Sir.*

Ash ignored her.

A handwritten sign on the second door off the foyer read: *Sleep lab — Quiet, please.*

Ash opened the door and entered. He found a moderate-sized, dimly lit room lined with computers and unknown monitoring equipment. At the far end were a pair of people wearing long white lab coats, both intensely focused on their work. They didn't see or hear him approach.

One of the two scientists was Mina. The man was probably her partner — the other person whose name had been on the hallway door.

Ash stood behind them, curious as to what they were watching. The spectacle turned out to be uninteresting: a young woman asleep in a bed inside an adjacent darkened room, visible through a window. The sleeper was strung with wires, all of them running into various machines. A monitor by the scientists showed close-up video of her face. Her eyes moved jerkily right and left under closed eyelids.

"Okay," said Mina to the man beside her. "Let's try again."

The man pressed a button. A red flash illuminated the sleeper's face three times. A light of some sort was mounted above her head, flashing at the scientists' command.

The sleeper's eye movements had been steadily side-to-side, but following the flash they changed to up and down for a few beats.

"Excellent," Mina said.

The man stepped over to a desk, noting something on a tablet.

Once Mina was somewhat alone, Ash moved closer. He

eyed the man, made sure he wasn't looking, then took Mina by the arm with a whisper.

"We need to talk."

She startled. Then she turned, calming only a little as she saw who she was facing: her homicidal, borderline-psychotic patient who'd broken into a place he shouldn't be.

"Ash?"

"Shh." The man still hadn't looked back, and Ash didn't want him to.

"Why are you here? Who let you in? You can't just—!"

Ash pressed the muzzle of his Beretta into her ribs. *"Please."*

NINETEEN

Hostage

There was a fire exit at the dim room's far end, but it bore no alarm sticker stating it was for emergencies only. Ash pressed into it and found another light-trap room beyond. Once the first door closed, they opened a second and went through that one as well. A moment later they were in a sunny courtyard, walled by the building on three sides.

Mina shaded her face and squinted, her eyes fighting the suddenly-bright light.

"What's going on?" It came out like a demand, but then she saw that what she'd thought was a gun was indeed a gun, and her moxie seemed to vanish.

Ash pushed her to sit at a picnic table, then stood between her and the exit. "Convince me that you're on my side."

She was staring at the gun. Her shoulders were rising and falling a little too quickly. Her eyes were wide, her mouth slightly open. A fear response — something Ash knew well from his time overseas.

He flicked the safety on and slipped the weapon back into his waistband, out of sight. "Now. *Convince me.*"

"What's this all about, Ash? Why did you come here? Jesus — *Why do you have a gun?*"

He told her everything that had just happened. He held nothing back. *Chuck. Jose. The crazy acrobatics and the verbal trick he'd pulled to turn one against the other.*

"Ash." She gave a nervous half-laugh. "That's ... very strange. You can't possibly believe—"

He lifted his pullover to show her the shirt underneath, clotted with blood and gore.

She looked up, her whole demeanor more dire. "Ash? What's that on your shirt?"

"What's it look like?"

"Whose blood is that?" She stared at his face, possibly seeking signs of a nosebleed. She seemed to notice his cut from the butcher knife, but that one had barely bled. "Why do you have blood on you?"

"I told you why I have blood on me."

Her expression was sideways and toothy — the look of someone feigning friendliness until they saw a chance to run.

"Chuck," she said.

"Yes. Chuck. He's some sort of an agent. In some sort of secret organization."

"You know how that sounds, right?"

"But the blood? That's Jose's."

"Your neighbor." Her tone suggested she just wanted to make sure she was getting this right.

"Yes."

"The one whose little brown dog keeps pooping on your lawn. The one who, when you confronted him about it, said, *'Oopsie!'*"

"I forgot I told you about that."

"*That's* whose blood is on you. That's who you ... who you shot?"

"I didn't shoot him. Chuck shot him."

"Chuck. Your best friend. Who you work with. The one who's a secret agent now."

"Are you patronizing me?"

Her eyes hardened. "Sorry I'm not being sensitive enough. Providing therapy as a hostage, after being dragged from my lab at gunpoint — it's new for me."

"I'm telling the truth."

"Ash ..."

"I'm telling the truth and you *know* it's the truth."

"Yeah? How the hell do I know that?"

"Antidepressants eliminate REM sleep, right? Eliminate dreaming?"

"Depends on the antidepressant and the dosage. It at least suppresses some of—"

"*My* antidepressants. *My* dosage."

"Usually, yes, but every patient has different bioch—"

"And Nyperal creates sleep paralysis."

"It tends to deepen REM-state atonia," Mina said.

"You know what I mean. It should stop me from acting out my dreams, but it's not."

"You said yourself that you had a false awakening," Mina countered. "You can't even be sure the things you said happened overnight actually happened. *Or* that you have today's events correct. Lucid dreams can be *incredibly* convincing, almost as if—"

"I shouldn't be dreaming at all, *doctor*," Ash persisted, "but I am. I shouldn't be moving around while I dream, but I am. I've told you that people are following me and you keep telling me it's all in my head. And look at you right now: I show up with blood all over my shirt and you think *that's* in my head, too?"

"No." She seemed to be fighting to present herself calmly. "Listen to me. *Something* obviously happened, but you need to consider the possibility that it's not what it seemed. Sleep deprivation is an incredibly effective form of torture, and you're *already* torturing yourself over what happened with Emily. Add sleep deprivation to that and the effects compound. You—"

"I slept! I slept the whole goddamn day!"

"Yes, but you—"

"How the hell can I still be dreaming? That's the real question. How the hell am I waking up in the middle of the night *running through my motherfucking neighborhood*?"

He'd said it too loud. He looked around for eavesdroppers, but it still seemed like they were alone.

So he sat beside her, but not close enough for her to grab. Maybe he should try again: a different approach, with less anger this time.

"Okay. Say I'm losing my mind. Say I really am imagining all of this. I'd still love for you to tell me why you're so terrible at your job." He looked back at the exit and scoffed. "*Sleep studies.* This is what you *do for a living* and still nothing works for me. You want to know what I think?"

"Ash, listen to me. You're mad at me because it's hard to be *this mad* at yourself. So you're deflecting. I don't know what happened today, or why you have blood on you," she reached into a pocket, "but the first thing we need to do is to make sure everyone's okay. Do you know Chuck's number? Or maybe we can just call the police?"

When she came out with her phone, Ash reached for his gun.

Mina's hands went up so fast, she dropped the phone into her lap. "I'm on your side, okay! Listen to me: I've only ever tried to help you!"

"Explain it, then! Explain why I have dreams! Explain why I'm still up and around, acting them out!"

"*I don't know!* Maybe it has something to do with …" She trailed off, thinking.

"What?"

"The thing you said the guy dropped. The thing that looked like a walkie-talkie?"

Some of the tension left Ash's gun arm. He let go of the butt, returning both hands to the table in front of him. "What about it?"

"Can you describe it?"

"It was the size of a walkie-talkie. There was no button on the side, but it did have some sort of display on the front. Not for the frequency. It …" Ash grasped at his recall. "I think it showed a graph …"

Mina was more upright. "What kind of graph? Like in high school geometry class?"

Ash shook his head. "There were actually *two* graphs. One showed steps moving up and down, like an uneven staircase. It went down, down, down, then all the way back to the top in one big jump. Basically a series of rectangles side by side, most of which were orange."

"Most?"

"The tallest rectangles were blue. Like they were special. And the other graph … It was like a heart monitor. A whatchacallit: an EKG."

"Could it have been an EEG?"

"What's the difference?"

"Heart versus brain. EKGs have sharp blips at regular intervals. EEGs can be long and slow, shorter and more active, sometimes full of spindle-like formations."

"Okay. *EEG.* Are you saying it means something to you?"

Mina held up one hand and went for her phone again. This time she moved with such certainty and assurance that Ash didn't try to stop her. She wasn't dialing a number. Instead she was delving deep into her photos, using extra taps to open what looked like a hidden album.

She stopped, then looked at him earnestly.

"Is *this* what you saw?" She turned the phone so Ash could see it.

Ash couldn't believe his eyes. On the screen of Mina's phone was the exact same device the man had dropped under the mailbox, then retrieved later by force.

Ash lifted his eyes from the picture to Mina.

He didn't like what he saw on her face.

TWENTY

Blip and Chirp

"You're going to laugh," Mina told him a half hour later.

They were in the break room of her lab. The large Indian man and small white woman were gone. Mina had sent them home, along with the grad student. Only the man in the dim room, who Mina confirmed was Associate Professor Bryan Waters, remained to watch the still-unconscious woman for her sleep study. Mina had told Professor Waters that she needed some deep-dive thinking time and to please not disturb her — to take the subject out quietly when her study was over without opening the break room door. She hadn't mentioned Ash.

After that they had the place to themselves, and were free to talk.

Yeah, Ash's paranoid half-thought, *IF you believe that. You didn't go with her. You didn't hear what she said to those people. She probably told Bryan to call the cops. Or she called your old buddy Chuck. You just signed your own death warrant, Ash old buddy. Give it ten minutes and that fat ginger bastard will storm right back in here, sighting down his silencer.*

But, seeing himself from the outside after Mina left the

room, Ash had made a monumental decision: He didn't want to keep living the terrified, always-watching-his-back way he'd been living. He couldn't. He'd lived in hopped-up fear for long enough … and honestly he'd rather Chuck (or anyone else) put a bullet his brain than to do it any longer.

Instead, he'd done something that felt naive and stupid: he'd decided to trust Mina. If she turned out to be bad, he'd be no worse off than he already was.

"I don't think I'm going to laugh," he told her in the break room.

She was considering the device in her photo with a confused expression. It was her own phone, but she acted like the picture had been put on it by someone else. She'd only known how to find that specific photo and show it to Ash out of luck or something. Ash could relate. He'd had similar unknown knowledge pop up recently: information he definitely knew … but had no idea *how* he knew.

"I don't remember when or where I saw this thing," Mina said, meaning the same walkie-talkie device Ash had held in his hand just yesterday. "I have no idea who showed it to me, or if anyone even did. Maybe I found it on my own. But if so, I don't know *how* I found it. Or where. Or what happened to it after I took the picture."

"Maybe you didn't take the picture. Maybe someone just sent it to you."

Mina shook her head, face still scrunched with concentration. "That's my hand holding it." She looked at her left hand now, eyes ticking back and forth to the photo. "That's my ring. That's the scar I got falling from a tree when I was eleven. But there's something else."

Her lips pursed, as if the photo was telling her things she didn't want to believe but knew just the same. "The more I think about it, the more I get the feeling someone was there with me. Someone *handed* that thing to me, then watched me document it. *Wanted* me to document it."

"That's … weird." Ash was thinking of the bat he'd taken to the head — a wound Mina had verified. Ash had been robbed of the walkie by force, but if Mina was right, someone had practically forced it upon her.

"It gets weirder. I … I think I actually know what this thing is. Ash … I think I know what it *does*."

Ash felt his eyes widen. That was the last thing he'd expected her to say.

"How?"

"I have no idea. The information is just … *there*. Once my brain looked in the right place, it all started coming back. Like remembering a dream. At first, you wake up and don't think you had any dreams. But then … but then it's like you spot a loose end. 'Why was a song stuck in my head when I woke up?' And then your focus shifts and suddenly you see the song, and you remember hearing it in a dream, and then the whole dream comes back all at once even though you'd *swear* a second ago there'd been no dream."

"But to know something like *this*, in your waking life …"

"I can only describe the feeling. I can't say why or how or what." She nodded to the phone in front of them. "But I also didn't know I had this picture. I *definitely* didn't know how to find the album it's hidden in. You can create hidden albums on any iPhone, but I seem to have installed an app that hides them a whole lot better. The album's encrypted. I needed a swipe pattern to open it. But … I didn't have to think about any of that in the moment. I just *did* it, like my fingers knew what to do even though my brain didn't. After I heard enough of your story, it's like you gave me the same kind of loose end as recalling a song. My focus shifted, and the information just popped right into me. I suddenly knew exactly how to get at the album, and that I was looking for this specific photo. Now it turns out I know what it's a photo *of*, plus a whole lot more. The knowledge is there, but I don't remember how it got there. It's like realizing I'm fluent in a language I've never actually spoken. You can't imagine how strange it is."

"Actually, I can," Ash said.

She half-smiled. She seemed to be accepting his story more with each passing minute. Discovering he could fight like a ninja and randomly knowing a codeword able to paralyze Chuck no longer struck her as quite so unbelievable.

She took a breath, then held the phone in front of them both. "I'm pretty sure this is called a 'Blip.' There's another piece that goes with it, called a 'Chirp.' The Chirp is the transmitter and the Blip is its receiver. I don't think I saw a Chirp, but I might have seen diagrams. I assume that's what you found plugged into your internet router."

Ash nodded. It was weird to accept something that even Mina couldn't give evidence of, but he did anyway.

"Both are unknown technology. Top Secret stuff. Governmental — an NSA or CIA cliché, like MKUltra or hiding aliens at Area 51. I half-wonder if I signed an NDA before seeing this." Mina laughed at herself before going on. "God. Turns out you're not the only one surrounded by secret agents and assassins. I am, too. Are we in the Matrix or something?"

They sat in silence. Then Ash said, "I have to ask. This may sound stupid, but ... Is it possible ..." It really *did* sound stupid. "Well, I mean, since you're the sleep and dreaming expert ..."

"You're wondering if it's possible we're in a lucid

dream. Because this is all so weird, and I told you how realistic a lucid dream can be."

Ash exhaled, relieved he hadn't had to be the one to say it. He felt like an idiot, but he also remembered standing in his bathroom that night, sure he was awake until he saw the changing face on his clock.

"It's not stupid. It is, however, untrue. I saw you looking at the clock. And the wall calendar. When you scratched your face just now, tell me the truth: did you plug your nose real quick, then try to breathe?"

It was Ash's turn to laugh self-consciously.

"The display on the clock didn't change, right? The text on the calendar didn't change, and you couldn't breathe when you closed your nose and mouth. So you already know this isn't a dream. But now tell me this: I think I saw you try to push a finger through your palm under the table."

Ash frown-smiled as if caught. "Just one more reality check."

"Finger-through-palm is a really common reality check for lucid dreamers, but I know *I* didn't tell you about that one because it doesn't always work. So. How did you know to try it? Did you look it up?"

Ash shook his head. He just knew, like hearing a silent song upon waking.

Mina nodded. "Uh-huh. I don't think you're new to lucid dreaming, Ash. I'll bet you know finger-through-palm because you used to use it as a reality check all the time. *You're* finding stuff you didn't know *you* knew and *I'm* finding stuff I didn't know *I* knew. Does that strike you as a coincidence?"

No. Not at all. But Ash still found it hard to dredge up what he needed to know, unlike Mina. He seemed to be on a need-to-know basis.

"Dreams," Mina said, almost to herself, like a conclusion she was reaching.

"What about them?"

"You're a lucid dreamer, even though you don't remember it. I'm a sleep scientist, specializing in lucid dreaming. Both of us with ... Oh, shit, I'll just say it: both of us with parts of our memories erased, as crazy as that sounds. There's no *way* it's a coincidence. I think ..." Mina considered the photo, then nodded to herself. "I think this is about dreams. All of it: *about dreams.*"

Ash waited while she gathered herself.

"The Blip you saw? This device right here?" She held up the phone. "Paired with a Chirp, they're devices for monitoring brain activity; I'm sure of it. But not *just* brain activity. Dreaming in particular."

"Dreaming? You're sure?"

She nodded, then zoomed in on the Blip's screen in her photo. "The top graph, here, is a rough, at-a-glance representation of a sleeper's cycles throughout the night. Sleep happens in phases. At the start of the night, you step down from wakefulness all the way into slow-wave sleep, then come back up to REM, which is a high-consciousness state close to wakefulness. It's almost impossible to tell the difference between someone in REM and someone who's awake using brainwaves alone. After a short REM period, you'll usually wake up briefly, but a lot of people don't remember it. A full cycle, from awake to awake again, takes around ninety minutes. Sleep phases are sometimes represented this way, as rectangles of different heights — like a staircase going down, then coming back up. The tall blue rectangles that go almost to the top are REM periods. REM gets longer later in the night."

She scrolled sideways, showing him wider rectangles to the right side of the graph. "I think that's what the top display shows: a simplified, graphic representation of a sleeper's progress through the stages."

She moved her fingernail down to show the Blip's lower graph.

"This one is an EEG. I remember being able to change the display magnification, and I know I zoomed all the way out and saw sleep spindles. Delta waves, too; the works. All the brain data someone like me would ever want to see."

"So it monitors sleep, like the wearable gadgets you hear about?"

"Much more than that. The Blip and Chirp are Wurtzman devices."

"Wurtzman!"

Mina nodded gravely. "There were experiments a while back by a Japanese lab. They were able to correlate certain EEG patterns with self-reports from lucid dreamers."

"If you say so."

She smiled, then dumbed it down. "In layman's terms, the scientists learned to 'translate' dreams by comparing brainwaves with what the dreamers said they were dreaming of at the time. But as you can imagine, the translation was very, *very* crude. Very little 'resolution,' as it were."

"So it's not like they could peek into people's dreams. Is that what you're saying?"

"Not at all. *Maybe* you could look at this and figure out how to tell a 'winter' pattern from a 'spring' pattern, but you couldn't tell 'car' from 'bus' — or even 'car' from 'planet.' It's landmark work, but not all that practical. If you wanted to get any resolution at all, you'd have to somehow make sense of individual, unique, specific firing patterns in the brain. *Very* specific firing patterns. If you wanted to 'see' dreams in any meaningful way, like you suggest, you'd have to parse an *unimaginable* amount of neuronal data. It's far too much information to make sense of. Far too hard to see patterns that are even *remotely* useful."

She paused.

"Until, that is, the Wurtzman Conjecture made finding patterns in huge amounts of data easy." Then she nodded at the photo of the Blip. "Until now."

"Wait. Are you saying that thing can *see* people's dreams?" Ash asked.

"Like you wouldn't believe," Mina said, awed by her own recollection. "Someone showed me a demonstration of what it can do. It was flashy more than academic, like they were trying to sell me on the idea. It felt like a salesman trying to close a deal."

Ash didn't comment. Combining "Top Secret" with "salesman" sounded like *recruitment* to him. Shadowy parts of the government had a history of recruiting scientists for questionable ends. It almost sounded like Mina had been tapped as this field's Oppenheimer. *Of course* the government would try to kill him over something like this, if he'd been involved. If dreams could be turned into a weapon.

"I watched a subject's dreams *on a screen*," Mina continued. "I stood in front of a giant high-definition TV and *watched someone dream*. I even think it might have been one of my own lucid dreamers, maybe right here in this lab."

She looked around, and something seemed to click. "They came with a bunch of equipment on a cart. It was *right over there!*"

She pointed through the wall at the sleep lab, then nodded as memories came faster. "I could show you the port they plugged it into. It uses something like wi-fi, which makes sense if you found a Chirp plugged into your router.

DR. MICHAEL BREUS & SEAN PLATT

It doesn't need wires or a skull cap, which is how we usually measure brainwaves."

"How can it monitor that kind of thing without wires?"

Mina was in full scientist mode now, remembering the details. "Every nerve in the body — including neurons in the brain — make tiny electrochemical signals that can be detected from a short distance away — usually just through the skull and skin, which is how EEGs work using a skull cap. A Wurtzman algorithm, though, is able to magnify the strength of those signals by billions. It can detect them from much farther away. *And* differentiate the simultaneous firings of millions of individual neurons *and* are able to make sense of it all like deciphering some enormous code. The permutations of that kind of thing are endless. Ten to the twentieth. Ten to the *one hundredth*, for all we know. But you've seen the news. Wurtzman makes dealing with big numbers easy."

"Are you saying that thing can pull dreams *from the air*?"

Mina's head bobbed. "I can't answer the engineering half of it, but I think the resolution is much stronger if its piggybacked on another EM signal, like home wi-fi. It can't just 'read dreams' right away, though. Everyone's brain is different, so the algorithm needs a lot of baseline data before it can do its thing. I was told the Blip and Chirp need to gather data from a subject for a few days before they can decode anything. They need to build a cypher key first. What 'dreaming of a lamppost' looks like in *your* brain is different from what it looks like in *my* brain."

Mina was only trying to make a point, but Ash didn't particularly like her phrasing. This wasn't theoretical for Ash. It *was* his version of 'dreaming of a lamppost' being decoded here.

"The observation phase gives the Blip and Chirp a

working vocabulary. I don't think they need the dreamer's reports like in the Japanese study. Every dreamer is unique, but there are enough similarities across the population that Wurtzman algorithms can figure it out. *Your* pattern for 'tall man' presumably looks similar to other people's patterns for 'tall man.' After they get their initial vocabulary from those first few days, they can translate with incredible levels of precision."

Mina looked haunted as she revisited her memory of the demonstration. "I remember the depth of what I saw. The *detail* it had. Ash … *It was like watching a movie.*"

"Do you know *why* someone showed this to you? *Why* they wanted to 'sell you on it'?"

Mina thought, then shook her head. She focused for a while, then finally stopped trying and gave him a shrug. The information, it seemed, had stopped flowing.

They were silent for a while.

Until Ash eventually spoke. "If everything you said is true, it answers a lot of questions. At least I know I'm not nuts. Everything I told you about actually happened. A pair of fake technicians *did* plant that 'Chirp' thing in my house, and they *did* send killers when I figured it out."

"When *part* of you figured it out, anyway," Mina agreed.

Yes. *Part*, because Ash hadn't realized anything consciously at all. It was his dreaming mind — his subconscious, which also held unknown fighting skills and immobilizing codewords, far more aware than Ash was himself — that had managed to assemble the pieces.

"But," Ash said, "now we have a much bigger question."

Mina waited.

"They were spying on my dreams, doctor," he said. "So what's in *my* dreams that they're so desperate to see?"

TWENTY-ONE

The Puppet

Mina was laughing again, but it wasn't a good laugh.

They'd taken Emily's car, driven in loops and made more unexpected turns, and tried in a probably pointless way to shake anyone who might be tailing them as they drove out of town. Maybe it was dumb to leave, but Ash wasn't sure what else to do. They couldn't stay inside the lab forever.

"What's so funny?" Ash asked.

"You saw what I was doing when you came into the sleep lab, right? With the woman in the bed?"

"Something with a flashing red light. I didn't understand it."

"Celina is one of my best lucid dreamers," Mina said, presumably referring to the sleeper. "We've worked with her for months to develop a two-way signaling system. We 'talk' with Celina while she's dreaming by flashing a light cue she learned while awake. We flash red lights at her when she's in REM. If Celina's in a lucid dream, she's usually able to recognize it as coming from the waking world and can 'reply' by moving her eyes up and down instead of the more typical left-right. I won't bore you with the ways it's different from similar work done in the seventies, but let's just say we were *so excited* to have made really dramatic progress in so promising a field."

"Why's that funny?" Ash asked.

"Because I'd *already seen* technology that makes our best work look prehistoric. I just didn't *remember* that I'd seen it. It's like if someone showed up one day and told you how to teleport easily, safely, and for free … and the next thing you did was to go out and invent the wheel."

She shook her head in frustrated disbelief. "Jesus, Ash. Someone walked right into my office and explained it all. They even let me take a picture. Why didn't I remember it *before* we wasted so much time drawing with crayons? I feel so stupid. We thought we were breaking new ground. We were ready to start trumpeting all about it, but now I see that my entire career has been pointless. Just one big joke."

It was a deliberate dig for pity. Unsure how to respond, Ash let it go. It took a few moments for Mina to do the same.

Then Ash said, "At least this isn't only happening to you. At least you're not alone." What he really meant was, *At least* I'm *not alone*, but it felt good (albeit a bit self-aggrandizing) to soothe someone else's nerves for a change.

She smirked. *We're in this together* was of little comfort when the *this* you're in is terrible.

"Do I exit here?" Ash nodded toward the road ahead.

"No. Still two exits up."

They were halfway on the lam; that's the way Mina had put it. The intensity of their new memories implied they should *do something*, but the question was how and what. Running, when things were otherwise so normal, felt ridiculous. If not for the gunmen who'd visited Ash, they might have stayed in and ordered pizza.

"Up here." Mina pointed to an upcoming exit.

It was an ideal place for a wife-killer and a scientist-doctor with no family or personal life to lay low. Both felt absurd leaving bills unpaid and plants unwatered on what still felt like a whim, but they lifted right out of their lives — at least for a few days — with an embarrassing ease. The destination was Mina's idea: an adjunct sleep lab she sometimes worked with upstate. Only Associate Professor Bryan knew of her involvement, and thanks to a fortuitous holiday at the lab, only Bryan would visit during the time they'd be there.

Mina didn't want to call Bryan to warn him off because calls left traces. So she planned to tell him that she was working on a private-sector project when he showed up this afternoon. Bryan was an academic snob and hated private-sector work. Even a mention would make him scurry back to the campus lab like a roach.

"There's something I need to tell you," Mina said as they merged onto a new road. "Something that worries me."

She glanced his way, but only fleetingly. Ash recognized the look as embarrassment.

"What is it?" Ash asked.

"I didn't give you Nyperal."

"Sure you did."

"*No*, I didn't." She paused, then continued. "Back at the lab, I started looking through my records for anything that might jar my memory. I came across something interesting. Something … troubling."

Ash looked at her profile, saying nothing.

"The university was part of the initial drug studies on Nyperal, before it got FDA approval. Drug studies always involve some participants being given the real drug and others being given a placebo. Placebos look and feel just like the real drug but don't contain any active ingredients."

"Sugar pills," Ash said. "What's it got to do with me?"

"The dispensary apparently still had some of the fake Nyperal. Anyone would mistake it for the real thing, but it's not."

Now he saw where this was going. "You gave me placebos instead of real drugs."

"Not on purpose!" She was clearly flustered. "You always got your 'Nyperal' from the college dispensary because it was so expensive at Walgreens. I sent the orders in myself, but …"

"But your orders were for the fake kind. And you didn't even know you'd done it."

"Ash …"

"Don't apologize. After the shit we learned today about our memories, it's easy to believe this wasn't your fault. Not your *conscious* fault."

She nodded as if this was good enough, but she was still looking straight ahead — still burdened.

"What?" Ash asked.

"There's more. Turns out your antidepressants are TCAs. They're tricyclics, not SSRIs like I meant to prescribe. Like I *thought* I'd prescribed." She wiped her forehead: an unconscious parody of sweating from nerves. "I mean, Christ, Ash. That's malpractice. I could lose my license."

He didn't feel like repeating that it wasn't her fault, that someone was clearly fucking with both of their heads. He didn't blame Mina, but he wasn't quite evolved enough, following this deceptive news, to forgive enough to coddle her.

Learning he'd gotten two fake prescriptions made him

furious, but he forced his voice to be calm. "What do TCAs do? The kind I actually took?"

"SSRIs typically blunt dreaming. TCAs, on the other hand, don't block dreams at all. They're meant to make dreams more pleasant."

"My dreams haven't been pleasant."

"Within reason. Your scars go pretty deep."

Ash sighed, wanting to pat himself on the back for not blowing his top at all this shitty news. "So let me get this straight. I kept dreaming when I shouldn't have been dreaming because I was on the wrong antidepressants. And I kept acting out my dreams because I wasn't actually on Nyperal like I was supposed to be."

"I'm so sorry."

"I told you not to be sorry." He took another breath. "Someone made you do it. Someone fucked with *you* so *I'd* keep dreaming."

He wasn't surprised; if shadow forces wanted to spy on Ash's dreams using the Blip and Chirp, he'd need to have dreams to spy on. "I understand the antidepressant thing if the normal kind blocks dreaming. But why give me fake Nyperal? Why would they want me to *act out* my dreams?"

"There's a strong tie between physical movement and memory. Maybe they thought it'd be easier for you to remember if you acted out your dreams."

"Why do they care if I remember my dreams?"

"I thought a lot about that," she said, "and I can only guess it's not about remembering the dreams themselves. I think they want you to remember something else."

"What do you mean?"

"A lot of neuroscientists think nothing is truly forgotten. You don't lose information; you just can't access what has moved into the subconscious."

Ash understood. "The subconscious is the realm of dreams."

Mina nodded. "What if they don't want you to *remember your dreams* so much as *remember something* through *your dreams*? What if they're using dreams as a way to access something you've forgotten? A memory that's been blocked … but that your dreams might be able to find?"

Ash thought about that. About how badly someone seemed to want something that was buried inside his head … perhaps using dream-spying to find it, with dreams themselves as the lever.

"What the hell's happening, Mina?"

She didn't have an answer.

TWENTY-TWO

Firewalled

Richard Quince (who'd started his day as Ash's mild-mannered doormat buddy, Chuck DeMona) stood inside the anteroom with his hands restlessly intertwined at his waist.

He'd never been to this part of the compound. He usually met with the Dispatcher, with whom he'd always gotten along. One exalted time, he'd even met the Unit Director. The UD turned out to be the most boring sort of government employee — a man who lived in brown and tan. The UD had a dial-tone personality, but Richard knew how much power he held and had respected it. He'd left that meeting not only alive, but also with a promotion.

But before today, Richard had never been to the Bespokery. Why would he? For the longest time nobody took the place seriously. Richard came up believing the Bespokery was either an exaggeration or a club that thought itself a lot more interesting than it was: nerds who'd discovered a legitimate way to play wizards for a living.

Somehow it worked; somehow the Bespokery had

scored a few lucky hits, earned some praise, and ended up with disproportionate egos. According to rumors, they even halfway believed they *were* wizards. It made sense, considering what the Tailors could do — but that wasn't *magic*; it was science Richard hadn't troubled himself to understand.

Tailors were really just off-the-books government workers with 401(k)s the same as Richard's. Everyone knew that, and for a long time all everyone had done was laugh.

Everything changed last year, when the upset happened.

Last year the far-more-respectable Agency, which Richard worked for as a junior operative, fell apart. All five of the full Agents were retired in incredibly complex ways. Afterward, the Unit Director found himself with the same funding but no Agents to spend it on. The Bespokery had ascended for one reason: the UD hadn't wanted a budget surplus. Lines on a goddamn spreadsheet: *That's* the reason the Bespokery was now something to fear.

It'd happened without a formal hand-over: Bespokery replacing Agency at the tip of the pyramid. The Bespokery had gotten its big office and sweeping powers in the way a mouse gets cheese. During the confusion of the post-shakeup power vacuum, the Tailors had sneaked in and stolen whatever they wanted. Nobody had explicitly told them *No*, so of course the Tailors had assumed *Yes* and dared anyone to say otherwise.

The UD allowed it. Even the general had allowed it. Richard supposed he shouldn't be surprised. That was government for you.

Now half of all field operations had to be cleared through this office. And here Richard was in that same office, about to bend his knee.

Across the anteroom, a small man sat behind a large

oak desk beside tall oak doors. Most of the compound was duller than the IRS, but another way the Bespokery had helped solve the UD's budget issue was to requisition themselves a large remodeling budget. It'd made the place more intimidating, which in turn made it feel more important than it was.

Everyone seemed to fall for it. Supposedly the NSA's Deputy Director was visiting next month. A rumor (Richard hoped it was *only* a rumor) said the Secretary of Defense had been here last week.

Maybe these motherfuckers really are wizards, Richard thought.

A light brightened the small man's desk. He put one finger to his ear, then looked up at Richard and said, "Director Baynes will see you now."

Richard nodded and moved toward the doors. Both opened outward on their own. As he walked, Richard didn't like the way he found himself casting a low gaze and making small, cowed movements. He should be standing tall. He'd been here long before Baynes and that little chimp she called a protege.

The inner office had large, north-facing windows and no dust. A single black chair — not too small or too large — sat in front of a broad black desk with barely anything on it. There was no other furniture or decorations, no rugs on the hard floor. The space had an echo, like a concrete warehouse. Even his footfalls sounded loud.

The doors closed. A well-pressed, reddish-brown-haired woman stood behind the desk. According to her dossier, Natalie Baynes was mid-forties, but in person she looked ten years younger. Testament to her time as a military unarmed self-defense instructor, he supposed.

"Have a seat," she told him.

"I'm good like this," Richard responded.

She smiled privately at his response, humoring his attempt at a power play. "Would you like anything to drink?"

He looked around. "You don't have a bar."

"I didn't say I was going to make it myself. Are you all right, Richard? You act like a man with nothing to give and everything to prove."

Her words were beyond pompous. What she'd just said was the sort of crap these wannabes yearned to say when they were pizza-faced teenagers, along with *abracadabra* and *alohamora*.

Still, it wasn't like he could laugh in her face.

Baynes sat again, without having shaken his hand or given any real greeting. Knowing the Tailors, that was probably an NLP trick designed to unnerve their opponents. And who's the opponent? Why, it's everyone, of course.

After a quiet moment, Richard decided to sit as well.

"It's probably overdue that we met." She gave an oily smile. "Do you know what we do here at the Bespokery?"

"Of course I know what you do here."

"Do you really? Or do you only *think* you do?"

Well. If she was going to be an overt asshole, Richard supposed he could be one, too. "I'd like to know why the hell I embedded."

Baynes shrugged. "Everyone's embedded."

"Including you?"

"Of course not me."

"O'Brien?"

She didn't answer. Mike O'Brien was almost surely embedded, but not with a trigger that was lethal in the way Richard's own surprise trigger had turned out to be. She'd probably embedded O'Brien with a trigger that would make him shine her shoes. Or wash her car. One to give him an erection so she could release her steel-balled pressure. Because that was a thing, too: Everyone knew there was something between Baynes and O'Brien, but any affair they had would be more violence than affection. Baynes was old enough to be her protege's mother, and "mother and son" was exactly how they acted. O'Brien, orphaned at seven, took naturally to his role in their little Oedipal mess. It struck Richard as gross. Maybe even unholy.

Baynes answered Richard's original question in a matter-of-fact way. "You were embedded because you're an asset. Automotive manufacturers chip expensive cars. Stores stick anti-theft stickers to the best merchandise so people can't just walk off with it. Valuable things *must* be protected, Richard. You should be flattered."

"You were worried I'd be stolen?"

"Not stolen. Misused. Misappropriated. Minds change. After the government's investment in you, it's in our country's best interest that yours does not."

"I shot Manuel. I killed him."

Baynes shrugged. "Only as much as Sanders killed his wife."

"Sanders was different. I had to watch what happened from inside my own head. *I felt my own finger pulling the trigger.* Do you have any idea how disturbing that is?"

"Stop arguing semantics. An *embedded command* shot Manuel. An *embedded command* pulled the trigger. If you want more absolution than the facts, you should probably see a priest."

"Goddammit, you can't just—!"

She held up a hand. "I'll stop you right there. First of all: *Yes*, I can. Second of all, the Agents got a much worse deal than you and the other junior operatives did. If you'd prefer to be fully locked-down, just say the word. For now I'd rather you weren't. I'd like to keep your value intact.

So. Are you through being indignant, or would you like to continue?"

Richard buried his irritation. Everything she said was correct; he just didn't like it.

"The fact that Sanders knew how to *activate* your trigger?" Baynes continued. "*That's* what we should be paying attention to. You said he wasn't breached. Manuel thought he was. So far I'm more inclined to believe Manuel. We have a big problem if Sanders is indeed breached. He'll be much harder to plunge if he knows what's out there. If he knows what happened, who he is, and *who* we are relative to all the rest."

"He doesn't."

Baynes cocked her head, waiting for an explanation.

"The man I played — Chuck? 'Chuck' was Ash's best friend. He leveled with me on the drive over to his place. I believe his sincerity. Hell, he wasn't even sure if what happened the night before — when he caught you and O'Brien rigging his junction box and chased you all over his neighborhood in plain sight of everyone—"

Baynes gave Richard a warning look. She knew he was trying to goad her, reminding him it wouldn't work.

"He wasn't even sure whether that was real or just a dream. If he hadn't remembered the doorbell camera, I would have had no problem convincing him it was all in his head. The shrink would probably back me up if he went to her later. It would strike her as crazy, and she *already* thinks he's crazy. She'd resorted to giving him knock-out pills. One step from thorazine and a straitjacket. Come on, Baynes. You saw his metrics. Did he look breached to *you*?"

Her lack of an answer was a BINGO for Richard.

"Come on. Think about it. Sanders was great at what he did. He was the best."

"Second best," corrected Baynes.

"He wouldn't be dumb enough to leave himself mnemonic cues designed to cause a self-breach. He knows the program better than that. He knows we'd've noticed if he tried to pull that kind of bullshit. I guarantee he followed orders just like all the others. He did a clean job. Created Chloe's chaperone just like he was supposed to. Maybe he saw the sweep coming and maybe he didn't, but he didn't leave himself a way out. He'd knew *we'd* know if he tried."

"I thought you didn't know Sanders before the shake-up?"

"I didn't, but *everyone* knew his reputation." Richard tried to keep the scorn from his voice. The Agency had been a reputable (if somewhat underhanded) organization. But the Bespokery was the oblivious new boss who decides that everything done by his predecessor was antiquated and wrong. They had no respect. Not knowing Sanders was flat-out insulting.

"Sanders *looks* breached because he's figuring things out on his own," Richard explained. "You and O'Brien were there, watching him on your Blip. You've got days' worth of calibration and ... what? Two, three days of his dreams? Unless you're stupid, you can see for yourself that he's still intact. He's *wondering*, sure. Anyone would. The difference is that Ash Sanders is not, and has never been, 'anyone.' Even intact, he's got his natural curiosity. His natural powers of deduction. Not all skills are stored in the cortex. Rehearse something enough and it becomes part of you. It's like we were saying about H.M. on the phone: learning is possible without really learning."

Richard stopped, waiting to see if Baynes would bite his head off for implying she was stupid. There were more rumors about her than dalliances with her barely-legal underling, including that she'd "accidentally" killed more trainees during demonstrations than during combat.

"Do you know where Sanders went?" she asked.

Richard tried not to show satisfaction. Deflecting to a new question was as close to an *I-guess-you're-right* as he was going to get from her.

He nodded. "Ash went to Irving's office right after leaving the residence. Some time later they both started driving west. Give us a few hours and we'll find them."

"*You don't know where they went?* You didn't get a tracker on him?"

"For some reason the Agency doesn't have the manpower or budget it used to. Maybe you should have GPS-chipped him like a Mercedes, so nobody could run off with him."

"Did he tell Irving what happened? About you and the commotion at his house?"

"No way to know. But does it matter? She's heard his rambling for months now. It's not like she'll believe him."

But did Richard really believe that? Irving had gone with him to the new place, after all. He had to hope she was a hostage.

Baynes seemed bothered. "I don't like that he's having lucid dreams."

"He's had *years and years* of training in lucid dreaming. It's not an ability you'll be able to erase now that he's figured out he can do it."

"The question is what *else* he'll figure out. Lucidity gives him access to his subconscious mind."

Richard laughed. "He'd have to know it was possible to *ask* questions of his subconscious mind for that to be a problem. He's figured out how to dream lucidly, but keep in mind the guy thinks he's a beginner. Every new lucid dreamer starts out preoccupied with flying and fucking. We have a while before there's any threat of self-actualization."

"It's disturbing, is all." Baynes was slowly shaking her head. "The algorithm sometimes interprets windows of awareness as directed attention. When Mike and I were watching him on the Blip, there was a moment where I'd swear he was looking right at us."

"*Looking. Chasing.*" Richard shrugged. "You kept a man with a documented REM disorder mobile. Did you think he *wouldn't* act out? You did this to yourself. If you'd left him paralyzed like I suggested — if you'd let the doctor prescribe him *real* pills instead of fake ones — he'd never have found the Blip. The hit O'Brien gave him with the bat and the cut it left behind were the clues that broke this particular camel's back. I tried to convince Sanders he'd hit his head falling off a chair, but would *you* have believed that if you were in his shoes? Throwing a few bucks at the floor manager and workers to keep them saying the right things doesn't change reality. Ash lost an *entire day.* Your story put him back at work like nothing happened. That—"

"We had to get him back on track," she said, defensive. "Back in the groove. If he wasn't allowed to dream normally ..."

"The 'normal' ship had already sailed. He was *fired,* for fuck's sake. That was *your man's* decision, by the way. You couldn't at least have kept him fired instead of trying to ret-con his life?"

"We needed you in play," Baynes argued.

"I *was* in play! I was his shoulder to cry on after he lost his job! Did you really think our interactions all had to be at the fucking *machine shop*? My backstory said we were war buddies! He would have called me. It would have been easy as hell for me to 'be in play' at his house!"

Her chin was firm, obstinate despite her mistakes. "You have to get back in there. Fix this."

"How, exactly?"

"When you locate him, go to him."

Richard stood up and headed for the door. Baynes reacted right away.

"Where the hell do you think you're going?"

"Find him and go to him," Richard repeated, turning before he reached the exit. *"He knows,* Baynes. He doesn't know *what* he knows, but he knows something. He knows *I'm* not who I said I was. That's not something you can erase. He won't believe that he fell off a chair again. You interfered, and now we don't have him. You couldn't trust the Agency to do things the right way, and this is what happened. No. Instead, you came into my house like I was just another subject and put a trigger command in my brain."

"We'll erase the trigger. And we'll change the trigger for everyone else so he can't control anyone again."

"Doors closed! After the cows left the barn! I'd have brought him in, and you could have had one of your freak-shows get what they could out of Ash the hard way. Now he's on the run. And what are we going to do when we catch him again? He was an *Agent*, for fuck's sake. He has an incredible firewall. They all did. We only had a short window to try — and I do mean *try* — to get what we need out of him by force. Now that window is closed."

Richard shook his head. "It's like you said. Ash has access to his subconscious mind now. But more importantly, *his subconscious mind* has access to his subconscious mind. You'd lobotomize him trying to get anything by force out of him now. So honestly, what's your plan?"

Richard gave her a moment to fail to answer, then went on. "Ash is the last Agent standing. Last of the original five.

You've checked every other lead, so you know by process of elimination that Ash didn't get the decoy. *He has what you need,* but your bumbling triggered his subconscious defenses. Forget sneaking in at this point. Your own actions have turned Ash Sanders into Fort Knox."

Baynes stared with eyes like emerald lasers. She wanted to disembowel Richard for all he'd said, but she also knew he was right.

There'd only been *one* way to retrieve what the Bespokery needed from Ash, and it'd been through the surveillance of peaceful dreams. But good luck with that now.

"Okay," Baynes finally said, nodding at some unseen idea. "Here's what we're going to do."

TWENTY-THREE

Sunshine Makes Everything Better

Ash slept.

He dreamed he was at a picnic.

Emily sat facing him across a red-and-white-checked blanket, picnic basket between them, packed to over-flowing with tiny rolls of obsolete microfilm and modern thumb drives.

"Pie?" she asked him.

Ash nodded. The picnic basket had become a golden-brown pie, steaming from the oven. Emily sliced into it, and microfilm dripped like juices from the edge.

"It's fresh. Look how fresh it is, Ash."

He looked. But now the filling was human heads instead of microfilm. The impossible geometry just seemed to work.

There were three heads in the pie. All of them were looking at him. None were as lifeless as they should be, for being severed. They also weren't simply *thrown-in*. All three, despite being in a pie tin, were lined up like some sort of committee awaiting his approval. And then they weren't even in the tin. They weren't swimming in baking juices and melted celluloid. Instead, they now seemed to be upright on a shelf. Ash's dreaming mind told him they'd always been on a shelf, never in a pie. When he'd thought "in the pie" before, he'd made a mistake.

The pie, without the heads in it, was now on a plate in his hands. A piece had been cut from the whole.

It smelled delicious. Probably would have been, if not for the eyeball in it.

"Don't knock it until you try it," said a voice.

Ash looked up to see one of the heads speaking to him. That head had one empty socket: no mystery about the origin of the eyeball. The head belonged to a dark-skinned man he remembered from somewhere but couldn't say where. His name started with an I, Ash seemed to recall. The head beside it was of a smooth-skinned woman with cat's-eye makeup. Beside that one was the last head of the three: a man who would be handsome if not for his bad teeth.

"Try it with some sunshine," Emily suggested.

Ash looked over. She was holding a red-and-white Reddi-wip can with a blazing sun on its label instead of the usual logo.

Accepting the offered sunshine-in-a-can made sense to Ash. He certainly couldn't eat his pie with an eye in it. So he raised his plate, presenting the slice as if for inspection.

Emily tilted the can and pressed the nozzle sideways. Hot, semi-liquid sunshine squirted out with the sound of whipped cream. She artfully piled it atop Ash's pie. The fusion heat burned his hands, lighting the pie on fire.

Ash looked up, surprised by this turn of events, and found Emily staring at him — right into his eyes as if looking all the way through him. It was the most intensity Ash ever remembered in a dream. And as that thought occurred to him, something shifted inside his mind.

The Sleeper

He thought: *I'm dreaming. This is a dream.*
Then Emily became Mina.
Became Emily again. Became Mina.
Finally settled on Emily.
And told him: *"Sunshine makes everything better."*

TWENTY-FOUR

A Bad Joke

Mina was searching PubMed for symptoms of sudden-onset psychosis (strictly a personal project — one that made her a little afraid) when Ash startled awake so suddenly and violently that she took up arms against him. Her fake Nyperal gaffe meant, technically speaking, that what had happened to Ash's wife could happen again.

Ash froze. So did Mina, now holding the putter Bryan kept in the upstate lab for cup-putting in his idle time. She wielded it like a scythe as they traded wide-eyed stares.

Ash barely seemed to notice. Then his focus broke, eyes darting hither and yon around the early-morning lab. He suddenly leapt past her, eliciting an involuntary yelp, and started digging through desk drawers.

"What are you looking for?" Mina asked, lowering her weapon a little.

Ash didn't answer or look up. He was mumbling under his breath, his focus intense and obvious.

"Ash?"

He found a blank piece of paper and a pen in one of the drawers, then slapped the paper onto the blotter and began writing very fast. His words were indecipherable from Mina's vantage.

"Ash?" she repeated.

"Wait."

"Are you ... Are you awake?"

"Just ... Yes! *Shh!"*

Mina relinquished the putter. Her pulse, which she hadn't noticed spiking, slowly returned to normal. She sat, waiting five minutes or more until his sudden missive was finished. Even afterward, she waited for Ash to speak first.

His pen stilled. He paused thoughtfully, tapped the sheet a few times, then jotted another few words. He repeated the same loop two more times before finally stopping.

"Okay," he said. "I think that's all I'm going to get."

"Get from what?"

"I had a dream."

Mina was unsure how to reply.

"Like Martin Luther King," Ash said.

"What?"

"'I had a dream.'"

Pause. "Are ... Are you joking?"

Ash closed his eyes and sat heavily, like a man just back from his sprinting. His eyes went to the paper he'd left on the blotter. He offered a tiny nod, practically out of breath as he stood: exasperation, not fatigue.

"Yes. It was a joke. A bad joke. And yes, I'm awake. Really. I'm okay." It must have dawned on Ash what he looked like now, or had five minutes earlier. "I'm sorry. I needed to write it down before it fell out of my head."

"Fell out of your head?"

"You know. Like dreams do." He picked up the paper.

"What was the dream?"

"Me and Emily. And three people I keep seeing. One's

a dark-skinned man with medium-length curly black hair. Indian, maybe. Or Middle Eastern."

"Afghani?" Mina asked.

"Maybe. But not in the way you're thinking. This guy's not symbolic. He's not 'the Afghanistan war' in my head."

"How can you know that?"

Ash went on as if he hadn't heard her. "One of the others was a Black woman. Light-skinned. Maybe half Black? Short hair. Very pretty, with dramatic mascara. The last was …"

He stopped, but his most recent almost-thought had eluded him. "The last was … I don't know. A man. White. Maybe Eastern European. I have no idea how I'd know that, but it feels right. Ring any bells?"

Mina took a few seconds to think, but then she shook her head. The small desk lamp threw her oscillating shadow against the far wall. "Not that I can think of."

His face pinched, frustrated. He retrieved the pen and tapped its point on the filled page as if to jar something loose.

"I keep seeing those same three people, over and over. In my dream. Emily …"

Then his eyes shot wide.

"What?" Mina asked.

"Oh. Oh shit." He scribbled another word frantically on the page as if afraid this new epiphany might suddenly flee. Then he looked up. "Do you remember that dream I told you about? When I was the jumper on the roof?"

"Sure," she told him.

"I read in a magazine yesterday that something *just like that* happened for real. Some guy jumped off a building downtown. They said it was suicide."

"Yes. Suicide. I read about it too. You probably read

about it, then created your dream without realizing the connection. I was concerned—"

"Look it up," Ash said, nodding at Mina's laptop. "See if you can find any pictures of the jumper."

After a moment, it became clear he was serious, so Mina searched until she found the story and turned the screen toward Ash.

She didn't need to ask if the photo meant anything to him. His expression — equal parts victory, revelation, and fear — said it all.

The jumper was white, and would probably be handsome if not for a mouthful of terrible teeth.

"He was Russian," Mina read. "His name was—"

"Alexi. His name was Alexi Solokov."

TWENTY-FIVE

A Mnemonic Cue

"Have you ever heard of the Memory Championships?" Ash asked Mina after she decided to brew coffee in the new lab's break room. It was almost dawn anyway, and she'd seemingly gotten all the sleep she was going to get.

With the overheads on and sunlight finally visible through the windows, the overnight spooks haunting her had mostly departed. She was tired, but felt otherwise normal again. Well. Normal*ish*.

She took a sip and shook her head.

"It's one of those weird competitions you see some-times, like the World's Strongest Man where they lift Atlas stones and drag trains. Emily loved it. Sincerely. I mostly thought it was funny. Ridiculous, really. These people, who call themselves 'mental athletes,' compete in a series of events like memorizing the order of a deck of cards in a few minutes, or a zillion random digits, or the names and faces of two hundred strangers and everything about them after only meeting them once. It's impressive, but useless. Who needs that kind of memory outside of a bar bet?"

Mina smiled and took another sip.

"I think it appealed to Emily's constant desire to improve herself. She was an optimizer, always wanting to learn new things and find ways to do the things she could *already* do better. So of course when she learned that 'mental athletes' existed, she wanted to be one. Or at least learn a few of their techniques. I asked why. Writing our grocery list on paper like normal people had always worked fine. Besides, she ..."

He pinched his brow. "She ..." The pinch became a scrunch. "It's so strange. You know how you couldn't remember who told you about the Chirp and Blip? Or why?"

"Still can't." She'd been trying all night.

"I've got some of that, too. Gaps in my memory. After the thing with Chuck, I tried to remember how he and I met. You know how he told me yesterday that we'd only known each other a few months — not since before the Army like I thought?"

Mina nodded.

"Turns out I can't *remember* how we met. Isn't that strange? The memory seems to be there until I look right at it ... then it's gone like a mirage. I just 'know' that Chuck's been my friend for years, but I can't prove it. Or pin down the details. Or say exactly where or when or under what circumstances. It's like forgetting a dream."

"That's how it is with my gaps," Mina said.

"Look. I have to ask again ..."

She smiled, seeing what he was about to say. "This isn't a dream, Ash. As long as you can think to ask the question and do the reality checks, you can't get trapped. 'Getting trapped in a dream' is Hollywood fiction."

"There's no way *at all* for it to happen?" Clearly the past few days were forcing him to reconsider insanity. Even

185

though they'd already been through this, he seemed to need the warm blanket of hearing it again.

"You notice the strange things around you in a lucid dream, and you know by seeing them that where you are isn't real no matter what it feels like," Mina told him. "*Non*-lucid dreams never feel entirely real because there's effectively no present moment in them. If you were in a dream right now, this conversation would probably *make* you lucid. Look at the clock. Go to the restroom and stare in the mirror. How could you be wrong about what you see and experience during your reality checks? If I was some evil person determined to make you *think* you're awake when you're not, I'd have to fake the clock. I'd have to somehow fake what you see in the mirror. How is that possible?"

Ash looked at his hands. Then he read and re-read his own handwriting, checking the clock twice to be sure.

"Anyway," he continued as if deciding to trust her instead of truly believing, "my memory gaps are like that. *Like* a dream, if not one. I've noticed gaps everywhere since I started thinking about Emily again."

Mina made a sympathetic face. There were two things that Ash, to his therapy's detriment, had never wanted to examine in detail. They were that day in Afghanistan … and his late wife.

"Now that I'm remembering the Memory Championships, I have this feeling that Emily *trained* more than *dabbled*. I think she became kind of a brain-hacking whiz. Even weirder, I think we might've done this *together*. Not memorizing cards; I know I told her I'd never do something as useless as memorize a deck of playing cards. But we *did* learn to do other things — mentally — that most people can't do. And now, after having a lucid dream or two …"

He stalled, seemingly on the edge something.

He shook his head as the thought eluded him. "Anyway. It feels like maybe we *both* got kind of good at memory stuff. I even think we might have played some Memory Championship games after she got interested in the sport. Just a little. For fun."

Ash crossed his legs and leaned back, eyes intermittently toward the ceiling as if answers might be woven in the drop tiles.

"There was one main technique the memory masters used. It was called a 'memory palace.' It's also called the 'method of loci.' Basically, you take a mental picture of a place you know well, and you insert images of things you want to remember inside that place. So for instance, if I wanted to buy eggs, beer, and bread at the store, I might imagine a ton of eggs, a huge bottle of beer, and someone baking bread at three different places inside my childhood home. Then, when I want to remember those things again, I just take a mental walk through the home. The exaggerated pictures I stored inside it would come right back to me. It's actually not hard, and kind of fun."

Mina nodded, waiting for the punchline.

"My problem with the memory palace was establishing an initial trigger for the memories as a whole. Basically, I had a hard time remembering that there even *was* something I needed to recall. Emily never had that problem. But she wanted me to play the game with her, so she wouldn't let me leave myself notes or tie a string around my finger. There *was*, however, one method we found effective — one good way of reminding me that there was something buried inside myself and where to start looking for it."

"And what was that?"

"A mnemonic cue. A phrase she'd say that woke my brain up and made me remember."

Mnemonic. They both sat in silence with the idea. Ash

claimed he'd spontaneously recalled a mnemonic trigger for Chuck during the melee. He'd said a specific word to Chuck, and it'd changed his brain for a while.

"What was the phrase?" Mina asked.

"I couldn't have told you yesterday, but my dream reminded me." Ash looked into Mina's eyes very seriously. "It was 'Sunshine makes everything better.'"

TWENTY-SIX

Things You Need to Know

Ash and Mina were weighing the revelation when someone knocked on the outside door. Both startled. Mina spilled half of her coffee, almost dropping her cup as hot liquid spilled over her knuckles.

But even in the quiet that followed, they kept staring at each other with wide eyes.

Emily had a trigger for Ash, same as Ash had trigger for Chuck. She used it to wake him up. To make him remember.

If that was true, then somehow Emily was still trying to nudge her husband — to wake him up — from beyond the grave. But what was Ash supposed to remember? Why? Why *now*? Was it really possible she'd planned to kickstart him in the future, having set a failsafe before she died?

The knock repeated. It wasn't particularly gentle. The sound was more urgent than casual, like a police officer's knock.

Mina put her hand to her heart, trying to calm it. "It's probably just one of Bryan's grad students."

"Wouldn't a grad student have a key?"

She shook her head. "Bryan's not a trusting guy. He left

the college lab before us yesterday, but you can bet your ass he came back after we were gone to make sure I didn't accidentally leave the door unlocked. Grad students are only allowed in the lab when one of *us* is in the lab. It's really inconvenient sometimes."

"Then maybe it's Bryan," Ash guessed. "You said yesterday that he'd come up today."

"*Bryan* has a key."

"Maybe he lost it?"

But it wasn't Bryan. When the knock came again, a female voice came with it.

Ash stood, then moved toward the break room door.

"*Ash!*"

"We can't just sit here," he said.

"Of course we can! It's why we came!"

Ash stopped, but Mina wasn't making sense. If it was a killer outside, they'd break in eventually. And besides, why would a killer knock?

They should at least see who was there.

As they both came to the same conclusion, Ash stepped into the hallway. The outer door was hardly secure. It had a deadbolt, but there were six-foot glass panels on either side of it, easy enough to break.

Mina shoved past Ash, seeming to know he wasn't convinced. "At least let *me* look. We *know* someone's after *you*."

So she went forward. The sun was fully risen now, its angle blinding. But the hallway farther down was dark without windows. Unless the person outside pressed their face to the glass, it would be impossible to see inside but easy for Mina to peek out. So she did.

"It's a short Asian woman," she reported, keeping mostly against the wall. "A short Asian woman driving a monster truck."

That pulled Ash forward. He actually laughed a little. Peeking out himself, he could see the truck in question, parked halfheartedly at the foot of the steps instead of in a slot. Not quite a *monster* truck, but very large with tall, knobby tires.

"Jesus Christ," he said. "It's Emily's friend Daisy."

He didn't even need to see her face to be sure; only one diminutive Asian woman in his world owned a ride that fit her so strangely. Daisy had won the truck in her divorce. She hated the thing, but her husband had loved it more than he'd ever loved her, so of course she'd fought tooth and nail to get it. She'd originally planned to set fire to the steel beast and send her ex photos, but with a life lived low to the ground, sitting behind the wheel of something so big was a power trip for Daisy.

Ash's smile became half frown. Even though she was harmless — even a friend to Ash, despite everything — Daisy absolutely shouldn't be here.

"Who's Daisy?" Mina asked.

But Ash was already unlocking the door. Already opening it. Already ushering their visitor inside and embracing her small frame with his six-three one. Hugging Daisy was like eating her. She often called herself a firecracker: small but mighty.

"Ash, thank God!" she gushed.

"Why are you here?" Ash asked her.

"I saw the story on the news. About what happened at your house." She didn't say, *About what you did.*

Daisy was one of only a handful of people who truly believed Ash had never meant to kill Emily. Others *said* they believed him, but they were believing on faith. Daisy, on the other hand, had a sleepwalking disorder. She'd woken doing pushups in the park, baking plastic in her oven, and stepping into a scalding-hot bath. She knew exactly how possible it was to do strange — even terrible — things while sleeping.

"*How* are you here? How did you know where to find me?"

"LoJack," she answered.

"Lo …" Ash looked into the parking lot, but of course the car his eyes sought wasn't there. With stacked paranoia he'd stowed the SUV beneath a maintenance overhang behind the building and leaned metal scrap all around to hide what he could. "Emily's car has *LoJack?*"

"Of course it has LoJack. This is Emily we're talking about. You didn't know?"

Mina cleared her throat.

"Oh. I'm sorry." Ash turned sideways to both of them. "Mina, this is Daisy Zhao. She was Emily's secretary."

"Assistant," Daisy corrected, extending a hand.

"And this is Mina Irving. She's … She's a friend."

"'Friend,'" Daisy repeated, eyeing them both.

"Yes," Ash repeated. *"Friend."*

Daisy shrugged. "If you say so."

They went silent after that. Obvious questions streamed from Mina's eyes into his. The three of them looked from person to person as if only now realizing that there was something seriously wrong with this picture.

"Look," Daisy said. "Is there somewhere we can talk? There are things you don't know. Things you *need* to know."

TWENTY-SEVEN

Tossed

They returned to the break room, nestled deep in the building. It was windowless and felt safer than the outer rooms — like taking shelter in a storm.

"We should check the thing while we're up." Mina gave Daisy a thin smile and, before he could protest, dragged Ash into the adjoining room and shut the door.

"What 'thing'?" Then he saw Mina's face and his own fell. "Oh. There is no 'thing.'"

The room seemed to be Bryan's office. It was small and dark with the blinds drawn, strewn with unpacked banker's boxes and half filled by a modest desk dominated by framed photos of a family, Bryan in all of them.

Mina flicked on a desk lamp that did little to brighten the space.

"You just *let her in*? Who the hell is this woman?" she demanded.

"I told you. She was my wife's secretary."

"Assistant."

"See? You don't need my help."

"How do you know she was *really* Emily's assistant?" Mina asked.

"*How?* Because she was, that's how."

"And you're sure about that?"

"Of course I'm sure. She's a family friend. She was in our wedding."

"Uh-huh. Was *Chuck* in your wedding?"

"What's that got to do with—" He swallowed. "Oh."

"What makes you so sure she's not a plant?"

"Because she doesn't have leaves." The joke landed so poorly, he may as well have insulted her. "Sorry. I just don't think she is."

"*You don't think so,*" Mina repeated.

"Did you sleep?"

"What's that got to do with it?"

"You tell me, Doctor Shuteye. I heard that sleep deprivation can cause all sorts of mental fuckery. Like paranoia."

"You think I'm paranoid?"

"Takes one to know one, I guess."

"And you're *not* paranoid," she said.

"Look. Daisy was one of Emily's best friends."

"Like Chuck was yours."

"This is different."

"How?"

"I just … I remember how we met." He wanted to snap his fingers with epiphany.

"So?"

"I told you before. I *don't* remember how Chuck and I met. If I start there, the whole relationship starts looking suspicious."

"And the Daisy situation isn't?"

Ash sighed, thinking hard. He wasn't articulating well,

but the difference between his histories with Chuck and Daisy felt perfectly obvious. Two days ago he wouldn't have thought fake memories were possible, but even though they both had strong reasons to doubt their memories now, Daisy was still legit. He just ... *knew*. Now that he understood what to look for in false memories, he felt confident being sure.

"I *know*." Then he had an idea. "Here."

He went to the desk and woke Bryan's sleeping computer. He opened the internet browser and navigated to LiveLyfe. He searched for his account, then scrolled through photos until he reached his and Emily's wedding pictures. Emily appeared onscreen, stunning in white. And yes, Daisy was three women down from her on the bride's side, plain as day.

"You've never heard of Photoshop?" Mina asked.

"Look at the timestamp." He pointed. "I don't think LiveLyfe is in on this. The picture was posted exactly when it should have been."

"That doesn't mean—"

"Yes. It *does* mean. You know how my head feels right now? Tossed. Like a salad. I can tell by looking at you that yours is even worse. We have to draw a line somewhere, Mina. Is *Bryan* in on this? Maybe you don't know him. Maybe *he's* a plant."

"Ash ..."

"I remember meeting Daisy. I know our origin. Live-Lyfe has timestamped proof. That's good enough for me. It *has* to be good enough for me. Because ..." His stern tone faltered and desperation bled through. "Because I can't keep going without something to stand on, Mina. You should understand that more than anyone."

It was hell for Ash, living with himself these days.

Dealing with all the guilt and loss. Finding it so impossible to go on that sometimes he thought about eating a bullet.

Mina looked at him for a long moment before she finally replied. "Okay," she said with a sigh. "If you think you can trust her, then I will too."

TWENTY-EIGHT

Briefing

Mina lingered behind, her hand still on the doorknob as she looked back into Bryan's office. It had always reminded her of what the inside of her partner's head must look like. Bryan had always been a mess, but also dependable.

The thought made her wonder where he was. She'd thought the knock might be Bryan at first, too — maybe he'd lost his key like Ash supposed. Bryan was a creature of habit. He *always* came up on the weekends, and he always came early. She'd thought he might even beat the sunrise. So where was he?

Conspiracies. Killers in the shadows. Maybe Bryan's a plant after all, just like Ash said.

But no. He couldn't be. If Ash could be sure about Daisy, then Mina could be sure about Bryan. She remembered first meeting him. She remembered their history. Just because Bryan hadn't known Ash was in the college lab yesterday didn't mean he would have killed him if he had. Just because Bryan hadn't shown up here yet didn't mean he'd realized yesterday's mistake … and was late because he'd taken extra time to load his guns.

Mina blinked into the office and its absent demons. She'd barely slept. She really was sleep-deprived. Maybe she *was* paranoid.

She took one final look into the empty office, then decided to take a leap of faith

(I can't keep going without something to stand on)

and closed the door.

By the time she entered the break room, Ash and Daisy were already talking. Daisy acknowledged Mina's arrival with a friendly but still-businesslike nod, pretending she didn't know Mina had been casting doubt on her only moments ago.

"You know I'm not one for bullshitting," Daisy was telling Ash. "Taking what's on the news at face value, I would normally think you killed your neighbor despite knowing and loving you."

"But … you don't?" Mina asked.

Daisy's eyes flicked to Mina, then resumed speaking to Ash. "I drive a truck tall enough to climb over traffic jams, but I'm still a practical girl. I follow the rules. I obey laws. I even drive that shit-heap no more than five miles over the speed limit. The *last* thing I'd do would be to illegally use LoJack to find you if I didn't think something was fishy. If I didn't think you were innocent."

"How *did* you get LoJack to tell you where the car was?" Mina asked.

Daisy finally looked her way. "I was Emily's assistant for two years. I have all her codes and passwords. This isn't 1980. LoJack has an app and it's not hard to use. Now, please. I really don't want to be an asshole, but it's clear you don't trust me. I need to know if that's going to be a problem."

Mina couldn't help but admire Daisy's style. "I guess not."

"I'm four-eleven. I'm in yoga pants. Nowhere to hide a weapon. If I'm bad news, I'm sure you two can take me. So please. Let me finish. When I'm done, you can decide if you need to truss my little ass up like a turkey. But until then. Please. Just let me talk to Ash."

Mina sat back, less offended than she should be.

Daisy turned back to Ash. "Do you believe what I said?"

He nodded.

"So the fact that I'm here should tell you that I *know* you didn't kill that man."

"How can you *know* I didn't kill him?"

"Because I know who did. The real guy was on the news, walking past in the background."

"What 'real guy'?"

"Richard Quince."

"Who's Richard Quince?"

Daisy was already fishing her phone from her pocket. Then from where she sat, Mina watched Daisy's fingers navigate to a hidden photo album much like the one in which she herself had stored the Blip photo.

She selected a picture from the album, then showed it to Ash. "What's this guy's name? Who is this man to you, Ash?"

"That's Chuck." Ash's eyes were confused as he gave his answer. "Chuck DeMona."

Daisy shook her head. "His name is Richard Quince. He's NSA. Or a subdivision of NSA."

"NSA!" Mina had technically known that the National Security Agency was a thing, but still thought of it as something from the movies.

"Yes." Daisy nodded at Mina. "Richard's a bad dude. He was put with Ash as a kind of chaperone. The people who ... *interfered* with you? They needed someone to stay close to you, to make sure the bullshit story they fed you held up."

"I have all these memories of him ..." He took Daisy's phone to look more closely at the photo. "But as 'Chuck.'"

"Those memories are—"

"—fake. We know." Ash nodded to include Mina in the discussion.

Daisy looked from one to the other. She seemed impressed, and thus to have deemed Mina worthy. "How much have you figured out?"

Ash's eyes flicked to Mina. The biggest thing they'd figured out, but barely unboxed, was the mnemonic cue Emily seemed to have left for Ash. But that discovery was still too new and too unknown, and his second-long glance at Mina promised to keep it a secret.

"Something's wrong with our memories," he said instead. "I've forgotten a bunch of stuff I thought I knew. Things I *should* know. At the same time, I remember a bunch that's not even real. I thought I'd known Chuck for years. Since Afghanistan."

"What do you remember about Afghanistan? Do you remember the Afghani general?"

"*What* Afghani general?"

"The Afghani general whose wife slit his throat. The one who'd been scheduled to lead a major intelligence incursion against CIA interests in the region before he died."

Ash blinked.

"So you *don't* remember," Daisy said. "What about that lieutenant in the British army? The one who kept bucking the command chain? Do you remember him? The one who ended up being poisoned by his own daughter?"

"Excuse me," Mina said when a dumbstruck Ash didn't

answer. "Maybe this is rude of me. But *who the* fuck *are you and what the* fuck *is all of this?*"

Daisy looked at Mina, silently promised to answer her question, then took both of Ash's hands in her own. "Ash," she said.

"Yeah?"

"You've been erased."

"I know."

Daisy shook her head. "You *almost* know. You're in what Emily called no-man's-land. I can only imagine how disorienting that must be."

"Emily?" Ash repeated. "What does Emily have to do with this?"

"I'm sorry ..." Her entire body seemed to exhale. "You'll have to forgive me. I never thought this was a briefing I'd have to make."

She took another deep breath. "You and Emily are the reason that all of this is happening."

TWENTY-NINE

Sleepers

"Emily used to say that dreams were windows to the soul," Daisy told them as they walked through the building, turning on lights with her in the lead.

Daisy entered a new room, flipped the switch, then scanned the place before entering. The facility was bigger than it seemed from the outside, due in part to the basement. Room after room came up empty as they searched. Daisy had suggested they check the building. She wanted to be sure. Ash could use the distraction, and her promise of answers made it feel like time well spent.

The large building was surprisingly mundane. Ash had imagined Mina's lab as filled with sci-fi contraptions: sleep vessels shaped like chrome dentist's chairs placed head to head, perhaps, to link sleeping minds in magical ways. The truth turned out to be boring. Stripped of the monitoring equipment and what looked like miles of wire (and perhaps with yard-sale art added to the walls), the place could just as easily have been a fourth-rate motel.

With the click of a final switch, Daisy stepped back and

surveyed the last room's perimeter. She nodded to herself. Then she looked at Mina, who nodded back.

"Do you remember her saying that?" Daisy asked Ash.

"Emily said a lot of things," he answered.

"About dreams?"

"I don't remember anything in particular." He shrugged. "She wasn't terribly interested in dreams."

"You're wrong," Daisy told him. "She was *extremely* interested in dreams. Professionally so."

"Wasn't she an accountant?" Mina asked.

Daisy was watching him if waiting for him to answer. Finally she said, "Ash?"

"I ... I'm not sure." One thing he did recall were reams of paperwork on Emily's desk every March and April — but then again, he also remembered Chuck in Afghanistan.

Daisy nodded as if his non-answer was expected. "The process used to alter memory uses a lot of the same biological machinery that makes it hard to remember dreams after waking. There's a hormone that causes forgetting. MCH, I think."

Daisy made a frustrated face, trying to be sure, but she'd already told them Emily was the expert. She really had been an assistant — but in their line of work, assistants seemed to know more than professors.

"Anyway. Emily said that when you eventually tried to dig information out of yourself, it would feel like trying to remember not just *any* dream, but a dream from *last week*. Without all of your training, you'd *never* be able to get at it."

"I didn't train," Ash said.

"You both trained. Primed yourselves to retain things that most people forget. It's probably why your memory started to return in the first place."

Ash filed that away for later consideration, but it

seemed Daisy didn't *really* know why he'd started to remember: not because of training, but because of what they'd learned involving Emily's mnemonic cue.

He was starting to get the impression Daisy had come here expecting him to remember almost nothing. She was only guessing as to how the seal had broken. Only Ash and Mina knew about sunshine and how it made everything — specifically Ash's memory — better.

They walked on. Ash found his mind drifting. The dim basement had no windows and the atmosphere itself was sleepy. His mind was untethering from the world, slowly spinning like a Lazy Susan until it came to rest facing a misplaced universe. He was surprised to discover it'd been lurking just to one side of his old universe all along: out of focus, visible only after he thought to look there.

But once he did look — once he *did* focus — what Ash saw in his real past was unmistakable.

Emily hadn't been an accountant any more than Ash was a machinist. She wasn't even good at math. Until the shop, Ash had barely used a drill. So what had their lives actually been like?

He saw it bits of it now, as his grip on that unseen place resolved.

He remembered snippets of sensation before anything concrete: detritus in the stream of his existence.

Sitting in a classroom setting, as an adult, while someone in charge revealed secrets to him. Sneaking around in the dark. He remembered guilt, then rationalizing his guilt into mist. The feeling of cold metal, scored like a pistol's stock, in his hand. Discussions with Emily that only deepened the shroud of conspiracy. A room packed with colleagues and friends. A woman with feline makeup. A handsome man, minus his bad teeth. A dark-skinned man, with intelligent eyes.

Ash looked up at Daisy, his rivulet of memories becoming a stream. And he said:

"Wait. You didn't work at Emily's office."

Mina's eyes widened, seeing treachery. But that wasn't what he had meant, so Ash added, "Not at her *office*, I mean. Emily didn't *have* an office."

"Not the normal type," Daisy said, nodding with encouragement. "What else do you remember? Trust your gut, Ash."

"We ... We worked for ..."

The taste of an unknown drink on his lips. A hollow sense of grim duty. Something unfortunate that had to be done. And far too many lies. Even in this forgotten world, he had always hated lying.

Seeing him struggle, Daisy gave him the answer. "For the government. The NSA specifically. You and Emily were part of an NSA division simply known as the Agency."

"What do you know about ... about 'the Agency'?"

"The name's all anyone ever gave me." Daisy shrugged. "Unfortunately we're about at the limit of what I know. Your bosses? They were my bosses too. It was you, me, and Emily, and they kept me mostly in a bubble. It's like I said: I really was her assistant, and assistants don't get full keys to the vault. I only know there was some sort of trouble, and because of it both of you were made to forget who you were and what you did. You became Mild Mannered Mr. and Mrs. American. The things I'm telling you now, I only know because Emily made sure I knew before it happened."

"Why didn't they erase *you*?" Ash asked.

"Em and I were closer friends than our bosses realized. Everyone working in our circles was subject to regular psychological profiling, present company included. But I was just 'the help' — lowly enough to not be worth the expense and red tape of an erasure. My psych profile showed I was loyal. Their mistake was not thinking to ask who I was loyal *to*. My friend and boss, not the brass."

"You still haven't told me who the brass is."

"The government," Daisy said with something like irony. "It's truthfully no more specific than that. Even 'the NSA' was just a convenient slot for us on the org chart. Really we belonged to nobody — not so much 'unacknowledged' as 'forgotten.' This isn't Orwell's *1984*. It's more like that movie *Brazil*, where a big, dumb machine runs the people instead of the other way around. The bureaucracy behind this country is massive, faceless, and redundant. It's carved into sections — small departments with their own budgets and purpose — but there's no one at the top. Nobody understands it all, and I do mean *nobody*."

She laughed to herself. "The Agency was the bit left behind after all the carving was done. We functioned like scavengers. Our funding was the remainder of everyone *else's* funding. Our leaders were the defense employees not assigned to anything else. The brass, the Agents … We're all the very definition of 'nobody.'"

The feel of a pistol in his hand. Moving around in the dark. Moral questions in spades. And three people — one leaping from a building in what was definitely not a suicide.

But now Ash knew there hadn't been *three* people. There'd been five. Because he'd been one of them, and so had Emily.

They'll know we stole it, said one of them as all five Agents sat around a table.

That's why we have to hide it well, someone else had replied.

But what was "it"? Why had they taken whatever it was? Where had Ash and the others decided to hide it?

"What did we do for the Agency?" Ash asked. "What was our job?"

Daisy nodded as if she'd been waiting for the question.

"You manipulated people's dreams in order to brainwash them. The Freak-Outs you've seen on the news? Every one of them is a sleeper agent your group created."

THIRTY

Two Men

Ash told Daisy to stop.

After another few sentences it became apparent how much blood was on his hands — but curiously, hearing about that blood didn't make him want to curl into a ball and hate himself. That's what amnesia movies always got wrong. Ash wasn't *learning about* his old self so much as *becoming* his old self. And that old Ash had made peace with death long ago.

He didn't feel guilt just yet (if he ever would), but he did feel surprise. Old Ash was out of focus. New Ash needed time to accept his arrival. The combined Old-New entity he was now had the task of tracking two biographies at once, and the process was neither easy nor comfortable.

So he took his leave from the women. He paced the silent maze of sleeping rooms on the lower level alone, giving his memories enough space to return. What the media called "Freak-Outs," Ash remembered now, the Agency had called "Sleepers." They were ordinary people who'd been programmed, through their dreams, to do whatever the Agency needed done — like assassinate problematic Afghani generals that the Sleeper alone had access to.

A wife killing her husband.

A daughter killing her father.

The dream-manipulating process used the Blip and Chirp. Mina's understanding of the tech was spot-on according to Ash's slowly returning memory. The devices could read dreams from a person's head in real time, using a Wurtzman algorithm to display them on a screen. Ash hadn't worked out how observing someone's dreams turned them into a Sleeper, but he thought it had something to do with influencing those dreams from the outside.

Even Mina's work proved that sleeping people noticed stimuli from the real world: a flashing red light, a song in the room — maybe even someone whispering in the sleeper's ear.

Maybe brainwashing worked like that. If a man dreams about his controlling father, playing the father's voice for him in the real world might worsen his dreams. Maybe debilitatingly so. And perhaps that process, done consistently, could unhinge the man enough for the Agency to apply leverage.

Manipulate dreams and you change the subconscious. Ash thought he remembered someone saying that.

It even made sense. It'd just be an advanced version of what Mina had been doing in the lab when he'd arrived with a gun and a grudge. Maybe they used post-hypnotic suggestion. Although … the more he thought about it, Ash decided he'd *never* fully understood his work. Emily had been the genius. She might even have developed some of the tech herself. Hard to know with so many gnarled memories.

He made himself stop pondering. Thoughts of Emily were still a spear through his chest. He didn't strictly remember murdering her (he'd slept through it, after all), but his imagination had filled in the blanks. The result was an almost-memory: a vivid re-creation his treacherous mind had made of the actual event.

I'm an Agent, he kept thinking. *Not the victim, but the cause.*

He almost wished he could still believe he was a Freak-Out rather than the Freak-Outs' creator. Freak-Outs had their programming as an excuse. But nobody had programmed Ash. His memory had been erased, but he knew deep-down that Agents couldn't become Sleepers. They knew too much about how it was all done, and their minds had built aggressive defenses against it.

Ash was a killer without anyone's help. *His* choices had caused him to join the Agency. *His* sleep disorder had squeezed the life from Emily's throat.

One way or another, Ash was at fault.

THIRTY-ONE

Catastrophizing

Mina paced the floor like a caged animal.

Evening had come again already, and in waning light the lab was desolate and far too quiet. How had so many hours passed? Time was supposed to crawl through boredom, but today had disappeared as if stolen. Ash was on the lower level by himself — and as his therapist, knowing what he must be going through, Mina had decided to let him be until he decided to come back up.

She just hadn't expected him to take so long. She didn't know Daisy, and selfishly wanted the comfort of someone familiar. She felt awkward — idle for so long without Ash. There was no reason to feel chased here in the upstate lab, but still Mina felt a looming threat. The lab's emptiness was a bad omen, but they had nowhere else to go.

Bryan still hadn't shown. And Mina hadn't called him. Using the office phone felt like a security risk, and her smartphone felt even more so. He wasn't involved in this, and logically speaking she saw no reason to endanger him to soothe her nerves.

Still, she kept thinking: *Why didn't Bryan come in? He's so dedicated. Such a workaholic. So very predictable.*

But the counterargument went: *He changed his mind and decided to stay home. It's the goddamn* weekend, *Mina. Even dedicated and predictable workaholics needed the occasional rest.*

The silent and dragging hours were a boot on her neck. She'd forgotten to bring a charger, and her phone's battery was critically low. She might need it before this was over, so she made herself stop using it entirely and thus had no distractions to numb her. She was sleep-deprived, and confused due to the deprivation. Truthfully, she wasn't even sure how her day had been spent. And yet still it was gone.

To kill time, she'd spent hours behind Bryan's computer to try and answer some (or even *one*) of her million questions. Researching their situation would have burned a lot of time, but Mina had barely started when overwhelm hit her. The CIA and NSA could spy on anything. What would it look like, if she googled what she most wanted to search?

"I need some fresh air," she told Daisy. "I'm just going to duck outside for a minute. I'll stay close."

Daisy gave Mina a nod. Thankfully, she didn't ask to come along.

Mina traversed the main hallway to the back exit, then let herself into the rear parking lot. The door was heavy; she had to prop it open with a brick to keep it from locking behind her. Using the back exit felt safer than the front — this despite knowing she was being ridiculous and had nothing to fear.

You know, maybe it's all *ridiculous,* she tried to tell herself. *Maybe every bit of this is jumping at shadows. You don't know this Daisy person. She could be crazy. Maybe it all sounds so insane because it* is *insane. Just look at yourself. You've run away with one of your patients to play spy-movie. Do you really believe that Ash was some sort of a secret agent? That he and the wife he killed were part of a Shop-type organization responsible for the Freak-Outs? It's crazy, Mina. Things like that just don't happen in the real world … and even if they do, they certainly don't happen to* you.

It was a tempting explanation for all that had happened, and Mina very much wanted to believe it. But then she remembered how she, too, had an abundance of memories that didn't feel like they'd been made by her. That *she*, too, had somehow been mentally impregnated and erased.

So what was *Mina* in all of this, with her odd, comprehensive knowledge of dream-stealing technology? Was she a Sleeper? Did the dangerous information in her head mean that *she* might snap like the janitor in Hoboken who'd Freaked Out a few days ago, knifing a businesswoman who always walked through his building's lobby?

Stop it. Just stop it.

Mina breathed in, then out. She hugged herself, tightening the light sweater around her, thick hair lifting in a nighttime breeze. She'd told Daisy she'd come out here for fresh air. Maybe she should make it true, and actually get some.

She stepped away from the building and started to walk.

Fresh air began to clear her head in a second. Night was a difficult time, psychologically speaking. People tended to make things worse in their heads when the sun wasn't shining. The phenomenon even had a word: *catastrophizing*. Mina had been shut in with her thoughts all day, and now that it was night she'd been catastrophizing plenty.

She noticed that a pair of eyes was staring at her from a slit in the mostly closed dumpster.

Fear came hard, but then Mina stared it down, knowing with the gagged part of her logical mind that she was only seeing things. A dumpster would be an absurd place for someone to hide. Even if someone *was* watching, they wouldn't keep staring after Mina saw them, which was how it still appeared.

She exhaled slowly, making a low whistle.

You won't need people to torture you if you keep torturing yourself, she thought.

So she stared the dumpster down.

Face your fears. Don't let your brain fuck with you, Dr. Irving.

A utility light cast a dim yellow pool around the dumpster. A car revved a block away. The air was tinged with the sour reek of trash, wafted forward by a breeze rolling leaves past her ankles.

She drew a breath and lifted the lid to confront her mental demons, and of course found no spy inside the dumpster.

Instead, Mina found something worse.

THIRTY-TWO

Berserk

Ash was deep in thought when he noticed someone approaching in shadow at the end of the hallway. Lights down here were motion-activated, and he'd wandered away from the nearest one long enough for it to die. For a moment Old Ash took over and he forgot his situation. An internal voice told him: *That could be anyone.*

His hand shot to the small of his back as if there might be a gun there. Pure instinct, like flinching at an oncoming fist. But then the newcomer spoke.

"Ash!" The words were whisper-shouted: the kind of thing a person does when they don't want to be overheard.

The sensor tripped and the lights came on. It was Mina.

Ash's hand moved away from his rear, under conscious control again. He'd left his pistol in Mina's purse after her protest that he'd "shoot his ass off." So why had he gone for it so automatically now?

Then he remembered: He used to carry a concealed weapon there more often than not. It was always cocked and safetied with a round in the chamber. He was an ace at flicking the safety with his thumb mid-draw so he could fire on a dime. If he'd been carrying the same gun the same way today, he might have ended Mina's life.

God. Who had he been in his last life? His *current* life?

Mina came forward slowly at first, then faster once she was sure it was him.

But how could it not be him? Other than Daisy, who was a foot and a half shorter, who else was here?

"Ash, is that you?"

"What's going on?" he said.

"We have to get out of here. Now."

"*What?* Why?"

"I was just outside. I needed some air." Ash watched as she blinked rapidly, eyes darting and breath disturbed, her hand shaking. "Some trick of light at the dumpster was freaking me out. I knew it was just me being ridiculous, so I decided I might just go over. Face my fear and all, like looking in a closet to prove there's no monster inside, you know? And … And …"

She fought harder for breath. Ash could feel her thundering pulse as he tried to steady her. She seemed to have run down to find him, winded and scared.

"Inside. In the dumpster. It was …"

"Mina. It's okay. What did you see?"

She looked him full in the eyes. "Bryan. My partner. He's …"

That's when Ash noticed a blot of fresh blood on her right sleeve. He didn't need her to say it. *Dead. Bryan's dead in the dumpster.*

"Mina. Listen—"

"We have to go! We have to get out of here right now! I think … I think maybe—!"

A deafening whip-crack startled them both.

Ash's gaze shot past her to the end of the hallway, his

pulse slowing instead of gathering speed: a self-cooling battle mode; a hypersensitive calm that Old Ash had trained himself into.

He knew the sound was a gunshot, not something dropped upstairs.

He grabbed Mina and dragged her as another shot fired. She protested, trying to say ten things at once. The last of her composure disintegrated as he dragged her to the hallway's end — *toward* the gunshot instead of away from it.

Ash barely noticed. He was focused on the fact that the shots were from his own weapon: the Beretta M9 he'd left in Mina's purse. He knew its sound even though he'd never pulled its trigger.

"*Stop!* We're going the wrong way!"

There was another trio of shots. His calm deepened. Then something happened that Ash couldn't describe: It was like time slowed down while possibilities dilated in front of him. He didn't feel like a man reacting so much as one delving into study, taking his time to research a hundred courses of action in a blink.

Upstairs. Left, then right. First room. The corner office's wall angles add protection. There are eleven shots left: full magazine to start, plus one in the chamber. Get eyes on the shooter. Almost for-sure it's Daisy — her eyes are sharp enough to recognize the M9's shape and weight in the purse. She'd take it out only under duress. She's trained. Won't panic fire. If she's shooting at something, she for damn sure has a reason.

They climbed the stairs as another pair of shots fired, Mina still chattering in panic. Adrenaline was in charge, not Mina. If Ash held her wrong, she'd hit him. Kick him. See him as the enemy instead of whatever was up there. *Out* there.

The office has a closet. Without intending to, Ash apparently had the blueprint memorized. *Find a line, then secure the civilian.*

Ten seconds. His vision tunneled. He ignored the periphery. He could count his heartbeats: *one … two … more.* A *larghissimo* metronome ticking off measures.

He entered the office and eyed the shooter in a mirror room across the hallway.

Daisy as predicted, sighting through a broken window with five shots remaining. Ash, who'd been a different person when he'd left home, hadn't thought to pack a second magazine. Daisy hadn't seen him, so he couldn't sign. He *definitely* couldn't shout. Without recon, he dared not speak above a whisper.

Shoot slower, he wanted to tell her.

Everyone in the Agency's orbit could shoot, and that meant Daisy was relatively calm and collected. Problem, though: Those who fired only on ranges didn't develop an Agent's situational intelligence. Daisy needed to be counting, but Ash knew she wasn't. She needed to know she had less than a tumbler of rounds remaining. Nerves could make you shoot too fast. She was almost redline now, and had to conserve her shots.

"Get in the closet," Ash whispered to Mina, pushing her to make his point. "Shut the door."

"*Ash!* You—!"

He didn't want to hear it. *Couldn't* hear it. Old programming was driving his mind, and right now he was on rails. Ash had no time for a panicking civilian, nor the manners to deal with one.

He shoved Mina into the closet and closed the door. When she tried to push it open, he took a letter opener from the desk and stabbed it into the space between door and frame. It wouldn't hold her forever, but that was the point: he might be killed or taken in what came next, and he didn't want her to suffocate.

Mina's words became shouts, muffled by wood. Ash left the room and raced for Daisy, still counting shots. He rushed in, waving for her to stop.

Too late. He reached her just as she loosed the final round and the slide locked back smoking.

He went to the perforated window, approaching it sideways, flipping his gaze back to Daisy after two seconds glancing into the dark. "Tell me."

"Our old friends activated some Sleepers to come and say hi."

Ash ducked back as a fresh bullet shattered glass from the outside. "How many?"

"I don't know."

"More than one?"

"Yes."

"Where?"

"I don't know."

"Then why were you shooting?"

Daisy's semi-fluster vanished in light of all this straight talk, her voice now tinged with anger. "Goddammit, use your eyes."

She pointed. Ash understood.

His ears hadn't properly registered the shot tracking from below, but now with more clues in sight it made sense. She'd fired the first shots from the back hallway, not this room. A dead man was there now, holding a machete. Bloodied handprints were on the door's surface: evidence that Daisy had closed the door after yanking the first man clear of its sweep.

Daisy had then apparently run to where Ash found her and seemed to be spraying cover fire across the front lot. An overly zealous but mostly correct choice. The front door was flanked by glass panels, so if outsiders wanted in, breaking them would be easy. Defending that weakness from the other side of the panels would have gotten her killed. Although the shot that'd barely missed Ash was the first from the aggressors as far as he'd heard, Daisy must have seen their guns. This was the only room from which to cover the front without leaving herself in the line of fire, and the only way to do it without sightlines was to lay down cover — blindly, if needed.

"You didn't leave us any ammunition," he said.

"What the fuck was I supposed to do? Let them in?"

"What exactly happened?" Ash asked, acutely aware that whoever was left out there could enter the building now.

"Someone propped the back door open with a brick. That one walked right in."

Ash looked at the dead man, part of his mind hearing the walk and drag of more outside. The corpse didn't bother him. Sleepers were all or nothing. The ordinary person that this man used to be was gone forever. Already dead, whether Daisy killed him or not.

"And then you started shooting? Without knowing what you were shooting at?"

She shoved the pistol into Ash's hand as if it still had value. "It was *cover* fire. I'm not a field operative, asshole. If you wanted to play hero, maybe you should have been up here watching the perimeter instead of walking the dungeon and feeling sorry for yourself. I did what I could. You're welcome for saving your ass."

Ash ducked low so he could reach for Mina's purse. It was covered in glass and wood splinters.

"She doesn't have another mag," Daisy said. "I already—"

"That's not what I'm looking for."

Ash came out with a fistful of keys. Emily's. There was something troubling out there, more than the numerous bodies. This was a coordinated attack, and he'd seen from the window that they'd somehow taken out every outside light on the property.

Ash flipped through the keys until he found the SUV's fob. He hit the panic button, setting every light on the vehicle to flashing and the horn braying.

Ash peeked through the window. From the SUV's concealed position, its flashing lights illuminated just enough for him to see the depths of their trouble. There weren't just five or six Sleepers in the lot. There were at least fifty.

A sound of breaking glass came from the front door. Ash snatched the dead man's machete and marched forward without thinking, retreating only when a bullet nearly took his face off.

Reversing course, he slammed the small room's door and locked it as tromping feet invaded the hallway. Not that one flimsy interior door would hold long. Thinking of it now made him wonder if Mina was being quiet in her closet. If she wasn't — and if they heard her — she'd be dead or accosted within minutes.

"Where's Mina?" Daisy asked, as if reading his mind.

"Across the hall. In a closet."

"That's your idea of protecting the perimeter? I don't feel so bad about my plan now."

Ash barely heard her. His mind was working as the SUV's panic alarm turned the parking lot into an apocalyptic discotheque.

He went to a small card table that was folded in the corner, then turned it upside down and kicked the legs against their pivots, snapping each of them free.

"What the hell are you doing?" Daisy asked.

Ash didn't have time to explain. Sleepers were repurposed people, and there were actions in any situation that almost no rational *person* would expect — actions like a target charging *toward* his attackers instead of away from them.

Ash planned to do the irrational thing, counting on the shock of momentum to open a hole in his favor.

Sleepers were in the hallway now, just outside the room. Standing beside the door, on the side where it was about to break open under a fusillade of hammering blows, Ash held the legless table like a shield by one corner bracket. He held his machete in the other.

"Get behind me," he told Daisy. "Stay close. If I fall, get as far away as you can."

"But what—?"

The door gave way. Its sudden failure sent Sleepers spilling into the room. Ash wedged into the space behind the first wave and kicked them forward with one booted foot.

Six of them, thus booted, spilled to the floor.

Then he swiped at the startled second wave with the machete, opening one woman from neck to waist with one swing and nearly severing a man's arm — bone and all — with another.

Time slowed again.

Ash pinpointed three attackers before they could turn to face him, then put the table-shield in front of himself and shoved his body into the mob like a battering ram. Those he struck wobbled like tenpins, falling into rooms along the hallway or slamming flat against walls as the Ash Train with its Daisy Caboose stormed past.

Ash dealt with the few who were cognizant enough to come for him from behind with his elbows and feet.

Three or four of the Sleepers fired guns, but for the

most part quarters were too cramped for gunplay. Shots went wide, firing limbs deflected when the table struck them. One bullet clipped the corner, causing the metal beneath cheap wood to flower at the edge.

Seconds later Ash and Daisy were down the final hallway. Ash turned and threw the table like a frisbee at the Sleepers who'd managed to round the corner behind them. Then he wrenched the door open and they both stormed through.

The rear parking lot beyond was mostly clear. Sleepers still in the lot saw them and rushed forward as the SUV's lights illuminated their flight.

If Emily's car had been a key-start instead of a push-button activated by a fob, he and Daisy might not have gotten away. Even then it was a near thing: Ash had to hold his door halfway closed, driving left-handed, because a pair of Sleepers were clinging hard enough to keep it from latching.

Even driving at twenty miles per hour, the on-hangers kept trying to yank it open from the outside.

They finally shook loose. Ash ran over them both (legs for one, head for the other) as he peeled away.

Daisy leaned back, relieved. Ash looked into the rearview and saw just how many Sleepers there had been: maybe a hundred dazed killers, silhouetted by the city lights far behind them.

Now that they were clear, his pulse finally began to rise.

Not because Ash was afraid for himself ... but because they had left Mina behind, choked in the middle of that murderous mob.

THIRTY-THREE

Bad and Worse

Mina waited fifteen minutes after the last of the sounds ended before trying to extricate herself from the closet. Any sooner than that and she might break out of one bad situation just to enter another.

There had been gunshots. Door-breaking, shouting, tire-squealing, and howls of pain. She'd been furious when Ash shoved her in here and locked the door, but now it was clear that he'd done her a life-saving favor.

What exactly had happened? Had there been more deaths? There'd already been one she knew of: poor Bryan, left in the dumpster. Had *anyone* survived?

Through it all, she'd at least taken comfort that no matter what, she had her phone in her pocket as a lifeline. Turned out there was no reason for comfort; the thing was useless. Service at the upstate lab had always been spotty, but inside the closet it was nonexistent. She'd put the phone in Low Battery Mode earlier when it reached critical levels, but now she considered shutting it off entirely.

Before the chaos, saving the last of her battery had felt smart. Now it felt essential. If she could get out of the closet, she could always use the lab's landline ... but whatever happened tonight had sounded like an armed invasion. Once she saw what was out there, she might not want to stick around. She might want to run like hell — and how important would her last few percent be *then*?

She checked the time and was just about to power the phone off when a silenced notification caught her eye:

21:00: DISCO DANCE PARTY.

Mina wasn't much of a dancer. And not at all into disco. Even if she was, why would she need to set herself a reminder? This wasn't an invitation. It was from her Notes app. And why was it in military time?

Despite her situation, Mina laughed a little. Some smartass — probably one of her own grad students — had gotten hold of her phone and added it as a joke. A weird way of saying, *Loosen up, Mina.*

She was still staring at the bright, battery-sucking screen fifteen seconds later. Despite knowing better, she still hadn't shut the phone down because a new problem had occurred to her, and it was the Ghostbusters problem: *Who ya gonna call, Mina?* She didn't want to call 911 once she got out of here; with NSA fears on her mind, that was a last resort. So who, then? *Ash?* If he was still alive — and had been in the car she heard driving away — then Ash was the logical choice. But she didn't know his number. If her phone died, she couldn't even call him from a landline without access to her contacts.

She had to look up his phone number now and write it down for later — just in case.

She surveyed her tiny surroundings, using precious screen light to do it. The closet, which was more *linen* than *office supply*, contained no pens or paper.

And so, with no immediate solution to her problem, Mina went back to staring at the dance party reminder for unknown reasons. An off-white rectangle on her lock screen kept insisting it was time to disco, and she found herself inexplicably unable to ignore it.

The screen dimmed on its own. She was again in near-perfect darkness.

Focus. You need to find a way to memorize Ash's number. If you can't write it down, you need to use your head. You need to put those digits in your memory, and somehow make them stay there.

She thought of Emily Sanders. Of how Ash had recently remembered a unique bit of trivia: Emily had been into memory games. Although, was it really *that* unique? She had thought so at the time, but now Mina found another bit of her own buried mind returning: she knew a thing or two about memory games, too.

It was weird, but the more Mina thought on it, the more she knew it was true. Why the hell had she learned such a pointless skill? Had she carved out time in her already-too-packed academic schedule for self-study, or had someone taught her?

Mina blinked in the darkness and found some of those previously unknown skills returning.

There was a trick to remembering numbers, she recalled. You were supposed to turn each of the ten digits into consonant sounds, then string those sounds together to make words. One of the digits was tied to the sound *T* or *D*, for instance, and another to *M*. Vowel sounds didn't count. So a two-digit number that started with the *T* digit and ended with the *M* digit might form the words *TOM* or *TIM* or *TAME*. Any of them was okay. You'd then employ the kind of visualization Ash had mentioned when he'd told her about the memory palace technique: Imagine the thing you want to remember in a strange place or doing something unusual. In this case, you might imagine your friend Tom in some strange circumstance as a way to remember the number that "Tom" represented.

Mina frowned. She didn't just *know* this. She knew it *well*. She knew every one of the consonant/number pairs; she even knew they were called "the phonetic alphabet."

Weird. She woke the phone again, preparing to unlock it and find out if she could use any of this to commit the number to memory. But she stared at the lock screen instead. At the reminder for the disco dance party she was currently missing.

Hey. Dummy. You need to hurry. You need to get the number, then shut that phone down before it dies.

But Mina *couldn't* hurry. *Couldn't* shut the phone down. An unknown thing was rattling around inside her head, its presence magnified by sensory deprivation.

Ash. His wife. Their memory games.

In her mind Mina saw hands — not her own — unlock her phone and program that reminder into it. Her memory's point-of-view was side-on; she'd watched someone else type it for Mina, for later.

Disco dance party? Mina had asked.

It's a precaution, said the person entering the reminder, *in case you don't remember on your own.*

The phone powered down in her hands.

"Fuck," Mina told the closet. Forget about retrieving Ash's number now.

She looked at her wrist. She still wore her Mickey Mouse watch, and its hands still fluoresced enough to read in the dark. She was getting later and later for the joke of the disco dance party, and something about it really bothered her.

But what? She scratched at new memories ... of learning the phonetic alphabet, of who'd typed that reminder into her phone, of why. But there was nothing.

Her mind went to Bryan. She hadn't just seen him dead. After opening the dumpster, another thing she'd discovered was exactly who'd killed him.

It was Daisy.

Bryan's body had been strangely dressed. His shoe, which had kept the lid from closing all the way, was ordinary. So were his blue jeans, belt, and neatly tucked oxford shirt. Only his neckwear had struck Mina as strange. She'd never known Bryan to wear Lululemon, and yet there he'd been: dead with a Lulu hoodie wrapped around his neck. He'd been strangled with the thing. It'd been size XS or smaller — far too small for Mina, but perfect for a small woman with a little torso and tiny shoulders.

You don't know that Daisy killed him. Even if you were sure it was Daisy's sweatshirt, which you're not, anyone could have choked him with it.

But that wasn't true. Mina *did* know. After seeing the body, she clearly remembered hearing some unknown person's doubts about Daisy — probably the same person who showed her the Blip and maybe the same person who taught her how to memorize numbers.

She'd be the perfect Sleeper. If they suspect me at all, they'll turn Daisy for sure.

Mina had heard Ash's exit from the building. She'd told herself she wasn't sure what'd happened out there, but she knew at least part of it. Ash had been shouting to the only other ally he'd thought he had.

To Daisy, who'd started the shooting. Daisy, who despite her name wasn't the delicate flower Mina apparently was, and hadn't needed to be hidden in a closet.

They'd left together. Mina was sure of it.

Ash didn't know what Daisy had done. The shots had begun after Mina told Ash that Bryan was dead but before she could tell him who'd done it. And that wasn't even the worst of it.

Mina's resurfacing memory was filling out by the second, and now she could remember the rest of what that shadow person had told her regarding Sleepers. Regarding Daisy, if they turned her into one.

The Tailors started with what we did and took it further. Now they're trying something new. They think they can develop a new kind of Sleeper that's not all or nothing. They call it "fractional activation." They'll be able to click Daisy on and off like a light switch. Off, she's herself. On, she's whatever they need her to be. Then off again … and when *she's off, even Daisy won't know what she's done.*

Was that why Mina had been shown the Blip? Why she'd been brought into this at all? It was starting to feel that way. One group had developed some terrible things, but then another group had taken over and planned to make those things even worse.

Mina didn't know what was worse than brainwashing, but she was starting to know something else: The second group — "Tailors," apparently — had crossed a line. Bad was bad, but worse was unforgivable and had to be stopped by any means necessary.

Panicking now, Mina began slamming her shoulder into the closet door. If the bad guys were still out there, so be it. She couldn't just sit here.

It was terrifying to feel the certainty that something was going horribly wrong … and she had no idea what it might be.

They'll learn where it's hidden, that other person had told Mina. *By the time you remember any of this, it'll only be a matter of time before they figure out what's there.*

Mina had only pieces of the puzzle, but for now that was the least of her worries.

They'll turn Daisy if she's the only one who can get it out of him. Don't let her get it from him, Mina.

She understood enough.

Daisy had come here for Ash … and now she had him alone.

THIRTY-FOUR

Higher Purposes

Mike O'Brien racked his weapon, but Natalie put a hand on his arm and said, "Not yet."

Mike looked over. She was in the driver's seat as usual, and to Mike the arrangement always felt somehow punitive: like he wasn't *allowed* to drive due to his immaturity — like he always drove too fast or did other things wrong.

The only respite from their usual state of affairs (Natalie breaking balls; Mike with his balls getting broken) came when they were in bed together — or against an alley wall together, or being cheered on by a crowd of horny bikers together. Because Natalie liked a break from being the boss sometimes, Mike was allowed to be as sexually bossy as he wanted. Although all the demeaning things Mike did to Natalie were still her idea. She told him *exactly* how to tell her what to do.

Was it really winning if even her break-time masochism was a form of control?

Pull my hair. Punch me. Make me bleed. Bitch. What if he didn't *want* to be an asshole? What if he wanted to be nice sometimes? Luckily the question hadn't come up. At least so far, Mike hated her exactly as much as she wanted him to.

Sometimes he wondered if theirs was a healthy relationship. He'd probably have read up on it if he didn't loathe himself so much.

"We don't need the Sleeper anymore. Let me kill her, at least," Mike told Natalie now. His hand was still on his weapon.

Her silent response managed to convey both exasperation and disappointment until she finally spoke.

"What's the goal, Mike?"

"To get Ash Sanders."

"What's the *real* goal, Mike?"

Mike considered the answer as Natalie drove away from the motel where Sanders (who apparently wasn't the *real* goal after all) believed he was hiding unseen with Daisy. Sanders, Mike felt, was disappointing. He'd been the Agency's best man, and yet he'd chosen to conceal himself at a roadside dump. In the 1980s, this was where the sax would come up and the two fugitives, exhausted and barely having escaped, would start getting it on with clothes-ripping abandon. It was trashy. And obvious. Maybe Sanders should get a pass because he still didn't have all his memories: he didn't *know* how stupid and obvious it was to hide where he'd hidden. Or maybe he shouldn't get a pass at all. All Mike knew was that he wanted *something* dead tonight. Exercising the restraint Natalie insisted on was giving him blueballs.

Natalie pulled onto the highway. Apparently they were heading back to the compound — or perhaps to a trashy roadside motel for passionless stress-relief with a 1980s sax in the background.

"What's your problem?" Mike asked.

"What's *your* problem, Mike? Sometimes I wonder if I made a mistake saving you from the Agency purge."

"You didn't save me."

Natalie smirked as if deciding not to state the obvious: that she very much *had* saved him. Mike found the smirk hot on her. She was old by a young man's standards but had the body of an athlete half her age. Mike was addicted to debasing her. Even her patronizing got him hard.

"I didn't want this clusterfuck any more than you did," she told him. Mike tried not to laugh; clusterfucks were awesome. "And I like Quince believing he was right even less than you do."

Now it was Mike who decided not to state the obvious: Richard Quince *had been* right. There was no matter-of-opinion there.

"Maybe we should have given the Sleepers at the lab guns," Natalie went on, talking somewhat to herself. "Maybe that was the right move. Maybe if they'd had guns, Sanders wouldn't have gotten out of the building and everything would've been a lot easier to contain. Until we could deploy Protocol, I was worried a group of 1.0 Sleepers that big might kill him. But don't you get it, Mike? Killing is the wrong choice — for *any* of them. This is a delicate situation. Killing is *last* thing we want right now."

Mike said nothing. Was she seriously saying there was a time for *not killing*?

"The little Chinese girl's proving that fractional activation is possible. She's basically proving Protocol can work, at least in beta. And that right there is the *second* reason we should let this play out, Mike. Daisy's metrics suggest she's not fully activated. I think she went right back to her base state after killing the scientist and throwing him in the dumpster. Maybe lifting the body was too much exertion for her. Maybe it snapped her out of it. She probably thinks she's legitimately helping Sanders right now."

"But if you ever want to use Protocol on anyone else …"

"Of course. But we can't ret-con the Protocol blueprint from Daisy's install, and we're not going to find the original blueprint without Sanders."

"That's plan A, anyway," Mike said.

"No." Natalie looked over like he was an idiot. "That's the *only* plan."

"But couldn't Protocol eventually be written from scratch? Like, just … rediscover it, like it was discovered the first time?"

Natalie scoffed. She'd tried to have protocol "rediscovered." It wasn't that simple. Protocol was an elegant work of neurological and psychological art, but the single Protocol-knockoff she'd attempted had turned out to be more like a battering ram. Could her brute-force version do some interesting dream work? Sure. Was it also likely to fry the brains of anyone connected to it? Definitely.

"No, Mike. It can't just be rewritten."

"Why not? It was written the first time."

Natalie didn't feel like explaining. Protocol's origin was beyond proprietary. A one-in-a-million moonshot, not something to simply be 'done over' without Sanders. "We need him. *Alive*. How stupid are you?"

"I wasn't actually planning to kill him," Mike sulked.

"Just beat the shit out of him, huh? Just let him know we're right behind him? Just let Sanders know that *everything he does is being watched*? His top is almost popped, you know. If we do finish the job, we'll find out where the Protocol blueprint is … and *then* you can do whatever you want with him. But we have to be smart until that happens.

Right now, nothing's more important than sweet dreams for Sanders."

"I know."

She gave him another of those hot mothering looks: one that meant she was about to condescend to him again.

"Then you know how important it is that we leave it alone. Quince got his way, and maybe it's good that he did. We can't risk scanning Ash actively anymore. But I think that's okay. I think he'll talk to Daisy. She's been coached, so she'll know what to tell him. Sooner or later Sanders is going to figure out what's in his head — and when *he* finds out, *we* find out. His defenses won't matter if he says it out loud."

They were quiet for a while. Mike found himself pondering. Was there seriously nobody he could hurt tonight?

"Doesn't it piss you off?" he finally asked.

"What?"

"Quince. You said no to him, but he did it anyway."

Apparently Mike's strategy, in the absence of someone external to hurt, was to injure Natalie emotionally. Quince had wanted to send in Daisy, who'd been conditioned with the Protocol beta before Protocol's blueprint was stolen. Natalie had wanted to ambush Sanders with Sleepers. So Mike was just poking the bear.

"I mean, were your orders *optional*?" Mike continued. "How does it *feel*, to have a piece of shit underling like Quince lie to your face and do exactly the opposite of what you ordered him to—?"

"Shut the fuck up, Mike!" Natalie knew exactly what he was doing.

But then she answered his question anyway.

"Yes. It bothers me. But Quince is a dead man walking. Even the general knows it. I just want to find Protocol before we kill him. Whatever gets Protocol back is fine with me."

"And what if Protocol turns out to be bullshit?"

"It's not bullshit in Daisy. She's able to go in and out of Sleeper mode, and that means she's not pretending. She actually believes she's on his side when she's inactive. You don't see the benefit of something like that?"

"Sure, but—"

"And keep in mind Daisy's only got the beta. It was almost finalized the last time anyone saw it. The things they said the new algorithm would be able to do …"

"You seriously think it's possible to *enter people's dreams*?"

Natalie nodded. "It's all just math. Supposedly programming Sleepers is just like programming a computer, tracking neurons instead of bits and bytes. One of the subjects from Sanders's team in Morocco was the target's *son*. Six years old, and they got him to stick a needle through the Councilor's eye after conditioning him with … what? A half-dozen dreams? And they did it through two solid feet of stone? So yeah, it's absolutely possible; the question is maximizing resolution and minimizing lag. That's just about crunching bigger and bigger numbers, which the right algorithm should be able to manage. Do that with two dreaming subjects — feeding high-resolution dream data back and forth in real time — and you basically put both people in the same place. That's all it means to 'enter a dream.' Just like *Dreamscape*."

"What's *Dreamscape*?" Mike asked.

Natalie sighed as if to say, *Fucking kids today.* "Fine. *Inception*."

"What if Sanders doesn't know where Protocol is?"

"He does. He *has* to know it, whether he *knows* he knows it or not."

"You said that about Alexi."

"Alexi was unfortunate. I really thought Alexi had it. Still his own goddamn fault he had to be retired."

Mike looked over, wondering what that meant.

"Oh, come on. The *Magic Mirror*? An Agent *that* seasoned, and a fucking trick mirror convinced him he was dreaming? I don't care how many reality checks we faked; his mind should have known the difference. I wanted to keep Alexi, but in the end he thought he could fly off the rooftop like a goddamn amateur. I guess he wasn't as good as they said he was."

Well, that was one way to hide your department's human housekeeping: by making executions look like suicides. Another was to make it look like the subject's husband did it. Accidents and scapegoats were so much easier to explain than murder.

Mike looked at his hands, and not just to see if he was dreaming. Mike was born for this kind of work. For one, he didn't have fingerprints, which was why none were found after he was in Sanders's home the first time. Daddy had burned them off when little Mikey spilled his beer and got punished with twenty seconds spent having his hands splayed on a red-hot griddle.

Mike flexed his anonymous hands, remembering the feeling of life ending between them.

He'd get to do it again, before the night was over.

THIRTY-FIVE

Spy vs. Spy

Ash put the motel phone down, shaking his head. His call to Mina had gone straight to voicemail … again.

Daisy looked over, her face full of judgment.

"You know what a bad idea that is, right? You remember enough about who you're dealing with by now to not use a phone?"

Ash shrugged. His guilt at leaving Mina was a dagger in his chest and he didn't need a lecture.

"Is it as bad an idea as stopping at a motel five miles down the road from where they came at us last time?"

"Insider information." Daisy tapped her head. "For now, I know how the people chasing us think better than you do. Nobody would expect us to be here, knowing what we know about them. Besides, I want Mina back, too. If we stay close, we can keep watch and move back in when the way is clear."

She looked at the beds, then Ash. The place wasn't as disgusting as it had every right to be. "You need sleep."

"I slept last night. Mina didn't."

"Don't feel guilty. Try to remember that you're the target, not her."

"That doesn't mean she's not in danger."

"Okay. Then here's a question: If we get caught trying to rescue her, will she be in *less* danger? Or more?"

Ash looked away.

"We'll go back for her," Daisy said.

They'd actually already tried. A few times. The mass of Sleepers surrounding the lab had broken up, but a few were still in the area, patrolling the streets. They'd need a different car if they wanted to get anywhere near the place without being obvious, and even that was a massive risk.

"What do they want from me, Daisy?"

"I don't know, but I do know they want you alive."

"What makes you so sure?"

"Because they went to the effort to erase you and give you 'Chuck' as a babysitter."

"That was before I figured out what was going on," Ash said.

"Yes, but you said Jose tried to strap you down with a zip-tie. He came up behind you. Had the best bead on you in the world. Wouldn't it have been a lot easier to shoot you than to detain you?" Again she nodded toward the beds. "I'm serious. You need sleep. This is fucked up. We both need your wits to—"

"What about you?"

"I need sleep, too, but someone should stand guard. It's okay. My brain wasn't blown today. It must be hard, remembering everything."

That was an understatement. It felt like running a marathon.

Ash moved to one of the beds and sat on it. Daisy sat opposite him.

"Ash. I need to know. Why did you run off with

Mina?"

"I guess because other than Chuck, she was the only one I thought might believe me."

"That's not what I was asking. I don't mean it like you were looking for a shoulder to cry on. You might not remember, but you're a lot more analytical than that." She shifted on the bed. "I was watching your LoJack signal for a while before I caught up with you. You were at a building on the college campus when I turned it on. That was Mina's other lab, right? You didn't go to wherever you had your regular appointments."

"She wouldn't have been there. She was at the lab, so I went to the lab."

"My point is, you went out of your way to find her. Her *specifically*. I'm not sure I believe it's just because you thought she'd believe your crazy story, or because she was some garden variety therapist. There had to be another reason. Is it because she's a sleep scientist? Was she treating you for your dreams?"

"I've been thinking about that," Ash said.

"Thinking about what?"

"These people ..." He paused, only now remembering that as much as they'd discussed the Agency and dream work, his own dream-stealing hadn't come up. "Well, you know how you said the Agency used to manipulate people's dreams?"

"Yeah?"

"They were *watching* mine." He told her the short version: Tailors she'd already identified as Natalie Baynes and Mike O'Brien posing as internet techs, planting a Chirp in his home to spy on him. "Do you know what 'Ark-Tek' is?"

"It's a cover the Agency used. They sent ArkTek vans out on dream surveillance."

Ash bobbed his head. That fit.

"Jose called someone when they had me at gunpoint. I think it was Baynes. Chuck told her I might be 'breached.' 'Breached,' as in 'leaking.' It sounded like they were worried that whatever they did to erase me was coming apart. That makes sense, right? Because my erasure *is* coming apart. Little by little I'm remembering everything."

Daisy seemed to consider. There was no question his erasure had broken, but because he'd never mentioned his thoughts on Emily's "sunshine" trigger to her, Daisy had needed to guess *why* it'd broken. She couldn't buy that training made him immune. The people who did this knew he'd been trained, and would have surely accounted for it.

"What?" Daisy asked, reading his face. "Did you realize something else? Something that might give us some answers?"

Despite everything, Ash's gut told him to keep Emily's trigger to himself. He heard the memory of her voice in his ear: *Sunshine makes everything better.*

Come to think of it, Ash had said that exact phrase in one of his Mina sessions just before the trouble began. Before the *breach* began. If he hadn't thought he'd heard Emily whisper it one morning weeks ago, he'd probably never have thought about it again. Pain made him want to forget all things Emily. Despite that, he'd seemed to hear her in a half-dream that morning ... and Mina, being the therapist asshole she was, had forced him to confront it.

Was Ash's speaking those words aloud the beginning of all of this? Before she died, had Emily somehow planted a trigger in Ash just like someone had planted a trigger in Chuck ... and had his own repeating of the phrase set it off?

Daisy's original question throbbed like a neon sign: Why *was* his first instinct to go to Mina?

And the answer: *Because Mina understood dreams.*

Daisy said there'd been an upset at the Agency. Some sort of a coup, it sounded like. She'd also said that he and Emily, both of them Agents, were the reason for all of this. And Ash had wondered, earlier with Mina, why his dreams were so important to the watchers.

Mashing all of it together now was connecting some dots for Ash. Dreams were doorways to the subconscious. Ash had been erased, and that meant his memories were *hidden* in that subconscious ... where only dreams could reach them.

Mina's voice: *What if they're using dreams as a way to access something you've forgotten? Some memory that's been blocked ... but that your dreams might be able to find?*

Dreams as tools. The sunshine trigger. This was all starting to look like a game of Spy vs. Spy between the Tailors and Emily — with his unknown secret as the prize.

"What's in your dreams, Ash?" Daisy asked. "What do you dream of these days?"

Afghanistan. Mostly the bombing that I'm starting to think didn't actually happen ... but still always Afghanistan.

Then, after Ash's internal voice was finished, another voice spoke. This one was strong, insistent, and feminine:

Yes. You dream of Afghanistan. But Ash? Keep it to yourself for now.

"Emily," he answered. "More than anything, I dream of Emily."

Daisy seemed disappointed. But then she looked up. "Emily told me that if anything happened and whatever they did to you started falling apart, there was something else I should tell you about. One more thing I'm supposed to remind you to try."

"What's that?" Ash asked.

"An acronym," she said. "Do you remember MILD?"

THIRTY-SIX

Orders

Richard Quince stared at his orders. They were onscreen in black and white, and still he didn't understand.

The Agency had liked to use VPN-masked IP addresses, disguised in various non-IP-seeming ways, to convey its orders. The Bespokery — unoriginal parasite that it was — tended to do things the same way. And so earlier in the day, Richard had been slipped what looked like a phone number by a man he'd passed on the street. If Richard dropped the first digit of that phone number and added periods at the appropriate places within the remaining nine digits, he'd have the IP address he needed. All he had to do was add *https://* before it and type the prefix into any web browser, and he'd end up where his orders would be.

There was security, of course: a password based on an easily findable but changing metric: the day's temperature high combined with the fourth "Down" answer on the day's *New York Times* crossword puzzle, perhaps. That part had been easy, and as such Richard had received his orders lickety-split.

That was the moment he'd started wishing things *hadn't* gone lickety-split. He'd felt so much better before reading what the brass wanted him to do.

Richard stared at the screen. He then began committing the orders to memory, forbidden by procedure to write them down. The page he'd visited would last for 120 seconds once accessed, and after that it would self-delete.

He really needed to start memorizing. The orders had punched him in the face a bit too hard, so he'd gone blank for a while. He had thirty seconds left at most. The general behind those orders wasn't fond of repeating himself when field idiots failed to commit them in time.

A single line of text read: *SEED 55 AND MONITOR. SCRATCH 401, 302, 11. NO PINGBACK. 0222+3.*

The code wasn't difficult. There were only so many persons-of-interest on Richard's docket, and he'd memorized their identifier numbers long ago. The command words in the message were simple and clear. There was, unfortunately, no ambiguity here.

SEED 55 AND MONITOR meant that Richard was supposed to begin dream surveillance (usually just installation of a Chirp) on person-of-interest number 55: a local city councilwoman. The councilwoman in question had been stonewalling on re-appropriation of land that one of the defense contractors needed, and the Bespokery's intent was to change her mind. Once enough baseline data for the Wurtzman algorithm had been gathered, the orders (for someone else, not Richard) would change from SEED to INIT: from passive to active influence.

The end of the message was similarly clear: *NO PING-BACK. 0222+3.* That just meant Richard shouldn't reply to the message ("no pingback" was standard) and should watch for his next orders at 2:22 a.m. three days from now.

The lack of trailing GPS coordinates meant those orders would be delivered to him in the usual place.

It was the middle instruction *(SCRATCH 401, 302, 11)* that Richard didn't understand. Or, more correctly, that was the part he refused to believe.

SCRATCH was Bespokery code for "kill," which Richard had made clear he would longer do. He'd paid his dues as a trigger man, at the time morally bound to execute only enemies of the state or people he could somehow *justify* as enemies of the state even though there were, technically speaking, multiple sides to every story.

Richard was long past the obligation to murder people and the government damn well knew it. He'd been adjunct to the Agency for *fifteen years* now. That was an eternity for a career like this. He'd earned his seniority, dammit, and the tenure came with a right to choose his targets — or to choose no targets at all. A man could only stop so many beating hearts before he could no longer see himself in the mirror.

That's how seniority *used* to work, anyway. The old Agency had respected such things. Baynes and the Bespokery? Not so much.

Richard's final assassination assignment, years ago, had been POI 992: a nuclear smuggler who'd seemed by all rights to have it coming. Unfortunately for Richard, the smuggler's four-year-old son had walked into the room just as Richard was finishing the guy off. The Intel department had somehow missed the kid, assuming the smuggler would be alone. After Richard secured the room and reported the error, Intel had helpfully offered new orders: *Kill any witnesses.*

Or in other words, *Kill the kid.*

The idea was profane, and pointless. The kid had been

so traumatized and frightened in seeing his father's murder that he couldn't have identified Richard's species.

Richard had briefly — incredibly, *incredibly* briefly — considered doing as he'd been told, but every time he blinked between that consideration and his eventual decision, his own son, Connor, appeared in the darkness behind his eyelids.

Connor, just like the smuggler's son, had recently turned four. Were the smuggler and Richard really so different? Were their *children* so different? One day, an assassin might come for Richard. That assassin might find the same intel mistake, the same loose end.

That was the only time Richard outright refused an order. Instead of doing as the general wanted, he simply ran away. He slipped back into his vehicle a half-mile down the street, then spent ten minutes freaking out in plain sight. He couldn't drive for those first ten minutes. He could barely stop shaking.

Nothing had come of it, of course. The boy never said a thing about what happened to his father. Richard faced a harsh reprimand from the general, but that was all. At the time he'd been considered too valuable to lose.

The next day, Richard had marched into the general's office to play his seniority card. He told the general he was too old for active field assignments. He'd joined the Agency as a psychological manipulation specialist, then ended up in murder because assassination was like hazing for the department: it was just kind of what everyone did. Richard had never wanted anything to do with assassination. He was a friendly man when he wasn't ending lives — great at making friends. Instead of sending him out as an assassin, he told the general they should use him the way he'd been intended: for PsyOps.

It was dangerous, basically telling the general what to

do, but after the kid incident Richard had been beyond caring. He'd *rather* they killed him, if the alternative was to keep pulling triggers.

The general had green-lit a transfer, and Richard had retired from assassinations for good.

Except that "for good" turned out to mean "only until the Bespokery overthrew the Agency." When Baynes took over, she hadn't respected any of the old agreements. Richard's agreement with the general was no exception. The general, for his part, didn't stand up to Baynes. He never really had. Secretly Richard wondered if she had leverage on him.

Before the Bespokery, there was honor among thieves.

Richard hadn't worked with Ash, Emily, and the other Agents directly, but he'd known their reputations. They did necessary (even honorable) work: the kind Richard felt lived on the justifiable side of good and evil. Once the Wurtzman Conjecture made dreamtech possible, Richard gained new visibility as part of the psychological team, and *still* he found the Agents' work more necessary than treacherous at first. They did brainwash people, sure, and *that* was probably uncool … but of the people they ended up killing (directly or through Sleepers), Richard still felt those folks threatened too many lives to keep on living.

The day that Ash Sanders thought he and Richard (as Chuck) had witnessed an IED bombing, their ArkTek van was actually parked fifty meters from a Kandahar hookah bar patronized by a nasty terrorist cell. One of their number suffered an extremely vivid nightmare thanks to that van. Convinced post-nightmare that the world was ending, the terrorist had triggered his cache of explosives early just like the Agency wanted him to.

There'd been heavy collateral damage after that one, which was unfortunate. An old woman lost a leg when shrapnel ripped through the bar's wall and into her home. But overall, the balance still remained fair enough for Richard to sleep through the night … at least for the time being. Now that he was a ninja at rationalization.

Post Blip and Chirp, there'd been a slow, department-wide creep toward assignments that were both messier and in more of a moral gray area. At first one civilian casualty per mission was acceptable, so long as they got the bad guys. Then a fatality was okay. Then *two* fatalities. Meanwhile, the focus of the Agency's work shifted to more ambiguous targets. Instead of killers and terrorists, they started going after people with unpopular opinions — people who weren't *bad* so much as *in someone's way.*

Richard rarely left HQ in those days. His job was profiling and dream design, but still he heard stories of grumbling agents not long after the change. They, like Richard, had noticed the shift from work that let them sleep at night to work that kept them awake. He supposed it was ironic, for dream specialists.

Still, though, things might have been okay … until work on the Protocol algorithm got going.

Protocol promised to change everything. Pre-Protocol Sleepers were like rockets once triggered: the Agency could launch them, but what happened afterward was fingers-crossed. Protocol would allow the Agency to turn Sleepers on and off at will. That single change opened the door for long-term manipulation campaigns — personalized propaganda, in other words.

The subtlety of it was, in Richard's mind, a slippery slope.

The old way of doing things — even with 1.0 dreamtech — required killing the targets. Protocol assignments, once Protocol was ready for prime time, would be different, more about influence. Removing a lot of the murder made Protocol easier to sell to the higher-ups, but that wasn't a good thing. Whereas previous Agency assignments were tightly controlled and overseen, the same wouldn't be true of Protocol assignments. Why bother micromanaging, if nobody had to die?

It meant there'd be no restraint once Protocol was ready — not from the generals, and not from the upstart who'd come out of nowhere to advocate it: one Natalie Baynes. Those who saw Protocol's potential for personal gain salivated and sucked up to Baynes right away. Forget moderation; Protocol was everyone's chance to change everyone else's minds over to their way of thinking.

Protocol could make liberal senators more conservative or turn conservative judges liberal. The EPA was a real pain in the ass for big business these days, but Protocol could change that. Protocol could pull any string it wanted: make gas prices rise and wages fall, or shoo the bleeding hearts from Big Tobacco's back and get kids smoking again like they did in the cool old days.

But even *that* was only the beginning of Protocol's promise. Soon, said the dev team, it would allow Agents to enter their targets' dreams: the ultimate form of brain-washing.

Forget about *influence*. Dream-entry would herald the beginning of *control*.

It was the final straw for the Agents. They hadn't liked dreamtech's slow creep, they hadn't liked Protocol, and they definitely hadn't liked Baynes and her bullheaded ambition. Not that the Agents' dissatisfaction came as a surprise to the government. The brass knew they had an Agent problem waiting to happen, and so a brief period of tense stand-off began with both parties unwilling to flinch: Agents versus government, eye-to-eye in a cold war.

When the overthrow came, it came from both sides at

once: the government fucking the Agency while the Agency, prepared but not prepared enough, fucked them right back.

It took a long time for the chips to fall. The Agents disappeared at first, then reappeared in civilian lives with their memories erased weeks later. Their reappearance shocked everyone: why hadn't Ash and the others been killed?

It took some sleuthing for Richard to learn the answer: before the government closed in on the Agents, they'd somehow stolen every copy of Protocol. To this day — even without their memories — those smart-ass mother-fuckers *still* held it hostage.

There'd been a no-win arms race between the government and its former employees ever since. This despite the erased Agents not having the slightest clue anymore that it was happening.

To fill the power vacuum — and with a promise to recover Protocol — Baynes had established the Bespokery in the Agency's place. It was a fitting name. The so-called "Tailors" who worked there (forced to use old dreamtech until Protocol was found) didn't poke the world so much as custom-fit it to the government's preference.

These days Natalie Baynes had the big office, the Agents were gone, and Richard Quince was apparently back in the murder business.

401.

302.

11.

Person-of-interest 401 — the first of Richard's three targets — was DeShawn Jackson. Richard didn't want to kill anyone, but if someone had to die, he didn't mind it being DeShawn. An ordinary asshole, not any sort of government. DeShawn hadn't known Richard was a plant

— only that he was being paid to pretend Ash had worked there forever. As a boss, Richard found DeShawn lacking. He liked to fondle his female employees while they were machining metal, knowing how dangerous it would be if they moved their hands to stop him. He called Richard "Chucky" and made allusions to his round, redhead's face as being like a certain murderous doll's. DeShawn's favorite restaurant was also Applebee's. And *fuck* Applebee's.

302 wasn't terrible either, as far as murder went. It was Linda Solara, who worked at the shop with Chuck, Ash, and DeShawn. Richard didn't know why she was a target while none of the other shop workers seemed to be, but he didn't particularly care. Linda regularly pissed in the break room coffee pot because she thought it was funny. She also liked to break into lockers and steal things. That might be the reason she was on the chopping block, actually: maybe she'd broken into Ash's, locker — or Richard's, or DeShawn's — and found something that raised eyebrows.

He could deal with killing DeShawn and Linda if he had to, but Richard drew the line at his last target.

Number eleven was Charity Goddard: a small, round woman with a broad smile and a newborn eternally slung across her chest in one of those Baby Bjorn things Richard's own son had wanted nothing to do with. Unlike Connor, Charity's kid fell asleep in his baby hammock and stayed that way for the entire day while Cathy worked at her desk in the shop office. She just went around all day with baby in tow, helping wherever her aid might be needed.

There was no person in the world less deserving of an unkind word — let alone a bullet — than Charity Goddard. So why had she been targeted?

The room seemed to darken as Richard realized the

reason: *Baynes*. This was Baynes punishing him for going over her head and sending Daisy after Ash.

But what was he supposed to do? Her plan was to send hordes of Sleepers after Ash instead, and God knew what kind of attention they'd draw or what damage they'd do. Sending Daisy was far more elegant even if Baynes didn't want her sent.

Daisy was the only Sleeper still around who'd been trained with Protocol's beta, meaning she could be activated and then deactivated again. Ash was smart, and would get a whole lot smarter as his old memories returned. He'd see through any double-agent they sent his way, or any ordinary Sleeper. *Daisy*, however, could be turned off on arrival. She'd come to Ash as her usual self, leaving Ash nothing to see through in the first place.

They could turn Daisy on beforehand (to make sure the lab was empty of all but Ash and Mina) and after (to deal with Ash once they were alone), but during primetime, she'd be the same Daisy Ash remembered … and trusted.

Even Baynes had to admit Richard had been right by now … but still he'd embarrassed her, and that wasn't the kind of thing a woman like Natalie Baynes could let stand.

SCRATCH 11 … and meanwhile fuck you and your disrespect, the order seemed to say. *You think you can disobey me? Fine. Now Snow White dies, and you get to kill her.*

Richard stewed, trying to think his way either out of or around this.

Could he just ignore her again? No, Baynes would catch and torture Cathy if he refused to kill her quickly.

He had no options.

But then Richard decided that maybe — if he was very clever — one outside-the-box option still remained.

THIRTY-SEVEN

Nine Digits

21:00.

Disco dance party.

In a way that was downright compulsive, Mina absolutely needed her phone to work again so she could check that reminder on her lock screen. The one she'd stared at in disbelief until the phone finally died in her hand.

Letting the phone run dry was an incredibly dumb thing to have done. Now Ash was with Daisy, and Daisy was a killer. Although Mina had broken out of the closet, she didn't even have enough juice to send him a text and warn him that his new best friend was bad news.

Contacting Ash was vital, and for that reason it struck Mina as impossibly strange that she didn't care *nearly* as much about contacting him as she cared about the Disco Dance Party reminder. In fact, if she'd had only enough battery left to see the reminder again *or* text Ash (but not both), she'd choose the stupid, nonsensical, who-the-hell-cares reminder.

Why?

She couldn't shake the feeling that it meant something. She had a lot of missing memories, and Ash had them, too. They'd been right about Emily's "sunshine" expression being a trigger; Mina had decided that much was true. It was a cue to help Ash's memories return, right? So what if the same was true of Mina?

"Sunshine makes everything better," she said aloud.

Nothing happened and no memories came back. But maybe that wasn't how it worked. Or maybe she was an idiot, seeing codes and tricks where there was only banality.

Chuck, with an embedded trigger that allowed Ash to commandeer him. Ash and Emily, playing memory games.

Everything lately was puzzle boxes. Everything lately had at least two meanings.

She went to the blinds. One of the room's overhead lights had been shattered in the melee and the other hadn't been turned on to start with. Invisible in the dark now, Mina crouched low. She peered through a slit between the blinds just above the sill.

The streetlights were back on, and she could see a silhouette standing beside a lamppost, looking like the poster for *The Exorcist*. Peering around the lot, she saw other figures as well. There were still Sleepers out there — not many, but a few for sure. They seemed to be watching, not waiting to attack again. Mina took it to mean that she'd been right; *Ash* was the target. They weren't watching Mina's position so much as keeping an eye out in case Ash returned.

It meant Mina was trapped. She could still call 911 on the lab's landline, but strong instinct told her that calling anyone other than Ash would be a terrible idea. He should still have his phone; she could call from the landline if she knew his number. The phones still worked (she'd checked), and might be bugged. She could probably speak artfully enough to keep any spies on the line confused while still letting Ash know what he needed to know.

But Mina *couldn't* call Ash from the landline because like every other modern person, she'd let her phone memorize his number for her. If only she was a world-class memory champion like Emily and Ash Sanders.

But she couldn't memorize numbers by turning them into words, then envision them with multi-sensory clarity the way mental athletes memorized thousands of digits into pi.

Mina stepped away from the window, wondering how she even knew those things. *Mental athletes? Memorizing pi?*

But she *did* know those things. Because someone had told her about them, just like someone had explained the Agency's dreamtech to her in detail.

Just like someone had let her take a picture of the Blip, then told her to hide the photo.

Just like someone had maybe programmed her with a memory trigger, same as Ash.

She knew who that someone was. She was sure of it. It was Emily Sanders.

Mina thought: *Pi's value is 3.14.*

She knew what to do with "3.14" to remember it, she realized. It was a trick Emily had taught her. She needed to use the phonic alphabet, which gave each single-digit number a different letter sound. That would turn the relatively meaningless sequence "3.14" into a word, which (unlike numbers) she'd be able to visualize ... and hence could remember a lot more easily.

I don't know how to do that, she thought.

Yes you do, she thought next.

She remembered that the first digit, *three*, was assigned the M sound. *One* was T or D. *Four* was R. If she put them together, she ended up with three sounds she could use to compose a word or phrase: M, then T or D, and then finally R. Inserting some vowels (which weren't assigned to any numbers), she turned M-T-R into the word *"meter."*

So she visualized a parking meter inside her mind. But that wasn't quite enough; her parking meter would only be memorable if she made it odd or exaggerated. So instead of imagining the meter at the side of a city street where parking meters belonged, Mina instead imagined it growing out of some poor kid's math book: *math*, because pi was a math term.

That was all it took to memorize numbers: making memorable mental images and linking them together. Now if Mina ever wanted to remember pi's first three digits, all she'd need would be to look at her mind's image.

Math would lead her to *meter. Meter*, in turn, was made up of three consonant sounds: M, T, and R in that order. MTR translated back to 314 ... and voila, pi was memorized forever.

Mina closed her eyes, feeling the memory more closely. She remembered Emily Sanders now, back when Emily had shown her everything.

Not bad, Mina, Emily's voice said inside her memory, *but everyone knows the first three digits of pi. See if you can memorize some more.*

That's when Mina realized she hadn't needed to *add* the meter/book image to her mental landscape because that exact image turned out to already be there.

What's more, she saw now that her mind insisted on seeing a dollop of sour cream perched atop the meter.

"**D**o**L**lo**P**," or D-L-P, of course translated to 1-5-9. Not

1-5-5-9. When consonants were doubled, it only counted as a single sound instead of two, Emily said.

That meant pi wasn't simply 3.14. It was 3.14159.

Fascinated, Mina's mental image pulled back. In her mind's eye, a sprocket-holed frame appeared around the image of book, parking meter, and sour cream.

When Mina had first constructed this image sequence under Emily's tutelage as an example, she'd apparently chosen "in film" as the next words in the sequence. *iN FiLM*, decoded using the phonic alphabet, was *2653*.

A *MeTeR*. With a *DoLloP* on it. The whole thing *iN FiLM*. That made pi's first digits 3.141592653.

She could go on if she wanted (the images continued), but she didn't bother now that she understood the point. Instead, encouraged by all this sudden recall, she turned her mind toward a much bigger question: *Why had Mina and Emily been meeting in private?*

It couldn't be about Ash. Ash had considered working with Mina before Emily died, but started only after the court forced him.

It doesn't matter why you met with Emily, Mina told herself. *Like it or not, you're part of this now. The Agency's work was in dreams, meaning Emily's work was in dreams. You're an expert in sleep and dreaming. That must be why she came to you. Can't worry about why. Not yet. You knew your stuff, and you were close to Ash, and that must have been enough for Emily. She must have given you the basics, right? Maybe you know them, Mina: Ash's name, rank … and phone number.*

Mina concentrated, but nothing came. She needed her phone. Scary memory skills or not, she required her contacts to recover the number.

She looked at her dead phone, then at the landline on the desk, and finally at the draped window. There was a CVS down the block that surely sold iPhone chargers.

Maybe she should risk trying to get there. It felt very important all over again.

Then something struck her like a brick.

Disco dance party. Programmed into her phone. She hadn't registered it consciously at the time, but Mina was now sure that her nine p.m. reminder about the party had gone off at least ten minutes before the hour.

What if *Emily* had programmed that reminder on Mina's phone? What if it wasn't really a reminder?

She scrambled for pen and paper. She then scribbled fast, double-checking her work until she was sure … of what, Mina didn't know.

DiSCo DaNCe PaRTy. Using the phonic alphabet, it translated to *107120941*.

Mina counted nine digits. Was it a truncated phone number? She wasn't sure, nor was she sure that was all there was to the code. The reminder had been set for 21:00. Not nine p.m., but 21:00. It had also gone off early, not actually triggered by the time. So maybe "21" was significant?

She tried 21107120941 first. In phone number format, that worked out to 2-110-712-0941.

Except that no phone number started with a two. You didn't even need to start them with a *one* these days.

So was it a country code?

Along those lines, might it be a non-US number?

Mina flipped it around, trying the number backwards. It looked more phone-like that way: 1-490-217-0112. She got excited, tried to call, and got bupkis. If the number (or, for that matter, "disco dance party") meant something, it must mean something else.

Thinking, Mina rolled her chair toward the desktop computer, no longer caring if its screen light gave her away or if her watchers knew she was searching the web. She couldn't just wait for Ash to come back for her. With Sleepers at the perimeter, she couldn't let him walk into a trap.

The solution had to be somewhere. What good was a code left for Mina if Mina couldn't figure it out?

The computer's screen powered on. Something strange happened: she found herself unable to look at the computer without imagining it covered in a huge fishing net. The picture had come to her like the math/meter with its sour cream on top: *just there* as if Mina had anchored that exact image for herself in the past.

Could she have left herself the *net-covered-computer* image on purpose? Was it part of this odd mental cascade?

The frown fell from her face.

The time in question was 21:00 — twenty-one hundred hours.

21 translated to *NeT*. (Or *NeD*, but that one didn't seem too likely. The only Ned she knew was Flanders.)

So instead of searching for phone numbers and exchanges, Mina entered the string of digits into Google just as it stood. She was increasingly certain as she did so that she was correct: Her mysterious nine-digit string had something to do with the *net*. With the *internet*.

The search results that came up were useless, though. Most were technical specs and serial numbers, all too numerous and random to be whatever she was after.

Frustrated, Mina did the most inane search possible, asking Google for the goddamn answer already: *What do numbers mean on the internet?*

The top search result made her sit back in her chair, agape.

"Oh, shit …"

Nine digits.

"Disco Dance Party" must represent an IP address — a

machine number used instead of *www.something* to access a
website.

Mina had left herself — or Emily had left her — an IP
address.

She was as sure of it as she was her own name.

THIRTY-EIGHT

Sweet Dreams

For Ash, hearing Daisy talk about dreaming was like discovering he could speak a language he'd never heard before. Despite remembering almost none of it at first, he was sure he could do what she described — or had once been able to.

"MILD," she told him, "stands for 'Mnemonic Induction of Lucid Dreams.' It's a technique involving what's called 'prospective memory.' Basically, you set an intention *now* (before going to sleep) to remember that you're dreaming *later:* after you're in a dream. Is any of this ringing a bell?"

"Sort of. It's like trying to recall a vacation I took when I was a kid. I have the feeling of it but not much else." Then he shrugged. "I guess I'm waiting for the punchline. Emily wanted you to tell me about *this*? About lucid dreaming?"

Daisy nodded. "I think the Bespokery is looking for a memory that's inside you somewhere, but that you can't consciously reach. A memory like that might be available through your dreams."

"You mean, I might *dream* about whatever-it-is even though I can't remember it?"

"Right."

This was the part Ash didn't get. "Okay. But why would I dream about some random piece of information? Doesn't watching my dreams and hoping the specific thing they want will *just kind of show up* strike you as a little needle-in-the-haystack?"

"That's just it," Daisy said. "I don't think it's random at all. Knowing Emily, the kind of memory we're talking about is something you'd've deliberately stored before you were erased … probably *because* you thought you might be erased. If you went out of your way to protect it, it's important. And the kind of thing that pops up in dreams all the time even if you don't remember or recognize it."

Ash thought about that. He still didn't remember all of who he'd been before the erasure, but what Daisy said rang familiar. It felt entirely possible that he'd done what she described. Their memory games involved creating private vaults to store important information.

"Okay," Ash said. "So. This important information I stored and can't remember. How do I get it back out?"

"Dreams. You've been a lucid dreamer for as long as I've known you. The best lucid dreamers can practically browse their subconscious minds like a library. You just need to get yourself into a lucid dream, then ask around for what's important."

"Wait. You want me to 'ask around' *inside my dreams?"*

"It's not as crazy as you think. The mind knows a lot more than you do, and it sees all the things you don't pay attention to. So for instance, if you can't find your watch, you could go into a lucid dream and ask someone in the dream where you saw it last. Dream characters are all parts of you, and they have your whole mind at their fingertips. *They'll* know where the watch is even if *you* don't."

"So the Bespokery has been trying to poke around in my head and find something I've forgotten?" Ash corrected himself: "*Intentionally* forgotten?"

She nodded. "Except they can't do it for you. *They* can't poke. *You* have to do the looking around and the poking, because it's your mind. They can only try and manipulate you. Push you to the point that you'll look where they want you looking."

"How can they do that?" Ash asked.

"They could remind you of your war memories, maybe, or anything else traumatic. Get you scared, so your defenses go down. The dreams you've had over the past few weeks and months … Were they vivid? More so than usual? Were they troubling? More bad dreams than good?"

"Like nightmares?"

"No. Nightmares would wake you up. They'd want you asleep so you'd keep digging. I'm talking about dreams of oppression. Maybe you're being chased. Or questioned. Anything to get you thinking. Searching for answers."

"And these would be *lucid* dreams?" The phenomenon still felt new to Ash, even if Daisy said he'd done it forever.

She shook her head. "These would be normal dreams. All dreams involve the subconscious, so any dream could do what the Bespokery wants. They wouldn't *want* you lucid. They want you unaware that you're dreaming so you don't ask questions they don't want asked — and again, so your guard is down. They want your mind on important things without knowing they're important."

"Still feels like a crapshoot," Ash said.

"I think they know the *kind* of thing they're looking for," Daisy answered. "It's probably an 'I'll know it when I see it' situation. I'm sure it involves a lot of guesswork and being patient, but still with a method to the madness."

"What if the thing they want just never comes up?"

Daisy shrugged. "No idea. We're above my pay grade at this point. All I know is they got it out of Alexi Solokov. If they hadn't, he'd still be alive."

"Alexi killed himself."

And Daisy replied, "I don't think so."

They sat with that.

"There's good news, though," Daisy went on. "As far as we know, you haven't been under dream surveillance since you found the Chirp, and right *after* you found the Chirp, they had plenty of chances to kill you but didn't. That tells me they haven't gotten what they want from you yet."

Ash tried and failed to take it as good news. Mina was still trapped, and going back for her seemed to be exactly what the bad guys wanted him to do. If he returned to the lab, they'd capture him and probably torture the information out of him. His only option was to stay with Daisy, where he was safe.

"Emily told me to find you if things went bad," Daisy said. "That I should help you find what's hidden inside your head before *they* do."

Ash nodded. That made sense. If he knew what he was hiding, he'd have options. Until then, he could only be a victim. Or a pawn.

"There's something else you should keep in mind," Daisy said.

"What's that?"

"Has Mina tried to help you remember your dreams?"

"She's a sleep therapist. So yeah. It's most of what we talk about."

Daisy nodded knowingly.

"What?" Ash asked.

"Does she have you on any medication?"

"Antidepressants."

"Antidepressants usually blunt dreams and make it nearly impossible for them to recall."

"Not the ones I'm on." He remembered having this discussion with Mina, but not its outcome. Things were happening too fast, and he'd been managing two lives that were merging like traffic lanes. "I still dream a lot."

"Uh-huh." Daisy gave another nod. "She have you on anything else?"

"Nyperal." He didn't mention Mina's mistake involving the Nyperal placebo. No point in throwing her under the bus for no reason.

"Nyperal is a benzodiazepine. Why were you on a benzo *and* an antidepressant?"

"It's supposed to keep me from acting out my dreams. To paralyze me or something."

"REM atonia," Daisy said, nodding. "And? How well does it work?" She asked like she already knew.

Again Ash didn't want to shit on Mina and admit the truth, so he waffled. It must not have been convincing, because Daisy nodded as if she'd heard all she needed to hear.

"So your therapist has you on a drug that's supposed to stop you from dreaming, but it doesn't. She also has you on a conflicting medication that's supposed to keep you from acting out your dreams, but that one doesn't work either. Have I got that right?"

"Are you implying that Mina's a plant? Like Chuck?"

Daisy's shoulders rose and fell: *You tell me.*

Not wanting to, Ash let Daisy's insinuation sink in. In the past day, he'd fielded Mina's suspicions of Daisy and now Daisy's suspicions of Mina. Seen objectively, Daisy's arguments were better. Although Mina claimed to be sorry for the ways she'd misled Ash and wrongly prescribed his medications, she'd still done those things. Daisy, meanwhile, hadn't misled or wronged him at all.

So why haven't you told Daisy about Emily's trigger? About sunshine making everything better?

Ash ignored the voice. He couldn't reopen the door to paranoia now. "So what's with that 'MILD' thing you were talking about?"

"It's a way of inducing a lucid dream. It *might* be a way for you to find what the Bespokery's looking for before they find it. I was just thinking: Here we are, in a room with beds. It's nighttime and you need sleep. Strikes me as good a time as any to try it."

"Are you sure that's safe?" Ash asked. A week ago he hadn't known dreams could be snatched from the air like broadcast TV. What else might be possible?

"We know they're not watching your dreams now."

"How do we know that?"

"Because now you know they *were* watching before, and that means your defenses are up. The Blip won't work if you know how to protect your mind. If they find us and capture you now, they can't just let you sleep and see what comes. They'll have to … to take a different approach."

Ash didn't want to know. "My defenses don't *feel* up."

Daisy gave a smile: *It's cute, how naive you are.* "Oh. They're *up*. You were an *Agent*, Ash. Your defenses are formidable; trust me."

He must have looked doubtful.

"It should be safe to dream," Daisy said, "but don't let me convince you. *You* need to feel it; otherwise you won't let yourself get anywhere near what you've been hiding. So *do* you feel safe enough to enter a lucid dream?"

"I …" How was he supposed to answer that? "I guess so?"

"Then I think that's our next step: You need to dream. And you need to give whatever is hiding permission to come out."

"How the hell am I supposed to do that?" Ash asked.

"By setting an intention in line with the MILD technique. Tell yourself you want to find your best-guarded secret in your next dream. Then tell yourself that the next time you're in a dream, you'll remember to recognize that you're dreaming."

"The next time I'm in a dream, I will realize that I'm dreaming," Ash repeated. The phrase felt familiar on his tongue, as if he'd said it countless times before.

Daisy nodded. "Exactly. Normally a person has to practice and practice to get lucid with MILD or any other technique, but you won't. This is something you could do in your sleep, no pun intended."

"I'm not sure that's a pun."

"Go to sleep. Get lucid. Then ask one of your dream characters if they know where something was hidden. Keep asking and searching until you find it. Remember, these aren't strangers. You're asking yourself."

Ash sighed. "Okay. Fine."

"Kick off your shoes." She moved over to him, pulling at the sheets. "Shirt and pants off. Do you want me to look away?"

"It's fine. I'm in boxers."

"Get under the covers." She rose and began turning lights off.

"Okay," Ash said once he was under the covers.

Daisy stood over him. "Good. Now go to sleep." She put her hands on her hips as if she planned to watch it happen.

Ash laughed. He'd never felt less like sleeping.

"You used to do this for a living," she said. "You can

meditate yourself to sleep. Your body will remember how to relax under duress."

"I don't know how to meditate."

Daisy refrained from contradicting him. She came over and sat on the bed at his side. "Begin breathing like this …"

She began to breathe in long, slow measures.

Ash followed her pace, mimicking her ins and her outs.

"Now we're going to start by focusing on—"

"My toes," he finished.

She looked him in the eyes. "You remember."

"I'm starting to."

Daisy pulled a chair from the desk and moved off the mattress. By the time she was sitting, Ash found he was growing tired despite being agitated just minutes ago. She was right; his body did remember this.

"You forgot one," Ash said, meaning the dim lamp on the end table.

"I need one light on," Daisy told him.

"Why?"

"To watch your eyes. I need to see when your eyes start moving, so I know you're dreaming. But it'll be a while before you dream long enough to help us. Until then, you'll be lost in the valley."

"So I just fall asleep? How do I …?"

Ash didn't finish. He was already drifting off. The process was eerily fast.

He saw shapes in the shadows behind his eyelids. He saw colors. He saw lines and human silhouettes as if they were coming to get him.

Then he heard a beep: the sound of Daisy starting her phone's stopwatch.

"Sweet dreams," she told him.

After that, he heard nothing.

THIRTY-NINE

Don't You?

It'd been over an hour since Mina's epiphany: nine digits on the internet had to be an IP address. Addresses could be longer or shorter, intra- or extranet, with port controls appended to the end or naked, but by and large nine was the common number.

Disco dance party. 107120941. With dots inserted, it became 107.120.9.41.

She was guessing at the format, but that one seemed to make Bryan's machine chug a bit differently than the others. It didn't entirely work; she got a page telling her that the address was invalid.

On closer inspection, she saw another clue: this wasn't a *real* error page so much as a page pretending to error.

Research followed. She had more success when she added the *https://* prefix for security, then even more success once she added an anonymizing thingamajig called a proxy. She was tired as hell, and all this geek work hurt her head.

Finally, exhaustingly, she was rewarded: two full hours

after Ash and Daisy had left her, Mina found herself staring at a web page that required a password to proceed.

A password, of course, that Mina didn't have.

"For fuck's sake," she said aloud.

She stood from the chair, glaring at the monitor. She wasn't a hero. She shouldn't even be on this stupid adventure. She had run off with a patient, found her partner dead in the dumpster, then been attacked and shot at by a horde of zombies before being locked in a closet. All before she was required to play Secret Motherfucking Agent.

It was too much. This wasn't her business. Ash was a patient, and she barely knew him. She was a non-player in this. She would, upon successful extrication from this mess, solemnly swear to say nothing about any of this espionage bullshit to anyone.

But none of that was true.

You ARE part of this, Mina. Emily erased your memory, too. For all you know, you could be an "Agent," too.

(Or a Sleeper.)

Carefully, Mina lifted the blinds. Two figures still patrolled in the shadows, so she couldn't leave if she wanted to. Instead she sat heavily, now on hour forty of being awake, her brain barely working.

This was all so uncool. So completely unfair.

She didn't know any goddamn password. She was exhausted and tech-weary. She'd barely figured out the IP thing, then gotten her "proxy" going out of what felt like sheer luck. How the hell was she supposed to come up with a—

Mina stopped. A thought came to her, insistent.

No. Wait. Think about this for a second, will you? Emily wanted you to see whatever's on that page, and she wanted it pretty badly. She taught you how to turn words into numbers. She left a reminder on your phone about it. The password is probably there only to prevent brute-force discovery: a machine on the web scraping every server while searching for gold. You were the only one sent here. You were the only person Emily wanted to see it. Doesn't it stand to reason that she'd have made it possible for you? Easy, even?

An easy password, Mina thought. Just a speed bump to derail search robots.

She typed: *Disco dance party.*

For a moment nothing happened. But then the page reloaded and Mina found herself looking at a black rectangle with a right-facing arrow in its center: the universal symbols for *Embedded Video* and *Play*.

Mina clicked the Play arrow, realizing only after she did so that she'd been holding her breath.

The video began. As it did Mina saw a room: domestic with files littering the background; probably a home office. The video was from the perspective of a built-in camera atop a computer monitor. An empty black chair was visible in the foreground.

The camera jarred as someone struck the computer's desk. A second later, an attractive and thoroughly no-nonsense woman entered the screen and sat.

Mina recognized her immediately, though she had no memory of meeting her other than in fractured memories of Blip and Chirp. The late Emily Sanders was speaking to her from the past.

"Hello, Mina," Emily said, smiling like a friend. "I guess right about now all you want is to run away. That's what you told me you'd be thinking when you finally saw this."

Mina's mouth was hanging open.

"But you're too important to run," Emily said. "You do remember that much ... don't you?"

FORTY

David Gitz

Ash had been asleep for a while before Daisy looked at her phone again — or so she thought.

She suddenly blinked, confused. She hadn't fallen asleep; she'd just zoned out completely. She had no idea how long she'd been that way, but it felt like hours. It'd gone on until a door-slam elsewhere in the motel interrupted her reverie.

Wondering, she glanced down at her phone's dark screen. It was hard to tell how much time had passed while she'd been staring at the far wall, but the motel room right now felt like the kind of place where time disappeared. There were no ticking clocks. It was the perfect temperature even without AC. No humming mini-fridge, and the room itself faced away from the road. With just one light on and the blinds drawn, Daisy half-felt like she was in a sensory deprivation tank.

She woke the phone and frowned at the screen. The stopwatch was just passing eighteen minutes. How tired *was* she?

She looked at Ash, dead to the world. No surprise

there. He was probably in Stage 2 or 3 of NREM — might not even get a noticeable REM phase this early in the night.

Going under had, of course, been no problem. Agents, trained in the original techniques, were basically sleep ninjas, using lucid techniques to understand the experiences of their subjects. *Do to thyself as thy do to others,* went the unwritten motto. All five Agents had become hobbyists and quick self-studies, unwilling to let their subjects have all the fun once they saw how cool lucidity could be.

Daisy had only worked for Emily, but she also believed she'd worked with all five of them. She knew that Emily had told her very little, but it still didn't strike Daisy as strange that she knew far more than she should about the Agency and its programs.

All of those contradictory beliefs coexisted neatly inside Daisy's mind. The brain seldom asked questions unless it was forced. She didn't know she'd been tampered with. The truth and the lie had yet to knock heads.

Daisy stood. *What lie?* She didn't tell lies. The troublesome thought dissolved like mist and was gone.

Daisy had all of Ash's metrics, which she now displayed in a custom app alongside the running stopwatch. His sleep cycle time was exactly ninety minutes. According to EEGs from his time at the Agency, he also exhibited a near-prototypical sleep progression. The man's sleep graph was neat enough for a textbook — not the messy thing most humans spit out when hooked to machines and wires.

Ash lived in the exact center of the bell curve; that's what Richard had told Daisy yesterday … and what Daisy's altered mind believed *Emily* had told her long ago. The briefing she'd thus-far conveyed to Ash had been given to her by Richard, not Emily. Emily had probably made plans, but Daisy didn't know them if so. The plans she knew weren't actually Emily's. Daisy was *Richard's* spy. *Richard's* soldier. She just didn't know it, believing Emily had sent her.

Her mind believed all those things. It was a forest of contradictions that somehow worked exactly as Protocol wanted.

Meanwhile Daisy was still staring at her phone's screen, only a tiny bit confused.

You had Emily's LoJack login, someone *(richard)*

had told her. *That's how you knew where to find Ash. And here's what you'll say — what you'll tell Ash when you meet up with him. Tell him that Emily pulled you aside. Tell him all the things I told you, but you won't remember it was me; you'll think Emily told them to you. Tell Ash that Emily made plans. Tell him she set up contingencies in case things went bad. In case someone came for them in the way they came for Alexi.*

But at the same time, Daisy remembered meeting with Emily — not Richard — quite clearly.

You will believe Emily explained all of this to you, someone *(richard)*

had said. *You can see her in your mind's eye. You can smell the soap she used. It was on such and such a day. At such and such a time. In such and such place. See it in your mental theater, Daisy. You're going out there to help Ash; that's what you believe. Of course you're only there to help.*

Daisy caught herself staring. Her screen had gone dark again.

She woke the phone to see the timer past twenty-four minutes. The slippage of time she felt was slightly troubling.

She decided the room was too quiet. She should turn on some music. It wouldn't wake Ash, and Daisy sort of needed an anchor to help her cope through the blankets of silence. With no sound or stimulation, she kept losing minutes. She kept catching herself staring into space, thinking about the time when Emily told her everything.

It'd happened on April 22nd, 4:12 p.m. In the reservable conference room at Panera Bread. Emily had told her all about everything while smelling of Dove Lavender.

A sound broke the stillness, and Daisy startled.

It was her phone, but with a custom ring she'd never heard despite hearing it several times before. The caller was a man named *David Gitz*, according to the screen. She didn't know any David Gitz. Why was he in her contacts?

Her mind slotted into a new configuration as she listened to the ringing. It was a hypnotic sound. Daisy felt something inside herself like the rearranging of a puzzle box. She let it ring four times, feeling that rearrangement, before she answered.

When she finally did answer, she felt differently than she had before. Serene. Her mind had never been clearer. She no longer thought about Emily. Right now she barely knew her own name.

She didn't speak even though the call had connected. David Gitz also said nothing, and Daisy knew why. She understood, like instinct, that she never spoke to David Gitz within earshot of anyone. Talking to David Gitz around anyone was forbidden; everyone knew that.

So Daisy left the motel room. She walked into a shallow grove of trees and only then spoke into the phone.

"Ready," she said.

"Report," came a voice.

"Ash Sanders is sleeping. For the past," she looked at the phone, toggling over to the app, "twenty-seven minutes thirty seconds. First cycle. No REM yet."

It didn't occur to Daisy how strange David's voice was.

When she'd spoken to him back at the sleep lab (before Ash and Mina arrived but after she'd eliminated the man who was already there), David had sounded like a woman. Now, he sounded like a kid barely out of his teens. But sound didn't matter to Daisy. She did what David Gitz told her to … *period*.

His special ringtone always made Daisy feel peaceful. Almost like she was floating. Like it was okay that she hadn't talked to Emily Sanders, but had instead spent a lot of time being talked-to rather convincingly by Richard Quince. She'd liked talking to Richard. He'd even played David Gitz's ringtone for Daisy before they got going.

"Do you have a Chirp?" the young-man voice of David asked her now.

"No. I was instructed not to use one."

"By who?" David Gitz sounded angry. David got angry a lot.

"Richard."

"Richard doesn't tell you what to do. I do."

"Richard told me not to use a Chirp," Daisy repeated. The trees were so pretty at night.

"I don't care what Richard said. *Use one.* Hook one up right fucking now."

"Richard took my Chirp. He said Ash would know if it was used."

"How could Ash possibly know?"

"Richard said he can see its interference now that he's starting to remember. In his dreams."

"That's ridiculous. Nobody can detect—"

"Richard said that's probably half the reason Ash breached," Daisy interrupted. "It's probably how Ash caught that dipshit Mike O'Brien outside his house in the first place."

The line went quiet. Sometimes David Gitz got mad

when anything was said about Mike O'Brien. She'd never met anyone named Mike O'Brien. Nor Natalie Baynes, which was the other person Richard often spoke about after he'd played the dial tone and was giving Daisy instructions.

According to Richard, Natalie had no understanding of her job and had an ass filled with solid iron. These were the things Richard told her. And Daisy always listened to Richard after she heard the ringtone. David Gitz liked to tell her what to do, but Richard had trained her, even though she got the feeling he hadn't wanted to.

David Gitz began to argue with himself on the other end of the line. Daisy could hear his two voices bickering: the young-man voice and the female voice having a row. David's male voice said it wanted a Chirp delivered to Daisy, but David's female voice thought the male voice was a real cockswaddler for thinking that wouldn't break cover. David's female voice further opined that David's young-man voice should get about the business of jumping up its own asshole.

"Daisy, listen," said David's female voice, shoving the young-man voice aside and coming to the fore. "You'll just have to record whatever Sanders says. No Chirp. No instruments. I'm talking about a simple voice recorder, like on your phone. Richard was probably right about Ash's ability to tell when dreamtech is being used. We've … seen it."

"Yes," said Daisy.

"The record shows that Sanders never really has a usable REM period in the first cycle. There's a solid REM block at two and a half or three hours in on most nights, though, during the second cycle. I want you to give him twenty minutes or so of rapid-eye movement when that happens, then wake him up and ask him what he was dreaming about and if he found anything. Oh. And you're to stop answering to Richard Quince. Do you understand?"

"Richard plays the ringtone."

"We've rerouted the number, so he can't call you. Do you understand, Daisy? You don't listen to him anymore."

"I listen to Richard," Daisy said.

There was an argument on the other end of the phone between the Davids.

"Daisy," said the female voice.

"Yes."

"If you answer to Richard anymore, your mother won't be happy."

Daisy felt instantly cold. *"Mommy?"*

"She'll beat you. Do you understand? Beat you with the belt, like she used to."

Daisy's face broke. A tear spilled. She was shaking. Terrified.

"In the closet, Daisy. She'll lock you in for days. Remember?"

Daisy remembered. At first she thought she'd had nightmares about Mommy, thinking that maybe Mommy had been dead for a long time, but then she realized they weren't nightmares at all. Mommy was tough. She was a survivor. Daisy was beaten by Mommy all the time now, the old girl not dead at all. Sometimes it happened every night.

"So listen to me, Daisy," David's female voice continued. "You listen to me now. *You only listen to me. Not Richard.*"

"Richard sent me. Richard told me to go to the lab. Richard—"

"Yes. Richard sure does think he's some sort of a fucking genius, doesn't he?"

"What?"

"Never mind. Richard sent you, but now you only listen to me. You know this part, Daisy. We taught you all about it. Time the cycles. Watch for when his eyes move. He knows how to hold onto his dreams. He'll remember MILD, but if this thing drags into the morning hours, tell him about WILD. His metrics on WILDs are even more compelling than MILD lucid dreams. If he still hasn't found what we're looking for by six or seven, wake him right as REM starts and have him run through it. He'll know. That will do it. And Daisy?"

"What?" she repeated.

"Your kit contains an audio-only surveillance bug embedded in a pink semisolid that resembles chewed gum. I need you to stick it under the bedside table so I can hear what you say to Ash and what he says to you. Do you understand me?"

"Yes."

"And lastly, I need to hear you say it. This is your test of prospective memory."

"Jesus," said David's male voice, apparently annoyed at his female voice.

"Shut the fuck up, Mike," said the female voice, mouth away from the microphone. "Daisy was friends with the wife. You've seen the reports on some of these fucking betas. I don't want to have to trigger her again if she ends up needing to kill him."

"She's a Sleeper," said the male voice. "You *tell* her to kill him and she'll kill him."

"Not a normal Sleeper!" snapped the female voice. *"She's the last of our Protocols!"* Take a Sleeper in and out of state and it gets a fuck of a lot more complicated!"

Female David Gitz spoke into the phone again, his voice soothing once more. "Daisy. I need you to say it, okay? Prospective memory, just like a MILD. I might not be able to call you in time, so if Ash finds what he needs, and then somehow things go bad … Do you know what I mean by 'things going bad'?"

"Yes."

"If things go bad, if it's after Ash finds what he's looking for and you've written it down or recorded it, I need you to kill him."

"I killed the other man," Daisy said. "For Mommy."

"Yes. But you have to kill this one, too."

"But I won't want to."

"*Won't* want to? Or don't?"

What Daisy felt on this particular sticky issue was hard to describe. When she was talking to David Gitz, the world made perfect sense and she knew exactly what to do … but after hanging up with him, she didn't know he existed. During those times, Daisy felt differently and had new, confusing thoughts and forgot many things. After she'd killed the first man for Mommy and put him in the dumpster, for instance, she seemed to have forgotten all about it. Only the ringing phone had made her remember again.

It wasn't that Daisy *didn't* want to hurt Ash Sanders. Right now she very much *did*, because she didn't want to end up in the closet with Mommy and the belt. But that might change when the call ended — when David Gitz stopped existing again. At those times, she *liked* Ash. Without David and Mommy, she might not want to kill him. David never seemed to understand.

I won't want to was a different statement than *I don't want to*. She could control the latter, but the former sometimes felt out of her hands.

"I need you to say it, Daisy," David repeated for the third time. "If you say it, everyone you know here will believe you."

"Okay …"

"Say it."

"If things go bad after Ash Sanders has found what you want," Daisy told the phone, "I will kill him."

"Do you promise, Daisy?"

She hesitated. Then: "Yes."

"Are you sure?"

"Yes."

David paused. "Good. Because later tonight I'm going to pay a visit to Ash's friend Mina, and she's just ten minutes away from you. If you're a bad girl, I'll come and see you ... And Daisy?"

Daisy shivered at what was coming.

"Mommy will be with me."

FORTY-ONE

Drastic Action

Mina lived in a bubble of time while watching Emily's video.

The office from which Emily Sanders spoke to her from beyond the grave was strangely familiar — a place Mina recognized despite feeling she'd never been there. She also knew that it was in an unseen corner of that same room that Emily had shown Mina the Blip and Chirp without authorization, then told her all about them.

That had been their first encounter, forgotten entirely until Mina found the hidden photo on her phone. That first time, Emily had come to Mina as a source more than an ally. Emily, who'd helped build the devices, had been reckless to consult an outsider ... but with no one left inside her organization whom she could trust, she must've felt trapped without options.

I don't know if I can trust you, Mina remembered Emily saying that first day, *but Ash respects you and so I have to trust you. I need to know how much damage this technology will cause if it ever sees the light of day.*

Emily had been talking about something new. Not the

Blip and Chirp themselves, but an advance involving both that made dream observation like playing with blocks. Whatever that new technology was, it was close. Soon everyone would be using it in Emily's community of shadows.

Emily, who Ash often described as unflappable, had been plenty flappable that day. She'd struck Mina as extremely worried. Details about the new tech hadn't come back to Mina yet, but she thought now that it'd been something better able to penetrate dreams and waking psychology than the naked Blip and Chirp, which were passive. This new thing was active. It might force psychosis. Maybe control motivations and scramble minds like eggs in a skillet.

Emily had probably justified the work that she, Ash, and the others did as matters of national protection. But then something had changed, and she'd found herself facing orders that were so much harder to justify. She'd needed an unbiased opinion on what the Agents were being asked to do — and Mina, who had no government baggage, was perfect to give it.

It seemed Emily had committed treason by spilling her guts to Mina before this all began ... and *still* she'd reached out from beyond the grave to spill them again.

"I can't know how much memory you've gotten back," Onscreen Emily told her, "so I'll give you the quick version of everything."

She drew a breath.

"First things first. At the risk of stating the obvious, your memory has been modified. By the time you watch this, Ash's and mine will be, too. So if you come to see me after you watch this, don't be surprised if I don't know who you are at first. It may take me a while to remember what's going on, or understand your questions."

Mina sighed, one of her wonderings now answered: Emily hadn't expected to die.

"Ash and I have agreed to have our memories erased by our employers. They don't know about you, though, so not long after I record this, I'll erase you myself for your own safety. If it's any consolation, you agreed to it. You said that you didn't really want the burden of knowing about this shit if it wouldn't make a difference anyway, after Ash and I have forgotten."

Mina smirked. Though she'd have to take that on faith, it sounded like something she'd say.

"The erasure Ash and I will undergo is part of a compromise. You know the definition of a compromise, right? It's an arrangement where neither side is happy. Unless something goes wrong, we'll go underground and stay there. I hope that's how it went. I hope you'll never see this video. But I'm a glass-half-empty kind of girl, and my work has taught me to think that anyone is capable of anything."

"Sorry," Mina told the screen, her presence justifying Emily's pessimism.

"Ash and I work for a governmental bureau called the Agency. Our job is to monitor the dreams of persons of interest, then act according to any intel we uncover. Sometimes it's only surveillance: we watch and learn. Sometimes we learn useful things, like terrorist plots. We've stopped two airline hijackings using this tech. Coups have been stopped. Bombings have been avoided. I guess I'm telling you this because I want you to know we aren't all bad. I hope we're both adult enough to admit that secrets and rule-bending are sometimes necessary. Due process has its place, but the bad guys don't follow all the rules. If we sweat every technicality, a lot of people die.

"I've shown you the Blip and Chirp. If you got my

reminder on your phone and were able to figure out what it meant, I'm sure you already found the hidden album. Look for one if you haven't; it contains photos you took in my office. You're not anyone of interest, Mina, so there's no reason for anyone to look at you twice. Nobody's after you."

Mina looked around the shredded office, particularly noting the blood visible in the hallway. She laughed.

Emily looked down, consulting a slip of paper in front of her. She must have made notes to avoid missing anything important.

"Ash and I implanted a mnemonic in all three of us so that we'd be able to recall what was buried — not really *erased*, only *buried* — if we needed to. Mine is different from yours and Ash's. The flow I've designed takes a leap of faith, but if you're here now … Well, I guess it worked.

"'*Sunshine makes everything better,*'" Emily quoted with a scoff. "I never once said that. Maybe Erased Emily will have a Pollyanna personality once they reassign me as a waitress or whatever, but Agent Emily is kind of a hardass. I barely believe in sunshine. That's one reason I'm hoping that simple-minded expression will stand out for Ash, as his recall trigger. Maybe he'll remember me saying that all the time and think, 'Wait. *Emily* said something that you only see crocheted into oven mitts? I don't believe it.'"

Emily laughed. Mina laughed with her.

"You may remember my interest in memory sports. The people who compete in those sports use all sorts of tricks. I know a lot of them, but the one thing I could never solve was the issue of *prospective* memory. Prospective memory is what helps you remember to do things in the future without being reminded. I always need *some* sort of a reminder, even if it's just a string tied around my finger. After I see the reminder and know there's something I need to remember, I'll absolutely remember it. But that first step? The step that reminded me I'd memorized something in the first place? Without a string around my finger, I never had a clue. If I wanted to tune into a webcast at noon, it was no problem to store 'webcast: noon' in my memory palace … but then I'd forget to check the palace. I'd only remember my noon appointment hours after it was over. What's the solution, if you don't want to cheat and set a reminder? How does a person *remember to remember*?"

Good question, Mina thought.

"So I started playing around with environmental triggers. The most useful was my wedding ring. I look at my hands a lot — part of a ritual called 'reality checking' — and whenever I do, I notice the sparkle. So I made it my cue. Whenever I saw my ring, I was supposed to check my to-do-list memory palace and see if anything in there needed action. It was a pretty good solution. Soon the time-sensitive stuff started jumping right at me whenever I thought about my palace. I only needed the slightest nudge to help me out, and then my memory was off to the races."

Mina nodded to herself, admiring Emily's solution.

"What I did with Ash's trigger was similar. We worked together to create a false memory so that if he ever felt mortally depressed — we're talking suicidal-level depression — he'd think of a thing I 'always' said to cheer him up. We planned it that way because if the government broke our deal, they'd want to kill us but wouldn't want to draw attention by doing it themselves. Instead, they'd try to get us to commit suicide by dream persuasion. Using the exact tech I invented.

"So the way the trigger worked was this: If the government broke the deal, they'd use dreamtech to make us feel suicidal. Once Ash felt suicidal, my stupid phrase would pop into his head. We conditioned him so that until he said the Sunshine phrase aloud to someone, he'd grow more and more obsessed with it. You were the logical person he'd eventually say it to, seeing as you're the one helping him with his parasomnia. His saying it and your hearing it would trigger both of you. If we did it right, it'd poke your prospective memories like my diamond ring pokes mine. It'd send your minds inward, looking to recover your erased memories. Ash then knew how to undo my erasure, to bring me back to normal."

Emily stopped, then consulted her notes for several long seconds.

"This all happened because of an internal shakeup at the Agency. The Wurtzman Conjecture made the detection of patterns within enormous amounts of data possible, which is the reason dreamtech exists. Billions of neurons fire to create the sensory experience of waking life, same as billions of neurons fire to create the rich sensory experience of dreams. Sorting patterns from that much firing used to be impossible, but Wurtzman made it simple. Soon enough we could watch a subject's dream on TV, then find ways to exploit what was in those dreams."

Mina didn't think *simple* sounded like the right word at all.

"I won't sugar-coat it, doctor. We learned to brainwash people, and we did it well. That work created the first Sleepers, which the press are calling 'Freak-Outs.' Sleepers are just ordinary folks, influenced to action because they can do things and get at people that Agents can't. They've killed for us. They killed bad guys … but yes. We've done murder secondhand. And what about the Sleepers? Mina, it's not lost on me that we've ruined lives."

Emily stared into the camera, and it seemed to Mina

that she was looking right into her eyes: no white knights here.

"The use of Sleepers forced a schism in the Agency. Some, like the five-Agent group Ash and I work with, wanted checks and balances: reports required before deployment, plus some degree of accountability. A system like that would at least ensure we couldn't change a person's mind without anyone knowing we'd done it. We had a responsibility, holding that much power."

Emily shook her head, then kept going.

"At first, the big questions were always espionage-related: *Who do we have assassinated? How deep into their minds should we go?* I wanted a case made for every target we went after — but one woman, Natalie Baynes, argued that accountability would hold the Agency back. She argued that the more we hesitated, the less effective we'd be when fast and decisive action was needed. She got the ear of a few friendly generals, and that made her loud. She rounded up her followers, and soon had a whole tribe of Yes Men."

Emily drew a sober breath.

"At some point, someone somewhere gave Baynes an operating budget and authorized her to create a team of very aggressive dream workers. She formed her own department working parallel to the Agency, calling her people 'Tailors' because they were talented at designing directives that were custom-tailored — 'bespoke,' as it were. The Agency was more senior, but Baynes's 'Bespokery' was louder and created bigger and more visible results. Officially, any mission rejected by us was theirs to consider, but then we heard that they were finishing jobs we'd never even *seen*. Soon they were creating ten times as many Sleepers as we were. Even more troubling, those Sleepers didn't have defined trigger events. They were being dropped into the world 'just in case.' On-demand assassins already in place, should they be needed. A small group at the Bespokery knew the activation codes for those 'quiet Sleepers' and could deploy them however and whenever they wished."

Mina felt a chill. That's exactly what'd happened here, at Bryan's sleep lab. Whoever this Baynes woman was, her minions were apparently those outside.

"A line was crossed right before we met, Mina. The Bespokery was already using all of the Agency's methods, but recklessly and with brute force. They had a lot of support from war-mongering, testosterone sorts up the command chain. But then the dev team told us they were working on something brand new, just for the Bespokery. It was a new algorithm for use with the Blip and Chirp. They called it 'Protocol.'

"Protocol applied Wurtzman to Wurtzman. It looked at the algorithm we'd perfected at the Agency, then used the math to find patterns inside of *that*. Once it was finished, Protocol would make customized brainwashing pushbutton-easy. The level of precision it promised was insane. The devs boasted it'd be able to make a person decide to switch the order of two keys on their keychain. It could watch the outcome of a coin flipped by a subject over and over again, then learn that subject's muscle-firing patterns and make him decide, subconsciously, to subtly shift those muscles so he always flipped heads. All of that was very interesting, even to us. But do you remember what scared the shit out of me when we spoke the first time, doctor?"

"Dream invasion," Mina said aloud. The answer just came to her.

"The ability to enter other people's dreams," Emily recited, nodding as if she'd heard. "They thought they'd found a way to 'match a pair of dreaming minds' to create a bridge between them. They'd just show *my* brain some of what *your* brain was dreaming and vice versa. Do that right and it'd feel like you were both inside the same dream ... except that now, a character in 'your own dream' would have a mind of his own. The invader could do terrible things that your own mind's characters would never do. The trauma is hard to imagine: being attacked from the safety of your own thoughts. Using Protocol, Tailors would be able to destroy their subjects from the inside out.

"But why stop there? If it's possible to take *one* person's dream and present it to someone else as *their* dream, why not bring a *lot* of people into a shared dream? And what if the dream they all shared was actually a dredged-up memory: the memory of something all those people witnessed in real life? So for instance, let's say you saw Kennedy's assassination and I saw Kennedy's assassination, and so did thousands of other people. All of those memories could, after a few more years of development, be scraped out of dreamers' heads and reconstructed using Protocol. Forget about an HD picture on a screen; assembling all those different memories from all sorts of different perspectives and viewpoints would allow Protocol to build a virtual reality scene. With that much data, that scene would be entirely complete, full of vivid sensory information that'd make it seem incredibly real. If the Bespokery did *that* — if they rebuilt the Kennedy assassination as a dream so that *anyone* could be sucked into it — they'd be able to rewrite the past, one person at a time. Think about it. What if they altered the memory so that Kennedy was obviously shot from the grassy knoll instead of by Oswald — or by the Cubans, or the Russians, or the vice president staging a coup?"

Mina sat with the idea, feeling cold.

"Dreams and memories are a door that swings in both

directions," Emily went on. "Dreams come from memory and memory is shaped by dreams. Anyone sucked into an altered dream like that would take it in and store it deep in their subconscious just like they would for a genuine, real-world memory. Soon, people who'd been shown the altered version in their dreams would start saying they *knew for sure* that the vice president was behind JFK's shooting. They'd be *positive* because deep down — probably not even consciously remembered — they'd feel like they'd 'seen it happen.' You've heard of the Mandela Effect, where people are *sure* the past was one way even though history says they're wrong? This is that. Give Protocol a few more years of development and I worry the Mandela Effect could stop being a conspiracy theory and become the real thing. One person at a time, the Bespokery could change 'reality' from its roots. It'd be the ultimate DeepFake, and the internet would spread it like wildfire. In time, the altered version of past events would simply become the truth."

Emily paused there, but to Mina it seemed she'd had to force herself to stop. She'd been working herself up with talk of Mandela'ing the past, but the story she'd begun telling wasn't yet finished.

"Anyway," she said, "after we'd all spent enough time worrying, our team's leader — a man named Alexi — got all five Agents together off-record and out of sight. He'd anticipated the worst and had already taken action. *Drastic* action. Specifically, he'd gone into the Sleeper computer system shared by the Bespokery and Agency to do some *Mission: Impossible* shit I still don't understand and steal a copy of the Protocol algorithm. Then he scrambled what was left, making *his* copy the *only* real copy."

Emily looked right at the camera: "Protocol was so sensitive that even most of the generals didn't know it existed. Alexi said there were three local server backups and a single copy stored in a Defense Department cloud-base that had been decommissioned and was therefore immune to prying eyes. That was all. The paranoid types had kept Protocol close, limiting copies and keeping the wider system far from it. That was good for us. Not only did it make it possible to find all the copies — if you had Alexi's access and skills, anyway — but it also allowed Alexi one other bit of trickery: instead of *erasing* Protocol from the four places he found it, he *replaced* it with bogus code that looked almost identical but would fail when someone tried to use it. He hoped doing things that way would give us time. We—"

Every light in Mina's room suddenly died. Emily's voice stopped mid-sentence as the monitor turned black. Mina heard a bang and sizzle from outside: the sound of a giant dropping meat in his pan to fry.

She startled, half-falling and half-diving toward the floor. Her heart accelerated. The intrigue of Emily's video had spellbound her, so the sudden intrusion of real-world stimuli was like a brick to the face.

Mina crawled until she was under the window. She peeked outside and saw that in the lot's corner, a light on an electric pole was casting its cone of illumination on a parked car. Something large and metal lay sparking on the concrete nearby: the now-severed transformer that'd fed the building, she guessed.

Someone was on the pole, climbing down from where the transformer had been cut away. It had to be a Sleeper — a stupid but strong one: he could have cut the wires instead of the transformer's mount.

Other Sleepers milled — silhouettes in the darkness.

As the man descended the pole, two people emerged

from the car, clearly agitated. One argued; the other pulled a pistol with what seemed to be a silencer on the end.

The muzzle flashed.

The pole-climber hit the pavement.

The taller of the people from the car, who was unarmed, turned toward the one with the pistol and started shouting at him. *Scolding* him, really. From this far, Mina could see that the taller person was a woman with red hair and the other was a man, younger and small.

It was the pair after Ash. The fake technicians who'd broken into his home. And after all she'd just heard from Emily Sanders, Mina knew who the woman pretty much had to be.

Natalie Baynes, it seemed, had arrived.

FORTY-TWO

Protocol

Natalie's phone buzzed. It was the encoded one that almost *never* rang — certainly while she was in the field. She snatched at it, eyed the building covertly, and said, "What?"

"An inauspicious greeting," said a velvety voice. "You sound frazzled, Baynes."

Natalie almost snapped a salute and smacked the phone against her forehead. Mike, who was still wiping blood spatter off of his cheeks, looked over with an emotion that was possibly pity, possibly ridicule, and definitely lust.

"General," she said. "I didn't mean for anyone to bother you."

That was an understatement. The general was less militant about his job than he was about his health and habits. He ate only organic food raised by ranchers he personally knew. He took a bevy of questionable supplements daily, and slept more than she guessed anyone in his position ever had. Sleep was vital in the general's mind. Everyone knew not to disturb the general's sleep ... *ever*.

His being awake at … What? … after two a.m.? It was like disturbing a demon baby.

"I didn't mean for it either," he replied in a calm voice more intimidating than any shout.

The general's delivery was too soft and controlled for a man in his position. In all the time Natalie had known him — with all the atrocities committed and backs stabbed to please him — she'd never once heard him raise his voice. It'd been the same with her father. Dad used to punch Mom unconscious in the most courteous way, then calmly ask his children if they wouldn't mind cleaning the kitchen of all the blood because he really needed to unwind with his crossword puzzle.

"Well, sir, if *anyone* in my command bothered you—"

"There *is* no one in your command, Baynes," he said, cutting her off with the same smooth tone. "It seems you mean to keep it that way."

Natalie's accusing eyes shot to Mike O'Brien. *Mike* had woken the general, hadn't he?

"And don't look to blame your monkey," the general said as if he'd witnessed her glance. "You yourself said that if O'Brien had as much skill at his 'job' as he had at servicing your undercarriage, he'd be shit at his job indeed." He paused and then commented, "Not a very good metaphor, really."

Natalie had said that yesterday. In her office. She and Mike had been alone and she hadn't been offering feedback so much as demeaning him during their sex play. Of course the general had her office wired.

"Perhaps you'd care to explain why I've been receiving threatening calls from Senator Buckley?" the general asked.

"Shoshana Buckley?"

"*Senator* Buckley," the general repeated. "Seems a small

local police force was called off of one of their small, local cases by the FBI."

He had to mean Ash Sanders. Ash's little dust-up with Richard Quince and the fake neighbor had caused a ruckus. After Ash waved his gun around in plain sight of the entire block, some fucknut had called the VA and complained — as if the VA controlled all combat veterans and their rights to wave their weapons at local fucknuts. The news had somehow gotten a different version of the story. The local cops had gotten yet another. After that the "FBI" had stepped in to restore order, but it hadn't really been the FBI. The "special agent" who took over at Ash's home was actually Natalie's secretary. They'd pulled false credentials for him from the FBI's system using the general's not-entirely-approved authority.

"I'm sorry, sir." Natalie had already turned, subtly taking steps away from the parking lot's only overhead light. "O'Brien didn't ask before giving that order."

"I'm trusting you to fix this," the general said.

"Yes sir. Of course sir."

"I'd like to remind you that although there was once record of the Agency, the Bespokery does not officially exist."

"Yes sir."

"And that in order to facilitate your heading of the Bespokery, *you* were made to no longer officially exist as well. According to the unarmed defense school at which you trained prior to this engagement, you were officially shivved in the anus by a disgruntled trainee."

Damn. They shouldn't have let her choose her own cause of death. It'd seemed funny at the time. "Yes sir."

"As far the paperwork is concerned, the current messy issue can be solved very easily."

Natalie's hand was shaking. There was sweat on her forehead despite the chill. "Yes sir."

There was a long pause. Then his tone shifted back to business. "Since you have already disturbed my sleep, perhaps you can give me an update."

"Yes sir!" Natalie was suddenly eager to please, not nearly as cool as the cucumber she wanted be right now. She walked back to where Mike and the Sleepers were standing. "Sanders is with our beta Sleeper. The one trained with Protocol. The *last* of the Protocol betas."

"I see. And why is that?"

"Sanders has a lot of his memories back, sir. If we sent in an ordinary, activated Sleeper, he'd see right through them. Fortunately we made a wise choice in choosing who we entrained. This woman was already a friend to Sanders and his wife. He'll trust her whenever her conditioning is turned off. Meanwhile, we stay firmly in control."

He didn't congratulate her cleverness. He didn't say anything at all.

Natalie continued: "The problem is, Sanders has compromised our ability to watch his dreams. He—"

"Of course he has."

She stumbled at the interruption, then recovered quickly. "Because we can no longer surveil his dreams, we're looking at another solution. The beta has convinced him that going through a few REM cycles and dreaming lucidly is the best way to locate what we're trying to get from him, thinking he'll beat us to the punch. In truth, he'll relay whatever he finds to our Sleeper. She's informed him about some key intel that will guide his search — enough to show him where he needs to go once he's under, but nothing he could use against us."

"And *you* provided the beta with this 'intel'?"

In truth, the answer was no. Richard Quince had set

Daisy up from end to end. Natalie's idea was the failed one: storming the lab and capturing him. But Quince wasn't here, so the general didn't need to know that.

"Yes, sir," she said.

Again, no response.

"Our ... our goal is for Sanders to learn his drop's location and then self-report that location to the beta Sleeper, sir. After we know where he made his drop, I'll send someone to recover the drive immediately. With your permission, sir."

"With my permission," the general repeated.

"Yes, sir."

"Recover it immediately."

"Y-yes, sir."

Natalie heard the general adjust something on his desk. "My board shows a lot of active Sleepers close to you, in a residential district. Have you surrounded your target with Sleepers? Are you just outside his location?"

"No sir. We're at a separate location."

"Why?"

"The woman that Sanders ran away with, sir — his therapist, Dr. Mina Irving? She was left behind when ..." Fuck. Natalie couldn't admit to *that*. "Irving was separated from Sanders, sir," she said, pivoting. "We're at Irving's location. Daisy is watching Sanders a few miles away, at a nearby motel."

"*Daisy,*" the general repeated. "The woman holding Sanders, by herself ... is named 'Daisy.'"

"She's tougher than she sounds, sir."

"Of course. If 'Daisy' is keeping an eye on the primary target while you are busy massing governmental property and a creating another PR problem around yet another loose end, I'm not at all concerned. I'm sure you have it well in-hand, Baynes."

"There's a bug, too! An audio bug!"

"*A bug.* Quaint."

"No, no! It's one of the new ones. The X2s? They're fully equipped for—"

"Stop it, Baynes!" he snapped, his cool voice suddenly breaking. "This is my fault. I made a mistake with you. I mistook your cutthroat ambition for talent. Don't tell me the rest; you'll only embarrass yourself. I shouldn't have needed to call and lambast you in the field. I would've preferred to wait until I was rested, but the man who was supposed to watch your lines overnight is apparently asleep at the switch, wasting our money again. Where is he?"

"I'm—"

"I called the operators before I called you. They told me more than you have in one-third the time. I *know* you've deployed in two locations. I *know* there have already been reports of shots fired at your location earlier tonight, and that we now have police to pay for falsified reports. I imagine there were bodies as well?"

"Um …"

"Of course there were."

"Sir! If I could just say something?"

"You already *are* saying something. Would you like my express permission? Perhaps I can wipe your ass for you as well."

"Sir, I know this operation hasn't gone smoothly. The way we handled Alexi Solokov was a mistake. I wanted it to look like a suicide."

"You *wanted* to play with all the expensive toys," the general corrected. "It was an unfathomable lack of judgment. He could simply have been smothered in his sleep, or a Sleeper could have taken him out."

"But a suicide …"

"Suicides still get press," the general insisted. "*Especially* in a metropolitan area. *Especially* when they involve jumping from the top of a building."

Natalie wasn't sure what to say. Alexi had, more than anything, been her attempt to raise a middle finger at the Agency. Alexi used to lord his superior ability to dream lucidly over Natalie, arguing that an Agent (because back then, she'd nearly been one) couldn't do good work unless she knew and respected her field. So Natalie's thinking had been: Alexi thought he was a ninja at going lucid? The perfect fuck-you would be to die because he couldn't tell reality from a dream.

"But sir! We're right this time. Sanders had the real drive. I'm sure of it."

"You were sure before."

"This is different. *Obviously* it's different!"

"Obviously?"

She pretended to hike up her pride. "Yes. Obviously."

After a long silence, the general said, "You have the rest of the night to clean up your mess, Baynes. *Sunrise;* do you hear me? No longer than that."

"Of course sir. Thank you, sir. I won't let you down again, s—"

The call ended. Natalie waited until its screen was blank before she found the courage to say, *"Asshole."*

She spun on her heel. "O'BRIEN!"

Mike looked up, then came toward her.

"Tell Daisy to give Sanders three more REM cycles to search for the drop location. After that, we pull the plug."

Mike's face was scandalized. "Wait, what? What if he doesn't give her anything by then?"

Natalie looked at her watch. "It's 2:04 and he just came out of REM ten minutes ago. Three more cycles should take us to … what? 6:30? 6:30 is long enough. If he hasn't given us anything by then, we cut the cord. Have Daisy finish him off."

"But N—!" Mike stopped himself just in time. "But *Baynes*! We know he's got it! You can't be sure he'll even remember how to do any of this by then! What if he needs time — to figure out how to lucid dream, to locate the drop, or whatever else? We can't just *give up* if it doesn't happen tonight! We can hold the fort here, and tomorrow night Daisy can try ag—!"

"6:30," Natalie repeated.

The problem here was that Mike didn't have all the information and Natalie didn't plan to tell him. 6:30 was the last REM period Sanders would have before sunrise. If he hadn't delivered the drop's location by then, Natalie would need her few remaining minutes to make other plans before the general's men came for her — because by now she'd pushed him far enough, and *come* they would.

Protocol was *Natalie's* baby. *The Bespokery's* baby. If Natalie couldn't get it from Ash's mind, the general would forgive it because he'd never truly believed in Protocol to start with. But all the attention this operation was courting? All this *mess*? The only solution was to scrub the problem away at its source — by ending Sanders, Irving, and all the other loose ends together.

The general had ordered Natalie to clean things up by sunrise, and she planned to obey that order one way or the other.

Come sunrise, she'd wipe up Ash Sanders with a mop herself if she had to.

FORTY-THREE

By Sunrise

Ash's eyes darted back and forth under closed lids.

Daisy watched and waited. Per his usual profile for this time of night — in the middle, where REM and deep NREM were mostly in balance — Ash likely had another few minutes of dreams remaining. If he didn't wake shortly on his own after his eye movements stopped, she'd wake him to ask what he'd found.

She blinked in exhaustion.

She wondered how Mina must be faring back at the lab. She hadn't slept the night before, so a second night without rest would be inhuman. Daisy had slept great last night, and still felt beat to hell. Probably looked it, too.

She pulled a compact from her purse, then used it to check her eyes. Not too bad. They didn't look baggy or red. In a way that made sense, because despite *knowing* she was tired, Daisy didn't *feel* fatigued at all. Her sense was more of an intellectual thing. She was tired because "being tired" fit the symptoms.

Symptoms like zoning out for long periods of time,

snapping out of it after ten or twenty minutes had passed her by.

Symptoms like what Daisy could only think of as blackouts, though the term frightened her. An hour or two ago, she'd smelled dog shit and looked up to see muddy tracks on the motel carpet. Ash had gone into the nearby thin strip of woods to scope the place, probably picking up some literal crap. But his shoes were clean. Hers were caked with mud ... and, of course, a reeking surprise. The mud was fresh, and yet she hadn't left the room since they'd arrived.

She might be seeing things. Once when she'd snapped out of her reveries, Daisy had remembered a fragment of some other world in the way a person remembered dreams. On instinct, she'd gone for her phone, sure somehow that she'd just hung it up even though she had no memory of doing so. In her recent calls list, plain as day, had been an incoming from a David Gitz.

But then the entry vanished as if it'd never been there, right in front of her eyes.

Her certainty triggered another thought: the name had to be in her contacts.

So she searched ... and yes, she had one *David Gitz*. His number was somehow obscured — no way to call him. And she knew no David Gitz.

She stared into the compact. Exhaustion was the only explanation. Even though she didn't feel tired, Daisy was clearly sleep-deprived.

A strong hand grabbed her wrist, causing her to fling the compact toward the desk. The hand was as unyielding as a pit bull, hurting her. Ash was staring right at her, half upright and propped on his free elbow, eyes wide open, his mouth forming a scowl. His gripped hand reeled her forward.

"It was *you*. It wasn't me. It was *you*."

"Ash! Stop it!"

"You came in here. Stood over me. And you—!"

Daisy drew back and slapped him as hard as she could without thinking.

Ash blinked. His face reset and he dropped her wrist with abject embarrassment.

His intense, murderous expression dropped like an anchor, replaced with a look of surprise and repentance. "Daisy! I'm sorry. I … I was dreaming."

Her spitfire was rising; she wanted none of his apologies. She'd scared herself to death in this Twilight Zone of a room, and then here he came, scaring her further.

She lashed out, slapping him again. "The fuck is wrong with you?"

He kept stammering, trying to articulate himself despite having just woken up and feeling correspondingly confused. Something about the "just woken" part pinched her — pinched her *hard*, and with purpose — but Daisy was too angry and afraid (and angry *because* she'd been afraid) to grant him an inch of slack.

She let him stammer, daring him to make sense.

Slowly, he did. Once Ash finished explaining himself, she almost felt bad.

Daisy had known about his condition — that his body didn't always shut down when he was unconscious and instead tended to act out his dreams — but for some reason she'd forgotten.

How did a person forget something like that? Especially considering that Ash had killed his wife in the grip of one such dream-animated episode?

But didn't you hate him for it? asked a goading voice inside her. *Didn't you know about his condition, and believe the press when they said he didn't do it on purpose — that Ash hadn't been in control of his actions? Didn't you know all of it from A to Z (his therapy for REM disorder, Emily's worries for him) and still found yourself unable to look him in the eye after the funeral? So why hasn't it come up since you've been with him? Huh, Daisy? Why did you greet him like an old friend when your resentment is still burning hot?*

A good question. As Ash gaped at her, silently begging forgiveness, an answer surfaced in her mind. She hadn't come because Emily wanted her to — If *that's* the way things had gone, Daisy would remember hating him plenty. Emily's request alone wouldn't have bleached it from her mind.

So why had she come? And if Emily hadn't told Daisy all that she'd so far conveyed to Ash (which, interestingly, seemed to contain stuff even *Emily* hadn't known), who had?

That's when Daisy remembered her mother. The belt and the broomsticks. Sometimes just her hands, gripping Daisy's wrist.

Mommy had told her to come, and *that's* why Daisy hadn't thought twice about how she used to hate Ash Sanders. Mommy's demands stood above everything.

You didn't *think* when Mommy wanted something; you simply *did it.*

"What?" Ash asked, having gone from penitent to curious.

Daisy supposed she must look strange, having been mute for more than thirty seconds already. "I was thinking about my mother."

"You were?"

"She's been dead for thirteen years."

"I'm … sorry?"

She felt the oddest emotion. "I'm not. Ash. I have a weird question for you. If the Agency wanted someone to do something that …"

His eyes went bright as he bolted out of bed. "FUCK!"

"Ash?"

He was fully upright, mania personified. Bent at the waist, digging through a small pile of books and snacks she had made on the end table while watching him.

He finally found the notepad, but was apparently still looking for the pen that was by the pad before she'd buried it.

"Just tell me!" She fumbled for her phone. Clicked to the voice recorder app, hit record, and thrust it at him. "Tell *this*!"

The second worst thing a person could do if they wanted to remember their dreams was to enter into another discussion before writing them down. The *worst* thing was to get agitated. Get emotional and burn adrenaline.

"O-okay." He forced himself toward a parody of calm, rubbing his face. "I was dreaming about ... Emily. I think it was Emily. I was ... Maybe it was my house, I don't know. Or here." He grimaced, then shook his head. "SHIT!"

Daisy felt terrible, thoughts of her mom and mind control banished. They'd had *one* job here tonight, and setting about it hadn't been easy. Ash had found sleep despite some rather tall odds, after remembering enough of his old self to do so.

But dreaming was only half of things. Ash had to *remember* his dreams to be useful. Now she'd ruined it. She'd been agitated, putting herself before the greater good, reacting instead of calming him and coaching his recollection.

"You said it was me," Daisy told him.

"What?"

"When you grabbed my wrist, you said, '*It was you. It wasn't me. It was you.*'"

"I was asleep."

"I know you were asleep! Goddammit, you were *dreaming*!" She took a breath. "You *said* 'Emily.'"

"I dreamed about the night she died. The night I killed her."

Daisy tried not to flinch, hearing murder stated so plainly.

"Except that in the dream, I didn't kill her. Did I say anyone's name when I grabbed you?"

"Anyone's name?"

He nodded. "I feel like I was saying his name. Like it was someone I'd recognize."

"Ash. It was a dream."

"It didn't feel like a dream. It felt ... It felt like when I caught those cable repairmen outside my house. The woman and the ..." He stalled out, his face inscrutable. "It's gone. I can't remember. I don't know if I knew his name, but he was familiar."

"Listen," said Daisy. "You were right here. *Right here* in this bed. Emily's been gone a long time. Obviously it was a dream. What else could it be?"

"A memory."

She blinked. In the microseconds of darkness, Daisy saw her mother.

She hit the *Stop* button on the recorder, then pocketed the phone. She drew a deep breath, then put a hand on Ash's chest to return him to bed. He complied easily enough, both of them silently deciding to close the issue until later. His guilt ran fathoms deep. Of course he'd dreamed of exoneration: some other vaguely known person killing Emily instead of Ash himself.

There was bound to be some confusion on the way back to his former self.

"Do you remember anything else? Anything about the reason you went in?"

He shook his head.

"Were you lucid?"

"No."

"Then it doesn't matter. You have to be lucid. It's okay. It's time to try WILD."

"What's 'WILD'?" he asked.

She saw some recognition in his eyes, but it was still small, still hiding in the obscured recesses of his mind. "It means a 'Wake Initiated Lucid Dream.' You go directly from being awake, right into a dream."

"I thought it was 'mnemonically induced.'" His eyes ticked to their upper corners as he searched for the word. "*MILD*. You called it 'MILD.' You said I needed to remember to realize I was dreaming or something. To set an intention."

She shook her head. "It's WILD. I said WILD. Not MILD."

"No, you said MILD. I'm sure because I was thinking how boring it sounded. Some of Emily's memory tricks are coming back to me. Without meaning to, I pictured myself literally being bored to death."

Daisy brushed it away. "Then you misheard me."

"I didn't mishear you, Daisy. You said *MILD*. Then you spelled it out. I know *that* because part of the acronym was 'mnemonic,' and that's not a word you hear very often. It made me think of … Well, there was another mnemonic recently that it reminded me of."

"What's it matter?" She didn't understand why this was bothering her. *Just correct it and move on*.

But no, she couldn't. Because Daisy, now that she

thought about it, was *also* sure she'd said MILD. And that was strange, because she wasn't an oneironaut and had never been one.

Yet she knew all about lucid dream induction. *All about it*. And when Emily

(Mommy)

had told Daisy one oddly specific bit of information about Ash (that he'd always done better with WILD than MILD), Daisy too had misheard the terms. She'd had to ask Emily

(Mommy. David Gitz)

to explain the difference.

"I guess it doesn't," Ash said. "Just tell me what to do."

"So you don't remember?"

He shrugged.

"Should I know this? Should I know the difference between them?"

"Clearly you don't. Don't worry about it. Time's wasting. I'll have trouble getting back to sleep if I don't get to it."

"No. You won't."

Ash had to look up at the sound of her certainty.

"You won't," she repeated. "Your wake-back-to-bed times during training were the lowest the academy had ever seen. You always did better with WILD. You had to have at least one non-lucid dream first, but when you followed the WILD protocol after, especially if it was late into the night, your hit rate was over seventy-five percent. Into the morning, it was almost perfect. Why do I know it, Ash? Why do I know these things?"

"Emily told you."

"I think ... I think my mother told me."

He started to sit up, his face concerned at whatever he must be seeing on hers.

Get it together. This is more important than you. More important than how exhausted you are. "Never mind."

"Are you sure?"

"It's creepy here," she told him. "There's no sound. I don't like the shadows of the trees through the windows where a parking lot and highway should be. I'm an assistant. I'm just freaked out. It's got me confused."

He watched her another minute, trying to decide if she really meant it.

"Come on," she said. "Lie down. I'll tell you how to do it. You used a simplified version of WILD and you just came out of REM so you might be able to drop right back into it. I'll explain. It's easy. For you."

He waited another moment, still watching her, then lay flat.

His eyes closed, then opened again. "Daisy."

"What?"

"Turn on the TV. I don't mind. It won't bother me."

"It might pollute your dreams. You'll hear the sound."

"It's not the first time I think I might have seen through a dream into the real world." He paused, but didn't elaborate on that strange bit of miscellany. "Turn it way down. Just enough to keep you company."

Daisy nodded as he closed his eyes again.

"The WILD variation that always worked best for you was to replay anything at all you can remember of the dream you just came out of. You said you were in your bedroom. Forget the other man. Forget the rest. Just be in your bedroom. Then see yourself realizing you're in a dream. Picture yourself looking around and thinking, 'I'm dreaming right now. I'm—'"

"And Daisy …" This time his eyes stayed closed.

"Yes?"

"Thank you. Not just for me, but for Emily too."

Daisy needed a moment before finishing her instructions and sending Ash back into dreamland — lucidly, hopefully, this time. She felt a speck of dust in her eye. Like she might cry, though she couldn't say the reason.

She thought of Emily.

Of her mother.

Of Emily again.

And of Ash, who suddenly didn't seem as guilty of murder to her as he used to.

FORTY-FOUR

Tough Decisions

Mina had no idea how much time passed after the power was cut. The lab had once been a constable's office and as such had standard government wiring: wall clocks fed by current instead of batteries. The computers were off and Mina's phone was still dead. Without the sun to mark the passage of time, she might have been waiting for minutes or hours.

Baynes — if it *was* Baynes outside — had barely moved.

Emily's video had been interrupted before the punchline. Unable to finish now that the power was off, Mina couldn't stop thinking about its ending. The story had reached an exciting apex: Alexi had just stolen the dangerous Protocol algorithm and corrupted every other copy. What would he do with it? Did the theft of Protocol have something to do with the "deal" that got the Agents erased instead of killed? Mina had been on the edge of her seat when she lost her chance to hear the rest, and now she was dying to know.

She felt like a little kid denied the end of her bedtime story. Season finales weren't this cruel with their cliffhangers.

The power couldn't have been cut *because* she was watching the video, right? The timing had to be a coincidence. If that was true, the video wasn't gone; Mina simply had no power to reach it. She needed to find another way to watch.

But how? She was low on options. The building didn't have a generator, so lights, heat, and computing wouldn't be returning any time soon. Her phone was dead and she didn't have a charger — not that she'd have a live outlet to plug it into if she did.

Ash was with a killer and Mina had no way to warn him or enlist his help. She didn't know where Ash and Daisy were. She herself was surrounded and the car they'd come in was gone. Daisy's truck remained, but Daisy had the keys. The only escape was on foot, but she'd be spotted the second she stepped outside.

Maybe I could call an Uber.

She laughed at her own thought, exhaustion turning it funny.

When had she last slept? Mina more than anyone knew just how poorly a person performed when sleep-deprived. Sleepy as she was, she had no chance of out-fighting or out-thinking Baynes when Baynes finally decided to come for her — and of course, she wouldn't be coming alone.

Even now Mina could barely think straight. Her emotions had grown too intense. Her heart was pounding too hard, exerting too much effort.

Maybe you could use this time to sleep since you can't do anything else, she thought. *Maybe you should sleep, if they're just going to sit outside waiting for God knows what.*

But that was an even bigger laugh. Exhausted or not, Mina would never be able to sleep with enemies outside. Plus, her mind was preoccupied by her compulsion to know how Emily's story ended. Somehow, in all of this, *that's* what mattered most to her now.

Would the landline work without power? Maybe it was time to call 911 after all, risks be damned.

She picked up the nearest handset and pressed a few buttons. But no, either the lab's elaborate phones needed current to work or they'd cut the lines outside.

Needing something to occupy her mind, Mina began inspecting the offices, staying low as she moved from one to the other. None of the phones — all the same high-end model — had a dial tone. So Mina rifled through desks, hoping hard against the odds that someone had left a charged phone behind. Obviously, no one had.

If only she'd brought her charger. If only, before this began, she'd thought to charge her battery.

Battery! This time, the word rang an enormous bell inside her head. Because Laptop computers were also powered by batteries.

She ran into the next office, no longer bothering to stay low. She made for a MacBook in one of the RAs' offices, perfectly centered on an old-fashioned blotter. She grabbed the thing, sat on the floor, and powered it on.

When the screen lit, she almost cheered.

But … No, wait. Mina was being stupid. Without power to the modem and router, even a live laptop couldn't connect to the internet.

She could play solitaire if she wanted to.

Your hotspot, said a voice.

Yes, yes, her mobile hotspot could connect to the internet, but only if her phone wasn't dead. If her phone had juice, she could connect the laptop to it as a source of wi-fi.

But that just put her back where she'd started. If her phone was live, she wouldn't even need the laptop.

But it wasn't live, so she was just as fucked.

Live laptop, but no internet connection.

Dead phone, but no power source.

Mina stopped, looking at the USB ports in the laptop with sudden realization.

She shot to her feet and began ransacking the office.

She soon found a charging cord buried in one of the drawers, feeling idiotic that she hadn't thought to search for chargers long ago. Things just hadn't seemed dire enough to invade her labmates' privacy before the gunfire began and bodies started showing up in dumpsters. She'd had a few percent left before night fell, and back in those simpler times she'd still thought she'd go home in the morning.

She used the cord to plug her phone into the laptop, then waited. Eventually the *No Power* screen gave way to the Apple logo, and two minutes later Mina was frantically swiping to activate her hotspot.

Live laptop. Live phone.

Even wi-fi between the two, if she preferred to use the laptop's larger screen.

Mina was back in business.

She took a few deep breaths to calm herself, then navigated to Emily's IP address and re-entered the password. She was terrified until the video reappeared, sure the message had self-destructed after her first viewing.

But moments later she was scrubbing the video to the point where she'd been so rudely interrupted. Onscreen, Emily's comforting presence continued her story.

"—of *erasing* Protocol from the four places he found it, he *replaced* it with bogus code that looked almost identical but would fail when someone tried to use it. He hoped doing things that way would give us time. We knew they'd discover the swap eventually, but Protocol was still in its infancy, and between the need for departmental secrecy and Baynes's paranoia, few people knew it existed. They couldn't do much more with the algorithm until they had a clear path forward, and guess who was standing in the way?"

Emily pointed both thumbs at her chest. "The Agents. That's who."

Mina found herself nodding. This still felt new, now with a wink of the familiar.

"The team developing Protocol couldn't proceed without top-down support, which Baynes had already more or less secured in secret from a general overseeing both programs. That gave us an edge. Until the Agents were out of the way, nobody had any reason to look at Protocol again. They wouldn't notice that it'd been swapped out, for a while at least.

"The hammer *always* falls in our line of work. But our knowledge bases contained information the Bespokery might need some day. *We* built the program; Baynes just put herself behind its wheel. She didn't really understand it, and was smart enough to know that. Keeping the real version of Protocol *intact* but *hidden* was our long-term insurance policy. If they ever hoped to find it, they'd need what was inside our heads."

Smart. Mina couldn't help but admire the Agents' thinking. Still, something had clearly gone wrong. Something Emily and the others hadn't anticipated.

"Alexi put his copy of Protocol on an Agency storage device that had a long, technical name I don't remember. Around the office, we just called them 'cry-out drives' because they were made to 'cry out' if the drive was destroyed. If damage was detected, a drive like that used an amplified NFC signal that prompted a feedback loop in any wi-fi or cellular signal within …"

Emily stopped, then waved a hand as if this was too much. "It's really complicated and doesn't matter. Cry-out drives are made such that if they're destroyed or information is erased from them after the initialization period, anyone with that drive's device code will know it happened. It's kind of like signing the sealed flap of an envelope so you'll know if anyone opens it.

"We queued-up a delay-send message to Baynes. It included the cry-out drive's device code and told her that *One*, the Agents had the only copy of Protocol, *Two*, we'd put it on a cry-out drive and hidden it, and *Three*, if the drive was destroyed or Protocol was erased, she'd know because we'd given her its code. We wanted her to be sure Protocol still existed somewhere — and that if she played fair, there was always a chance she'd get it back."

Mina paused the video. She'd heard something outside, but from the office window she couldn't see Baynes's vehicle or the streetlight above it.

She listened to the quiet for a half-minute, decided she was jumping at shadows, then scooched back and kept watching Emily:

"As you can imagine, hiding anything from professional spies isn't easy. We couldn't just stuff the Protocol drive into someone's sock drawer. Cry-outs can't be back-traced, but there were other ways Baynes might think of to find it. We were being watched, and *still* we had to find a way to hide that little bastard. We only had one chance. We knew they'd catch us and erase our memories soon, so it's not like we could move the drive later. We wouldn't even know there *was* a drive. Or who we used to be."

Mina paused to absorb the weight of Emily's message in a bottle, then heard something outside again.

Paranoid now, she checked all the exits before resuming the video.

"We made as much smokescreen as we could," Emily explained. "We initialized four empty cry-out drives to act as decoys, then tossed all five into Chloe's hat and each of us took one. Nobody knew if they had the Protocol drive or a decoy. We scattered, all of us carrying multiple fake passports and traveling under the radar ... and *even then* we went out of our way to create false trails, always ducking in and out of cover. Some of us met in public, swapped drives, then parted again. Sometimes we met but didn't swap drives at all. In the end nobody knew where anyone else did their hiding. Hell — in the end, *I* barely knew where *I* did *my* hiding. The whole thing was a global shell game. Five drives ended up scattered to five different corners of the planet, and even then there was no way to know which one contained Protocol. I suppose it was a masterwork of espionage, but mostly it was just the best we could do. I can only hope it was enough.

"In the end, the only way to find any one of the drives was to learn where they'd been hidden from the people who hid them." Emily tapped her head. "But see, we break into brains for a living, so we know how to lock them down. They wouldn't be able to get the locations out of us by force. Certainly not without drawing a lot of attention, and trust me: Baynes and the general behind her can't afford attention. Because they couldn't know who'd hidden the real drive — even *we* didn't know who had the real one — we had to hope they wouldn't be willing to gamble on breaking into us one by one. Something like that would cause problems for Baynes and the people around her. Although the Bespokery became an enemy, we have friends in the government, too — and those friends wouldn't be happy if they saw Baynes breaking the deal we ended up making: for erasure, not torture and death."

Mina considered. Apparently Emily had been wrong; either the Bespokery was just fine with taking that gamble or it had turned out to be a whole lot better at breaking into brains than the Agents thought.

But at the same time, the Agents' ploy *was* still winning. If it wasn't (if the Bespokery had already found the Protocol drive), they would have killed Ash instead of simply spying on his dreams, still fishing for secrets inside him.

Onscreen, Emily seemed to reset.

"There's one last thing. My fellow Agents were extremely intelligent people. *Good* people, considering the tough decisions we were forced to make. But they didn't know Baynes like I did. And the thing about Baynes is—"

Mina hit pause again. Now she was *sure* she wasn't imagining things. Someone definitely *was* snooping outside the doors and windows. She just heard tinkering from the far side of the building, and it wasn't her imagination this time.

Mina quietly closed the laptop, then pushed it under a couch along one wall: out of sight just in case. Then she crept across the hall to the opposite office, and from its window she could now see activity in one corner of the parking lot.

It was dark there, though; she couldn't make out what was happening. Whatever-it-was made a banging sound: hard but high-pitched.

She moved to the next office and learned the truth thirty seconds too late.

Directly in front of her, the headlights of Daisy's hopped-up truck blazed to life. Mina was exactly in their middle. Maybe it was because the people outside had known exactly where she was — and exactly how to entice her toward the target's center by revving the engine.

A shape behind the wheel slammed on the gas, and tons of American steel barreled toward her.

Mina ran as fast as her feet would go, diving into the hallway as the wall behind her detonated in a bomb made of wood, glass, and plaster. She fell, then dragged herself forward in the milliseconds before the truck's momentum sent it crashing through one office, then through the hall and into another.

Mina turned, dodging back into the long central hallway. She hit the front door, remembered it was barricaded, then reversed direction and sprinted for the rear as what sounded like hundreds of Sleepers began to attack from the outside.

The truck now blocked the central hallway. Mina vaulted its hood like a stuntwoman. Meanwhile enemies spilled through the new hole Daisy's truck had made, swarming into the hallway behind her.

Ahead, the back door broke inward. The people who entered then weren't all Sleepers. Mina saw O'Brien leading others — others who reminded Mina of Men in Black.

From three directions at once, they came at her in a furious crowd.

She dodged left, causing a few of her pursuers to collide behind her.

She reached the break room window, prayed it wouldn't stick when she tried to open it, and heaved.

The window slid up as if greased and a second later, Mina was through.

She fell hard to the concrete. As she found her feet, Mina realized she'd been surrounded by a half-circle of assorted men and women. They were led by a well-dressed redhead: the infamous Natalie Baynes.

Mina met the woman's eyes. They were green and hard, like emeralds glaring back at her.

Baynes smiled. "Doctor Irving, I presume."

FORTY-FIVE

En Route

Fifteen minutes before Mina was led to a black SUV at gunpoint, Richard Quince was hauling ass down a nameless stretch of road. His coded phone rang and he answered slightly outside of convention with a simple and friendly hello.

"Quince," said the general's polished voice. "Do you need a minute?"

"No, sir. I'm ready when you are."

The general read him a twelve-digit number, which Richard managed to transcribe onto a Sloppy's napkin with minimal swerving. Writing was easier than trying to type the identifier into the X2 receiver directly, especially while driving.

Richard had grabbed the X2 bug receiver from a depot after his first conversation with the general — a conservation Baynes didn't know they'd had. It looked like it'd been built by aliens. Richard himself was a low-tech guy. The only surveillance bugs he knew about came from 70s movies and required an entire comm van to listen in.

"Read it back," the general told him.

Richard read the number back.

"Officially, I didn't give you that bug's identifier number and I didn't assign you an X2 receiver; understand?" the general said. "I don't want Baynes knowing that you're listening in, or how you even *could* be listening in on the bug her operative planted."

"Daisy is actually my operative, sir. Baynes commandeered her."

The general said nothing, but Richard knew the man tended toward strong and silent. Natalie's story about Richard, Daisy, and what had gone down at the lab likely differed from Richard's, but instead of hashing it out now, the calculating general would consider the comment on his own time.

"Regardless, I don't want her to know you can hear what's going on in Sanders's hotel room. Understood?"

"Of course, sir. Understood, sir."

They both knew Baynes was dangerous, but they saw that danger through different lenses. Richard's fears were more existential — more philosophical and world-threatening. In Richard's mind, Baynes's problem was the classic *you-have-no-idea-what-you're-playing-around-with* scenario so popular in science fiction movies.

Specifically, Baynes didn't understand the subtle psychology of Sleepers — and she *really* didn't understand the *even more* subtle psychology of the only Protocol-entrained Sleeper the Agency had left. Even brainwashed, both kinds of Sleepers were human beings with thoughts and emotions of their own.

Daisy, who'd loved and respected Emily, would not be easily turned from the simple watch-and-report mission Richard had sent her on to the much more demanding stalk-and-kill required by Baynes. Yet Baynes had bulldozed ahead, counting on the hypnotic "David Gitz" ploy to somehow make it all work. Baynes didn't understand how dangerous *that* ploy was, either. In order to get what she wanted RIGHT NOW, she was shaking Daisy like nitroglycerine.

"Are you en route?" the general asked.

"Yes. But I won't arrive for ..." Richard looked at his GPS. It tracked both Baynes's phone and the bug, which were a few miles apart. "Just under an hour and a half. Have you listened to the bug's audio at all, sir? Do you get the feeling I *have* that much time?"

"I haven't listened. But I gave Baynes until morning."

Morning might not be enough time. Without dreamtech at her disposal, Richard knew that Daisy was trying to get Ash to self-report ... assuming dreams showed him the location of his cry-out drop at all. Her requested timeline required a crash course: first Ash had to re-learn the trick of lucid dreaming, then the more difficult trick of finding buried information in his subconscious mind.

Still, it was possible. Ash had always been a prodigy, and his memories were returning fast. He might well find his drive-drop by morning — or by the end of the dream cycle he was in right now.

How much was left of that cycle? Richard did the math, accounting for time of night and the lengthening of REM that began around three a.m. He'd studied Ash's old metrics, and knew his cycles were regular as a German train schedule.

So how much *was* left? Ten more minutes before Ash woke again? Fifteen at the outside?

Richard half-wished Protocol was already in use, and worked from distances. He'd insert himself into Ash's dream now if he could, then tell him to play possum.

Hey. Ash. Listen. I know I almost killed you. I know I might still end up killing you. But if you could just sandbag on this "drop location" thing for one more REM cycle so I have time to get there before you spill the beans, it'd really help me out. Just tell Daisy you didn't find it yet. Tell her you need to go back to sleep. Because buddy? If you tell her where you hid that drive before I get there, all hell will break loose. For me and probably for Dr. Irving, but for you most of all. So maybe just play dumb until I show up. Can you do that for your old fake war buddy?

"I'll do what I can, general."

"You understand I can't interfere. I can't order her to do anything more or I'm putting myself on the line."

"Yes, sir." Richard understood the politics in play. The powers-that-be still mostly stood in the Bespokery's corner, even if they unofficially hated it. Everyone privately rooted against Baynes while publicly raising her flag. It was a fine example of why being an assassin beat life as a politician. Killing was so much more honest.

"Sanders is inconsequential," the general told him. "The goal now is containment and damage control. I don't want Baynes leaving loose ends for the press to grab. If she dispatches Sanders, clean it up. If she doesn't, separate them and bring him in. Either way, keep in mind that you're only officially aware of the non-negotiable parts of the agenda. You know the only reason I involved you in this."

"Yes, sir."

"And Quince."

"Yes, sir?"

"When this is over, unless Baynes pulls off a miracle, the Bespokery will be yours to lead."

The general wasn't much for pleasantries. He hung up without saying goodbye.

FORTY-SIX

The Master Cypher

Richard's guess about Ash's dream timing was almost spot-on.

In reality, he had eleven minutes left before waking. Not that Ash knew it, or would have felt it as eleven minutes if he had. Dream time wasn't longer than real-world time like it was in the movies, but the brain's way of editing dreams sometimes made things seem that way.

He attained lucidity around the time Mina was remembering that phones could be charged from USB cords plugged into laptops. It wasn't wake-induced. Instead, he became aware while he was already under.

It began as an ordinary dream.

A cop was chasing him through a party. He was holding a long string of joints linked like shells in an ammunition belt, rolled into a toilet-paper-like cylinder. Apparently this was an arrest-worthy crime, so he spent long minutes visiting the dream-home's many rooms trying to dispose of his contraband.

Eventually he lost the roll, then panicked that the cop would find it with his fingerprints all over it. The scene ended when Ash, still not lucid, realized he could escape the cop by teleporting himself away from the party.

He found himself outside a movie set trailer, sitting on its scored-metal step, trying to covertly pass joints to Humphrey Bogart while the same weed-hating officer attempted to catch him in the act. Bogart would request a fatty, Ash would pull one from his pocket, and the cop would glance their way. Ash would hide the joint, and soon enough Bogart would make his request again and trigger the cycle to repeat.

Fucking cop, always trying so hard to bust him over some harmless—

But … wait.

I've done this already, haven't I? Ash found himself wondering. *This cop. This crime. Wasn't I just at a party?*

With that thought, something he'd told himself earlier clicked into place:

The next time I'm in a dream, I will realize that I'm dreaming.

The world grew instantly vibrant. Then something else happened that was nearly impossible to explain: *The past became the present.*

It happened with what felt like an audible snap. His mind had been storing the dream directly to memory: something he would later look back on as *having happened* without any memory of it *presently happening*.

But now Ash found himself *here* instead of preparing to look back on this moment as the past of an imagined future. The change felt like coming awake. The world around him grew real enough to be reality, and yet he knew it was not.

The moment of disorientation passed. This wasn't Ash's first lucid dream; he knew it now plain as day. The dreams he'd had before the O'Brien kid dropped the Blip weren't even his first.

No. He'd done this hundreds of times. *Thousands*. Maybe *tens* of thousands.

How far back did his lucidity go? Dream logic made real-world logic hard to fathom, so in the moment Ash had no idea. His mind still found a way to an answer: in tiny, screen-shaped vignettes, some of his prior lucid dreams replayed around him.

Himself playing hockey, which real-world Ash had never played.

Himself and Emily having a perfect evening together: a lucid dream he'd created after meeting her but before their first date, so he could practice.

SCUBA-diving without a SCUBA, so deep that only the lantern fish had lights.

And, prominent among its fellows, Ash saw the first lucid dream he remembered, as a kid of unknown age. It had come not long after he saw *Back to the Future* for the first time, and featured himself learning to fly with Michael J. Fox.

"Truth," Ash demanded using his dream voice.

This dip into his subconsciousness — done intentionally and with context now — had reawakened many buried revelations. He found himself recapturing entire forgotten skillsets in a blink. He knew WILD, MILD, and DILD, alongside a dozen other -ILD induction methods that internet dream explorers had ripped off or invented.

Ash remembered the way he'd once been able, on certain late mornings, to practically *meditate* himself into a lucid dream: waking induction on Hard Mode.

He remembered his real life with Emily.

At his request for *Truth*, the wall of childhood screens filled with the sinister dreams of adults.

"So you remember," someone said.

Ash turned to see Emily standing beside him. They

were on a grassy hill with an electric sunset sizzling the sky in many shades of red, seeped with canary and tangerine smears. It could have looked ominous, if not for the majesty.

"I won't ask if I'm dreaming," Ash told her.

"Of course you won't."

"I've kept you away. I'm sorry."

"You're apologizing to yourself, Ash."

"I know."

A moment passed. The sky became gold and the ground concrete. Then they were in a bare-bones building, maybe a garage.

Ash *did* know he'd been apologizing to himself. He also knew that dream characters were almost always oblivious about what they were, and almost impossible to control. His mind effortlessly spooled back to his first training with the Agency, after he'd already become dream-adept as a hobbyist. The bosses wanted Agents to demonstrate command of their own minds, and the most failsafe way was to get an Agent to dream lucidly, then attempt to convince the others in their dreams that they weren't real — that they were figments of his own mind.

Those attempts had gone hilariously awry until Ash gained the mental control to get it right. But things weren't *going wrong* now, with this projection of Emily. She was a part of his mind, and yet she knew it was so.

Maybe it was because he was projecting her faithfully. In life, Emily had always known exactly who she was.

"We didn't only *watch* people's dreams, did we?"

Emily shrugged. "The others did. But you did more."

"Why don't I remember?"

Because now it felt like he remembered everything, and yet the sense that he'd been more than an observer of dreams was still only that: *a sense.* Ash had wondered why the Agents were required to lucidly dream even before he'd entered his mind this deeply, but now it struck him as a compulsion that refused to lie still.

Ash had more knowledge of the entire program now than he'd had when they'd erased him, his watching mind having subconsciously stolen nuance from everyone he'd met since. With that new knowledge, he understood the ways in which the Tailors worked differently now. He also remembered one of his skills that the others never understood: Ash alone could tell when his dreams were being monitored.

He was special. But *how*?

Then that same strange sixth-sense about being observed showed Ash a peek into what they all called Protocol.

"*Protocol*. They used Protocol on me, didn't they? That's what makes me different."

Emily shook her head. "It was never *used* on you, but a ghost of Protocol is still *in* you."

"Why?"

"Because you were its inspiration," Emily explained. "There were patterns to your brainwaves that only became apparent as unique once Wurtzman math existed to see them. Those patterns were turned into an algorithm. The algorithm was weaponized, and that weapon became the first version of Protocol. But it began with you, Ash. Protocol was born from the patterns your mind made naturally."

"*Which* patterns?"

"Nobody knows. Not even you. Most people believe in intuition but not ESP. Why? They share a spectrum. On one side is a hunch. On the other is verifiable knowledge. The same people who were so taken with MK Ultra were rather enamored with your brain, Ash."

"I'm psychic?"

"It was more subtle than that." She smiled. "You guessed well. You've always been lucky. It was subtle enough that it took Wurtzman analysis to find any of it."

"So they wanted Agents to be lucid dreamers even though we didn't need to dream to do our jobs because …"

"Because they wanted to see if what *you*, *Ash Sanders*, had could be trained into other people. Turns out it couldn't. You don't remember giving birth to Protocol because you were your own first subject. It's not usually possible for a person to forget something on purpose. The best most people can do is *repress* a memory: to shove it so far down that it's never seen again. And yet you were able to outright erase one. Of course the generals were excited. Your ability to so precisely excise thoughts suggested a truer form of mind control than was previously thought possible. Protocol was fast-tracked. The Bespokery was created. We at the Agency didn't want Protocol to see the light of day, but the joke's on us because we were its source. We buried *ourselves*, Ash. We never had a chance."

"But if my memories of all of this were erased …"

"Then how am I — a facet of your own mind — able to tell you about it now?" Emily almost rolled her eyes. "Come on, Ash. Use that *intuition* you were famous for."

"You're saying I got it back because I have special brainwaves? Because I intuited all of this without realizing it: intuition so strong, it's almost ESP? Emily … are you saying I *unerased* it?"

She nodded in concession. "Splitting hairs. Mostly, you were able to figure it out again from scratch. You were always an intuitive man with suspiciously accurate hunches."

"'*Hunches.*' So I don't *know*. I don't absolutely *know* that what you're saying is real?"

Emily smiled in a new way. "How much of life can you be absolutely sure is real?"

After a beat, Ash looked around the room. "This is Ishaan's garage."

"Yes. This is where we met after the trouble started. Ishaan built a Faraday cage inside the walls to block signals. He EM-swept it. Alexi managed to hack all of the Agency and Bespokery deployments before he hacked Protocol from the system, so while we were in here, we could be sure we weren't being watched."

The garage stayed solid in his vision, but three-dimensional scenes popped in and out of life on all four of the walls. The ceiling and floor found dimension next, soon displaying cycling images like the rest of the room.

Standing in the middle of all that shifting imagery felt like floating.

It was a metaphor. The images were Ash's higher mind thinking and deducing — running years of experience through the thought-nexus at hyperspeed. The scenes all around them were the algorithm, and everything he'd seen and heard and touched and tasted and smelled were its fodder.

"They killed Alexi," said Ash, reading what the thinking walls told him.

"You knew that already. They made him think he was dreaming, so he jumped off a building."

Ash nodded. He *had* known that. It was an elaborate, ironic, and ultimately cruel way to commit a murder. But Ash, in this space of mind, understood it fine. More than anything, Alexi had been killed by another person's ego. Someone had wanted to shame his work even more than they'd wanted him dead.

"They …" Ash looked at Emily, surprised for real this time. "They killed *you*."

"Stay focused. You knew that, too. Before you went under, Daisy commented that having the TV on might pollute your dreams. What did you think when she said that?"

"It reminded me of another time that I ..." He stopped, because the thing he'd thought so casually hours ago was suddenly full of new depth, new meaning. "Of another time I saw through a dream and into the real world."

He remembered it now. On the night Emily died, he'd had a blip of lucidity. He'd known for sure that where he'd ended up was a dream, and the real world was someplace else. Yet he could *feel* into the real world even without leaving the dream. He'd sensed ... someone there? With both of them, in their real-world bedroom?

At the time, Ash's dreaming mind hadn't thought much of it. Now he knew the truth: He really *had* seen into the waking world. He'd been asleep on his side of the bed, but his dreamsense (quiet ever since the erasure) had tried to warn him: *Pay attention, Ash. There's someone in the room with you and your wife.*

It was Emily's true killer he'd sensed that night. Ash hadn't hurt her after all. He'd merely been the man with a REM disorder sleeping beside a woman the Bespokery wanted dead — a man whose disorder made him the perfect frame for her murder.

But if someone had come to kill Emily, why hadn't they killed Ash, too? Was it only because they'd needed someone to blame?

No. It was because they could only deal with you one at a time. They needed to test each of you somehow before killing you, to see if you had what they wanted.

"*Focus*, Ash," Emily said. "There will be time for that later."

Ash tried to release his new sense of indignant rage, and to his surprise it went easily inside the dreamscape. Moments later he was floating again, watching Ishaan's walls cycle through their many images.

He thought: *Everything around me is my own mind. These images are my own private slideshow: a best-of reel of all things I've seen without knowing I saw them.*

"I kept watch for them," Ash said, realizing it was true. "For Alexi, Chloe, and Ishaan. Even after I was erased, my mind never stopped keeping an eye out for my fellow Agents. Storing away clues about them like nuts for the winter."

"Part of what makes you special, at work again." Emily nodded. "You're the algorithm. Where most people see noise, you saw patterns."

Through cultural osmosis, over months and years, Ash's mind had tended its archives. As he'd gone about his days, he'd seen so many things without taking notice: glimpses of newspapers and magazines, links on websites he'd visited for other reasons, the occasional overheard conversation on the street. His algorithmic mind had sifted and sorted all of it, plucking tidbits he'd later realize had been about Ishaan, or Chloe, or Alexi, or even him and Emily. It's why he'd dreamed of Alexi's death: his mind had noticed the story in the break room magazine, recognized Alexi, and shown him how it happened.

For months and years he'd built case files on the other Agents without knowing he'd done it. Images on the garage walls, floor, and ceiling were his mind now reading those files back to him.

Here's what happened, sir, an internal librarian seemed to be saying, *while your awareness was out.*

"Jesus Christ ... Chloe is dead, too, isn't she?"

Emily nodded. "She died under a false name. They

drugged her, assigned her a mental illness, then let her quietly expire in an overrun state hospital. The last time you came across her was as a barely glimpsed obituary in Seattle."

"I didn't look at the obituaries when I was in Seattle."

"Didn't you?"

"Besides, I was only there to visit Nellie—"

"—who lives in Tacoma."

"But … I didn't even *know* the fake name they gave Chloe!"

"Then why was it in your wallet?"

His mouth fell open. The dream was lucid, and still he was experiencing raw surprise.

On a garage wall, Ash saw a more recent memory: his own fingers finding a piece of paper in his wallet that he hadn't remembered writing, hadn't remembered putting there. He'd seen that note twice recently (once in Mina's office, then again outside her sleep lab), but only now did he understand its meaning.

There was a name on the note but no phone number: *Mariana Jordan.*

The name they'd given Chloe, after she'd been too intoxicated for contradiction.

Ash closed his dream eyes as another revelation came. He could see perfectly anyway: all six surfaces around him filling with stock images of a hangman's gallows.

And he knew.

Ash hadn't caught himself idly tying nooses last week because he'd planned to hang himself. If he wanted to die, he had a gun and knew how to use it. He'd tied those nooses because — just as with the Mariana Jordan note — his subconscious mind had been desperate to give him a clue.

"Ishaan hanged himself, didn't he?"

"Close enough," Emily said. "He was hanged, but he hanged *himself* about as much as your hands killed me."

The onslaught of truth was a weight on his throat: Alexi was the last of them. Emily was the first. *All four of his fellow Agents were dead.*

"They know." Ash didn't need Emily to confirm it because deep down he had known all along.

Ash was the source of Protocol: the codex and master cypher. "The generals, the Tailors — they know what we did and how to undo it, don't they? They didn't *need* to figure out who had the real algorithm and who had the decoys. None of that mattered because they figured out how to pry the drop locations out of our heads. They could just go through us one by one, hacking our dreams and narrowing it down." He shook his head. "We thought we knew how to lock ourselves down, but they found a way to get past our defenses, didn't they?"

"With a little help from *your* brain, I'm afraid." Emily nodded. "Some of the research must have survived. They probably scanned you first. There's not enough in you to re-create Protocol without Alexi's help, but the raw pattern-recognition inside you might have helped them tweak the old tech. Not enough to do what Protocol can do. Just enough to open the door."

But even worse was the implication. Emily, Chloe, Ishaan, and Alexi wouldn't be dead if the Bespokery hadn't *already* found their drop locations, hadn't *already* found their drives. It had to mean the others all had hidden decoys.

By process of elimination, Ash must have hidden the real Protocol drive.

Ash was the last one left — and the *right* one this time. The only thing standing between the Bespokery and victory was unlocking his brain and stealing the drop location inside it. He tried to remember his mission.

The only way out of this was to find the Protocol drive first.

How much time had passed? It couldn't be long before he woke up.

With that thought, his focus started to wobble, the dream beginning to end.

A sense of sudden, red-hot panic seized him. His calm departed and he found himself shouting out:

"Where is it, Emily? Where did I hide the drive?"

Just as the dream faded, Emily's lips opened and she said—

FORTY-SEVEN

Employee Empowerment

"—*QAHARAMANAN!*"

As he woke, Ash heard his own voice with his own ears as if another person had shouted out: another's mouth giving voice to Emily's answer. There was a millisecond of déjà vu between yelling and hearing, but then Ash remembered: he'd hidden his drive behind a loose board inside Qaharamanan's Bar in Kabul.

Duality filled him with vertigo. Had *he* shouted as he woke, or had Emily spoken? The phenomenon was strange. His lucid dream had separated mind from body in a way he'd grown unfamiliar with. Adjusting back to a mind-bound body was taking him a second.

Or more than a second. More than two or three. He couldn't even open his eyes.

Six long seconds later, Ash still couldn't move. A bizarre thought occurred to him: He should be happy. His REM disorder's hallmark was a lack of the usual dreaming paralysis, but for the first time since Afghanistan he was paralyzed.

Mina warned me about this. It's harmless. I just have to stay calm.

But he didn't have time to stay calm. He had to get out of here — had to somehow cross the ocean and get to Kabul for a drink and some data recovery.

Eight seconds. Ten.

Why was it taking so long for his paralysis to end? He knew panicking could worsen the phenomenon, so maybe it was urgency that hurt him now. Sleep paralysis could be a little different from person to person.

No big deal. Nothing to worry about.

It's in your head. Some people can't open their eyes, but you always could. Sometimes you could speak, even though everyone says that's not possible. Stay calm, Ash. You can open your eyes if you want to. But maybe you shouldn't. Everyone says that if you look around during sleep paralysis, you'll see demons coming right at you.

He opened his eyes anyway, and saw a demon holding a knife above him.

The demon was Daisy.

LISTENING in on his X2 receiver as he drove, Richard knew immediately what Ash's sleep-shout meant. The hiding spot he'd chosen for the drive was both idiotic and brilliant. Richard hadn't traveled with the Agents to Afghanistan (he hadn't even known Ash back then), but he'd processed their mission briefs. Qaharamanan's Bar was a place of interest and hence a place that those looking for the drive would know about. But on the other hand, it was also the most extreme example of a building in Kabul that you didn't enter without a few RPGs and an AK. It was sympathetic to terror organizations: an anti-American hotspot in the city's malcontented underbelly.

Ash, unlike most who traveled with the Agency, had

made a few friends among those the government considered enemies. Even after the most problematic regulars had been handled by that white ArkTek van, nearly everyone looked toward the bar and its patrons in a *don't-kick-the-nest-and-nobody-gets-hurt* sort of way … except for Ash.

Brilliant and stupid: everyone knew the place, but nobody dared go there.

Still, recognizing the drive's location from Ash's sleep-shouted word was a double-edged sword for Richard. The fact that *he'd* heard him yell it meant *Baynes* had heard it, too. The Bespokery had a presence in Kabul. To recover the drive, she'd only need a scrambled sat phone and a half hour — plenty of time to make the general's deadline. The sun was high in Kabul right now and Qaharamanan's was a nighttime place. Natalie's hired guns would barely need to knock on the door.

Richard actually pulled over to put his face in his hands, despite the theatricality. *This was it. The endgame.* He should just turn around and go home right now.

Richard had lost, and so had the world.

Natalie Baynes — and Protocol — had won.

IT WAS IRONIC. Less than five minutes after Natalie had the unimpressive and uninteresting Dr. Mina Irving zip-tied to the perp bar in her back seat, Ash Sanders served her salvation on a silver platter and rendered Irving's capture irrelevant.

Mike naturally had to ruin the moment.

"Did you hear that?" he purred to Mina, smiling evilly after Ash blurted his single word. "That's the sound of us killing you."

Jesus. His catch-phrases left a lot to be desired, and in Mike's case that said something because he practiced them in the mirror like DeNiro in *Taxi Driver.* She'd seen him do it after sex. Before sex. Sometimes *during* sex. Natalie should really have him executed and replaced, and maybe thanks to Sanders's revelation she'd finally have the clout to do so.

Because, *shit.* She was getting tired of ending up bound in their S&M games, then being told that Mike was the Terminator and that he'd *"be bahk."* The idiot would go for a sandwich, and she'd have to wiggle around in her cuffs and operate some shitty motel remote with her tongue for something to do.

"Get out of the car, Mike," she said now, ignoring his quizzical look.

She drove away when he did.

Once she could no longer see her supposed protege chasing her down the nighttime highway, Natalie pulled the SUV over, turned around in her seat, and faced Mina like they were about to have a casual conversation.

The good doctor then took her turn to ruin the moment by spitting in Natalie's face. Natalie hit her as hard as she could with a closed fist. She used to teach unarmed defense and knew how to hit like a battering ram. Irving would need dental work to be pretty again.

"I think you might be misinformed about how this works in the real world," Natalie told her prisoner while wiping her face and knuckles clean. "The spitters have always seen too many movies. It's all nice from a scripted point of view, you standing up to me like that. I guess the question is whether you think it's worth doing again."

Natalie moved more firmly between the seats, leaning close enough to feel Mina's breath. The leather squeaked as her body pushed into it.

"What'dya say, sport? You've got a mouth full of blood and I'm wearing white. *Spit at me.* I dare you."

Natalie waited. Unlike in the movies Mina seemed to have seen, bravery left her. Fucking people these days. Few had ever taken a punch.

"What? Not even a defiant scowl? You're seriously just going to let me get away with this?" Her eyes ticked down to Mina's feet. "You aren't even thinking of kicking me? Don't you have *any* fight in you at all? Just ... *saliva?*"

Natalie shrugged, then hit her again.

"Mike was right, you know," she said, slightly disappointed that Mina was rolling over so easily. "He's a fucking *idiot*, but right. I figured I'd use you for leverage. Your friend Ash got soft once they pulled his balls off, so I figured I could threaten you and get him to talk. Now that he's speaking up on his own, though, I guess I don't need leverage. He just said exactly what I needed to hear without so much as my girl needing to ask. And with time to spare."

Irving was sniveling. It looked like she might be fighting not to cry. Bitch.

"Hey. Get this. You know Daisy, right?"

No response.

"She's with me."

"I know," Irving told her.

"You do?"

Irving nodded.

"Hmm. That's really interesting, Mina. It's 'Mina,' right? Is that short for something?"

No response from Mina.

"What else do you know?" Natalie made like a schoolyard asshole and cocked her fist, seeing if she could get Mina to flinch. Mina still had that hurt puppy look, like she was waiting for someone to save her.

"Do you know that Ash is useless to me now?"

"You still have to find it," Mina said.

"What do I have to find?"

"The drive. With Protocol on it."

Natalie's eyebrows arched. That was interesting. "Who told you that? Ash?"

Nothing.

"Was it Ash?"

Still nothing.

"I *know* where the drive is. That word he shouted? It's a bar in Kabul. We've been watching the place for years. My people are ten minutes away."

Mina tried and failed to hide her hurt, but a lot of life had drained from her.

Natalie turned back around in her seat, sent a coded text to her team in Kabul, then returned to her contact screen and dialed Daisy. She looked back before connecting the call.

"This is nothing personal, *Mina*. I would really have enjoyed torturing you. Unfortunately, Ash just gave it up so there's no need. My orders are to 'clean up this mess,' and that means I should probably start with both of you instead of wasting too much time on the fun stuff. Pity, right?"

She drew her pistol and pointed it between Mina's eyes just to see her reaction. There was no smell of urine. So disappointing.

Natalie re-holstered the weapon, knowing she couldn't use it yet anyway. And certainly not at such close quarters — not while wearing white.

"I guess I should verify the drive is where I think it is before killing him," she said with artificial lament. "But hey. Those drives are indestructible, so if they have any trouble finding it, I can have them level the building and search the rubble. Ash spent some time with the owner. The guy had a nice office, by shithole standards. I'm betting it's in there. Do you want to get in on the over/under? I say we have the drive in twenty minutes. What do you think?"

Now Mina was sulking. Spoilsport.

"Do you want to watch him die," Natalie asked, "or would you rather pass?"

Mina's jaw wanted to work, but clearly it gave her too much pain. So, sighing, Natalie pressed the connect button and put her call to Daisy on speakerphone. She tipped her head back and forth as if pleasantly impatient until the phone rang to voicemail.

Then she made a *Silly me* face at Mina.

"Man. You know; I forgot. I gave Daisy a bit of autonomy I maybe shouldn't have. I pre-authorized her to make a choice on her own, about Ash and what she could do after he spoke up. In management circles, they call that kind of thing 'employee empowerment.'"

Natalie put the shifter into drive.

"He'll get away," Mina said from the backseat a minute later. But her voice was small, drowned by the rumbling of nighttime road under the wheels. "Ash is smart. He's strong."

"Honey," Natalie said, "Ash is dead already."

FORTY-EIGHT

Mommy

Mommy crouched on the mattress beside Ash, staring at Daisy.

Daisy tried not to meet her eyes.

"What are you waiting for, you little shit?" Mommy demanded. "I told you what to do. He *told* us what we need to know. What were you supposed to do now? Or did you forget already? Are you really that stupid?"

The knife's point was just far enough from Ash's neck to have room to quiver, trembling in her hands. Twice, Daisy had scratched his Adam's apple and drawn blood. She should have already finished the job. Tick one spot and she'd open his jugular. Another, the carotid. Even punching a nice-sized hole in his windpipe would kill him eventually.

But Daisy hadn't done it. Not even after Mommy started screaming at her.

At first Ash could only manage that one word — the strange, foreign word he'd shouted upon waking. Now, however, he was able to speak, and that wasn't a good thing. He kept trying to bargain with her, talking rudely over Mommy as if he couldn't hear her and didn't know what a bad idea it was to make her mad.

Now that Ash could finally move, he did so cautiously. His hands had risen in a pleading sort of way, seeming to understand that even as much as he outweighed her, he'd be lucky to avoid a mortal stabbing if he flinched the wrong way.

"DAISY!" Mommy chided. "Put it through his throat! Do what your mother tells you!"

Daisy couldn't look in Mommy's direction. Mommy was holding the belt. Looking her in the eyes now would be like challenging an attack dog. Instinct made her eternally guarded with Mommy nearby. Forever tensed against an inevitable blow.

Daisy flinched whenever Mommy yelled at her. Whenever Mommy moved. Her lower lip quivered. A long line of spit pooled on Ash's bare chest.

"Daisy," Ash said in his calm baritone. He spoke with a low-hertz tone that made people want to sleep. And oh *man*, did Daisy want to sleep right now. "Daisy, listen to me. You're not yourself. You don't want to do this. Put the knife down."

Daisy tried to summon anger. Tried to project her voice so Mommy would know she wasn't listening to his pleas.

"Shut up! I *am* myself! I *do* want to do this!"

"Someone got to you," Ash went on. "They messed with your head. Daisy? This isn't you. This isn't your fault."

"SHUT UP! STOP TALKING!" More saliva drooled from her mouth. She jabbed with the knife, opening a tiny wound. Ash flinched and finally, blessedly, shut his mouth.

"MORE!" said Mommy. "Stab him harder! Stop acting like a pussy!"

Daisy wished she'd followed her first impulse and killed Ash the second he'd said what David Gitz wanted to hear. She'd known what the strange word meant in practical terms, even if she hadn't understood it.

Mommy, of course, was on David's side.

Mommy and David Gitz were friends. They both wanted what was best for Daisy, even if it meant hurting her first. That's how it'd always been. Love came with pain. Affection was a bruise. Long nights spent crying in the closet, hoping Mommy never came home from wherever she went after sundown.

Daisy raised the blade. Held it with both hands. Her back and shoulder muscles bunched, her abdomen preparing to contract hard and deadly.

Ash's hands went up again. "WAIT! NO!"

But Daisy wouldn't be fooled. She knew to stab around his hands, before he rolled away. If she hit his hands, she'd hurt him a little but not nearly enough. He'd throw her like a rag doll. She'd hit the wall. Break the plaster. Instead, she had to kill him with the first stroke — in the mouth if his neck was too protected.

The door smashed open as if someone on the other side had heard Ash shout. He turned toward it, but Daisy had anticipated this sort of distraction — this sort of dummy's trap — and never broke her attention.

He flexed a beat after the door hit the wall, seeming to anticipate her distraction but finding none. Daisy's hands flashed until the edge of the knife, not its point, pushed hard against the now-exposed blood vessels in his neck.

She barely needed leverage. Only to slash. The edge was exceedingly sharp; she'd stabbed the cook in his stomach with a lesser knife while sharpening this one. Even trying to roll her off now would end him.

But the newcomer at the door was complicating things. It was a woman Daisy didn't know.

"What the fuck is going on?" she demanded, staring at the scene inside the room.

The woman had red hair. She seemed to be alone. Or *partially* alone. Her SUV was visible across the lot through the open door, its cabin light now dying. There was someone inside of it, but they might not be joining the party.

"That's it." Mommy leaned closer to Daisy. "That's good, Daisy. Now do it. Do what Mommy wants."

But then the woman at the door confused things again. She'd retrieved a phone from her pocket and must have put it on speaker, because suddenly Daisy was hearing David Gitz's custom ring. Her phone had rung with the same tone earlier, but she'd been too preoccupied to answer.

As Daisy listened to David's ring, the woman at the door turned into Mommy.

Mommy (now at the door, not on the bed where she'd been) looked at them both. She seemed to be analyzing the situation. She looked at Ash's hands and ankles, seeming to note that he wasn't restrained. Then she looked at his face, and seemed displeased that Ash was aware and awake. Finally she nodded slightly as if making a decision.

"Fine. Go ahead and kill him, I guess," said Mommy, now wearing a slim charcoal suit.

Daisy hesitated.

"I said do it! Do it if you're going to do it!"

"I DON'T WANT TO DO IT!" Daisy shot back, surprising herself. "I DON'T WANT TO DO IT SO JUST SHUT YOUR MOUTH!"

Then she started crying. Crying from fear and panic

but also from anger. *This wasn't fair.* She shouldn't have to do things like this. She was just a little girl.

"Goddammit, Daisy," Mommy said. "Do it or I'll do *you.*"

"Daisy," Ash said quietly from beneath her. He glanced at Mommy, looked momentarily confused, then seemed to understand the hold Mommy had over her. *"She doesn't control you."*

"Oh, for fuck's sake," Mommy said in a way that wasn't much like her usual self. Then she reached under her left armpit, distracted as she fished a pistol from a concealed shoulder holster.

A tiny, tiny voice inside Daisy said, *This is your chance to stand up to her.*

Daisy spun, obeying an irresistible impulse. She slashed wildly with the knife, opening a gash on Mommy's arm.

She saw a blip of surprise on Ash's face. It lasted a quarter-second before Ash bucked Daisy off, rolling down between the beds.

"I HATE YOU!" Daisy shouted at Mommy. *"I HATE YOU I HATE YOU I HATE YOU!"*

Wincing and furious, Mommy tried again to grab her gun. But she couldn't; Daisy had cut something important and her hand wasn't working right. So Daisy lunged and slashed again, this time catching Mommy's sleeve.

Mommy staggered back, trying to give herself room to regroup, then off-balanced into the wall. From her new, compromised position, she settled for tweezing the gun from its holster just enough to—

Daisy leapt at her, grabbing Mommy with both hands like a kid on a ninja course. Mommy elbowed her, dislodging her incompletely. From the corner of her eye, Daisy saw Ash stand, looking for weapons.

Mommy grabbed the gun and fired, almost dropping

the thing. Ash stopped searching and froze at the sound and sight, his eyes shocked.

Daisy watched Mommy's face. She seemed satisfied now, no longer fighting. Meanwhile white-hot pain bloomed in Daisy's side.

She fell away, looking down at her blood-soaked shirt, then up at her mother. She staggered, weak on her feet.

The pistol rose again, now pointed at Ash. Silhouettes had appeared outside: some of Mommy's friends, wading toward them like zombies.

"Asshole." Mommy said as she sighted on her target.

But Daisy wasn't finished with Mommy. She'd been shot; blood flowed like a faucet from her side. Still, she found one final reservoir of fight inside her, seizing Mommy's slashed arm and curling her modestly-nailed fingers into the wound.

Mommy screamed. She didn't drop the gun, but she lost every bit of her aim.

Ash's eyes darted to the people outside, about to enter the room. He took one last look at Daisy before going. That look was sad and pitying, but thankful as well.

After Ash had fled, Mommy cuffed Daisy to the floor. After that, Daisy could only lie in the warm pool flowing out of her. She saw Ash vanish between the dark trees — the same clutch of trees where she'd spoken to David Gitz.

Mommy looked toward Ash with irritation and regret, but for some reason she didn't bother to pursue him. Ash wasn't free just yet. Mommy would *never* give up, no matter how things looked.

But that was okay.

Daisy had stood up to her mother, finally and for once.

Now she'd never be afraid again.

FORTY-NINE

News from Kabul

Mike arrived on a bicycle. A goddamn *bicycle*.

Natalie didn't know if she should mock him or be appalled by his neediness.

He didn't even seem angry at the way she'd left him behind. Instead he came up like nothing had happened, still seeking her approval. The kid was damaged goods. She kept beating him, and still he came back eager for more.

"Where did you even get that?" she asked, meaning the bicycle.

He put his feet on the ground, then lowered the kickstand before stepping off. That was somehow the *coup de grâce:* lowering the kickstand on a stolen bike.

"Was that Sanders?" Mike asked instead of answering. He nodded toward the dust trail Ash had left when he'd sped off into the woods.

"Yes. But he grabbed his phone, so I know how to find him again." Natalie indicated her SUV, where Mina Irving was still cuffed.

Hilariously, Mike was still out of breath.

"Hard ride?" Natalie asked. "No wonder; you forgot your spandex and stupid helmet. Oh. And the flowers fell off your cute little basket."

The bike didn't have a basket. Mike ignored her again.

"You ran off before the news came back," he said.

"Why the hell did anyone call *you* with news?"

"They called the *team*, Nat. Why didn't you answer?" He looked toward the pocket where she usually kept her phone on vibrate. She must not have noticed it ringing while she was busy almost being murdered.

Mike saw her right arm. "Holy shit. Did Sanders do that?"

"No. His bitch."

"Irving?"

"His *other* bitch." Natalie simmered. Richard Quince's shitty work had come around to bite Natalie, almost literally. "Daisy."

"*Daisy* did that to you?" Mike looked aghast, moving to touch her arm before Natalie yanked it away. Even the yanking-away was agony. Daisy's fingernails had left her wound looking like a pot roast turned inside out.

"Was it news from Kabul?" Natalie asked.

"What?" Mike's attention was being diverted by her shredded forearm. Her fingers no longer worked correctly. She'd have a hard time hitting him for a while.

"*Kabul,*" she repeated.

"Oh. Yeah. The team in Kabul says they found the drive."

"Already?" Finally, some good news. How much time had passed since she'd given her order? Time flew when you were killing motherfuckers.

"Yeah. It was in the office, like you said. Behind a loose board."

"What time is it?"

Mike took out his phone. "4:40."

"Wow. Time to spare. Can they send over the data?"

"I don't think so. It's a cry-out drive. Can't be copied without military decryption. They're cracking it now. We'll have Protocol back in like, ten, fifteen minutes? They won't be able to upload it, but at least they can send you a screenshot of the verification. Think that's enough for you to show the general?"

Natalie wished she hadn't told Mike about the sunrise deadline. Having an expiration date made her look weak.

"It's enough," she said.

They looked toward the trees.

"Want me to go after him?" Mike asked.

"Nah. We got the drive. I'm really tired. We have time to deal with Sanders."

Mike looked at Natalie's SUV, parked away from the trees. Seeing Mina still inside made him frown.

"He didn't take her with him?"

"I don't think he saw her. Besides, she's zip-tied." Natalie's eyes moved toward the road, in the direction from which Mike had ridden his cute little bicycle. The path Ash had taken through the woods, she suspected, ran roughly parallel to that road. "But … do you want to hear something funny?"

Mike had peeked into the room. He didn't seem to have heard, because only now was he seeing Daisy dead and all the blood. *"Jesus,"* came his reply.

Natalie laughed, glancing intermittently toward Mina and her sad, puppy-dog expression visible even from here.

"Betcha I can guess where he's headed," she said.

FIFTY

The Vessel

Ash was still hoofing it double-time back to the sleep lab when Richard Quince arrived. Richard, unlike Ash, knew that Mina was no longer there. He'd been listening to the X2 bug's chatter the entire time he'd been driving, foot-down and daring highway patrol to stop him. He'd heard Baynes reach the motel room, heard Daisy go rogue just as he'd worried she might under pressure, and heard Baynes boast that she'd taken Irving into custody.

What Richard didn't know until he reached the lab was what a mess Baynes had made in order to accomplish that particular abduction.

He'd also heard from Control that the Sleepers on-scene had been called off and the area cleared of bodies, now that the building was empty. But Richard remained a cautious man, and approached carefully, crossing the parking lot with his weapon drawn.

The scene was a travesty. The general would not be pleased.

So much for subtlety. A Sleeper had driven a truck directly through the lab's wall. Although the body of the driver was gone, the footwell was filled with blood. Considering the way a piece of aluminum frame had impaled the backrest, they'd probably had to cut the bastard in half to remove him.

The truck's hood was still steaming. It was a heroic truck — jacked up and everything — but the wall was mostly brick and had proven the victor.

Richard circled around, staying wide. Then he moved closer, amused and professionally offended. Sloppy Baynes had left the truck idling. Richard reached in and killed the engine. Then he scoped the building's exterior with his elbows bent and gun aimed at the sky.

He was wearing an earpiece, but chatter from the motel bug had been uninteresting since O'Brien confirmed that Ash's drive-drop had been found. They had the drive in Crypto right now, trying to crack it and verify the contents. Not that there was really any question. Ash's was the final drive, all four of the other possibilities already crossed-off.

Ishaan with a rope.

Emily strangled in bed by Mike O'Brien, the whole thing blamed on Ash.

Chloe smothered in a mental ward, forcibly stoned out of her mind.

And lastly Alexi, tricked right off the roof of a building.

Ash would be joining them soon enough, Richard supposed. He'd bought himself some time when Daisy's conditioning failed and he slipped away, but Baynes was a bulldog with a grudge. She said she knew where Ash was headed — and although *Richard* had no idea where that might be, he was willing to bet that Baynes did.

It was almost a shame, the way things were ending.

Richard hadn't known the original Ash Sanders, but he

knew the man who'd emerged from the erasure quite well. The poor bastard was a sno-cone inside. He'd been morose and suicidal by the end — especially after his breach — but under it all Ash had a kind heart.

Believing that he'd ended Emily's life had broken him. Imagining he'd seen that kid blown up in Kandahar had crumbled him further. By the end he'd wanted death more than anything. But did his death really need to come like this? Richard would almost rather kill Ash himself than let fucking *Baynes* have the satisfaction.

At least Baynes may have managed to destroy herself, too.

On the matter of Baynes and her future, Richard gave her odds of surviving this debacle were fifty-fifty. Yes, she'd recovered the final (and hence correct) Agency drive, meaning it was just a matter of formality before she'd be able to say she officially recovered Protocol. But ... this lab? This destroyed truck? All this blood, and all the things the locals must have heard? Even Richard's own fumble at Ash's house was technically Baynes's fault: her operation, her blame. But which way would the general land, when Judgment came?

If Baynes lived and kept her job, Richard might just run off to Belize or something to avoid her in the future. If she was disposed-of or fired, however, he'd inherit the Bespokery, the big office, and a sizable promotion.

Richard could right the ship that Baynes had so effectively torpedoed. The Bespokery had become a parody of itself. Under his guidance, it might yet become the top-notch intelligence agency the Agency had been.

With his exterior circuit completed, Richard moved to check the building's interior.

The lab — easily accessible now that the truck had made a third doorway — appeared to be empty. Richard completed a thorough recon anyway, if only to prove that he wasn't sloppy and impulsive the way the world knew Natalie Baynes to be.

Downstairs, there was nothing. Upstairs was another story. It must have been a zombie-apocalypse kind of mayhem in here before the bodies were taken away. Richard found some barbaric weapons remaining. Bats, blades, and a big old machete.

Then, in one of the offices, he spied a laptop that'd been shoved under a couch.

It was cabled to someone's smart phone. The first cleanup sweep had really only carted away the meat. A second pass would come later … but until then, here was Richard.

Curious, he pulled the laptop from what seemed to be a hiding place and opened it. The screen lit. An internet browser was already visible on the display, loaded to a secure page identified only by numbers: an IP address, which was Agency stock and trade. There was a video in its center. Per the timecode at the bottom, that video was almost finished.

Richard had to double-take. The screen was paused on an image of Emily Sanders.

"What the hell?" he said aloud.

His attention moved to the cell phone cabled to the laptop. He turned it over and tapped the glass. It lit to show a lock screen. He couldn't hack it on his own, but Richard didn't need to unlock the phone to know whose it was. The displayed photo showed a pretty woman and a girl who might be her cousin or niece. The adult was Mina Irving.

Richard frowned. Then he looked from phone to laptop and back again, trying to piece together what he'd found. Irving had been bunkered inside this place, he knew.

Icons in the corners of both machines told him that the phone was being used as a hotspot.

So Mina had done this. She'd gone to great pains to do it, it seemed. What's more, she'd closed and hidden the laptop without finishing the video. Why? Had Baynes barged in, crashing a truck through the wall?

Yes, he thought that's what'd happened. Mina had been able to hide the laptop despite the interruption, so whatever Mina had been doing here, Baynes didn't know about it. The laptop wouldn't be here if she knew about it.

This hadn't been discovered at random. So Mina must have been led to it. Had Emily recorded whatever this was for her husband, but Irving discovered and watched it instead?

Or at least, watched all but the last few minutes of it?

The hotspot connection had timed out, but the video had already been loaded and cached. Richard hit play, and Emily's talking head resumed.

"—the thing about Baynes is, she comes off as fool-hardy because she's so ambitious, but she's extremely smart. Extremely capable, although I hate to flatter her. She's a fox, Mina. Don't underestimate her."

Mina. Richard frowned. So the video *was* for Irving, not Ash. *Why?* And *how?*

"There was always a chance that the Bespokery's tech would recover something from one of our minds — espe-cially with someone like Baynes behind the wheel. And if they found *one* thing, then they could find *everything*. In the end, I worried that even hiding four decoys wouldn't be safe enough.

"Now. If you're listening to this, it's because my Sunshine phrase is helping you and Ash to get your memo-ries back. But as I said earlier, that's only supposed to happen if Ash becomes suicidal. And that raises a very important issue, doesn't it?"

Emily leaned closer to the camera.

"Here's the thing, Mina. I know Ash very well. He listens to me. We're two halves of a whole, always balancing each other out. And so, I don't believe Ash would become suicidal — I mean *truly suicidal* — if I was still around. If I was around, I would have talked him down. And so I have to ask you a question: How did I die? Was it cancer? Or was I hit by a bus?"

Emily grew sober. "If you're watching this video, I'd bet money that I'm dead. I'd bet I was taken out by the Bespokery — maybe by Baynes herself. And if *that's* the case, Mina, *they know*. If they killed me, it's because they already found my drive. And if they could find *my* drive, they can find *all* of them. So. Here's one last thing you need to know."

Emily took a long breath, looked away from the camera, and then looked back again.

"Cry-out drives can't be destroyed, erased, or modified without sending a ping. I told you that earlier. But I *also* told you that cry-out drives require an initialization period. Straight out of the box, after you activate them but before they're put into service, there's a short window in which you have to do everything you ever plan to do. One short window in which you load the drive up before it locks itself down."

"Oh, you clever, clever girl," Richard said, understanding.

"All five of us were there when the drive was loaded. We put Protocol on it, then recorded the verifications so Baynes could be sure it was *that specific drive* she was after. But then, while the data was processing and the drive was still in its initialization window, I knocked a cup of hot coffee into my lap. It burned like hell. I stood up and screamed … and then, when they all turned to look, I switched the drive for another that had already finished initializing. Then I told the others I wanted to run to the bathroom and clean up, but I actually went into another room, dragged the real Protocol off the drive, and replaced it with another of Alexi's fake copies. I managed to do it just in time. Another few seconds and the drive would have cried out, but the transfer finished just inside the initialization window. So I quickly cleaned myself up in the bathroom, re-joined the other Agents, and found a distracted moment later to switch the drives back. The verified drive we set Baynes to chasing ended up full of gibberish just like all the others. So yes. *Every* drive was a decoy. *Nobody* hid a live copy of Protocol. It never went into the world at all."

Richard sat back, gobsmacked. Ash's drive wasn't the real deal, the way process of elimination insisted it had to be. Instead, that drive was just another red herring.

This changed everything. When Crypto finished decoding the drive from Kabul, Baynes was in for an unfortunate surprise.

"Now," Emily continued. "You may be thinking that I took Protocol off the cry-out drive so I could destroy it without anyone knowing. That's actually not true. The shadow-space of government the Agency works in has grown past checks and balances. It's not because of some evil plot — just red tape. In a bureaucracy this size, sometimes things just … *slip through the cracks*. Baynes is the kind of person who looks for those cracks, then crawls through them on purpose. So it's not like we could complain up the command chain about what the Bespokery was doing. There *is* no command chain. We also couldn't just take Protocol away and think it'd solve anything; give them time and they'd make something worse. Right now the

Bespokery doesn't really report to anyone — just a few opportunistic generals who are right-now taking Baynes's side. I realized pretty quickly that in order to bring the Bespokery down, we'd have to go outside the system. We needed public outrage. We had to show everyday people what they were up to. That meant keeping Protocol intact so that we could prove what we said — but always from a distance, so nobody could see how it worked.

"So yes. Protocol still exists. I've kept it safe until the right time comes to destroy it for good. I've done this because I've caused too much harm in my life — and if that life might end soon, I want to undo some of the damage I've caused before it does."

Now Richard understood why Emily's video wasn't more secure. Eventually, she'd *wanted* everything on it to be known. But that left one unanswered question: where *was* Protocol, if they hadn't hidden it on the drives or destroyed it?

Onscreen, Emily reached for the laptop she'd used to record her message. The camera's view pivoted to show the far corner of Emily's office. Seeing what was there, Richard, who wasn't easily surprised, actually gasped.

In view now was a wheel-out hospital bed. In it was none other than Mina Irving, asleep with an EEG tracing lines on a monitor by her side.

"You were a great student, Mina," Emily went on, moving back in front of the camera and speaking to the viewer version of Mina rather than the one in the bed. "And though you may never remember the times we shared, you were also my friend. I'm sorry we may never really know each other after they come for me."

She smiled a little.

"Soon you won't know me as anything other than the wife of one of your patients and I won't know you as more than my husband's doctor. With luck, it won't matter. We'll live out our lives and grow old, one day dying in rocking chairs. Maybe we'll meet again before that happens, as roommates in some old folks' home."

Emily blinked back latent tears, then crossed her arms and leaned forward to look directly into the camera.

"You probably haven't remembered yet, but you're an excellent lucid dreamer. You should be; I taught you every-thing I know. You *have* to be excellent, if I'm to have any confidence in what I'm about to do."

She looked to Mina in the bed, then stared into the camera once more.

"So do you have any guesses where Protocol ended up, Mina? If I wanted to hide something where nobody would find it until its job was done, have you figured out yet where someone with my expertise and interests might put it?"

Suddenly Richard understood. *Conditioning. Mnemonic triggers. Memory games.* All those mental tricks, coming together for Emily Sanders like a perfect storm.

"That's right," Emily said. "*You.* The last copy of Protocol is *in you.* It's funny. The government only cares what it can *get,* and that makes it miss a lot of obvious things. In a way, this was your idea. You taught me that sometimes it's better to think about what you can *give.* I thought a lot about our discussion, that night at Mozart's."

Emily laughed, forgetting herself. "Listen to me. You probably don't have any idea what I'm talking about. I guess you'll remember Mozart's when you remember. The point is, your way of thinking got me wondering. I designed the Chirp to *read* people's dreams. To *take* them. But what if the same technology could *give* something to a dreamer, too?"

She nodded to the room's corner, toward Sleeping Mina.

"Your mind will store the algorithm for us," Emily said. "Every digit. Every sign. Every linear regression. You just need to go deep if you want to find it. You know — or will remember — how. It'll take a lucid dream and a question. You'll never be able to rote-remember what comes out after you ask that question, but an ordinary Blip/Chirp setup can transcribe it for you like it would any other dream.

"You'll be safe until you're ready. Anyone who goes looking for a large data cache in your head will see it and understand how to extract it, but you're the *last* place anyone would think to look. You're a civilian, and until you gave me the idea, it never even occurred to *me* that my own tech could be used to implant something this complex. It shouldn't occur to anyone else. But ..."

Emily paused, then shrugged.

"In the extremely unlikely event that someone manages to breach every single defense we put in place and *then* somehow figures out what happened and tries to grab you, even *then* you'll hold all the cards. Because yes, lucidity *would* ordinarily be hard for you to relearn ... *if* we wanted to play by the rules. But where the Bespokery is concerned, I don't really want to play by the rules. Do you, Mina?"

A devious smile crawled across Emily's face. "I'm a woman of memory. Of triggers and mnemonics. And so I thought: 'All that lucidity training we did is still inside you, like any memory stays inside a person. So why not just give you a shortcut?'"

Emily kept speaking in the background as another thought dominated his mind — a thought that would change Baynes's odds of surviving this debacle from fifty-

fifty to one in a hundred ... and increase his own chances of taking over the Bespokery by just as much:

Protocol is still alive, and I know how to get it back.

Richard closed the video, erased the browser history, and pocketed Dr. Irving's phone just in case it came in handy later.

He knew where Baynes was, and which bad news she'd soon learn about the Kabul drive.

What a joy it would be, wiping that shit-eating grin from her face.

FIFTY-ONE

Bulldozer

"No," Natalie told the Crypto department. "You're mistaken."

"I'm sorry," said the voice on the other end. "We've run it three times."

Natalie refused to believe the drive was bogus. She'd spent forever on this quest and had already uncovered four bogus drives. There wasn't room for a fifth. What Crypto told her now was like learning there'd never been a red card in a game of Three-Card Monte.

"Maybe you're reading the drive wrong."

"With respect, we're quite certain we're not reading it wrong," the operative said. "The seal was intact. The signal was sent and received by our equipment. You were this particular drive's designated recipient, so I imagine you'll find that even *you* received—"

Yes, yes. Natalie had gotten the cry-out, and had been excited to confirm her victory: snatching Protocol back from those thieving, global-hide-and-seeking dickheads.

"I meant: maybe you *decoded* the information wrong."

"We're sure, ma'am," the voice insisted again.

"The algorithm is very precise. If you get just one digit out of place—"

"The cleartext is not ambiguous, ma'am. It's the script for *Robocop*."

"What?"

"*Robocop*. The 1980s movie."

Natalie squeezed her phone as if Hulk-smashing it would punish this idiot instead of sending pain into her forearm, making it seep blood through the bandage again.

She hung up on him, swearing in pain, then yelled for Mike to bring her a fresh bandage from his recently acquired stash. He'd run to an all-night market, because that's all he was good for. She couldn't take the agony of unwinding the old, bled-through wrap, so she had him apply the fresh bandage over its top.

"Maybe you should go to a hospital," Mike suggested.

Natalie walked away from him. She'd once again found herself in a deadly situation, but it was also seriously fucking annoying. She might die tonight. Worse, she might be demoted.

There must be a way to salvage the situation.

After a bit of thinking, she realized the answer: *Of course* there was still a way. It simply required dusting off a certain old underground program that nobody had authorized. The one that nobody *would* authorize, but that had done the job before.

When Protocol went missing, it was *Protocol*, ironically, that would have been required to hack the Agents' minds to unearth the truth of where it'd gone. But she hadn't had Protocol, so instead Natalie asked around until she finally found a neuroscientist willing to create something cruder: a smash-and-grab algorithm with all of Protocol's brute power but none of its precision.

Do you understand how dangerous this is? the neuroscientist had asked when the thing was finished. *It's not like Protocol at all. Protocol was a work of art. Protocol has safeties built in. Trying to do Protocol's job with what I wrote for you would be like trying to do dental work with a bomb when you can't find your little metal tools. Without a pattern to match, the damage it could cause is practically random. It's a bulldozer out of control. It might even …*

Yeah, yeah, Natalie had said.

Now, furious but with a purpose, she picked up her phone and started to dial Ash's number. But then she stopped, thinking better as she yelled to Mike O'Brien.

"Bring Dr. Irving over here!" she said.

Mike nodded, heading for the SUV.

Natalie's thumb moved from the button for an audio call to the video option instead.

"And rough her up a little more," Natalie added. "Let's get some fresh blood flowing for her boyfriend to see."

FIFTY-TWO

Preparations

The goal of Natalie's video call was to get Ash back from his dumbass errand. That part was easy; Ash lost interest in saving Mina from the lab once the call proved she wasn't there anymore. Seeing her broken nose almost made him beg — willing, now, to scamper back to the motel and trade his life for hers.

But there was more to it than simply turning Ash around. With the clock still ticking on her deadline with the general, Natalie also needed to get someone to rush over with equipment for the procedure she had in mind. Mostly, she needed a pair of Blip and Chirp prototypes, modified to handle her hacksaw of an algorithm.

Technically speaking, the rough-cut algorithm could already do the kind of dream invasion that Protocol promised only in the future. Natalie's neuroscientist partner simply needed to disregard that whole *do-no-harm* oath and stop caring if anyone survived its use.

The algorithm had never been tested because they hadn't yet found anyone disposable enough to test it on. But fortune was shining on Natalie Baynes today: Ash and

Mike were the *perfect* guinea pigs. Ash because Natalie didn't care if she killed him at this point, and Mike because he barely had a brain to lose.

If you ever actually try to use this thing, the neuroscientist had told Natalie, *keep in mind that your choice of operator will make or break the attempt. Given how rough the algorithm itself is, the operator will have to compensate by being extremely fine. You want a master pianist of an operator. Someone with the mental dexterity of a ballerina.*

Yeah. Well. Mike wasn't a master pianist or a ballerina. He was a lunkhead who'd tromp through Ash's cortex with muddy boots on. But oh fucking well about that: What did Natalie have to lose at this point? Only Ash and Mike, and that was no loss at all.

The motel itself was another problem. Whereas the site had originally been low-key and discrete, it was now becoming a spectacle. By the time Ash was escorted into the room next to his old one wearing a zip-tie like Mina's, a few more Tailors had arrived. By the time the dream link device that would allow Mike to enter Ash's dreams was set up an hour later, enough new personnel and spotlight trucks had arrived that the parking lot looked like a movie set.

Natalie hardly cared. All bets were off. After the tricks those asshole Agents had played on her, she didn't mind making a show of things and alerting the world. All that mattered was digging Ash hollow.

The motel's owner didn't share Natalie's enthusiasm for the circus the Bespokery made of her establishment. At first she asked politely what was going on. Natalie flashed her ID and said it was none of her business. Unfortunately the owner, like Mina, had seen too many movies, and had therefore challenged Natalie and demanded to inspect her ID.

When Natalie refused, the owner started quoting her Constitutional rights. She then got out her phone to film what was happening. Before she could record a single frame, though, Natalie solved the problem by grabbing the back of the owner's head and smashing her face into an exterior corner of the building.

She died on impact, but then of course she was right in the goddamn way.

Mike went to move the body. Natalie, huffing, told him to leave it. She was exhausted and sick of everyone's shit. There was a dead woman on the concrete, lying in a pool of copious nose blood. So what? Let it be a warning to others to do what Natalie wanted without being asked twice. Sometimes people needed a visual to understand these things.

To clear the rest of the motel, Mike went room to room disconnecting landlines and demanding cell phones, announcing himself to the occupants as FBI and insisting they stay inside with their doors closed. It would be obnoxious if anyone called the cops. Police always thought things like this were their business.

Then, with every person around finally crapping their pants like she wanted them to, Natalie got to work.

Sanders balked when he saw what Natalie had in mind, so she had to drug him. Even if she could somehow beat him into lying still on the bed, she doubted he'd sleep, let alone dream.

To solve the problem, she had the on-site doctor draw a medicinal cocktail and knock him out. Ash was still REM-deprived and they were nearing morning, so putting him under should send him almost immediately into dream sleep.

It didn't matter if Ash became lucid in the dreams that followed. *Mike* would be lucid, and Mike — thanks to the hacked-together algorithm — would be more than in-control. He'd plow through Ash's subconscious like tossing a safehouse.

There were no guarantees that Ash knew a goddamn thing as to Protocol's whereabouts, of course, but searching his brain anyway felt worth a shot. Worst case, Mike would give both of them embolisms. Natalie could live with that. She actually kind of *liked* that consolation prize. It was like giving a free massage to the loser of a contest.

Her odds of getting anything at all from Ash (let alone anything useful) weren't great, but Natalie had nine lives. She'd eked out of tighter spots than this one.

As the sedative took effect, Ash's eyes drooped. Then they closed fully and stayed that way.

"Yippie-ki-yay, motherfucker!" Mike squealed as a tech gave him a lighter version of the REM sedative, easing him into sleep.

Mike and his catchphrases. Natalie crossed her fingers, hoping for that embolism.

FIFTY-THREE

The Intruder

Ash found himself in his childhood kitchen.

His mother was making pancakes. The pancakes had a pattern on their tops that made them look like manhole covers. Also, his mother might have been two different people mashed into one body. It was hard to say.

Then someone else arrived. Ash decided the new arrival was the meter-reader. Did they still read electrical meters anymore? He supposed they must, if this strange young man had shown up in his childhood home.

Strange: Ash didn't think he'd been in this house for a very long time.

Also, the house was in the clouds.

Also, the meter-reader, instead of reading the meter, was running through the house waving his arms like some sort of wizard. What's more, he *was* actually magic: wherever the man waved his arms, cabinets blew open and drawers flew off their rails. It was like being ransacked: robbed by the power company.

The meter-reader began swearing. Shouting. His words were like punches, somehow able to summon the neighbors from the street and surrounding houses without them actually needing to walk through the door. Instead, all those summoned neighbors just sort of showed up — and when they did, the rude young man berated them all.

But something was strange about this young man. Ash had seen him before, hadn't he? But that time he'd seen through a veil, and ... into a different world? That part didn't make a lot of sense, but it felt right. Ash had been sleeping when he'd seen this man before, but also *not* sleeping. He'd seen/sensed him on the other side of ... the other side of ...

A thought came like a whip-crack: *The next time I'm in a dream, I will realize that I'm dreaming.*

And then Ash had it. In a blink, he had it all.

The dream took on the solidity of hardening lava, imparting a physical jolt that almost knocked him off his feet. The kid he'd previously thought was the meter-reader was actually Mike O'Brien: Natalie Baynes's sniveling runt of a partner.

O'Brien didn't shake with the world. That was because this was a dream, and the rocking ground was his mind interpreting sudden and complete recognition of the present. The things he felt were perceptual, not physical. It meant that even if the whole world shook, Ash didn't have to.

He took in his surroundings, now certain that he was in a dream without needing to check. But he checked anyway, lifting his hands and pushing the fingers of one through the palm of the other.

But why the hell was he dreaming of Mike O'Brien?

Recognizing dreams from within could be tricky — but for Ash, once he rediscovered the trick of lucidity, recalling the real world from within a dream was even harder. He used to set himself assignments for his dream adventures all the time: *Go to Pluto. Become a bacterium. Experience synesthesia by seeing tastes and hearing colors.* Doing those things was never difficult, but *remembering* to do them always was.

How did you communicate from the real world into the dream world? If you were Mina Irving, you used flashing red lights.

Mina.

Yes. He remembered Mina. But also someone else. He remembered someone small as well.

Daisy. You're thinking of Daisy.

Maybe that's why he was dreaming about Mike O'Brien: Mike had something to do with Mina and Daisy out in the real world. But what was it?

While Ash thought, O'Brien continued to toss the home using magic. He roughly interrogated Ash's mental neighbors — projections of Ash's mind, all of them. Although come to think of it, Mike's behavior was strange for a dream character. They were usually tame for Ash, after he was lucid.

But then Ash remembered.

Baynes. Mina, beaten and bloody.

They made you come back, Ash's real-world memory told him. *They put you in a bed. They put O'Brien in a bed beside you. Both beds are in a room that adjoins the room you had with Daisy. They drugged you both, then retired to the other room, door closed to keep things quiet. To keep you focused. To keep you from both from waking up.*

As if. Ash could feel his torpor. He wouldn't wake right now if a truck hit him, and it would only get worse with time.

Then: *Oh God.*

Ash found himself remembering more. Baynes had been talking about dream invasion when he went under: something that was only supposed to be possible with future versions of Protocol. She'd hooked up a device between them to act as a wireless relay. It'd looked like the teardrop thing. *The Chirp*, Mina called it. Was it really possible that Baynes had jury-rigged a dream bridge between them ... and therefore that the O'Brien Ash saw wasn't Ash's dream character at all, but was instead O'Brien himself?

No. It's not possible to put one person's mind into another person's dream. It'd be clumsy. Inefficient. Imprecise. And highly, highly unsafe.

But he was only fooling himself. That was the real O'Brien inside his dream, sure as anything.

Ash watched, strangely helpless, while O'Brien ransacked his dream house. The backgrounds around him kept bleeding into new backgrounds. They felt like opened seams: tears in reality. Ash could glimpse demons in the opened gaps. He saw eyes in the chasms. It became ulti- mate synesthesia: he could taste his fears as they percolated from some unknown abyss, like copper on the tongue.

He's looking for something. Rampaging for something.

It'd sounded to Ash, before sleep took him, like someone had fooled the Tailors. The cry-out drive Ash stowed in Kabul had been found, but the thing they so desperately wanted wasn't on it. How was that possible? Ash had no remaining secrets. He remembered the Agents' pact and their random draw from a pool of real and decoy drives. They'd verified the thing. Used an imperturbable drive. There was no way to switch one drive for another, and yet it seemed that's exactly what had happened.

This has Emily written all over it.

Yes. Somehow, Emily had fooled them all. What Ash saw now must be Baynes's nuclear option. She'd sent O'Brien into his mind on the desperate hope he'd find something — *anything* — that might lead them to Protocol's true location.

Unfortunately for Baynes and O'Brien, Ash had no idea where Protocol might be. He doubted Baynes cared. Time was running out, and her deadline had turned her reckless. There was nothing inside him, and yet O'Brien kept shredding his mind, searching anyway. Ash could feel his lucidity waning, his thoughts coming harder and harder. Mike was diving deep, using black-hat voodoo to open closed boxes that Ash never remembered having.

He was damaging Ash's brain.

Memories spilled from unknown voids like surprises from a grab bag:

A stuffed animal with dark meaning. But what had it been to him?

An image of his father, caught masturbating. Ash had shoved that one deep and forgotten all about it.

Ash could feel the damage spreading. If this went on much longer, his brain would turn into cottage cheese.

"Stop." His mind was foggy. He could think of nothing better to say.

O'Brien looked over, but he didn't so much as slow. How was that possible? This was Ash's mind, so shouldn't *Ash* be in control?

Stop him, said a voice.

I tried. I can't.

Then wake up. You're drugged to death, so they barely restrained you. If you can find a way to wake up, you can break free … and take him down in real life.

That's exactly the problem, isn't it? Ash thought. *I'm drugged to death.*

Long ago he'd learned the trick of reaching his mind into bodily awareness to feel his limbs while still dreaming. They were always like bricks. He did it now, finding them not just heavy ... but instead *so* heavy they felt bolted down. The drug was dragging Ash deeper into the abyss as O'Brien ripped him apart for evidence that wasn't there ... and there wasn't a damn thing Ash could do about it.

"I don't know anything!" Ash tried to yell, but his dream jaw had grown sluggish. It came out slurred. "I don't know where Protocol is!"

"I figured," O'Brien said.

Ash could only watch it all happen. The image of O'Brien searching in front of him flickered, intercutting with a different image of the same man making similar motions.

And then, Ash finally remembered.

It was HIM, that day in our bedroom. It was HIM I saw from my dream that day. It was fucking Mike O'Brien who killed Emily.

Rage flooded his system. He screamed and threw himself forward ... but this was still just a dream, and O'Brien laughed as Ash's best efforts failed to harm him. He guffawed at Ash's half-angry, half-mourning drawling of Emily's name.

"Do whatever you want," O'Brien said. "After today, you'll be as dead as I made her."

Ash's dream teeth ground. His dream fists balled into rocks. But he could do nothing.

It wasn't fair. He'd spent so long believing he'd killed Emily in his sleep, but it was a lie. They'd pinned her murder on Ash because he had a clinical history of doing such things without realizing. Like the time he'd caught himself sleep-boxing, or the time he'd nearly pulled his old girlfriend Mindy's hair out by—

The dream seemed to pause, though O'Brien kept thrashing.

The time you nearly pulled Mindy's hair out by the roots while you were dreaming.

The time you pulled Mindy's hair.

PULLED MINDY'S HAIR. WHILE YOU WERE DREAMING.

Jesus. Of course. He'd done that in the real world, but he hadn't woken until it was over. *He hadn't needed to wake up to hurt her.*

Right now, Ash couldn't wake up because of the sedative. And despite it, right now, Ash needed very much to hurt someone.

Sleepwalking. Parasomnia. Sleep violence.

By God, the disorder that had tormented him for years might turn out to be a superpower instead.

Inside the dream, Ash moved his hands in small circles at the ends of his wrists.

At the same time in the waking world, his real hands began to do the same.

FIFTY-FOUR

One Last Idea

They'd barely tied him down. There was no reason to. Considering how much sedative they'd given him, Ash would sleep like the dead for hours. His hands moved anyway, working the restraints in tiny circles. Thanks to his condition, he was asleep but moving just the same.

Ash worked blind, circling his wrists with nothing in the dream to circle against. He'd never been intentionally lucid *and* ambulatory before, so figuring it out took some doing. He'd managed to act out the movement of his wrists, but his dream eyes were open; it wasn't like he could re-open them now.

So on the motel bed his lids stayed closed, his hands moving on faith alone.

He'd seen his restraints before going under. They were leather, not plastic or metal. He'd seen how they'd stretch, if he applied enough tension. And so after a few minutes of experimental movements, his first hand came free.

He reached across his body then, and the other hand followed.

Inside the dream, Mike O'Brien took Ash's motions as random — or as an attempt to summon dream super-powers like fireballs. He laughed. Nothing can harm a person in a dream — and "in a dream" was exactly where the sedated Ash would remain. And so, with Mike oblivious, Ash kept working. He had to do it by trial and error, operating his real-world body on remote control. He'd become a curious sort of double-negative: a *lucid sleepwalker*, similar to a man awake.

He navigated the motel room by feel, his real-world senses confused by those in the dream. By stumbling and grasping, he finally found the second bed.

Then he felt O'Brien's arm, patting his way up its length toward the shoulder. In the dream, O'Brien did not understand. The waking world's signal telegraphed down to him as an itch. So he began to scratch, unaware that in life Ash was now standing directly above him.

Open, Ash thought. *Open, for the love of God … because I need to see this.*

His eyelids opened. Now he could see in two worlds at once.

He leaned over the bed — over his immobile, sleeping victim. Mike didn't have a REM disorder. Mike was normal. Mike didn't have a pathology that made him act out his dreams.

Poor Mike: powerless for all his tedious normality.

Ash leaned further. One after another, his hands wrapped O'Brien's neck just as O'Brien's hands had wrapped Emily's. In the dream, O'Brien's eyes darted as he felt the attack. He couldn't see Ash's hands from the inside, though; the squeezing sensation only confused him. His eyes grew afraid. His neck was constricting, but he didn't know how or why. The poor, murdering bastard didn't understand. To O'Brien, the dream world *was* the real world for the moment ... and you couldn't die in a dream.

"W ... what's going on?" he sputtered.

"I can see you," Dream Ash whispered.

He squeezed. Even in the dream, Mike O'Brien began to cough and choke.

It was too late by the time he finally opened his eyes.

NATALIE IGNORED the noises from the adjoining room at first.

The blurted location of his bogus drive wasn't the first thing Sanders had said. He constantly talked in his sleep. Even over the bug, back when Daisy was alive, Natalie had found it annoying. She was on her last nerve tonight, and if she had to hear Ash blabber and whine while Mike turned his mind to mush, she would lose her shit for sure.

Then something shattered in the adjoining room, and fresh adrenaline rolled through Natalie in a wave. Her fog and irritation evaporated. She became razor sharp, her hand instantly on the knob with fists ready for action.

She yanked open the door, expecting to find that Mike had lost his patience or control of his body. The sound she'd heard would be a breaking lamp, idiot Mike having sleep-thrashed it to the floor as his mind became kibble.

Instead she found Ash Sanders over Mike's corpse, looking like a zombie. How was he awake after all those tranquilizers? And why did he look so stupid and sluggish now? Before, with Daisy, Ash had tucked and rolled. Now he wobbled beside Mike's bed on unsteady legs, practically asking her to end him.

She drew her weapon. "HANDS UP!"

Ash didn't comply. Or stay upright. Instead, the effort

of throttling Mike must have drained every drop of his energy. He collapsed into a mess of limbs.

Mina Irving, tethered to a radiator in the original room, barked laughter. Natalie whipped around, her weapon still high.

"He was asleep," Mina said.

"Of course he was asleep!"

"No." And then that punched, slapped, bleeding bitch actually smiled at Natalie. "I mean he was asleep when he killed your little boyfriend."

"Fuck off," Natalie said, turning back around. She moved forward, preparing to poke Ash with her foot. What ruse was this? Did he really think he could kill her partner and then play like it'd never happened?

"Do you really not understand?" Mina continued from behind her. *"He has a sleep violence disorder.* Jesus Christ, lady ... weren't *you* the one who framed him?"

Natalie backed up, understanding without comprehending. Sanders had been tied down. Yes, he talked and moved in his sleep; she knew all of that, but those sorts of things weren't voluntary. How had Ash managed to free himself, then attack the right person at exactly the right time ... *without waking up?*

Mina was laughing.

Natalie closed her eyes. Her mouth became a straight line. Her blood boiled.

She spun on her toes and marched at Mina, gun aimed right at her. Safety off. Hammer back. And still Mina kept smiling.

Natalie pressed the barrel against her scalp, but she didn't even flinch.

"How did you know that?" Natalie demanded. "How did you know we killed Emily Sanders?"

Mina smiled wider. She'd lost more than one tooth.

"He told you something, didn't he?" Natalie could hear her voice rising with a loss of control. "Earlier in the car you said something else, didn't you? You know about Protocol. You know about the drives. What did Sanders tell you? *Where the fuck is it?*"

It kept getting funnier and funnier to Mina. Her eyes ticked toward Ash's sleeping mess, almost giggling. "Why don't *you* go into his dream now? Why don't *you* just go back in and mind-rape him? Maybe you'll have better luck than your dead little boy toy!"

Natalie wanted to hit her again. And again and again and again. Mina was taunting her. *Nobody* could go into Ash's dreams now. The sedative was progressive; that first REM period had been Mike's only chance. Ash would remain irrevocably dreamless until well past Natalie's expiration date. What the hell could she do now? They were only an hour or so from sunrise.

Mina leaned forward and pressed her forehead harder into the gun. "If you're going to kill me, just fucking kill me already."

Natalie's window for intimidation had passed. She'd have to beat Mina hard to get more than the weather out of her now. It would be easier and more satisfying at this point to kill her. So she touched the trigger. Pressed ever so slightly. At the same time Mina tipped her eyes upward, her gaze unblinking into Natalie's.

Natalie's trigger finger increased its tension. It would be such a relief, to end Mina's smart mouth.

But before she could shoot, a man's voice came from behind her.

"What the hell is going on here?" it demanded.

Natalie looked back and saw Richard Quince, glaring at this diorama of executioner and eager penitent.

She didn't back off. She didn't feel like bowing to

Quince's judgment right now. She'd dug herself a deep hole already, so was it really going to get worse? She could make this quick. She was already half-squeezed on Irving, she could just pull, rotate, pull a few more times: eliminate Richard Goddamn Quince while she was at it.

And why stop there? After handling Mina and Quince, she could head into the other room and do Sanders. And since she was dead anyway, she might as well take a shot at the general when his ass finally showed up to reprimand her.

But she'd hesitated too long. From the corner of her eye, she saw that Quince had drawn weapon.

"Shoot and I shoot you," he said. "Believe me?"

Natalie didn't answer. She made a face: reluctant acquiescence. Then, when her gun hand moved to comply, Quince barked again.

"Safety your weapon *before* you take it off her skin!"

Boiling, Natalie did as he wanted. She flicked the safety using her thumb, then holstered her weapon instead of threatening him. Quince kept aiming until he saw the scene for what it was. Then he did the same.

"This situation is bad for all of us," Natalie told him, her calm returning with a deadly edge. "Bad for the Bespokery. Bad for the general. Bad across the board."

"Whose fault is that?"

"Tell me, Quince. If we close shop without getting what I came for, do you think *any* of us will have a job tomorrow? Did he promise you my position? Did he tell you that you could lead the Bespokery after I'm gone?"

Richard didn't reply, but his face gave her the answer.

"The press won't stay at bay forever. Sooner or later someone will sneak through the barricade. Sooner or later, they'll get a drone past the spotters. So what do you think,

Richard? Will this be easier to explain *after* the sun comes up and they can see for miles? Or will it be much harder?"

Another beat of quiet. Then Richard said, "I've been listening in. I know everything. You can't find Protocol with Sanders knocked out. Not before shit hits the fan."

"Close the door," she told him. "I've got one last idea."

FIFTY-FIVE

One More Try

Richard wouldn't let her kill Ash Sanders, even though she very much wanted to.

There was no justification for his death beyond her anger, Richard claimed, and although all Natalie had said about the threat of press and exposure was mostly true, the government had an excellent record of wiggling out of sticky situations.

Their only chance was to somehow resolve this before morning — just not in the way Baynes wanted. Killing Ash would be severing the best source of information the departments would ever have on this debacle.

So they tied Ash up — very well this time. Then they unshackled Mina Irving and dragged her to the bed where Ash had been before his little magic trick had let him kill O'Brien without either of them waking up. They tied Mina to the bed, more tightly than they'd originally tied Ash.

Baynes would go in this time. Rather than leaving the room as always-sloppy Baynes had done when O'Brien had tried to do this, Richard pulled up a chair to watch and stand guard.

"I'll be okay," Baynes told him, looking up from her half of the dream bridge. "The procedure didn't hurt Mike."

Richard looked at the corpse, which was still slumped beside the second bed.

"You know what I mean," said Baynes.

A junior operative entered the room, then moved toward O'Brien. "Ma'am?" he asked Baynes. "Where do you want the body?"

"Being buggered by homeless people," she answered.

The operative waited.

"Out front," she finally said. "Put him beside that nosy cunt of an owner."

Yes. The owner. Richard had noticed the owner's body on display outside the room and had very much disapproved. Everyone here was supposed to be a professional. You didn't use dead people as scarecrows no matter how much they'd pissed you off.

Richard took a moment to think as O'Brien was dragged outside. He'd have to play some of this by ear. Emily Sanders had made it sound like the copy of Protocol stored inside Mina would blink like a strobe light if anyone thought to look for it, but Richard wasn't sure what "looking for it" entailed. It couldn't mean using Protocol, seeing as Protocol was still tucked away.

Richard looked toward Mina as the doctor slid a sedative needle into Baynes. They'd both need the drug to dream before time ran out, but the doses would be much lighter than before.

He looked over and saw Baynes. Her eyelids were starting to droop, staring wordlessly at him.

"Richard ..." Her voice was uncharacteristically soft, as if the sedative was lowering her defenses.

"Yes?"

"If that bitch so much as twitches," she said, meaning Mina, "I'll have your balls cut off and shoved down your throat."

Rolling his eyes, Richard moved toward the other bed. He was leaning over to tighten Mina's right restraint when a commotion exploded outside: men and women chattering, protesting, yelling at someone to step away — to get back.

Richard was about to rise and reach for his service pistol, but then the door opened and he froze in place. A small boy was standing in the doorway, dressed in footie pajamas. He looked around four years old: his son Connor's age exactly.

The kid must have slipped behind the armed guards outside. Richard felt a chill. In order to get past them, he'd've needed to crawl over the bodies: Mike O'Brien on one hand ... and a woman that almost surely had to be the child's mother on the other.

"Mister?" the kid said to Richard, tears already licking his eyes. "Can you please help my mommy? I think she's sick."

Nobody said a thing.

Except for Baynes. "Get that kid the fuck off my scene."

Richard started to rise. He stopped halfway, his hand still on the leather buckle as Mina Irving's glare finally speared him.

"What are you doing over there, kissing her?" Baynes said to Richard as the child was led away.

"I'm just tightening her straps."

She scoffed, sleep drifting into her voice. "Tell the bitch I'm coming for her."

Instead, before Richard pulled away, he told Mina something else.

FIFTY-SIX

A Masterwork of Astonishing Power

Mina found herself in what appeared to be a small diner with red-velour booths along one wall. A window looking out on a concrete-floored playground was on the other wall. The lot outside was half basketball court, half rusty swings. An intercom was fixed to the wall perpendicular to both. It was a large, boxy hand dryer according to the rules of this world — so although Mina *was* in a diner, she was also in a large industrial restroom.

She'd been in the diner/bathroom for hours now and had yet to snag a waiter's attention. She had also just arrived. There was no past here. Only future.

A voice came through the intercom: "WAKE UP, BUTTERCUP." It was a strange thing for anyone to say, let alone over an intercom.

Mina stopped. One moment she was thinking about ordering a pecan waffle, and the next she was paralyzed, remembering a stranger she'd once known intimately.

In the memory, she and the strange woman were sitting across from one another at a small metal table beside a wooden railing. It was evening, the sun just set. Beyond the railing was a broad and night-blue river, with boats tooling by.

The next moment, the memory was no longer a memory. Instead, Mina was suddenly *there*, at the place with the round metal table. At Mozart's. With the woman she knew but had never met. With Emily Sanders.

"Do you remember this?" Emily asked, meaning everything around them.

Mina considered. She understood now that Emily had been one of Mina's best friends for a while now — not that they'd ever been able to hang out in public. There'd been just this one time, because their ends were dawning and the time for their forgetting was near. Even then, they'd come at night so nobody would see them.

"*Mozart's*. This is Mozart's, isn't it?"

Emily nodded.

"And we're in a dream." The knowledge was dumbfounding. Despite her work in sleep and dreams (lucid dreams in particular), Mina herself had never managed the trick. She'd never really been able to imagine what a lucid dream might be like, outside of what her subjects described when they woke. They all agreed that such dreams — if you focused while inside and if they were stable — could be as real as anything in waking life.

Mina had known all of that, but only on an intellectual level. She'd never felt it deep down. Never really *gotten* it. Until now. And yet it required her full attention to hold onto those oh-so-real surroundings. The effort was like clinging to awareness itself. Non-lucidity stood to one side: always a threat of returning.

"Yes," Emily answered. "We're in a dream."

"I thought all of this," Mina waved to indicate her surroundings, "was a memory."

Emily shrugged. "Somewhat. But mostly, it's the way your brain is processing my shortcut."

"What shortcut?" Mina asked.

"The shortcut that unlocked you the rest of the way. That reminded you how to dream like this in seconds instead of months. The shortcut, Mina dear, that helped you remember *everything*."

And yes. Mina really *did* remember everything now. The voice on the intercom *("Wake up, buttercup"* — in Richard Quince's voice for some reason) had triggered her recall. Newly unlocked memories had been steamrolling through her ever since.

Now Mina remembered every one of the times she'd met Emily, each encounter fully rendered. There was no blink of epiphany. She went from knowing nothing to knowing it all.

Emily had come to Mina one day in the lab, bearing technology the world didn't know about and asking for help. With nobody left inside her circles to trust, Mina had been her only hope. Ash trusted Mina, so Emily decided to do the same. Not that Ash ever knew about their friendship. *Nobody* could know about their friendship.

Throughout their many visits, Emily had explained how dream observation worked. And Emily had convinced Mina that if Ash was ever made to forget, she should do everything in her power to help him remember. If Ash needed meds to suppress dreams, Mina should prescribe drugs that percolated them to the surface instead. If he needed help with his sleepwalking, she should give him sugar pills, not medication to stop it.

Not that Mina would know she was doing any of it, with her memories gone so soon after Mozart's … but her deep mind would remember.

And her subconscious? Why, Mina's subconscious would remember the biggest secret of all.

"The shortcut," Mina said. "Your 'shortcut' was a mnemonic trigger."

Emily nodded. "I told you I'd leave you a video with the mnemonic phrase in it. If you found the video, it meant things had gone bad. You'd need to relearn how to dream, and the trigger would let you do it almost instantly. You especially needed to know how to defend yourself. How to arm yourself inside your mind, in case someone tried to get anything out of you."

Mina remembered. *The beds. Ash's mind invasion. Mike O'Brien, dead by a vengeful husband's sleeping hands.* Emily's "shortcut" had given her brass knuckles and pepper spray to fight the mind rape in a way even Ash couldn't do. *That's* what the shortcut was for — at least in part, maybe in whole.

"You did this so I'd be able to defend myself against Baynes?" Mina asked.

"Or someone *like* Baynes," Emily allowed.

"But the phrase wasn't in your video. It—" But now she remembered. Back at Bryan's lab, she'd been interrupted before the video could finish. "Wait. How did I hear the trigger, if I didn't get to the end of the video?"

"Richard," Emily said.

"Richard?" Mina repeated.

"The man who arrived. You knew him mostly as Chuck, but his real name is Richard. When he bent over your bed to tighten your straps, he whispered the trigger phrase in your ear. It manifested as a voice over the intercom, back when this dream began."

Mina nodded. After the intercom spoke, that's when she'd become lucid. That's when she'd started to remember. That's when she came here.

"But … how could *Richard* know the phrase? How could he have any idea what it would do? And even then, why would he say it, reminding me how to protect myself? He's on *their* side."

"I don't know. *You* don't know. It doesn't matter."

A bright glow caught Mina's attention. She turned toward it and saw an enormous red sphere — like a dim second sun — rising from the river.

"Do you remember *that?*" Emily asked, meaning the new sun.

At first Mina thought the answer was no. The thing over the water was just a sphere, nothing else. But then she found herself able to feel into it, and she remembered the corresponding feel of the same sun being fed into her bit by bit sometime in the past.

She remembered Emily's plan, and the way Mina had volunteered to be a part of it: as a sort of organic storage vessel — a cry-out drive in human form.

"It's Protocol," Mina said, taking in the glowing sight of it. "I had it all along."

"I told you there wasn't anyone else I could trust."

Emily watched it rise. The sphere became semi-transparent, revealing inside itself a clockwork of tremendous complexity — a masterwork of astonishing power.

Terrifying, in the wrong hands.

The sphere moved toward them, shrinking as it came. Down to the size of a golf ball before it settled in the cup of Mina's outstretched palm.

A new light — bright white this time — shone from the other direction. The river vanished. The decking below them disappeared, along with the table and chairs. But it seemed Emily and Mina were already standing, now in an all-white space that seemed to yawn on forever.

The light had started life as a small rip, but now it expanded to encompass the world.

"She's here," Emily told her, eyes afraid. "You have to protect it from her, Mina. Don't let Baynes get her hands on Protocol, no matter what."

A new door, made of blackness, opened in the void. Natalie Baynes came through it, then came forward. She was much larger than she was in life. She had the same proportions, but they were magnified — towering above Mina like a behemoth.

"Emily, I—" Mina began to say.

But Emily was gone.

FIFTY-SEVEN

Death Blow

I can resist her, Mina thought. *Emily taught me how.*

But that was whistling in the dark, telling herself stories she didn't believe.

Baynes came forward with purpose. With zero doubts, zero hesitation. O'Brien had talked of "searching" inside Ash's mind, but Baynes had cleared the noise from Mina's mind with barely any effort.

Mina had nowhere to hide. Nowhere for *Protocol* to hide.

Baynes was staring right at her pocket, where she'd slipped Protocol's bright red marble. Mina could feel it radiating heat, as if this woman's will alone could summon it. Baynes had sniffed its hidden presence the second she'd entered Mina's dream.

Mina watched her come, half-forgetting that dreams couldn't hurt her.

Defenses up. Defenses UP!

She waved her hand over her head, summoning a dream shield between herself and Baynes. But it seemed puny; Baynes towered over Mina like a god.

Baynes raised a fist made of psychological strength. She sent it slamming down on Mina's shield of weaker ideals: hope, maybe ... or the weakness of love. The whole world shimmered. Hatred and purpose were so much more powerful than hope.

Baynes, half-demon in this impossible place, brayed with a bloodcurdling scream. Her teeth elongated. Her hair burned. Her tongue had grown a fork. Her sounds were pure animal as she raked at Mina with claws. Pounded and pounded on Mina's puny defenses, driven to frenzy by the prize she saw Mina so frantic to protect.

"GIVE IT! LET IT GO!" Baynes roared.

Mina pushed back with all her might, but hers was an atrophied muscle: a mental trick, not a spindle of fibers that could be trained with weights. Desperate and furious and bone-splintering as she came, it seemed Baynes was having no such issues in turning her intentions into action.

Mina could only brace herself.

God. Without the mnemonic, I'd be dead now.

Well. Not *dead*. Traumatized, maybe. Afraid of nightmares forever, maybe. A little psychotic when this was over? Probably. For sure she'd have been stripped of Protocol, which she was still only barely managing to grasp.

Thank you, Emily. Thank you, Richard. You did what you could. But she already saw that it wasn't enough.

What was giving Baynes so much strength? Why was she so much better at this — so large, so strong? This was *Mina's* head, *Mina's* goddamned dream!

And yet right from the start, Baynes had mastered her.

Another blow. Another barely-there defense.

Mina reached into her pocket and found the Protocol marble hot to the touch. It was pulling upward and away from her, stretching like a line of invisible taffy toward Baynes and her greedy open hands.

Mina could see the Chirp connecting them from within the dream, just like Ash had taught himself to see it — maybe because Mina was gifted, or maybe because Emily had taught her, too. She could see the device's influence, tipping the world toward Baynes. Something in this particular Chirp liked Natalie Baynes very much. She was being somehow fed from it, whereas everything Mina tried to do worked to starve her.

This was a battle of minds. Tailors had made the device connecting them, but even without help Ash had handled Mike.

You're not an Agent, Mina. Emily gave you some tools, but let's admit something before its obviousness kills you: Her kung-fu is stronger than yours. You should have stayed away from Ash Sanders.

And Emily, bless her heart, should have planned better. She'd underestimated Baynes twice now. Twice Baynes had cut through the Agents' defenses, and along the way she'd built this … this *thing* that adored her. This reaper's scythe.

Mina.

She heard Emily's voice. It was her own projection of her once-good-friend, cobbled together by recollections, estimations, and assumptions.

You're intuitive, the Emily-projection whispered as Baynes landed another blow, nearly shattering her dream shield. *So intuit. What do you see? What do you already know?*

Baynes struck again. Even in this unreal place, Mina felt her legs buckle, taking her will along with it. Meanwhile Protocol kept rising up, almost too strong for Mina to stop it from ascending to Baynes's possession.

Use your head, Mina!

Instead of being encouraged, Mina wished the Emily-voice would shut up. She hadn't learned to defend herself after all, it seemed. She hadn't raised any definitive arms. She was useless despite everything Emily had done, with the shortcut, to prepare her. This fight was already over. In any practical sense, Baynes was the victor already.

You're not listening, said Dream Emily.

Again Mina found herself sitting at Mozart's with Emily across from her. Baynes paused. Time stopped.

"Don't you remember what we talked about?" the now-solid vision of Emily said into the gap. "The Agency used to work on a paradigm of *get*. We *took*. But you told me about *your* dreamers — the ones you worked with in your lab. You said that everything started coming together once the dialogue could go both ways. Once dreamers could talk to you *and* you could talk to them. The paradigm went from *get* to *synergize*. That inspired me to redesign the Chirp. To make it more efficient by rethinking what mattered. Do you remember?"

Time resumed. The attack resumed, Mozart's gone again. Another of Baynes's blows landed. Mina's shield was in tatters.

Do you remember?

Why the hell did it matter what she remembered? Mina was getting murdered. Protocol was at the tips of her fingers, almost lost. She was straining as hard as she could to hold on as it rose toward Baynes.

But then in a blink, Mina understood.

She and Emily *had* had that discussion. Mina, with her knowledge of the body, had explained that functional natural systems didn't only *take* from their environments. They *gave*, too.

Few systems worked in only one direction. After the epiphany, Mina's lab had begun working with the natural order instead of against it. The change paid off; advances came faster. All it'd taken was a simple flip in thinking. Everything clicked once researchers learned the trick of talking back to the dreamers instead of simply reading what the EEG gave them.

Every natural system, Mina had told Emily that night at Mozart's, *is push and pull. Give and get. Agonist and antagonist. We finally asked: Why would we ever want to work against nature?*

As she held on for her life, Mina wondered why the memory struck her as so persistent now. Why was she thinking about it at all, and why was the Emily inside her so insistent that she stare that single discussion in the eye?

The real Emily had found Mina's ideas intriguing enough to redesign the Chirp based on what felt to her now like juvenile findings. But who cared about it now? Baynes was doing just fine with one-way aggression. Her Chirp was singularly focused, with Baynes's singleminded intent as its fuel.

The strongest form of intent was *anger,* and Baynes was pure rage. No wonder she was winning. Mina had no chance to be angry when she felt this afraid.

But does that mean Baynes is right? What natural system takes more than it gives?

Who gave a shit? Was she supposed to shoot for a moral victory while Baynes kicked her to the curb?

Don't you remember, Mina? The plan changed the plan. Can you stop her? Is it even possible?

And Mina thought, *No. No, I can't stop her from taking it. It's a lost cause. A dead end. Protocol is as good as gone.*

So why fight? Why try for what can't be done? Are you a fool?

Mina strained, dream fingers losing the last of their grip on Protocol.

Why fight the inevitable? Emily's voice persisted. *What's the point? Push and pull, Mina. Give and get.*

Something inside her clicked. Then Mina exhaled in a sigh of surrender.

What *was* the point? She lost either way.

So Mina opened her hands, opened her mind, and let go.

As she did, her guard shattered. Baynes's giant red hand reached past her, through her, and took what she'd spent every ounce of herself protecting. The demon roared with victory, raising the small red ball to the sky. Then she ran for the exit, and was gone.

Mina fell to the dream ground, exhausted and defeated.

Once Baynes was gone and her mind's scenery emptied into another void of pure white, Emily reappeared beside her.

"She took it," Mina said. "After everything you did, she still beat you."

"Yes ..." Emily nodded, then reversed direction and shook her head too, "... and no."

FIFTY-EIGHT

Friendly Headshots

Ash woke with the buzzing of a thousand sleepy hornets in his ears.

He sat up, but a hand on his chest pushed him back down. His eyes hurt. Something to one end of his visual field was nuclear bright. He might need to throw up. His entire body was vibrating, jarred from every direction at once. It wasn't helping his nausea.

"Easy," said a female voice. "Take it easy, Ash."

He complied, moving halfway back down but stopping himself short on bent elbows. His clearing mind had identified his surroundings as a van's rear interior, and the jostling as the vibration of driving. There was something beneath him, springy and plush. It smelled of copper, and when he looked to see what it was, he saw a mattress half covered in blood.

For a moment he felt even more nauseated, but then an internal presence seemed to slap him in the face and tell him to get over it. He'd seen far worse. In the name of God and country, he'd *done* far worse. He knew that now. There was no more lost memory. Ash remembered every single thing the Bespokery had made him forget, plus the lies they'd put in place of the truth.

His eyes had closed. He was supernaturally tired. Nobody in history had ever been this exhausted, and yet the last thing he wanted was to sleep.

He opened his eyes again and saw Mina sitting beside him like a nurse, holding a water bottle. But drinking felt impossible.

"How's your head?" she asked.

"Detonated," he told her.

"You should drink something."

"Never."

"You should really drink something, Ash. You've been asleep for sixteen hours."

He sighed, then sat up further and tried to comply. He'd done longer stints asleep before, and nobody had been there to coach him upon waking. Here and now, Ash did it mostly for Mina. She looked so worried. And she'd been so badly beaten.

"What happened to you?" he asked.

"You don't remember?"

Oh. Yes. He remembered now. His older memories had acquired the transparency of crystal, but last night was pieces floating in soup. It was returning now, but only slowly.

"I had the strangest dream," he told her.

"Yeah?"

"I'm not sure if it *was* a dream."

"How do you know you're not dreaming right now?"

"Very funny." But still he sneaked a glance at some writing on the van's interior walls — three times to be sure.

"Tell me what you remember," Mina said. "I'll tell you if it really happened."

"Daisy."

Mina nodded soberly. Her eyes ticked to the mattress, and Ash knew it was Daisy's blood beneath him.

"What else?" she asked.

"Did Baynes really have some sort of a … a *dream link*?"

"Yeah. Worked pretty well, too, if you didn't care about precision. Or control. Or human rights. Or safety."

"I think I dreamed about that young guy. Mike."

"True. You dreamed of Mike."

"He was killing Emily. Or …" Time was still confusing. "He *did* kill Emily?"

"He did. They framed you, but he was the one who did it."

"Then I dreamed I killed him."

"You did."

"In my dream, or in life?"

"Both. Can you believe it? You've now killed exactly one person in your sleep."

He was too tired for gratitude. He was innocent of Emily's murder, guilty of O'Brien's. Everything was just data right now.

"Where are we going?" Ash asked.

"That's not the game we're playing," Mina told him. "Besides, I don't think there's a firm destination. I'm kind of afraid to ask."

That was a strange answer. He sat up more fully, trying to crane to see past the blaze outside the windshield. "Who's driving?"

"Let's get your head straight first."

Instead of asking again, Ash rolled onto one hip. Movement was a bitch. His mouth was cotton. His head was in a vise and his stomach was brewing a nice vat of acid. He kept clawing forward anyway.

Then he saw who was up there behind the wheel. It

was Chuck DeMona: Richard Motherfucking Quince. Richard saw Ash, too. He had the gall to smile his stupid cherubic smile.

Stumbling to his feet despite Mina's protests, Ash grabbed the closest potential weapon. It just so happened to be a good one: a tire iron, nice and heavy.

Mina tried to push between them. "Ash. Put it down and sit. I can explain."

He took a lunging step, but then his legs gave out and he fell sideways onto one wall, most of which was covered with electronic equipment. A window there had been mostly blacked out by a wraparound decal. It seemed he was in an ArkTek transport just like the good ol' days. How ironic.

"It's okay," Mina said once he was down and staring daggers. "Richard's with us now."

Ash glared harder.

"I should get you up to speed before you wake up enough to try anything stupid."

And then, settling in across from him in the van's rattling rear, she did.

HOURS LATER, the three of them were in another shitty motel. It wasn't fair. Ash stared at the TV, trying not to think. He wondered if maybe the expression was true: if ignorance really *was* bliss. He'd been neurotic, paranoid, and exceedingly depressed when he'd believed his mind was failing him. But the joke was on him: having his mind back wasn't any better.

Mina had already told Ash the basics: How Ash had managed to turn the lemons of his sleep disorder into a nice lemonade that'd let him act while still sedated and dreaming. She told him how after Ash's mind invasion came up empty, Baynes had rolled the dice on sticking her fingers into Mina's mind instead. She and Richard then explained Emily's failsafe plot, which Ash, even before his memory erasure, hadn't known. *Every* Agent had hidden fake drives. Protocol had been encoded inside Mina ... but at the last moment, Baynes had taken it from her.

And of course Mina told Ash about how Richard had arguably saved her sanity. A person couldn't be physically harmed inside a dream, but psychological damage was more than possible.

"Emily taught me how to hold my ground," Mina told him. "I didn't do much more than that, but it was enough once those skills came back to me, thanks to Richard. If he hadn't heard the last of Emily's message and decided to crack my memories open like she wanted in the first place, I'd probably be in a straitjacket. Or dead by my own hand."

"I guess in the end I just couldn't let it keep happening," said Richard. "When that little kid walked in, all I could see was my son. It's like I saw everything through Connor's eyes. I just ... couldn't be part of it anymore."

Richard briefly explained the rest, leaving details for later. As ranking Agent on the scene after Baynes ran off for unknown reasons, he'd taken command. He got his troops to clean the scene, then had covertly cut Ash and Mina loose. He and Mina put the only mattress they could move without unfastening tethers or being seen into the nearest fleet van, put Ash atop it, and drove away.

He'd run off without much thought, save a call to send his family into hiding until the heat burned off. At the very least it meant Richard had retired: done with being a monster who made the world worse for his son.

Ash gave Richard a neutral, noncommittal look in response. It would be a while before he could show the man formerly known as Chuck DeMona any gratitude or compassion.

"But Baynes got it," Ash said. "She got what she was after."

"Protocol," Mina replied with a nod. "Yes. I saw it happen. I was no match for her. That rig they used was attuned to ambition, and Baynes was nothing but naked ambition. I never had a chance."

"She woke a bit before Mina," Richard explained. "Then she went to the Blip's optical drive and pulled the card. I don't know how she moved that fast, even though she wasn't sedated nearly as much as you were, Ash."

He didn't like Richard using his name, like they were buddies.

"She'd draped her holster over the end of the bed. She pulled her piece and shot the guard who'd been in the room with us. Then she pointed it at me. I didn't see it coming. Couldn't even get to my own grip. I figured she'd just shoot me, but the guys outside were moving around, getting ready to bust in, thinking something had gone wrong. And I mean, it had gone wrong. But wrong *for* Baynes, not *with* her."

"So what did she do?" Ash asked.

"She talked really fast. She told them to arrest me. Then, before anyone could ask questions, she ran. It was a confusion bomb. Nobody thought to stop her until she was gone."

"Why would she run?" Ash asked. "She had what she wanted. Like a hero."

"Maybe," Richard said. "But if you ask me, the general's odds of sparing Baynes, even with Protocol, couldn't have been any better than fifty-fifty. She's always been a cockroach ... and roaches know how to survive."

It made sense to Ash. Baynes was probably planning to

get some space so she could politic herself a deal. She'd return to the Bespokery on her own terms once she could be assured of safety — and a promotion, of course. Richard would probably have to do something similar, though only after the dust settled and the blame game was over.

Heads would roll at the Bespokery. With luck, Richard would end up a good guy in the new management's eyes instead of a villain.

Mina's head was shaking: after-the-fact emotion finally peeking through her armor now that they were free of imminent peril.

"I couldn't hold onto it," she told the carpet between her feet. "Protocol. Emily taught me everything she could, and it wasn't enough to stop Baynes from taking it."

She looked up at Ash then, but instead of the tear-filled eyes he'd expected, grim determination stood in its place.

"But do you want to know the weirdest part?" she asked.

Ash looked at Richard first, but he had no idea either.

"I've been thinking about it all day. About Emily, and our talks, and about how smart she was and how she'd thought of everything. And the more I think, the more convinced I am. The more sure I feel."

"Sure of what?" Ash asked.

"That maybe — just maybe — I wasn't *supposed* to stop her."

BAYNES'S WORK appeared on the evening news. A very credible tip — supported by all sorts of hard audio and video evidence — claimed that second-degree murderer Ash Sanders was at large and had killed at least five more times.

A flashy graphic filled the screen, pictures of "Ash's victims" lined up like soldiers. On the motel bed, Ash took it all in. He saw friendly headshots of Jose, Daisy, O'Brien, and two people he didn't recognize.

"Who are the two on the end?" Mina asked.

"That's Clark Westing," Ash said, pointing at the first. "He's the guard she shot before nearly shooting me. I'm pretty sure the woman there owned the motel where it all happened."

"What about all the Sleepers at the lab?" Mina asked.

"Too many dead there," Richard said. "They just made all of that go away. Don't ask how."

Ash almost laughed. This wasn't Agency. Or even the government. Those folks always hid corpses, then denied themselves blue. Black ops hated attention. It had to be Baynes who'd leaked the tip, probably dropping edited bug audio and selective surveillance video to support her claim.

Baynes was smart, already building a case for those who'd ultimately decide her fate. She'd bridge the gap between the damage she'd caused and the chaos she'd cleaned up. Now that Baynes had done this, Ash wouldn't be able to go to the police. He couldn't blow any whistles that weren't already blown, taking any of this to the public. Because who would believe Ash Sanders now?

Mina's mouth was hanging open. Seeing a new on-screen graphic, he understood why.

"Sanders is confirmed to be traveling with two accomplices, against whom police say evidence is also mounting," announced the newscaster.

The new photos onscreen, of course, were Richard and Mina's.

FIFTY-NINE

Correction

A week passed.

Ash and Richard moved into detente, each agreeing to disagree on the remainder of their issues — mostly from Ash's side. Richard, annoyingly, turned out to have the same general disposition as his alter-ego Chuck. He was willing to accept all the blame that Ash wanted to give him.

It was hard expending the energy to loathe someone who never resisted.

The three of them ate takeout from dives. Richard's face had a way of disappearing into crowds, so he was able to pick up what they needed without raising eyebrows, wearing only a light disguise. They lived in a different motel every night — although on the books, only a man named John Smith (who looked like Richard Quince) was ever registered. They stayed only at places without internal hallways — where the rooms were far from the office, cash was accepted, and the clientele of hookers and cheating spouses all looked the other way. Twice they stole vehicles from long-term airport parking lots, gambling that the owners would be gone for a while, and hence that their theft wouldn't be reported in time to make a difference.

Living life as a fugitive who finally knew his past, Ash was able to sleep without tormented dreams.

MINA SLEPT VERY DIFFERENTLY.

She was lucid most nights now. It wasn't intentional. Some stubborn remnant of Emily lived like a splinter inside her mind, waking Mina within her dreams. That version of Emily acted like a spirit with a will of her own. Night after night Emily would poke Mina in the middle of an ordinary dream, and then they'd travel elsewhere in the dreamscape and have coffee together.

Emily (really a part of Mina that had learned and now religiously applied what her subconscious thought of as "Emily logic") always showed up with a knitted scarf that grew longer by the night. Through the peculiar logic of dreams, the scarf was made not of yarn, but of tiny logical conclusions.

Emily had explained her "knitting" process, but to Mina it sounded more like excavating an archaeological dig. That part of Mina's consciousness dug all day long, then returned each night with new threads to weave into the puzzle.

"It's mostly finished," Emily told Mina on their seventh night of meeting. This time they'd dream-met at a plain old Starbucks, unusual only because it balanced atop the enormous tower dominating Dubai's skyline.

"What is?" Mina asked.

"My inference." Emily held up the thing that was almost a scarf.

"Tell me the truth. Are you really a part of me, or are you somehow Emily herself? Are you actually just one last time bomb she left inside me? One last mnemonic hurrah?"

"Not at all. I'm you, Mina."

"Then why don't I know what you're doing?"

Emily gave her a *well-duh* face. "Because *you* don't know what *you're* doing."

"I don't know what to think about that." In truth, Mina wasn't particularly concerned. She had maybe one broken-up hour of conversation with Emily nightly now, and it felt exactly like trying to work out an impossible problem.

Still, she'd felt an odd inkling for some time now. It was impossible to say what that inkling was.

It'd begun after her strange last conversation with the first mental Emily — the one who'd more or less said that *Yes, Natalie Baynes got Protocol out of Mina's head*, but *No, that didn't mean she'd beaten Emily.*

Mina couldn't stop puzzling over how both things could be true, but the only clues seemed to be somewhere in that conversation's miscellany: notions of give and take, of push and pull, of agonist and antagonist being the normal modes of nature.

Emily had heard those things from Mina for real once upon a time, then changed her Chirp's programming to mimic the natural order. The old Chirps had only *taken* from the minds of subjects, but the new ones *gave* to them as well. Dreamtech was a two-way conversation these days … just as Mina's lab, before all of this, had been building two-way communication with its dreamers.

Mina had mostly quit trying to figure it out, but here was the same discussion again.

Emily said, "You couldn't have resisted Baynes when she invaded your mind."

"That's an understatement. She was Godzilla."

"What did it feel like, when she took it from you?"

That was a strange question. Mina made a face. "Why are you asking?"

"Because I keep finding bits of her inside you."

"Bits of the real Emily?"

"Bits of Baynes."

Mina sat back in her dream-Starbucks chair. Dubai became Seattle around them. "What?"

"A shared dream isn't a one-way thing any more than communication is a one-way thing," Emily said. "Baynes wasn't *in you* that day so much as you were *both in the same place together*."

She held up the logic-scarf and pointed to a section as if the answers were there. "Baynes *took* Protocol, but she did it using a modified version of my Chirp. Thanks to the insight you gave at Mozart's, the Blip and Chirp were designed for reciprocity. So when Baynes scooped Protocol out of you, she couldn't help leaving an impression of herself behind."

Mina folded her brow. "I'm not sure I understand."

"You saw Baynes's thought patterns when the two of you were in the dream together," Emily explained. "You also still have a copy of Protocol inside you, because *reading* your thoughts didn't *erase* those thoughts. Protocol was made to decode patterns. As far as Protocol is concerned, what you saw of Baynes's mind that day is basically a fingerprint."

Mina felt the edge of understanding, but it was only an edge.

"Think about that for a second," Emily continued. "*You have Baynes's mental fingerprint.* The only way you could have gotten that fingerprint was to let her take something from you. She exposed herself to you when she stole Protocol ... whether she meant to or not."

"And that's good, to have her mental fingerprint?" Mina asked.

"That depends on you, I suppose. A fingerprint of any kind is a way of positively identifying someone. So for instance, I'll bet you could pick Baynes's mind out of a crowd no matter how well she's hidden … assuming you have a Blip and a Chirp."

"Richard has a Blip and a Chirp."

Emily smiled. Of course she'd known that.

"Baynes hasn't turned Protocol in to the general yet," Mina said.

"No. She's still biding her time."

"She hasn't turned in the only copy of the only safe technology that makes dream invasion — and very precise thought and behavior manipulation — possible."

"Correction," said Emily. "It's one of *two* copies of the technology that does those things … *if* you have the equipment to use it."

"What are you saying?"

"I'm saying that the real Emily may have had a plan all along."

Mina felt the last pieces of the puzzle click together. She suddenly understood the inference that Dream Emily had been knitting. She knew, now, why a deep part of her hadn't accepted their loss, or that this was over.

"Emily *wanted* me to let Baynes win," Mina realized. "To *let* her take Protocol, so I'd get what I needed in order to find her later."

Dream Emily nodded. "*Find* her. And more."

SIXTY

Terrible Dreams

Natalie Baynes frowned at her phone.

She couldn't remember why she'd picked the thing up. It was like opening the fridge and having no idea why. Had she been meaning to call someone? Had she *just* called someone? The latter was ridiculous, but it also rang a few bells.

She was in a penthouse at the MGM Grand in Las Vegas, surrounded by empty bottles. Her plan was working well, but it was taking its sweet time. She needed to make sure that every box was ticked before contacting the general ... so until the time came, she waited. And drank.

There was really just one big problem to solve before she got back in the saddle: the general wanted her dead for the problems she'd caused and the press nightmare her operation had unleashed. Fortunately, Natalie was slippery; she had a way of greasing palms and making back-alley friends wherever she went. She had a lot of favors lined up already, and soon there'd be enough of them in the right places to protect her. But not yet.

Once those arrangements fell into place (conservatively,

another two or three days), Natalie would be able to come out of hiding. She could take Protocol to the proper folks at that point and, by doing so, make herself a hero. For now, she was holding it hostage. All this plotting and planning and hiding would be worth it, though. Once Natalie returned to the Bespokery on her new and carefully planned terms, the general wouldn't be able to touch her. Natalie might even find a way to put *him* out of a job — have him demoted to janitorial, maybe.

She'd been partying to pass the time until everything lined up — alone, but a party was still a party. Although maybe she'd been laying it on too thick. She spent most of her time drunk out of her skull, and the forgetting thing with the phone was a great indication that she'd gone too far.

Not that there weren't other troubling indications that she'd gone too far.

At first, it was just the dreams that bothered her. She woke most mornings shaking off visions of Mina Irving, who'd spent the night harassing and pursuing her. The dreams were bad enough, but yesterday Natalie could have sworn she saw Richard Quince in real life, sitting across Las Vegas Boulevard like Midnight Cowboy.

The cocaine was making her paranoid. The booze, too.

She told herself to lay off. To try easing herself back into the routine of a respectable civilian. Getting clean and sober was a simple matter of will.

At this point she'd do anything to end the dreams. In them, Mina was a phone technician, but she didn't actually repair phones. Instead, she worked inside a giant switchboard room that Natalie knew, in the logic of dreams, was actually her own head. Mina pulled phone cords and moved them from socket to socket all night long ... and as she did, Natalie could only watch in terror, sure that Mina was rearranging neurons inside her brain.

As Dream Mina pulled wires, Natalie felt herself thinking of her high school bully, Laci (with an i) Devereaux. She seemed to see Laci everywhere now — sometimes even in waking life, though Natalie tried not to believe that part. She got confused. Sometimes she thought about doing destructive, stupid things.

Why? Because Mina was working the switchboard, changing her mind in her dreams — while Laci waited nearby as enforcer.

But all of that was stupid. Laci had been killed in a car crash years ago and Mina Irving was a nobody who didn't even know where Natalie was. She wouldn't have the stones to chase her even if she *could* somehow find her.

No, Natalie's problems were her own. The drugs were making her jumpy. The alcohol. The dreams.

Also, she kept losing time.

Also, this new shit with the phone.

Still confused, Natalie checked her recent calls. At the top of the list was a call from a contact named Fuk Chu that Natalie didn't even know. She didn't remember getting a call from him, either — not in the least. Maybe she'd been drunk when she received it, although the log said he'd only called minutes ago.

It must be a glitch. Maybe that was the name of the Japanese guy she'd let slap her ass last night and call her geisha. He could have called, right? She'd just forgotten.

As Natalie watched, Fuk Chu's call log entry vanished.

She frowned. That was strange.

SOME TIME LATER, for reasons she couldn't have explained, Natalie took the elevator down to the lobby and hailed a cab. She left her luggage behind and told the driver to take her to the airport on a whim.

All the while, she kept thinking about Laci Devereaux. Laci had ruled the social ladder in high school. At the time, Natalie had been less than cool and Laci had hated her for reasons unknown — maybe because Natalie was new in town, or because she wore skorts instead of skirts. She'd made it her mission to make Natalie's life hell, with torments too numerous to recall. Natalie had mostly blocked them out under the umbrella of "childhood trauma," but she did know they'd involved explicit photos of unspeakable acts — usually performed atop the school mascot and always distributed to the entire student body.

But it was cool — Natalie hadn't had a hard time back then or anything. Not at all. She'd been tough. She'd never cried herself to sleep every single night, or even once. Her mother hadn't told her to get over it, then forced her to confront Laci in public: a colossal failure that'd led to Natalie's social blackballing and turned her into a basket case for a really long time.

Not that any of that was true. Things back then had been awesome. Natalie's denial insisted on it.

And still Natalie was dreaming about Laci so much recently. She kept thinking that Laci was going to expose her social awkwardness even now — especially to boys Natalie liked.

She might start a rumor.

Might even stick Natalie's head in a toilet.

And of course, the caller known as Fuk Chu agreed that all sorts of new torment were likely for Natalie now that Laci was back. Fuk Chu even had his own ringtone, he called so often. The ringtone was a beautiful sound that made Natalie sleepy. She always wanted to do what he said. Always.

Looking around now, Natalie wondered why she was heading to the airport. She decided she must have a plan; she'd just forgotten what it was. Maybe she planned to get away from it all.

She decided to purchase a one-way ticket to Washington D.C. It was as good a place to get away as any.

After her plane landed, Natalie decided of her own free will to go to the Capitol building. There she flashed her ID and was given access to the Senate; apparently she had a pretty heavyweight ID. The Senate was in session. Seeing this, she flashed her powerful ID once more, then bullied her way around until someone put her on the docket.

At first, nobody wanted to let her do the open mic thing on the Senate floor while C-SPAN cameras rolled live. But then Natalie said a few very interesting things that Laci Devereaux had told her would be a good idea to mention and everyone got a lot more engaged. Laci's idea wasn't a suggestion. She'd actually threatened to tell everyone she still wore diapers if Natalie *didn't* talk to the Senate — and as popular as Laci was, everyone at school would believe it.

In front of the Senate that day, Natalie chose for some reason not to give Protocol back to her bosses. It was so much more interesting to explain how it worked to the world just like Laci wanted.

She was a star. She was able to provide a concrete demonstration of Protocol without showing any of the algorithm itself. Thereafter, she found herself listing her own crimes and those of the people she worked with and for.

It was a free-for-all after that.

She did everything exactly the way Fuk Chu wanted, in other words. He worked with Laci, after all — and after hearing his ringtone a few more times, it seemed to Natalie that she could even *see* Laci in the Senate room corner. She didn't want her wrath. That tall blonde bitch would tear Natalie apart if she disobeyed, just like she always had.

As a final cherry-on-top, some of Natalie's confessions just so happened to exonerate Ash Sanders, Mina Irving, and Richard Quince — including for the murder of Ash's wife. Mike O'Brien had actually killed Emily Sanders — something Natalie could prove with the evidence on her person.

They led her away in cuffs, just like a lot of Bespokery people would be led away in cuffs over the next few days.

Tragically, that wasn't the end of things for Natalie Baynes.

She had terrible dreams for the rest of her life.

SIXTY-ONE

Choose Both

By the time Mina reached where Ash was standing, he already knew it was her despite never looking up from the stone. She had a slight shuffle to her gait that he could identify by sound. Ash kept thinking he'd learned everything from the old days, but that was yet another new one.

He supposed some people might find those surprises from another life intriguing. Exciting, even. But he loathed them. They were ties to a past he couldn't revisit — and wouldn't even if he could. There was only one thing he wanted back from his old life, but no amount of reminiscence would ever return it to him.

"It's over," Mina said as she came to stand beside him.

Ash was still looking at the ground. At the stone. Yes, it was over. It'd ended long, long ago. But that's not what Mina meant, so he answered her in kind.

"Baynes confessed?"

"More than confessed," Mina told him. "She took personal blame for everything that happened in your neighborhood, at Bryan's lab, and at the motel — but she also told Congress a lot about the Bespokery and Protocol. Her bosses aren't going to get off any easier than she will."

Ash nodded, but still didn't look up.

Mina's conclusion was a little naive. Baynes would burn because her actions at the Senate had set her ablaze, but the generals and others who'd been enabling her would slip back into the woodwork. The Bespokery wouldn't live to see another day, and what remained of the Agency would go with it. Good, but far from perfect.

"What was it like?" Ash asked.

"What do you mean?"

"Controlling her. Controlling the woman who tried to control us."

"It wasn't control. It was influence. I didn't enter her dream. The first version of Protocol didn't get that far. I just used the 'mental fingerprint' she left inside me to find her. All Richard and I did after that was no different than what they did to Daisy."

"*Control. Influence.* You know what I meant," Ash said.

"Sure I do, but it's an important distinction. Daisy had a good heart. They must've observed some demon from her past while watching her dreams, then used that ring-tone-hypnosis thing to make it seem to Daisy like her demon had returned. She wasn't bad; she was regressed, tortured, and most of all scared. Baynes, on the other hand, *was* bad. It wasn't hard to manipulate her because the dream programming we nudged her into didn't ask her to violate her moral code the way killing — especially killing *you* — violated Daisy's. Baynes only had to do something she'd normally think was stupid. But just ask Richard: He'll tell you Baynes did stupid things all the time. She was just good at weaseling out of the trouble."

Ash thought about saying Baynes might wiggle herself out of this, but he knew better. Jaded and skeptical as Ash had become, he knew a scapegoat still had to hang for this. One way or another, Baynes was finished.

Thankfully dreamtech was *also* finished. Of that, Ash felt sure.

During the week Mina had spent using the Blip, Chirp, and the Protocol inside her to influence Baynes's dreams, Ash had been sorting the Agency's old work into two piles. One pile was for dangerous tech like Protocol, which Baynes herself had hard-erased from the only drive in existence after she demonstrated it to Congress. The other pile was for technology Ash felt was safe, and he released that pile to the public on Reddit. Thanks to Ash's data dump, the lucid dream hobbyists out there were about to experience a renaissance.

Because the internet now knew the government's best lucid dreaming tricks, minds would be awake and subliminal defenses would be up if another Bespokery tried to use them. But there were still bigger bombs for them to build, and more toxic biological weapons to grow in petri dishes. So of course they would move on.

Now Mina was looking at the stone at his feet as well. On it was Emily Sanders's name, and below it her dates of birth and death.

"This is complicated for you, isn't it?" she asked.

Ash looked over, not understanding.

"You told me that you already mourned her, but your first period of mourning was full of guilt. Now you have to mourn her for real — new grief from a wound you thought was already closed."

She nodded toward the grave, upon which Ash had already placed a bouquet of lilies — Emily's favorite flower, forgotten until just yesterday. "I don't imagine you were ever allowed to come here, to see her, in peace."

Ash didn't answer that. It was obvious. He'd tried

only twice to visit Emily's grave in the month after her death, and both times the press and protesters had followed him. By the time the furor finally died down and he could come without incident, he'd already repressed his feelings. By then Emily didn't exist. He couldn't let her exist, because remembering hurt too much.

Still, Ash wanted to reply to Mina. He wanted to mock her simplistic statements — her boilerplate psychobabble. He wanted to do anything not to feel, but when he tried to speak it was like he was paralyzed again. His limbs had stopped working.

So instead he came to kneeling, and then to sobbing with his forehead on the grass above where his wife's heart would be. He *had* mourned her, but he'd done it wrong. Before, she'd simply been gone. Only now did he feel the truth of it: she'd been *taken*.

It wasn't fair, and revenge had solved nothing, but still life somehow had to go on.

He rose some time later. Mina hadn't moved, and she was wise enough not to comment.

"Something she said keeps coming back to me," Mina said.

Ash turned to find Mina facing him eye to eye. "What?"

"You never watched the video Emily left for me. Richard saw part of it, but when word got out, someone found it and took it down. Your old bosses, I assume. Couldn't have evidence just lying around on the internet."

"What about it?" Ash asked.

"She said that 'Sunshine makes it better' was your trigger phrase, just like we thought. They got to Emily, and they started messing with you, and the combination made you depressed. That released the trigger. You started remembering Emily saying that phrase, which she actually never said."

"Yeah." Ash nodded. "Now that I remember all of her, it wasn't a very 'Emily' thing to say at all."

"You got more and more obsessed until you finally told me about it, as your therapist. Saying it aloud was your trigger. Hearing it was mine. That's when our memories started to come back."

"We know all of this."

"Yeah. We do. But Emily thought she might still be alive when it came time to remember. So on the video she said you would know how to undo *her* erasure. *You* had a trigger that you were supposed to use on Emily, to let *her* start to remember. So I just keep wondering: Was there something you feel like you were supposed to say to her? Like the sunshine thing?"

Ash considered for a while, then shook his head slowly. He felt tired all of a sudden, so he stepped back and sat on a bench that ran at the foot of Emily's grave.

Mina did not sit. She put a hand on his shoulder and said, "You're free, Ash. Never forget that."

Then she walked away. He listened until her footsteps became the sound of a car door opening, a car door closing. Soon enough she drove off.

Only then did Ash stop to wonder at Mina's parting words. They were strangely open-ended, strangely subject to interpretation. At first he'd thought she meant that nobody was chasing him anymore — not overtly for the murders Baynes and her people had committed, and not subtly for the murder Ash had been found not guilty of once, by reason of REM disorder, and then a second time when O'Brien was revealed as the killer.

But then he started to wonder if that's what she'd meant at all.

In their sessions, Mina used to tell him he'd made himself a prisoner of his own mind — a prisoner of his past. She hadn't known was that he'd also had another past hiding deep inside him, with programming like a computer's. Now it was all over, and Ash was free of everything. Free to stop living without Emily if he chose to.

"It wasn't about sunshine," Ash told the grave. "I know that's not what I was supposed to say to help you remember. But, Emily." He smiled slyly. *Was it about dreams?"*

He looked at the empty half of the bench beside him. In no way was Emily sitting there, but for a long moment he tried to see her just the same. There was a curious trick to something like that: it was possible to see the truth and what you wanted to see in tandem. They weren't mutually exclusive. Emily and Ash had talked about that sort of thing a lot, doing the work they did. Imagination was thought, just like dreams were thought, just like the present moment was a thought.

Yes, there seemed to be a real world out there, but what a person saw of that world came through human eyes and was given meaning by the decisions of a human brain. What humans called "the personal experience of reality" was the same as the experience of dreams when you got right down to it.

Or so said Emily.

"You told me once," Ash said, "that thinking about yesterday is no different from thinking about the dream you had last night. You said that *that* realization was what let you believe lucid dreaming was possible, way back when you first started trying. You told me, 'Think about the dream you had last night, Ash. Now, think about yesterday. Do those two thoughts feel any different? If you hadn't already convinced yourself that yesterday actually happened but the dream didn't, would you be able to tell which one was real just by thinking back on the memories?'"

Alone in the cemetery, Ash imagined Emily sitting beside him, smiling and nodding at what he'd just said. And then he understood: *Yes, that would have been her trigger.*

She couldn't have her memory unlocked now because she was gone, though. She wasn't real.

Except inside Ash's memory.

Except, forever and ever, inside his dreams.

Emily would never be in Ash's present moment again, but every morning after he woke up, he would have new memories of her in the past … because each dream was the same as yesterday, and aside from the single blink of *now*, yesterday was all anyone ever had.

"If I could," Ash said, "I would live inside my dreams. Every night, I'd be awake with you. I wouldn't live in this world. If I could choose one world, it would be yours."

"Why not choose both?" said Emily's voice.

Ash did a double take at the other half of the bench. Of course it was empty.

He thought about looking at his hands. He thought about checking the time twice, to see if it changed. He thought about those reality checks and others, but he did none of them.

Maybe he was dreaming.

Or maybe the real world, like the lucid world of dreams, was what he chose to make of it.

The End

About the Authors

Michael J. Breus, Ph.D., is a double board-certified Clinical Psychologist and Clinical Sleep Specialist. He is one of only 168 psychologists in the world to have taken and passed the Sleep Medicine Boards without going to Medical School. He is also the founder of sleepdoctor.com. Dr. Breus does more than 300 interviews a year and has been in practice for 25 years.

Sean Platt has always been an entrepreneur but knew he'd rather tell stories. When his wife bought him a laptop for his birthday in 2007 he dropped everything to write fiction. Since making the leap, Sean has written hundreds of novels, penned dozens of scripts, and founded the IP Incubator Sterling & Stone, where more than thirty story-tellers work together to create world-changing IP.